I0647914

Nobody's Hero

by

Patricia Grigg

Grigg Publishing, LLC ~ Arizona ~ USA

Grigg Publishing, LLC
P.O. Box 6154
Peoria, AZ 85381

ISBN-13: 978-1-62555-007-1

This story is a work of fiction. Names, characters, places, and incidents are either a product of the author's imagination, or used fictitiously. Any resemblance to actual persons, living or dead, events, or places is entirely coincidental.

Printed in the United States of America

First Edition, 2025

www.griggpublishing.com

Books written by

Patricia Grigg
***

The Nothing Girl

Children of the Nothing Girl Series:

Windy With Hell

Nobody's Hero (This Book)

Soon to come:

Even Thoughts Hurt

When Darkness Falls and Night Has Yet to
Come

This book is dedicated to my children who have been willing to face down Officials and Hurricanes to reach me.

To John Andrew Grigg, Theresa Ann McClure and Joseph Orien Grigg

Acknowledgements

A special thanks to Ray Bilcliff for the beautiful cover picture.

Visit his site at:
www.raybilcliff.com

My family who continuously keep me going with their love and support.

All the dear friends and readers who give me the confidence to go on.

Chapter One

BABYSITTING

"Honor detail, my butt," Bobby Jay thought. This was punishment for being late two mornings, plain and simple. Where was the honor of watching over a privileged brat? Lord knew he had had his share of that sort of crap back as a newbie. Yet here he was trailing behind some puny halfway to being a man guy, watching for heaven only knew what might threaten his rich life. "Shoot me now," Bobby Jay grumbled, "before this guy met up with some idiot friends." Teens were the worst, always doing something stupid. Never let them know you were guarding them, or they would do their best to lose you. Oh yeah, honor detail, right?

The irritation boiling in his mind, Bobby did another sweep with his eyes of the surroundings. It was just a typical college walkway with kids rushing to the next class, nothing of interest, well, the busty blond girl with too much make-up. Nope, nothing of interest.

All the while, he kept the subject of protection in his side vision. It was something an old-timer taught him. He kept his eyes searching the area but was constantly aware of where the idiot was and what he was doing. What was he doing? Standing there in the middle of the walkway like a stone statue?

Bobby gave the kid a moment before concern crept into his gut like a bout of nausea, that feeling an agent gets in his gut when something is wrong. Carefully, he pulled a candy bar out of his pants pocket and shoved all the good parts into his mouth. Then he went to the trash can as if this was what tough guys did: put their trash away. Puny boy's shoulders slumped just before Bobby Jay got to the can. It looked as if he would faint for a moment. He straightened his shoulder and pulled out a cell phone. The kid began a whispered conversation with someone on speed dial. A drug problem, calling his dealer, Bobby thought. Why were the rich kids so stupid? Bobby made it close enough to hear part of the conversation by then.

"No, I don't know where it was happening, Mids. Some check-cashing place, if I had to guess. I know, I know, there should be something… none, if only I knew where… I could… anonymous… sort of thing. I'll call you if I find anything more.

"No, you don't need to come to stay with me. I do wish Dog was here," Eric said and laughed, his voice carrying the conversation typically. "Yes, I know." The bit about Dog had become a private joke between Middy and him. "Dog" was their mother's dog, a huge beast who had more than once taken out armed men threatening their family. They believed their mother made the dog. How did you make a live, breathing dog out of the air?

If only he didn't have the visions, at least not the scary ones, then maybe he could live an everyday life. He overcame the fear the visions brought on once before because he had to save their parents. But these random visions of violence just left him shaken to the core. He would feel so much better if he had a dog with him. Please make your own. Eric heard the echo of Middy's voice in his mind. If only he could. He didn't have time for what-ifs; classes were challenging this year, so it was time to get back to it.

The rest of the day, Eric attended classes and dodged other students. He was leery of letting anyone get close to him, for they always had an agenda of one sort or another. They came with one or more objectives to him, to butter him up to get to his mother or grandfather. They bullied him because he was thin and not very social. Or to look down on him for whatever reason. He didn't care if they snubbed or bullied him; the one thing he guarded against was being used to get to his family. That he would not allow. Eric's one release from all the stress of being around people was running, and that he could do.

The day's last class was always a heavy stress-related one for Eric. The teacher, Mr. William, had it in for Eric for some reason and always seemed to find fault with anything Eric handed in. The last paper he had re-written twice already. If he had to do it again, Eric wouldn't know how to improve the paper. It wasn't that Eric didn't want to perfect the paper. He just thought he had done it. Twice. His heart was thumping in his chest so hard Eric thought it would explode as he handed Mr. William this last effort to get things the way the teacher wanted.

Mr. William took the paper from Eric with a scowl as if he already thought the paper was unworthy. Eric held his breath as the teacher, Middy called Wee Willie, scanned over his work. Finally, Mr. William nodded and put the paper on his desk to mark later with a grade. "Next time, do it right the first time, Whiting." Mr. William said in a scornful voice. Eric nodded and returned to his seat. Never was he so happy to leave for the day when the bell rang.

A butterfly with one ragged wing almost flew into Eric's face as he left the college grounds on a badly needed run. It was good that he had not gotten up to speed, or the poor thing would have smacked into his face. Eric stopped and watched the butterfly, wondering if it was one of his mother's butterflies. His mother had told him, with that certainty and calmness she had, that the butterflies would look after his sisters and him while they were away from home. The thing is, he believed her. He watched the butterfly hover for a moment in front of him. It flew slowly off to the other side of the street, hovering over a muscular man tying his running shoes. Eric's mind processed the man. The butterfly wouldn't have pointed him out if Eric wasn't supposed to be made aware of him. He looked like... security. Eric closed his eyes and sent a silent thank you to the butterfly for letting him know he wasn't alone. There was a dog with him, the human sort. He gave the man a nod of recognition and took off on his run again.

Crap, Bobby Jay thought, the kid made him. Well, no sense staying out of sight now, Bobby told himself, taking off after the kid. Man, the kid was fast. He could not keep the kid in sight as fast as the puny guy was running. Just when he thought the kid was trying to shake him, he slowed down and ran in place, letting Bobby reach a reasonable distance again. From then on, the kid ran at a more sensible pace, thankfully.

Eric turned off the paved road to cross into a little park he had found one day on the run. The park had trees that shaded paths running around it, ending at a small pond near the far side. This was where Eric ran when he needed to find peace of mind and relax after a hectic day, and today, he needed that peace more than anything. Effortlessly, he ran around the park on the path under the trees, letting the peace and the feel of nature flow over him, releasing the day's tensions.

He slowed as he neared the pond, thinking the security guy probably needed to catch up and take a break right about now. So he ran in place, looking over the water to where some ducks were paddling; how he missed the farm, the animals, and his family. He idly watched as a man approached the pond on the opposite shore. The man was carrying a white bag in one hand and was striding with purpose towards the pond.

Kittens mewing and fighting to live as the water took them down and down flashed in Eric's mind. Forgetting the security guy on his tail, Eric ran around the pond even as the man threw the bag in his hand into the middle of the water.

Eric ran into the water without stopping to think and swam for all he was worth as that white bag sank beneath the surface. He was going to be too late to save them all. He knew it, saw it, hated it. Keeping that spot where the kittens in the bag sank firmly fixed in his sight, Eric pushed his body to dive under and find that bag, find it, save as many as he could, find it… find it… find it. His hand closed on the cloth, and Eric pushed to the surface as fast as he could. He dared not waste time. Turning to float on his back, he opened the bag to expose the kittens to the air.

All of them looked dead. They were limp, not breathing, dead or dying. Eric didn't even look around to see if anyone was watching before trying to pull off a miracle and heal the kittens. Eric had never been as good as his mother at healing, but he could heal a bit, and he needed that healing touch more than ever. Quickly, he felt each small body with a finger; all the while, he kept them on his chest and kicked his legs to get to shore. Only the last kitten was alive and responded. The little black body warmed beneath Eric's touch and finally mewed. "It is okay, little one, I've got you, I've got you." Eric soothed.

Bobby grabbed the kid roughly and yanked him along to shore. The damn kid knew how to ruin a day for him. What the hell was he thinking about going into the water like that? "Real dumb, kid. You might have drowned out there?"

The kid looked up at him as Bobby dragged him onto the shore. It was the expression on the kid's face that hit Bobby hard. "They died. I was too late," the kid told him.

Only then did Bobby Jay see the four kittens the kid held cradled against him. Damn! Bobby rubbed his hand over his face, shutting his eyes. He was saving kittens. The dumb kid risked his life for some kittens.

"Only one is alive," Eric told the security man. "I was too late."

"But you saved one; isn't that better than all of them dying?" Bobby asked. "Come on, we'll bury the rest and take that little black guy to the vet. He'll know what to do for it." The poor kid was punishing himself over dead kittens. How sad was that?

The weakness hit Eric fast after reaching the shore. It was the healing weakness he knew so well from watching his mother heal. She had died a few times from healing others. Death was better than losing a single life, and he had lost three of them, three little helpless lives. Heartsick and weak, Eric had no idea how he ended up in a car and headed to an animal hospital with the security guy. The driver of the vehicle parked in front of the animal hospital, and the security guy had Eric out of the car, leading him into the hospital with the half-grown kitten still clutched to his chest. It wasn't until the doctor on call had pronounced the kitten healthy and inquired about its vaccinations that Eric gave in to the healing weakness.

It hit him full force, and his knees gave out on

him. Clutching the exam table, Eric barely managed to keep from whacking his head on the table. Roughly, he was grabbed from behind and dragged to a chair to be plopped into it, and his head pushed down between his knees. "I'm okay." Eric protested, trying to wave off the security guy.

"Yeah, and I'm the King of England," Bobby Jay said, chuckling as the puny guy tried to laugh only to pass out. "I've got you, kid," Bobby said, keeping Eric from face-planting into the floor.

Bobby had Ralph Higgins, the agent driving the car he had called to pick up the half-drowned kid and himself from the park, help him get the kid back to the dorms and into bed. They were careful not to disturb the kid's clothing, but Bobby had taken the opportunity to check the kid's arms and between his toes for needle marks. If the kid was taking drugs, he was snorting or swallowing them. Once Higgins had left, Bobby thought about what to do next. He hated to leave the kid all zonked out like he was, plus he was worried the guy had some sickness. It could be that was the whole reason Old Man Stanley had his superiors give Bobby this crap job. And the kitten was sleeping beside the kid. There was no food, litter box, or toys for the little thing, and the least he could do was get the kitten supplies. It wasn't as if he was soft and starting to like the kid. It was just the kitten he was concerned about, yeah, right.

The nightmares started almost immediately after Eric's body had recovered from healing the kitten. First, it was a regular nightmare. Eric saw the man throwing the bag of kittens into the water and ran into the pond to try to help the kittens. Only this time, they all died. No matter how often he ran in and dove after that bag, all the kittens died. No little black body took a breath and mewed. All of them lost, lost. He fought, oh how he fought to get to them in time, but it was a nightmare, and things didn't go right in nightmares.

Just when Eric thought he could take no more, he woke up to be hit with a vision. A man and woman with a tiny baby walked beside the pond, laughing softly not to wake the sleeping baby. Another man, a mugger, came up behind the couple and drew a gun; he threatened to kill them unless they gave him their valuables. Eric cried out a warning just as the gun went off, once, twice, and the blood flowed. "No!" the cry of anguish ripped from Eric's throat.

Gun out, Bobby entered Eric's room, adrenaline pumping through his system. Carefully, he swept the area. No threat was obvious, but the kid's face was one of grief and terror. It had to be a flashback, Bobby Jay reasoned.

"It is okay, kid. You probably had a flashback to the kittens dying. It gets better over time. Breathe deep and think good thoughts." Tortured eyes looked up at Bobby, making him wish he was elsewhere. He didn't do well comforting idiots.

Eric's mind was half trapped still in the vision he had just seen. Seeing the gun pointed at him did more than all the words in the world to calm him down. This guy could save those people. He could stop them from dying. He put on his mother's face that cool, calm look she had even in the worst of times before speaking. "No, it wasn't the kittens. I mean, yes, I did have a nightmare about the kittens, but we have to save a couple before they are shot. Let me use the bathroom, then we have to hurry," he said as he swung his legs off the bed, still projecting his mother, the action she always took in a crisis.

"Hold on, kid, believe me, whatever you think is going on isn't. This is just the shock of the kittens dying. I've seen this happen to the strongest of men. They get it in their heads that something bad will happen. You'll see, in the morning, you may be shaky still, but time will help. Give it some time, kid," Bobby said.

Now Eric could see why you don't depend on anyone you can't trust. He had to admit he felt disappointed in this guy. Wasn't he supposed to protect people? Squaring his shoulders, he used the toilet, then went to the door, stopping only long enough to put on his shoes and place the kitten on his bed before leaving.

"Damn!" Bobby swore to himself, damn stubborn teens, no sense at all, not one tiny grain of sense in a teenager's head, as he rushed out to follow the dumb kid. I am taking the car this time, not chasing a kid on foot in the middle of the night, he thought.

Even in the car, it took Bobby a bit to catch up to the kid, but Bobby did catch him. Speeding up and swinging in front of Eric, he stopped and stepped out of the car. "Get in the car, kid. I'll drive you wherever you are going. Besides, you look as if you are ready to faint again," he said, not liking the wary look the kid was giving him.

His mouth twisted grimly; Eric went to the passenger's door and got into the car. "That little park by the pond, we have to hurry. It was a soon thing, " he said, not explaining more. He knew others would think him crazy—not his family or even some of the Secret Service guys who had been guards before this guy, but most everyone else it was risky to talk to about a vision.

To appease the kid, Bobby made good time to the small park and stopped on the street where the pond was. He half-listened to the kid whisper about a man and woman walking their colic baby around the pond and something about a mugging. Bobby suspected this was just a fear dream brought on by the kid seeing the man drown the kittens earlier in the day. He was here out of concern for the kid but was not on duty. Higgins had nights.

The park was dark and quiet, with no signs of life until they approached the pond. A man and woman were pushing a buggy around the pond, whispering between themselves as if afraid to wake the baby sleeping within the buggy. Eric's heart almost beat out of his chest. He was so terrified that this young couple would be killed and their baby left an orphan. "He is going to come up behind them and kill them both. You have to stop him." Eric said, his whole body shaking with terror.

This is nuts, Bobby Jay thought, like something out of a voodoo movie. Did the kid think he was a psychic? Still, Bobby checked his weapon for some reason, ensuring it was loose and ready to draw. Slowly, he surveyed the area; there was nobody except the couple strolling around the pond with their kid that he saw. That is until a shadowy figure emerged from the nearby woods to hurry up behind the couple.

Bobby yanked Eric back behind him before taking off to where the couple was walking. He drew and raised his weapon. "STAND DOWN! Get on the ground with your hands over your head," He ordered.

The woman screamed, and her husband stepped in front of her to block her from Bobby; behind them, the prep dropped to his knees, then laid down and stretched his arms out over his head. Bobby walked forward with his weapon steady on the mugger. He waved the man and woman to get behind him, then waited until he knew they obeyed him before going to the mugger. The dumb-ass was holding onto the gun he had drawn to threaten the couple.

"Drop the weapon, or I'll pop one into your skull," Bobby ordered. Once the mugger's gun was secured, Bobby pulled out his phone and punched one number. He glanced behind him to see if the couple and the kid were doing okay. "Get me some locals down here. I ran across a frigging mugger. No, he is secured, but the couple he was about to rob may need some counseling." To his surprise, the kid stood with his fist raised in front of the couple and baby as if protecting them. What the hell was with this kid?

The locals finally arrived, and Bobby explained how they encountered a guy trying to mug the couple. It was surprising how readily the locals believed his charge had needed fresh air, and they happened upon the mugging. It made it more believable that the kid looked so puny and sickly. Despite the jokes and ribbing Bobby knew he would be receiving from the others in his department, he was glad they had saved that young couple from coming to harm. What ate at him was how the kid knew the mugging would happen.

Eric was relieved when the security guy didn't question him about the mugging on returning to the dorms. Once they were back at the dorms, Eric went about taking care of the kitten. As Eric fed the kitten, Bobby set up a litter box for the little one. It was late, and Eric knew he needed to sleep before classes in the morning, yet his vision of the robbery at the check-cashing establishment was preying on his mind. He mulled it over in his mind repeatedly until he finally knew he would have to ask the security guy to help him again.

He waited until the kitten was settled, curled up in his lap, purring, before broaching the subject. "Sir, there will be a robbery at a check-cashing place. I don't know where it is, but it's somewhere in this city, and they're going to kill the clerk. Can you stop it?" Eric asked.

Tired of dealing with stupid kids with no sense in their heads, full of ideas without basis, Bobby stood biting his lip. His brow pooled down, almost as if his very eyes were in a frown, taking a moment to answer. "What are you, kid, some psychic? What is it? Do you have these dreams or visions and think they are real?" He asked.

Eric didn't hesitate to tell the truth; it was how he had been raised always to say the truth, no matter what others might think. "Yes, sir. They are real. The first time was when I was little. I saw our young nanny goat wrapped in wire around her leg; we managed to save our goat, and Mom healed the leg enough that Dr. Andy could finish repairing it. The next time was soon after that. Aunt Julian had her twins, and later, during dinner, I saw a bad man shoot my mother and father. Dad and Mom sent everyone to safety and laid a trap for the bad man. My sister Middy and I came back to help them. Mom's dog almost died that time; he was shot. But Mom saved him. Mother is a healer, you know. I can't heal as well as Mom, but I can do some of it. You can't tell anyone any of this, Sir, please, I'm trusting you here."

What a screwed-up kid, Bobby thought; the higher they were in the food chain, the more nuts they became. More than ever, Bobby Jay wanted to be reassigned; he just wasn't cut out to watch over rich kids. "Sure, kid, I'll look into it. You best get some rest." Bobby soothed. He knew how to play the game and didn't like having to butter up crazy people. He saw the hopeful expression on the kid's face as he headed off to bed, the kitten clutched to his chest. What a mixed-up kid. Who would believe such a wild tale as the kid had just told him? Still, Bobby knew he wouldn't rest until he looked into the kid's background himself and figured out just what degree the kid was screwed up.

Dawn was peeping in through the one window

in the room when Bobby finally closed his laptop. He hadn't slept much but was used to working on fumes in a challenging situation. What he had discovered, or instead hadn't found, had him feeling wired up. There were files, and there were files so secret it took every bit of skill he had to uncover them. Things were never simple, it seems. The first thing Bobby had done was to look up the kid's family. Right off, a million sites popped up with a video of what was labeled 'The Butterfly Wedding.' Bobby had to admit it was an incredible wedding. How they had pulled it off, he didn't know, but it must have cost a fortune to have that many butterflies flown in just for a wedding.

It wasn't until he started looking up official records, figuring he'd find something on mental illness, that he ran into the first roadblock. The thing with roadblocks, well, they just made Bobby determined to break them. Some while later, he was shaking his head and running his fingers through his hair as if trying to settle the whirlwind his brain was trying to tame inside his skull. Hidden deep, very deep where records should be, there was nothing. Still, that didn't make the kid a psychic. Did it? There wasn't anything on the kids, and it was as if they had been deliberately kept off official records. What the hell? Had they assigned him to some freak show? Okay, he could do this, would do this, and then get a decent assignment out of it. Mind made up, Bobby set his alarm to go off in one hour. It was time to sleep.

Bobby was carefully shadowing Eric the following day; for one thing, he didn't want to be cornered by the kid and questioned about the check cashing bit. He would have to try to look into that possibility so he wouldn't have to lie to the kid about it. Only how in hell did you look for a crime that hadn't happened yet? He massaged his temples as he waited for the day's last class to end and for the kid to exit the building. This assignment was giving him a permanent headache. He had been to places where, every moment, day and night, he had to be alert for a possible assassin. He had guarded men where all he had to do was stand at attention and keep an eye on the crowds during speeches while usually bored by the drone of those speeches. He'd take the boring speeches over watching over a voodoo kid any day.

He watched as the kids streamed out of the building, some forming little clutches and standing around talking, others rushing off to something that seemed to them in dire need of doing, but no kid. Just when he was beginning to think he had a situation on his hands, the boy walked out of the building, his arms loaded down with books and papers. The boy stopped walking and watched three girls talking and laughing out near the street, his face holding a look of longing. The old teen hormones, Bobby thought, the kid should go out on a date, and it might loosen him up some.

Eric sighed and walked on out to the street. He saw the security guy waiting for him and, sighing again, walked over to him. "I just need to pick up some fast food, and it is to the dorm. If it is okay, I'd like to do a run, not a long one, just until I unwind a bit from class," Eric said, walking up to Bobby.

Bobby threw a glance at the three girls before

saying anything. "You should ask one of them out," He advised. "Might be more relaxing than a run, kid."

Shaking his head, Eric looked away from the girls. "None of them are the one. They turn on my body, not my heart, and my father said only the one who turns on your heart is worth going after. He is a wise man, you know."

Poor kid, Bobby thought. He had delusions of people being honorable. It wouldn't serve him well during life, and the others would eat him alive. "Look, kid…."

"Eric, the name is Eric Whiting, and you are?" Eric asked.

"Bobby Jay," Bobby said, feeling like he had been blind-sided. You don't get up close with the subject you were guarding. Who was he kidding? The boy, Eric, got to him the moment he risked his life for a bag full of kittens.

Later that night, Bobby was on his laptop again, this time searching for checking cashing places in the area. He couldn't bring himself to believe in all this psychic bull without some proof it was real. Bobby had seen so-called psychics scamming people before; his grandmother had fallen prey to one. No, he couldn't believe this Eric kid, not without proof.

He leaned back and looked over the nearby places for check cashing. There were eight possibilities within the nearby neighborhood; only three were not in a heavy traffic area where anyone robbing them would be easily seen. Crap, he wouldn't be able to live with himself if one of the places was hit and somebody died. The kid was playing with his head, and that same head was pounding in pain. There was nothing for it but to do a patrol on his time off to be sure nothing happened to some poor clerk. Some nights, he hated being the way he was, the need to be confident, to protect idiots regardless of how nuts they were. It was his job, driving him to do what was right.

Taking care to go slow enough to check out the area, Bobby passed by the first of the three check-cashing places on his list. He surveyed the street and surrounding buildings as well as the lit interior of the place. It occurred to him that if he took a photo with his phone, he could show it to the kid and at least relieve the boy's worry. So he drove by a second time and took two photos before heading to the second place on his list. All this was just guesswork on his part; he had no proof that anything would happen at any of the three; he was taking precautions. He didn't believe anything would happen at all.

Bobby had planned his route carefully so he would pass by each place once, going in one direction, and then again, going in the opposite direction for a while. To anyone watching any of the shops, it would appear a person was passing to and fro when out shopping, not patrolling the area.

While Bobby was doing his self-imposed patrol, Eric had his troubles. In one of his classes, he was supposed to find a stray animal at the pound and kill it, then dissect it to learn about its internal organs, veins, muscles, and so on. He couldn't do it. He couldn't take a life. This dog or cat was to count for most of his grade in that class. Even though Eric knew he would be sinking his chances of becoming a Veterinarian, he wouldn't take a life. Besides, he already knew everything the task was supposed to teach him. When he was little, he witnessed his mother heal their goat, Billy, and he wanted to heal animals. It was hard for him at first, but soon, he could look into each animal and trace through their body to see any place injured or sick in them.

He just needed to be legally licensed to help the animals truly, but he did not have the strength to heal as his mother did. Sure, he could heal some small things, not the big heal his mom could do with a single touch. Thus, he needed to know about medicine and surgery. Eric was so torn up over the idea of other animals being killed by his classmates he couldn't eat his dinner. Throughout the evening, he studied his medical texts, convinced that he would lose his chance of becoming the doctor he wanted to be. Eric wanted to hear his father tell him it would be okay, but he wasn't the little scared boy he had been when he met his parents. Now, he'd have to solve this problem on his own.

Out on patrol, Bobby was still looking for someone robbing one of the three places he was checking upon. It was growing near the time for the check-chasing places to close as Bobby made one last trip between the shops. He didn't expect to find anything. The only reason he was out here was to be sure. A good agent covered every possibility, and Bobby considered himself a good agent.

It was only a shadow creeping around the corner of the store, yet it caught Bobby's glance and held it. His gut tightened intuitively, telling him not to dismiss that shadow. Pulling over, Bobby exited his car and ensured his weapon was loosened, ready for a quick draw. The gut tightening was seldom wrong in Bobby's experience. Carefully, he walked around the shop building, arriving just as a back door started closing. He was hyped now, adrenaline flowing through his system, making all his senses sharp. Slowly, he cracked the door open, checking what was on the other side of it. Sure enough, it was a man with a gun in his hand. That was all Bobby needed to know. He stepped back and pulled out his phone to call the locals.

Ultimately, it was a simple take-down; Bobby only had to identify himself to the prep, and the guy gave up. It was often like that with bullies and cowards who preyed upon the helpless. It was the crap afterward that was bad. Once again, Bobby had to explain why he happened upon a crime being committed. It did not go down well. Bobby didn't care. He had other things on his mind, like a voodoo kid or whatever weird thing was up with the boy who had visions.

The trouble was he was starting to believe the kid. Twice, the boy had been right in his predictions of trouble and, in the end, results, saved people from harm. Bobby needed to research the boy and his family again. Then, he could decide what to do about the whole situation. That turned out to be a considerable problem; any records on the mother and father were sealed so tight Bobby, with his clearance, could not get into them. The only trace of the family was an obscure note made by a doctor who had treated a guard working in a Maryland lab. The note was an odd scribble notation to never touch Fredrick Whiting's wife. That would be the kid's mother if Bobby weren't mistaken. Exhausted, glad that he had the morning off and the relief agent would be bored while waiting for the kid to wake up at noon or whenever kids wake up these days, Bobby gave into sleep.

Today was the first day of working weekends at Eric's new job. He was both excited and a whole basket of nerves. It wasn't an exciting job, but it would give him some experience working in an animal clinic. He'd be cleaning the kennels and bathing dogs, and the upside was he would witness the doctor as he treated the animals some of the time. Eric arrived early to meet the elderly doctor who had hired him and to be instructed in his duties.

Dr. Monroe showed Eric through the clinic; the examination rooms were just behind the reception area. Once you passed the two examination rooms, surgery was on one side of the hallway. Across from the surgery was a recovery room with autoclaves and cages, where sick or surgery patients could be cared for and checked on easily. There was another hallway on the other side of this area, which led back up towards reception; along this hallway was a prep room for the surgery and a radiology room. Stuck between the recovery room and the two examination rooms was a small lab for running blood samples and other things. All of this area excited Eric, but it was out back of the main building where Eric would primarily be working.

Exiting the building with Eric, Dr. Monroe explained that Eric would be responsible for taking care of the covered runs where some of the larger breeds would stay when being boarded or waiting for baths or procedures.

"You must come in early enough to clean all the runs and this building where we keep small boarders and bathe the dogs and cats. You will feed and water the animals, then let the dogs exercise in the yard individually. You must never let the dogs interact with each other. We don't need dogs fighting and hurting each other while here. Also, you must access the in-clinic list of animals on the computer before heading back here to see who needs what preventive medication. You will be responsible for giving those medications, most of which are heart-worm prevention. You make a list from their charts on the computer and list the animals going home that need to be bathed. Those will be the first animals you bathe, and they have to be ready when a client arrives to pick them up. You will be called up to take back any new boarders or animals to be bathed. You are to be polite and caring towards the clients. Understand?" Dr. Monroe said.

"Yes, sir," Eric said.

"You do know how to bathe a dog, right?" Dr. Monroe asked.

"Yes, sir," Eric said, watching the doctor's stern face.

"Alright, it is best to let the dogs out of the runs one at a time. Clean that run by hosing it down. All the waste and dirt will go out the back of the runs into this drainage area. Once a run is washed and dry, put the dog from it up and do the next run. When all are washed, the last dog walked, you scoop poop out of the yard, dump it in the drain and wash it all down the drain outside. You do the same thing in the inside cages, except for the cats; they have litter boxes. Be careful not to let a dog or cat escape; they can do so quickly. Now, get to cleaning. Oh, take this: we use these soft slip loops to catch up a loose dog; most of the ones here know the drill. Come back inside now, and I'll show you how to make a bath and med list. If you have trouble giving a pill, let me know, and I'll show you how to do it properly," Dr. Monroe said, heading back into the clinic.

List in hand, Eric returned to the kennel room and began to give out medications; it was all only what the owners would give at home, so it didn't require the doctor to administer them. He didn't know what sort of trouble the doctor expected him to have given out the pills. All he did was ask them to eat the medication, and they did. Next came cleaning up the cages and runs and letting the dogs exercise. This was as simple as the medicines had been. Eric told them to do their business and return. Things went pretty fast, and soon, Eric began giving the baths. He didn't like the shampoo, and the dogs didn't like it, so he made a mental note to pick up something they would like. The call bell sounded when he was on the next to last in-clinic dog. Since Eric hadn't wet the dog down, he put him back up and went up front to see what was needed of him.

Dr. Monroe stopped Eric as he headed toward the reception desk. "Be careful with that fellow; don't take any chances. Put him in the last run, and if you have to leave the noose on him, it will be okay. I'll come out and muzzle him for you when it comes time to bathe him. Give me a call when you are ready to go get him," he told Eric. Eric nodded to let the doctor know he understood.

When Eric stepped through the doorway into the reception area, a large Doberman was standing staring at the doorway. The dog's eyes were cold and calculating, as if looking for a weakness in Eric.

"Boy, you make sure Luther has his nails done this time. The last time, they didn't trim them. He scratched my arms up in bed. Take good care of him. I'll know if you mistreat him. Do you understand?" A middle-aged man told Eric as he slipped the soft loop over Luther's head.

"Yes, sir. I'll take good care of him for you," Eric said, letting a finger touch the dog. Luther was distraught at having to be here. The poor guy didn't like baths at all, and they dragged him in back to be bathed every time. "It is okay, Luther. You won't mind me bathing you, will you?" Eric soothed the dog. Luther looked up at Eric and wagged his stub of a tail at him. Eric had had a great deal of practice communicating with his mom's dog. He knew how to soothe a savage beast. He didn't jerk on the lead to get Luther to go with him; he just let him know they were going back. Luther trotted beside him to the kennels. Luther also didn't like being in the last run, so Eric put him in the second run on the left side. This way, Luther could see him working in the kennel room, bathing dogs, and he could see the clinic's back door. In other words, Eric included Luther in the circle of ongoing business. Luther needed to know what was happening; his instincts were to protect, and being shoved back away from everything was horrible to him; they kept him from doing his job.

Bobby Jay was waiting when Eric left the clinic; Eric smiled at him. At least this guy had checked out the visions for him. He had been worried when a new guy had shadowed him today, thinking Bobby had been taken off security on him. "You are back," Eric said, then thought how dumb that probably sounded.

"Yeah, I am. How was your first day at work, kid?" Bobby asked, inwardly laughing to himself. The kid was funny.

Eric became animated. "It was great! You should see all the dogs that came in. Luther, he is this big Doberman, was so good. I will buy some decent shampoo and rinse for the dogs. All the stuff they use here smells terrible and hard on the dog's skin. They don't like it at all. I promised them to get something nice. I got to hold a dog when it was being examined. It was great!" Eric remembered the class he was about to fail and sobered. "Anyway, how was your day?"

Bobby's forehead wrinkled as he watched the kid go from excited to grimly sober. Maybe he was still beating himself up over the check-cashing deal. The least Bobby could do was relieve the kid's mind on that score. "Oh, it was fine. By the way, I checked out the check-cashing thing you saw, and we caught the guy before he could hurt anyone. Good job on that, kid… I mean Eric," He said. The kid still looked filled with gloom.

"Okay, tell me what is bothering you, making you look like your cat died," Bobby said, immediately regretting using a cat as an example. He grimaced as the kid shook his head. It was like pulling teeth to get something out of the boy. "Tell me, kid, maybe I can help," he prompted.

Eric rubbed his eyes, then the back of his neck, and finally started talking. "There isn't. Anything you can do, I mean. I have this professor who says we all have to get an animal, a stray, and kill it and practice what we are learning about the body. I... I can't do that. I'm not going to kill something. It goes against everything, I believe. Anyway, I will have to drop out of college. Maybe I can find a way to heal things without being licensed. I don't know what to do.

"The thing is, I don't need a dead body to practice finding things in the body; I can feel where all the muscles, organs, veins, everything is in a body, just like my mother can. I love seeing how Dr. Monroe works with the animals in his care. He is a harsh man with people, but he cares about animals. Now, gad, I should let another student take the job," He said.

Eric hung his head as he spoke, looking so forlorn that Bobby wanted to reach out and pat the kid on the back. Instead of comforting the kid, Bobby was... well, Bobby. "Suck it up, kid. And don't whine about it. Go do something about it."

Chapter Two

EVERY DAY THINGS

Bobby was right, Eric thought; he had to figure out how to get through the class without killing an animal. Perhaps he could talk the professor into letting him use the body of an animal that had died a natural death or from trauma. It was worth trying. In the meantime, he had Sunday to look forward to at the clinic. It wouldn't be so hectic as there would be no patients coming in, and all he would have to do was clean and take care of feeding the animals.

When Eric arrived at the clinic, he first noticed two cars pulled up in a half-hazard manner in front of the clinic. He had expected Dr. Monroe to be there to check up on him and the job he was to do. The other car puzzled him where it stood with one of the back doors wide open as if the owner had been in a hurry. No sooner had Eric open the clinic door than he heard his name bellowed from an examining room. Rushing into the room, Eric saw the doctor and a large man wrestling with a Labrador Retriever.

"Eric, I need you to take over holding the head. I can't get a vein on Rip here with him fighting us. First, bring the machine and mask out of surgery. We'll try to mask and gas him," Dr. Monroe said, handing out orders.

"I can hold him for a vein," Eric said, slipping to the thrashing dog. "Here, let me."

Dr. Monroe looked ready to shoot fire out of his eyes when Eric didn't listen to his orders. Eric touched the beast, and the dog turned its head to look at Eric. "It is okay. We are going to help you. Trust me," Eric soothed the dog, slipping his arms around the dog's front end. Rip became still. Only the heavy panting and the heaving of the dog's chest indicated it was still in distress.

Dr. Monroe stepped away without saying a word and readied a syringe. "I'm going to roll the vein up and insert the catheter, then inject something to sedate Rip. You keep him still," He told Eric and motioned his head at the large man helping. "Tom, step away. Go wash up or sit in the front. We have this. I'll deal with you after we have Old Rip fixed up." The man, Tom, hung his head and left the exam room. Monroe gave Eric a stern look and told him to keep the dog still.

"I can hold the vein for you, Sir," Eric said, wrapping his hand around Rip's foreleg and rolling the vein up. He had gone with his parents when they took Dog to be repaired after a man shot Dog. It was forever etched in his mind how the doctor who treated Dog had told his mother how to place her hand and roll the vein up to the top of Dog's leg and hold it for him to insert a catheter. That was when certainty of what he wanted to do when he grew up solidified in his heart. When Eric touched Rip, he knew the dog had two broken back legs. It took all his concentration to keep from trying to heal the dog, yet he did heal one bleeder. All the while, he observed as Dr. Monroe inserted a catheter into Rip's foreleg, wrapped tape to hold the catheter in place, and gave the dog something to knock him out.

"Watch him closely while I get the machine and tube," Dr. Monroe said before striding off. The doctor didn't take long to return with the machine and a tube to insert into Rip's airway. Eric watched every move the doctor made and monitored Rip. Dr. Monroe had him hold Rip's mouth open while the doctor inserted the tube into Rip's airway, inflated the small balloon that would secure the tube in that airway, and connected the machine, regulating the flow of air and gas. The doctor went about things quickly, making it look so simple, and perhaps it was when you had the needed knowledge. That was what Eric needed: knowledge.

Eric learned so much that day, from how to take an X-ray to how to set broken bones. He watched in fascination as the doctor made a brace from a thick metal tube nearly as big around as Eric's little finger. Once the doctor was done, they placed Rip in a cage in the recovery room. Eric was dismissed to attend to his duties. He was reluctant to go but knew he had a job to do, so he left quickly.

Later that evening, Eric returned to the clinic to let the dogs out again and give them fresh water.

The first thing he did was check on Rip. The large Labrador was in distress. At the first touch of a finger to the head shoved against the front of the cage, Eric knew the dog needed to relieve himself but wouldn't do it in the cage. Problem one: how do you get a dog with both back legs in braces outside to pee? He could put a towel around his belly, hold the dog's rear up, and maybe get him out just walking on his front legs, but what if he hurt him? It came to him then, Bobby Jay. Bobby was strong and could carry Rip outside. Once outside, the towel trick might let Rip relieve himself, and then Bobby could bring the dog back inside and hold him while Eric cleaned the cage, putting fresh towels down for Rip to lay on. Eric knew Bobby was outside, watching the clinic to ensure nobody kidnapped him. He had helped him with the kitten, Bruce, hadn't he?

Bobby's nose twitched; something was up; it didn't feel like danger, just some problem. His phone vibrated in his coat pocket, causing a frown on Bobby's face. Trouble, it had to be trouble. Nobody called him except work. "Jay," he barked into the phone.

"Bobby, come to the front door of the clinic. I'll let you in. I need some assistance," Eric said.

"Are you in danger?" Bobby asked through clenched teeth. How the hell had anyone gotten past him? He heard the kid suck in a breath.

"No, Sir. I'm just not strong enough. Will you help me?" Came the soft reply.

Grumbling to himself for letting the kid get to him, Bobby went to the clinic's front door. Eric was there, waving him to hurry inside. He locked the clinic door back before leading Bobby down a hallway. The place smelled like a hospital; Bobby didn't like hospitals; they turned his stomach. Still, he was curious as to why the kid needed help. Maybe the boy wasn't cut out to work in this place of hospital smells. Eric stopped to point to a room with a handful of cages. In one of the cages was a large Labrador with its head and face pressed against the door. Eric turned to Bobby, his eyes too bright for this depressing place.

"He needs to pee, but you see both his back legs are broken and in braces… so…. If you carry him outside, I'll put one of these big beach towels around his chest. You can hold it to support him while I hold his rear up, and then he can pee." Seeing the doubt in Bobby's eyes, Eric quickly went on. "He has promised me he will pee right away. Once he is done, we bring him back in here; you'd only have to hold him a moment while I refresh his bed. Then you can go back out if you want to," Eric said, his face a portrait of hope.

Bobby sighed silently. First, it was a cat, but now it was a dog; he wasn't any pet sitter. "Sure, kid," He said. Carefully, he lifted the big Lab out of the cage and waited for Eric to open the door leading outside before following the kid. Bobby watched the kid as he soothed the dog and encouraged him to only stand on his front legs while peeing. It would be laughable if the kid weren't so serious. Sucker. That is what I am, a sucker, Bobby told himself. He was happy nobody could see him holding a dog up with a towel around its chest.

As they placed Rip onto his fresh bedding, the clinic's front door opened, and Dr. Monroe walked to the recovery room. "Just who are you, and what are you doing in my clinic?" the doctor demanded in a stern, angry voice.

Bobby was reaching for his identification when Eric stepped in front of him. Eric's face was so expressionless that Bobby wondered if the kid would faint. But he didn't…

"Back off, Doctor," Eric said, his voice going soft with a touch of deadly curling around it. "This is my friend, Bobby. He is helping me settle Rip back into his cage. Rip had to pee, so I called Bobby to help carry him out. You don't want him here, then you don't want me here, so back off, and we will both leave. By the way, the rest of the dogs still need to be let out," Eric said; he nodded to Bobby and started to step past the doctor.

Dr. Monroe blinked once, then stooped down and checked Rip out. After a quick look at Rip, he stood and realized that Eric was indeed leaving. "Hold it right there. You still have work to do, boy."

"Eric, his name is Eric," Bobby said, speaking for the first time. He was impressed at how fast the kid had come to his defense. Admittedly, he had gone a little far in quitting his job, but still, he had jumped in and defended Bobby. Not that Bobby wasn't more capable of protecting them than the skinny kid. It was just the surprise of it all. Never had Bobby had someone stand up for him in that manner. Usually, the person he was protecting was grumbling at him with one complaint after another. Eric had stepped up most unexpectedly.

Dr. Monroe stood before the pair, almost as if blocking their exit. "Go out and do your job. Nobody said anything about not wanting you here," He said, glancing at Bobby. "Your friend can keep me company while I check Rip out."

As soon as Eric was out the door to the yard, Bobby turned to the doctor, opening his identification so the doctor could read. "Bobby Jay, I'm here to protect Eric Whiting. You'll probably be seeing me around and about when he is working. Eric knew I was outside watching the place, so he called me to lift that dog for him. He is a special boy. If I were you, I'd use him to treat your patients," He told the doctor.

Monroe processed the information and nodded. "Fair enough. We've had people break in looking for drugs, so you may understand my concern about seeing a stranger in the clinic."

Bobby nodded right back at the doctor. "I'll go back to watching the outside now, sir," He said and made to exit.

"Hold on, give me a hand with Rip first," Monroe said. "I need to check to make certain none of the circulation is cut off from the tape slipping when… Eric took him out."

In the same manner, he had handled the huge dog before, Bobby carefully took Rip out of his cage and put him on the exam table, as the doctor indicated. As the doctor reviewed Rip's rear legs, Bobby thought long and hard about speaking up about Eric's problem. "Doc, you know Eric is a good kid with a kind heart. All he seems to want is to help animals. Did you know he would quit this job because he may fail one of his classes? He feels one of the other students should be allowed to gain experience here."

Although Dr. Monroe didn't appear to be listening, he suddenly stopped with his exam and looked up at Bobby. "My question is, why is he failing the class?" he asked.

In for a pound, Bobby thought before continuing. "One of his professors says he has to catch a stray, then kill it for the class. Eric refused, so the idiot told him he'd fail if he didn't. That kid is never going to take a life. It goes against everything he is. You know that kitten he brought here? He ran into a pond and dove under to retrieve it from a sack some thug had just tossed in the water. All the kittens were dead except for that one. Crazy as all get out, but that seems to be the person he is."

"Put Rip up, and thank you for your help," Dr. Monroe said. Stepping over to a locked medicine cabinet, the doctor unlocked it and took out a bottle of pills. In a matter of seconds, he poked the pill down Rip's throat before patting the dog on the head and securing the cage again. He turned and marked the time and amount of medication given to Rip. By the time he looked back up, Bobby was gone.

Monday filled Eric with dread. Things had to be decided soon as to what to do about college. He could either drop out, admit defeat, or figure out a different route to his goal of learning all he could about veterinary medicine. He'd be okay if only he didn't have to take that one class to advance. The more he thought about things, Eric realized he could drop the class and only do the academic courses. It would mean he wouldn't be legal, but if he set up a clinic and hired a licensed doctor, he could give advice and treat the animals, letting the hired help take the credit.

Mind made up, Eric looked around for Bobby as he left the dorm for his early morning run. Only a new guy was shadowing him today. Realistically, Eric knew that his shadows were constantly changing, but that didn't stop the little feeling of disappointment he felt when he let someone into his life and they left. Only the family could be depended upon to be a constant in his life.

Eric ran, not waiting for the new guy to catch up, nor slowing so the guy could keep pace. He just ran until his head was clear of all the disappointment and despair that had been his constant companion. At last, he turned around and headed back to the dorms. It was time to shower and go to class. He waved to the new guy as he passed him. The man was standing with his head down and his hands clutching his thighs as if that was the only thing holding him up. A memory of his mother's face flashed in Eric's mind, and he slowed down to give the new guy a break; it wasn't in him to be cruel to another person. Slowly, Eric fell back until he ran beside his new security guard, glancing at the guy to be sure that the man was okay. "Next time, use a car," Eric advised, then took off, reaching his dorm way ahead of the man assigned to protect him.

Bruce was waiting when Eric came out of the shower. The black cat that blocked the doorway was no longer the tiny kitten he had saved from drowning. Bruce grew at a fantastic rate and would become a large cat. Eric petted Bruce and felt the desire inside the cat to go with him the next time he went running. "Okay, tomorrow we'll run together. Right now, I have class," He told the cat. Bruce sat and stared at Eric while he dressed. He curled up on the bed, looking to be asleep, as Eric grabbed his book bag and left.

Ronny Croft was one of the football players who gave Eric a hard time. He didn't outright bully Eric so much as look down on him. Ronny was massive in size, tall, broad, and confident, all the things Eric wasn't… well, except for the height and confidence; Eric knew what he could and couldn't do. Mainly, Eric didn't envy anyone. As his parents had always told him, he was the one who controlled the person he became; no matter what others thought of him, he knew himself. Yet Ronny, like so many others, thought of Eric as weak, someone to look down upon.

For the most part, Eric ignored Ronny's smirks when he was in the same area as Eric. Except last night, Eric had one of his visions. He spent most of the day deciding what to do about the vision. The day was spent in turmoil over what might happen to Ronny if he wasn't warned not to drive his motorcycle. All day, the vision of Ronny with both legs broken and his arm nearly cut off overrode all other worries. He had forgotten entirely about his resolve to drop Wee Willie's class.

With some reluctance, Eric entered the last class of the day, his last class in this room. It was only fair that he told Mr. William that he was dropping the class. His parents had taught him to face life truthfully and not shirk his duty. Only a stranger, a woman, was behind the desk where Mr. William was always seated. She stood as the students entered and took their seats.

"Good Afternoon. Mr. William has gone on sabbatical. I am Amy Stone, and I will fill in for him for the rest of your time in this class. I understand you are at the point of learning the body through experience. With that in mind, I have arranged for animal control to provide the needed bodies so that we can explore firsthand the different areas and problems of the body. I have assigned you a table where you will find the tools you need and the subject you are to study. You are responsible for seeing that your subject is properly refrigerated and given the care needed to prolong the tissue until we finish our exploration. Here is the first list of what we will do, with your table number." Amy Stone said as she handed each student a sheet of paper. "Look your sheet over, prepare your subjects, and be prepared to show me exactly what is on your sheet for today's lesson. Remember, we will run late in this first class, so I expect you to keep detailed notes in your notebooks. I will examine your notes and your work at the end of class. Now go through the door and turn left. Find your station and begin."

Detailed notes: I can do that, Eric thought. He went to his station to find a tiny dog laid out upon it. Eric checked his list of what he was to examine today. Stomach contents, blood samples, and repairs to the stomach afterward. Eric opened his notebook. Okay, first, the stomach contents. He touched the little dog's body and searched what was in the stomach, carefully noting everything the little one had eaten for her last meal.

> Chicken
> Rice
> Eggs
> Stomach acid
> Water
> A roach

List complete. Eric checked the blood in the little one's body after making note of the elevated white blood cells and the heart-worm larva. He decided it would be best to draw the blood and empty the stomach. Touching the little dog, Eric explained what he would do and why. He asked the dog to forgive him. Only when he felt a small invisible tongue lick his hand did he draw blood samples and cut into the dog. Carefully, he preserved the stomach contents and closed the little dog up. Once done, he took his notebook to the teacher.

Amy was startled when a student approached her desk. She knew he could not have possibly done the assigned work in the short time the students had been working. Indeed, he hadn't accessed the microscope. "Yes, do you have a question?" she asked.

"No, ma'am. I'm turning in my notebook so you can go over the assignment. Do you want to examine the little dog now?" Eric asked her.

"Young man, you can not have possibly done

the assigned work already," Amy scolded the boy, then sighed. "Okay, let us go check your work."

Eric wondered what he had done wrong. He had completed the assignment and listed the results, so why was his teacher upset with him? Was every teacher in this class going to be upset with him?

Amy checked the stitching on the little dog's belly first. It was clear the boy had at least opened the abdominal cavity, but where were the slides from the blood work and stomach contents? "Why have you listed all these contents without proving your results? Where are the slides showing the results? You can't go around guessing what you will find. You have to have proof. Well, where are the slides?" She asked Eric, a stern look on her face.

His stomach was rolling with nervous tension, and Eric realized his mistake. He should have made some slides to show his results. They, other people, couldn't see what he saw. "My mistake, ma'am. I'll have those slides for you in no time. And be certain they are labeled so anyone can understand them. Please give me a moment to correct my mistake," he said, taking his notebook from the teacher. Behind him, he heard Ronny snicker. It was okay; Eric knew he had messed up, and it would not happen again.

"See that you list each slide in your notebook. Careful notes are critical," Amy Stone said, glancing around the room to include all the students.

Fifteen minutes later, Eric again approached Amy's desk, notebook in hand. "I've completed the slides and am ready for you to examine them," he said, nervous now that she would find another fault in his work.

Feeling put upon by a lazy student, Amy snatched the notebook from Eric's hand and marched off to look at his work again. She had no patience with students who did sloppy work, which could kill a patient.

Amy examined the slides Eric had made one by one. She had to admit they were well done. Each held just what was listed for that slide. The blood samples were well done, and the white count was exacting. Okay, so she had been wrong. The young man knew what he was doing, so why hadn't he done the job at the start?

"Normally, I would give you an A+ on this work today. However, you didn't do the work you were supposed to have done until reprimanded, so you have earned a B+ instead. Next time, do the work, understand?"

"Yes, ma'am," Eric said, pleased that, for once, his efforts were recognized.

Across the room, Ronny watched and listened to the exchange between the puny Eric and the teacher. The wimp hadn't even checked his slides before labeling them. What was up with that? Ronny had to double-check each slide, looking up what he saw in the textbooks to ensure he labeled his slides correctly. He would keep an eye on this tall shrimp of a guy. If he was that smart, he could be an asset.

Eric scrambled to catch up to Ronny. He couldn't stand by and not try to save Ronny from the vision he had of him lying broken on the road. Dodging the rush of his classmates vacating the building after the late-running class they had just finished, Eric finally managed to grab Ronny's sleeve. Ronny stopped and frowned down at Eric. "Ronny, do you own a motorcycle?" Eric asked.

"What's it to you, Shrimp?" Ronny growled.

"It is just… well…," Eric hesitated. He didn't tell just anyone about his vision; they'd think he was crazy, not that he cared if they did. Still, the visions were personal, a part of him that he didn't want to share with everyone.

Ronny's look changed from scorn to thinking about Eric's stumbling words. "Just spit it out. I'm listening."

"I don't know how to say this. It is only… well, I had a nightmare last night. It was bad, horrible. You had been on a motorcycle and were in an accident. It was terrifying. Your legs, man, and your arm. I know it sounds unbelievable, maybe it is, but try to stay off of motorcycles for a while, please. I know you hate me, but this is about you, not me. Please try. At least for two weeks," Eric was willing to beg, do whatever it took to keep Ronny from ending up as the vision showed him.

A crease furrowed on Ronny's forehead. He didn't own a motorcycle but was looking for one to buy. At Eric's words, the grim picture that formed in his mind sent a chill down his back. He was supposed to meet his best friend, Charlie. They found one to go try out that was for sale. Charlie had a bike and pushed Ronny to buy one so they could ride together on the weekends. He realized that what he was feeling was similar to fear. The little freak was mucking with his mind. Ronny sneered at Eric, "Get lost, Shrimp." Turning, he stormed off, leaving Eric in his dust.

"Please," Eric called after Ronny. He had failed. What could he do now? He'd have to keep begging him not to ride a motorcycle. "Please," he said under his breath.

The knowledge that you couldn't prevent everything that happened was heavy on Eric's heart for the next two nights. Twice, it had taken too long for Bobby to locate the victim of a crime Eric had foreseen. The failures were something Eric took personally. If only he had seen more detail or had the vision a day before it had appeared to him. The trouble was that 'if only' did not solve anything. He had to try harder and, in this case, work on convincing Ronny that he was sincere. First, he needed to download and print pictures of motorcycle accidents. That would be his project for tonight. The next time he saw Ronny, he'd be armed with gruesome evidence of what such an accident could do to a person. That should help Ronny see how dangerous riding one could be to a human without the body of a car to protect him.

It was a great-looking motorcycle, probably the best deal Ronny would ever find, so why was he hesitating to try it out? That damn skinny kid had gotten into his head was why. His legs and his arm kept popping into his head as stubs. His dad had come home from a tour in the service minus an arm, so Ronny knew what a stub looked like. Ronny straddled the machine and felt the beast's power between his legs; he could almost feel the wind whipping around his body as he and Charlie flew down the highway. Still, he couldn't bring himself to start the monster up. He shook his head and stepped off the motorcycle.

Charlie looked puzzled. "Don't you want to try it out, Ron? We could race down to the corner and back, then load her into your truck."

An expression of regret passed over Ronny's face. "I'm not sold on it. There may be something better waiting out there. It would be foolish to buy the first thing that comes along."

"But, Big Ron, you haven't even given this one a ride." Charlie protested. "It is a sweet machine. I'd buy it myself if I hadn't already sunk my money into Ronda Girl." Charlie reached over and caressed his motorcycle. "She might get jealous, but I will give this monster a spin. If you don't mind."

Ronny waved his hand, indicating Charlie was free to do as he wanted. The machine seemed to purr when Charlie started it up. With a wide grin, Charlie raced down the street, making a circle at the intersection to head back.

That was when it happened—a massive semi without a load plowed through the intersection right into Charlie. Ronny took off running as fast as his legs would carry him, with the bike's owner hot on his tail. Brakes squealed, and the smell of burnt rubber filled Ronny's nostrils as he reached Charlie. The semi's driver was rushing back to where Charlie lay. It was all a nightmare, a horrible nightmare, but no matter how hard Ronny tried to wake up, he couldn't.

The semi's driver had his phone out, telling the

police to hurry and get an ambulance there. The guy was still alive that he had hit. All of it Ronny heard and saw, the mangled bike, Charlie laying in a pool of blood, parts of him twisted in impossible angles. Blood, blood everywhere. All he could think was it should have been him lying there, not Charlie, not his best friend. If the kid hadn't warned him, made him doubt, he would have bought the bike and been the one lying here all broken in bits.

The police and emergency vehicles arrived, and Charlie was scooped up, hooked to an IV, and taken off. Ronny was numb and didn't speak except to tell the information needed on Charlie. He had to call Charlie's parents. The thought became urgent, the focal point in his mind. Once he learned what hospital they were taking Charlie to, he reluctantly took out his cell phone. This was one call he didn't want to make, and guilt was like a thick bile in his throat. It should have been him.

Once he was certain Charlie's parents were on the way to the hospital, Ronny got in his truck. He sat there, unable to start the motor, to think what he was supposed to do now. It was like his mind had lost the ability to think and reason. He never realized he was crying until his vision became so blurred he reached up to rub his eyes to clear them. Ronny's hand came away wet. For a long moment, Ronny stared at his hand, the wetness on his fingers, his tears. Coach's words before the last game, when he was playing injured, came to him then. "Suck it up. Get out there and carry your teammates home, boy." Charlie needed him now more than anyone else in the world, and Ronny would be damned if he would let self-pity keep him from Charlie's side. With grim determination, he started the truck and headed to the hospital, to Charlie.

It was a night-long vigil at the hospital. Ronny, his parents, and Charlie's whole family sat or paced in the waiting room as the surgeons fought to reattach Charlie's arm and save his legs. At 3:30 in the morning, a time that stuck in Ronny's head, the group of surgeons came out to talk to the family. Mrs. Burns, Charlie's mother, collapsed and wept in the middle of the talk. Charlie's dad stood firm and pale through it all, listening, once in a while nodding his head as he held his wife up. Ronny and his parents stood respectfully, letting the family have the news. Ronny heard snatches of the conversation. They hadn't been able to reattach Charlie's arm. Charlie's legs had been smashed with the bones in so many parts that they wanted to remove his legs. Charlie's father shook his head at that suggestion. Charlie was a runner. He loved track and field and running. He had planned to enter the Boston Marathon sometime in the future. His dad would not let them take his legs. He thanked the doctors for saving Charlie's life and sat down to hold his weeping wife, his face pale and drawn, relieved that Charlie would live. He had a long road ahead of him, but his life had been spared.

Ronny was absent for two days from the class he and Eric shared. When Ronny returned to class, Eric had heard about the accident and Charlie. He was relieved that Ronny hadn't been hurt, but he felt responsible because he hadn't seen the other boy getting hurt. He planned to see the boy and do a little healing on him. Any more than a bit of healing would leave him too depleted to make it back out of the hospital. How to get into the boy's room was the first problem to overcome.

It was Thursday before Eric worked up the nerve to ask Ronny if he would go with him to see Charlie in the hospital. When he approached Ronny in the school hallway, Ronny glared at him and turned away. Eric walked up to Ronny anyway and cleared his throat. "Uh... I was wondering..."

Ronny swung around and got in Eric's face, his face red with the pent-up anger and guilt he felt at Charlie being hurt instead of him. "You were wondering what? That you could screw with my head again? Or you could get another of my friends nearly killed, their lives ruined? What? What were you wondering?" Ronny snapped out.

Eric didn't back down or cringe away as Ronny expected out of a wimpy kid like him. He looked solemnly at Ronny. "If you could get me in to see Charlie. I can help him."

"Haven't you done enough? You've crippled him. Charlie lived for two things: riding Ronda Girl and running. He is never going to do either of those things again. His life is over," Ronny growled, so full of anger he was seeing red wanting to hit Eric, to make him hurt like Charlie was hurting.

"Never mind, I'll have to do it on my own. I am sorry, Ronny. If I had seen the possibility of someone else being hurt, I would have warned you. I know it is my fault for not seeing that was possible. I had only wanted to help you. Not to get anyone else hurt. I'll see him on my own and heal what I can. Don't worry, I won't bother you again." Eric said, his voice grim and filled with regret.

The moment Eric left, Ronny's anger went out. He had been a jerk to the kid. He knew deep inside the kid hadn't planned on Charlie being hurt. It had been his fault for even going to look at the bike. The kid had warned him. Why hadn't he listened? Because he is a shrimp of a kid, not someone Ronny could respect or listen to. What did that say about the man he was becoming? Was he going to be one of those jerks who never saw the people around him and self-centered?

That thought lay heavy on Ronny as he rode the elevator to see Charlie in the hospital that night. He had not felt enough guilt over Charlie; now, he felt guilty for how he had treated the wimpy kid.

When Ronny reached the floor Charlie was on, he saw Eric and a guy in a dark suit facing off against the tiny bulldog nurse who ran the floor and refused to let Ronny see Charlie every night. She was shaking her finger in the man's face, lecturing him. "I don't care who you are. No one but the immediate family is allowed to visit with Charlie Burns. Come back in a few days; perhaps the visitation will have changed by then."

The man was holding up some badge identification. He glanced at Eric and took a deep breath as if readying himself for battle. "Ma'am, I have the President on speed dial. Do I need to bother him this time of night?"

Bulldog almost stepped back at those words,

and you could see her resolve kick in. "Go ahead. As if I believed you."

Bobby pulled out his phone and pressed a number on it. You could hear the phone ringing at the other end of the call. The little bulldog nurse looked doubtful for a moment as the phone rang. Still, she stood her ground. "Sir, I'm sorry to bother you. Yes, sir, you are busy, but Eric has a problem. They won't let him in to see a critical friend in the hospital. Yes, sir, I'm sure he plans on doing that." Bobby held the phone out to Eric. "He wants to talk to you," he said.

With a grimace, Eric took the phone and placed it to his ear. "Yes. Yes, I'm going to try to help the guy. You know you can't order me around like you do the Generals and Senate members, don't you? I will be careful. Bobby is here. We are in a hospital near medical help, and I've filled Bobby in on what to do. I promise to be careful. I could come back and help in several short bursts if needed. Okay." Eric handed the phone back to Bobby. Bobby listened for a moment before handing the phone to the bulldog nurse.

"Hello," she said into the phone. "Are you truly the President? How do I know this isn't some setup to get him in to see Mr. Burns? No, no, it won't be necessary, Sir." She was pale when she handed the phone back to Bobby. "You may go in, but keep it short, and don't stress the patient out."

The nurse saw Ronny and shook her head to let him know he couldn't see Charlie. Ronny pointed at Eric, "I'm with him," he said. The nurse's face scrunched up as if she had tasted a sour lemon, and she nodded.

Bobby was shocked when he saw Charlie. One of the boy's arms had been amputated, both his legs were in weird gadgets, and his head was bandaged. He stopped Eric before he could touch the boy. "Eric, let me start that IV thing on you before you begin. Did you finish all your food earlier?"

"Yes, and I brought some of the protein bars. I'll eat one now while you set up an IV, as Dr. Andy told you," Eric told him.

Ronny barely heard the conversation between Bobby and Eric. All he could see was Charlie. It should be me, he thought again. He walked to Charlie's side, which had an arm with various tubes and monitors attached. "I'm here, Charlie," he whispered. He thought he felt Charlie react as if trying to squeeze his hand, so he squeezed back.

Bobby set a chair on the other side of the bed and began to rig an IV for Eric. He had Eric place one arm on the bed and inserted a catheter into Eric's arm. Only then did he let Eric touch Charlie. He knew from what Dr. Andy had told him that the first thing Eric would do was to assess the damage. And he would start to repair the worst areas. There was just so much damage that Bobby was afraid for Eric.

When Eric found a bare patch of skin on Charlie's side and touched the boy, Ronny finally noticed him and Bobby. Anger surged, and he reached out to remove Eric's hand.

Quick as a snake striking, Bobby had Ronny's hand in a death grip. He almost pulled Ronny on top of Charlie to get into his face. "You will not touch either of them. Eric is in enough danger without some snot-nose bully causing more. Stand in the corner if you can't behave yourself," Bobby commanded in his best voice of doom.

Ronny blinked. He hadn't seen the man move. How had he grabbed him so fast? Who the hell was he? Who were they both? Questions pounded at Ronny's mind as he carefully stepped back from the bed. It was then he noticed the IV going into Eric's arm. What the hell? The color blanched from Eric's face right about then.

"Eric, stop. Stop now!" Bobby ordered. He had listened for over an hour to Eric's doctor's instructions last night. The man had scared the shit out of him. He wasn't about to lose his subject here in a hospital.

"Just one more spot. A small one."

"No, stop and rest, then you can do more. Eat another bar."

Ronny was baffled by the exchange between Eric and the man dressed in black. His eyes moved between the two as they exchanged words. The Bobby guy won. Eric took his hand off Charlie and slumped back in his chair. Bobby reached into a backpack sitting on the floor and pulled out some protein bar, which he pressed on Eric. "I don't suppose you brought an energy drink to go with the bars?" he asked Eric.

"In the side pocket."

Eric drank and ate while under the watchful eye of the Bobby guy. Ronny kept his silence, wondering what was going on. Once Eric regained some of his color, he leaned forward and touched

Charlie again. He only touched him for a few minutes this time, but by then, all the color he had gained was gone. Eric started slumping into his chair when he finally lifted his hand from Charlie's skin. "It will do," he mumbled more than said. "I think he'll be able to walk again, maybe run his races. I'm not sure if he will require special physical therapy. Take me home, Bobby, I'm done for."

Bobby removed the catheter from Eric's arm, stuffing the IV into the backpack along with the remains of the energy bar wrapper and the protein drink. Once satisfied, the room did not show what they had done; he put an arm under Eric and helped him stand. "Take the backpack. We need to get Eric out of here without any doctors or nurses wanting to see him. Open the door and pretend Eric couldn't stand seeing Charlie like that."

Nurse Bulldog spied them before they managed to get to the elevators. She strode towards them with that bulldog look on her face. Ronny surprised Bobby by speaking up. "Come on, Eric, don't be such a wimp. You knew he was in bad shape before we went in. Suck it up and be strong for Charlie."

Eric appeared to try to stand straight, waving Bobby off as they approached the elevator. "You are right. Charlie will never let me live down, almost fainting. It was just such a shock."

Nurse Bulldog hesitated as they stepped on the elevator together. She remembered the call and talking to the President. She loved her job and wasn't about to lose it over some kid who fainted at the sight of someone in a sickbed.

On the ground floor, Bobby snatched a wheelchair for Eric, so the rest of the way to the SUV was easy. Nobody challenged them. Once Eric was secured in the SUV and was nibbling on another protein bar, Bobby took Ronny aside. "You are never to mention what went on in that hospital to anyone. To breathe so much as one word is to betray your country and end up in federal prison for the rest of your life. Just be happy your friend will be able to walk and run again. Are we clear?"

At first, Ronny thought the guy was funny, but something about his serious expression and tone of voice convinced him this was serious. "Who are you?" he asked.

Bobby did not look happy at the question as he answered. "Secret Service, I'm Eric's bodyguard. We are always watching him. Go home, put this all out of your mind. I have to get him home and in bed, or he won't be able to attend class tomorrow."

Class, right, Ronny thought. The kid did seem serious about class. He had noticed Miss Stone was tough on Eric. He had always thought Eric deserved to be treated that way. Eric breezed through the assignments while Ronny and the others struggled to complete each. Now, he didn't know what to think. He felt like he had fallen through the world and landed in some alternate universe. Before his mind went completely off the deep end, Ronny needed to find out what the doctors had told Charlie's parents. They would know what his chance of walking or using his legs was.

In front of Charlie's house, Ronny pulled up and turned the truck off. He wasn't sure the Burns even wanted to see his face again. He was the one responsible for Charlie's accident. They must hate him. Ronny knocked on the door, feeling like he was about to play the most brutal game of his life. The door opened a small crack. The next thing Ronny knew, a hand reached out and snatched him, dragging him through the door. Mrs. Burns wrapped her arms around Ronny and nearly strangled him. "Ronny, Ronny, thank you for being there for Charlie. You don't know how much it means to me to know what a true friend you are to Charlie."

For a moment, Ronny couldn't speak. He was so overwhelmed by emotion. Finally, he cleared his throat and took a deep breath. "Would you tell me what the doctors are saying about Charlie? How bad are his legs? Do they think he'll be able to run again?"

Tears form in Mrs. Burns' eyes. Her lips trembled as if she was about to break down and sob. She seemed to get control of herself. "They don't expect him to be able to walk. Running will be a distant dream for Charlie from now on. We must see him through this and let him realize his life isn't over. There are many things a one-armed man can do… many…," her voice trailed off as if she didn't believe in what she was telling Ronny.

Ronny held her and patted her back. "I'm going to see to it he walks, and if at all possible, he will run one day, you'll see. Don't give up hope. Okay?" He was stringing his promise on what Eric had said in the hospital. Ronny had to believe the impossible would happen. He would make it happen somehow.

Mrs. Burns nodded her head. "Okay," she whispered in such a lost voice that Ronny felt like a heel for giving her hope.

Friday loomed damp and dismal. The land was covered in a fine mist, making the world look eerie in the early morning light. The bit of hope Ronny had felt last night seemed to die in that damp mist as he walked across the campus to his first class. He had researched ways to help Charlie the previous night and was depressed with the results. The words significant nerve damage kept spinning around and around in his mind. Mrs. Burns had told him this was what the doctors were saying. They had patched together Charlie's bones as best they could to save his legs, but the nerve damage was something they couldn't fix. He would be dragging around dead weight for the rest of his life.

It was as if the day was playing some ironic joke on him when he entered the last class of the day, and the assignment was to locate the nerves in the dogs' legs. It was almost too much for Ronny to bear. He hesitated to make the first cut, glancing over to where Eric was working away with that calm certainty he had when working on his dog. He hated Eric at that moment. Why was it so easy for Eric and so hard for him? He wasn't dumb. He scored at the top on his IQ test. So, he had to be as bright as Eric. Yet some of this was almost beyond him. Never had he felt like such a loser before. He was so absorbed in his self-pity that it was a moment before he noticed Eric was standing beside him.

"What do you want, shrimp?" Ronny was not

in the mood to be pleasant.

Like before, Eric did not back down. "I want to show you something essential to Charlie's recovery. Do you mind staying after class?"

Ronny felt like he would sit in hell if it would help Charlie. He nodded and began his first cut—the rest of the class crept by for Ronny. As usual, he had to double-check to be sure he had located the nerves Miss Stone had assigned. Several times, he glanced at where Eric had worked or had pretended to work. He noticed Eric had stopped taking notes and was carefully fiddling with the dead dog's body. He didn't call Miss Stone over to check his work as he usually would have done. Something was up with him. Finally, Ronny completed his assignment and called Miss Stone to check on his work. She frowned at a couple of his cuts but passed on his work.

Eric immediately called her over to look at his work. As usual, she could find no fault with his work. Grudgingly, she approved his work. By then, Eric and Ronny were the last of the class in the room. Everyone else had closed up the skin on the legs and put their animals away for the night. "When you two finish, turn out the lights before leaving." Miss Stone told the two boys. She had pressing business elsewhere.

Once Miss Stone left, Eric immediately motioned Ronny over to his table. He pointed to the tiny muscles in his dog's leg. "You see these muscles? How are they attached and here?" he asked Ronny. Ronny nodded.

"These are the muscles you have to exercise in Charlie's legs. You have to do the whole leg, but these were almost destroyed on Charlie. The larger muscles will take a long time to recover, but he is less likely to walk if you don't start exercising them. It will help strengthen the larger muscles. Usually, the surgeon takes care of them, considering the long muscles more important. In Charlie's case, you must start with these small, healed muscles. I didn't have the energy to heal the larger muscles completely, so I concentrated on the nerves and these little guys. The large muscles are patched as much as the surgeons can patch them. They will heal over time, but until they do, you need to work his legs gradually this way and that, slowly increasing the bend and stretch of the leg muscles. Understand."

"Not really, but I'm willing to do anything to help Charlie walk. Are you certain this will help?"

"It has to Ronny. The only other thing I can think of would be to bring my mother here to have a go at him. I don't think Dad will agree to that. He is super protective of her. She… uh… died a couple of times. I don't think he could take it happening again. Giving this all you have would be best to pull it off. I'll have Grandfather talk to the hospital, and they will let you work on him after that. I can't risk showing up there again. That nurse knows my face. She is more likely to accept you, but I doubt she will accept me interfering again. I certainly can't risk the exposure. They'd take me out of college and put me in some secluded cabin like my sister Susan.

"Work the legs like this. Here, lie back and relax your legs so I can show you. Then you can have a practice on me."

Like a fool, Ronny lay on the floor, trying to

relax his legs. Eric picked a leg up and slowly moved it. He showed Ronny all the little moves he would start with, explaining that later on, he would show him more advanced moves. Then Eric threw himself down on the floor to let Ronny practice on him. "Just pretend it is Charlie's leg. Remember, his legs are still healing, so you must be gentle. Carefully lift the leg and slowly flex the foot for a while, then bend the leg the slightest bit. You will want to bend the leg more each time until you can flex it with no pain for Charlie. Do repetitive actions five to ten times to start. You also want to flex the foot as if pressing down on something. This added tension will help greatly. Got it?"

"I think I understand what you are saying. What if I put too much tension and damage the muscles?" Ronny asked.

"That is why you must start slow; the muscles are bunched in healing mode, trying to hold themselves together. A certain amount of ripped and torn parts are seeking to grow back together. But they need to be encouraged to relax and stretch out, which is what you will do. Massage the muscles before and after each session with Charlie to encourage them to relax. Okay, lecture over. Call me any time, day or night, if you have questions." Eric stood and began to prepare his dog's body for storage.

Ronny was still trying to figure out what Eric was telling him. He grasped the idea but lacked confidence in himself. Self-doubt had never been a problem for him; now, it ate at him like a flesh-eating bacteria. What if Eric was blowing hot air, and he ended up hurting Charlie's chances of walking? On the other hand, if he didn't try this, Charlie might never be able to walk.

Chapter Three

FLYING UNDER THE RADAR

Summer had arrived, and Eric had a few weeks to concentrate on his job at the clinic, run with Bruce, and send Bobby to save lives. Of course, nobody knew that the reason an SS guy just happened to interrupt whatever tragedy that came into their lives was that Eric had sent him. They were too happy that the whole thing was over. Bobby always silently withdrew once the locals were there to take over. He and Eric flew under the radar, people who were never known or just disappeared from the scene.

For his part, Eric was just happy to be doing well and having the freedom to run at night with Bruce. Bruce surprised Eric at first with his speed and ability to keep up. Now and then, the cat would detour to catch a rat or mouse, but he always managed to catch back up.

Bobby fretted over his fear of losing sight of Eric. One night, he thought a shadow was stalking

Eric and ran forward with his weapon drawn. There was a shadow, a deep black shadow shaped like a cat. Spying the gun in Bobby's hand, Bruce attacked the SS agent. The agent went down with a panther, pinning him to the ground by his throat. That was the night they learned that Bruce could shift into a panther. This was both a relief and a worry for Bobby. The cat was another protection for Eric… provided he didn't eat him.

Bobby still had trouble keeping up with Eric, so he made Eric carry a tracking device in case they became separated. The tracker meant Eric did not have to worry about losing Bobby. On a Tuesday night when the moon was hiding away in the sky, such a separation happened.

That Tuesday night, Bruce made such a detour while Eric continued. Eric planned on cutting through an alleyway, running around the block after exiting the alley, and heading home. He didn't notice Bruce had fallen behind until a burly man with a gun stopped him in the alleyway.

"Give me your money," the man demanded.

"You are making a big mistake here, sir," Eric said in his most calming voice.

"You are the one who made the mistake, Buddy. Hand the cash over, now." There was no mistaking the menace in the man's voice or the threat of the gun.

"Listen, why don't you just leave while you are in one piece?" Eric reasoned.

For an answer, the man pointed the gun at Eric's chest. At about that time, Bruce arrives. A growl, low and dangerous, echoed through the alley. "Now you've done it," Eric said, still using a calm voice. "You've made my cat mad. Stand perfectly still and drop the gun."

"I'm not afraid of no cat!" The man bragged. It was then Bruce came around Eric. The panther crouched, his lips drawn back, showing his huge fangs. Bruce's eyes seemed to glow in the darkness of the alley. "What the hell?" The man yelled. Bruce was on him in one bound, knocking the man down and clamping his mouth around the man's throat. Thankfully, Bobby arrived, his gun drawn, ready to take down whatever threatened his subject. There was the stink of fresh urine as Bobby reached down and secured the man's gun. Bruce ducked behind Eric and changed back to cat form.

"Shoot the devil cat! Shoot it, shoot it," the man raved while Bobby handcuffed him.

"What? You want me to shoot this little cat? Man, you are one sick bastard," Bobby said calmly as Bruce weaved around him. "I have an attempted assassin cuffed here. Please send a car to take him away," Bobby said into his phone. Other agents in the area would see to it the man with the gun went away for a very long time. Bobby winked at Eric, "You can't even do a run without finding trouble," he joked with Eric. "I think our run is over."

It was the first time Bruce had changed to panther form while they were running, other than when Bobby was the victim. It seemed to give Bobby some satisfaction to know Eric was protected by his cat. The marks on the gunman's throat would fade fast. Bruce hadn't even broken the skin. Although

Bobby knew the man would speak of a panther attacking him, there was no evidence to prove it. Bobby pointed to Bruce when the man started raving about the monster cat to the agents who arrived to take him away, and they all laughed. There would be no report of the attack, and this man would silently disappear into some forgotten cell. He had attempted to shoot the President's grandson. His life was over as a free man.

The gunman was the action Eric saw most throughout the summer. Most days were mundane: going to the clinic to help with the animals, running and studying in his free time, and telling Bobby about one of his visions—everyday stuff. Once in a while, he heard from Ronny on Charlie's progress. Perhaps the biggest highlight of the Summer was when Ronny called to tell him Charlie had moved his legs. Charlie had a long road ahead of him and was lucky to have such a good friend as Ronny.

There was the new girl at the clinic, Betty. She was shy and asked to be put in the back, cleaning kennels and washing dogs. Eric had already been helping with many surgeries and medicating the animals under hospital care. Even though he was supposed to work just in the back, his remarkable ability to calm animals so they could be treated had him being more called up front. The doctor was happy to put the shy girl in the back and move Eric to the front. This caused some resentment among the older helpers. They seldom spoke to him and never offered to help him. Eric didn't appear to notice they were snubbing him. He had always been the weird kid, the one people hated just because he was alive. So he did his job and sometimes went back to help the girl, Betty, lift the big dogs. They seemed to work together well. To Eric, life was wonderful.

Eric's senior year loomed ahead of him. The break would soon be over, and Eric and the other senior students would be working on live patients. They would be under the supervision of certified doctors. They were expected to diagnose and treat patients, from bovine to rats. They would spend several months in each department, trying their hand at surgery and treating colossal draft horses. Eric was excited and looking forward to this year. Afterward, he'd spend a year as an intern at whatever clinic that would take him. Life was indeed excellent.

How do you get a girl to like you? That question was burning in Eric's mind most often these days. He had no solution. It wasn't like a sickness he could see and maybe heal. But a nagging thought which plagued him at odd hours during the day. He had three days before returning to class to figure out the solution. Three days to maybe find a way to forever. Hopeless, that is what it was, utterly futile. The more he thought of it, the more confident he was that his life wasn't something he should foster on a woman. There was the problem of Bruce shifting. How do you explain something like that to an innocent woman? There were his nightmares and premonitions. Could he subject a woman to the horrors he went through? Beyond hopeless, it was unacceptable. He dare not even tell Ronny his true nature. The world would look upon him as a freak of nature, something unholy, a thing they'd lock away, perhaps killed, shun most certainly. What right had he in asking a girl to share that life? Eric realized he had talked himself out of ever having a relationship with the girl he had instantly fallen in love with. Gloom and depression settled on his already heavy-laden shoulders.

Dr. Monroe and Bobby both noticed the change in Eric's demeanor. He was quieter than usual, even though he was already a quiet young man. This silence from him was getting on Dr. Monroe's nerves. He had grown used to Eric speaking up when he thought a patient needed a different treatment than Monroe was giving it. Usually, the boy was right in his diagnosis, something Monroe had reluctantly acknowledged to himself if to nobody else. His respect for the boy's insights and magical way of calming animals in distress grew daily. He decided that once Eric had finished interning, he would ask him to be his partner, something he had never considered with any other young want-a-be-doctor. The trouble was that Monroe might change his mind about that partnership if the boy didn't leave his gloom soon.

Knowing he only had three days before returning to intense work at college turned a switch inside Eric. He no longer feared doing little things for Betty. At lunch, he bought a plant with substantial bell-shaped flowers of brilliant purple edged in white and placed it in the kennel room by Betty's things.

The next day, he brought a book he had seen of weird animals that were real.

On the last day of working full time, he left a
hair clip shaped like a butterfly. Silently, he left that
night, knowing that he still had some weekends when
he could work at the clinic but feeling depressed all
the same. Bruce greeted him with extra affection.
The cat had been a great pal to him, even saving his
life. Still, his life would not be fully lived if he didn't
have this girl he was so taken with in his life. Yet he
couldn't bear to think of her in his life either. He felt
he was being torn in two directions with huge trucks
called doubtful fear and love battling inside him. He
couldn't have love without the other truck running
over him and smashing Betty. And that he couldn't
let happen.

Bobby Jay was worried about Eric. Something
was going on with this young man, whom Bobby
had sworn to lay down his life to protect if needed.
Only Bobby couldn't get a handle on the cause of
the problem. Dr. Monroe had confessed he was
worried about Eric. They decided to surprise Eric
with a Back to the Grindstone Party. They had
invited everyone from the clinic and that boy from
college that Eric had taken to, Ronny. It was simple
for Bobby Jay to arrange for the restaurant Eric liked
the most to be sold out for one night. After all, he
did have a little pull from the guy who had stopped
a robbery there. Of course, Eric had seen the theft
happening in his nightmares. So it was arranged
that there would be just enough cars in the parking
lot not to give away the surprise. All in all, Bobby
was pleased with the arrangements they had made.
Yet Bobby was worried about Eric. Something was
wrong with the boy.

Riding to the restaurant, Eric looked like the world had ended. Bobby shook his head, not knowing what they could do besides the party. He could call Eric's sisters, but he knew that each had their troubles, and there was no way he would add to their burdens unless all else failed.

It was weird, Eric thought. The place was nearly empty except for Dr. Monroe, sitting alone at a table. He waved them over as if the place was crowded instead of empty. When Bobby and Eric reached the table, Dr. Monroe stood up, as did people from the clinic and Ronny from under the tables around the restaurant. "Surprise!" rang out from everyone. Welcome to your Back to the Grindstone party," Dr. Monroe said.

There she was, his Betty, with the butterfly hair clip in her hair and one of the blossoms from the plant he had given her stuck in it at the end. Eric tried not to look at her, not to care, not to want the impossible, but he failed. He pulled out a chair for her to sit down, smiling. He had to stop, to do better, not care, not care, not care. And the gloom was on him again. So he faked a smile at the others and tried to look like he was enjoying himself for their sake.

Ronny joined them at their table—well, they all joined him, pulling tables together so they could all sit at one long table. Ronny noticed when Eric glanced at the girl. She wasn't pretty, not someone he would have dated, but Eric seemed to like her one moment, and the next looked lost. So Ronny joked and played nice with the girl and the others. These were Eric's friends. The thing is, Ronny hadn't known Eric had any friends.

As everyone was saying goodnight, and the enormous grindstone-shaped cake on the table was demolished, Betty had a chance to talk to Eric. She didn't know what to say. How could she thank him for the little gifts he had given her? Nobody ever ever gave her gifts. She braced herself to say goodnight, for she couldn't ever thank him, not him. He would be someone important, a famous doctor, someone people admired. It was her turn to say goodbye. "Th…ank, uh, thank you for the gifts."

Despite all the promises he made himself, all the resolve in his body and mind, despite feeling like his life was ending, Eric smiled. "You are welcome. I'm glad you like them," Eric said. The sun had suddenly shown even though it was night outside.

This was Eric's final year of college, and it looked grueling. Despite having some classes, each pupil was expected to spend long hours at the college hospital diagnosing cases and helping the real doctors with treatments, surgeries, and repairs.

The first day Ronny and Eric teamed up, they would work on everything put before them together. It could be worse, a lot worse. Eric could have been teamed with one of the few rough bullies in their class. Ronny, at least now, considered Eric human, and he often talked to him about the work on restoring Ronny's friend Charlie's legs. The work on those legs was now entirely up to the hospital therapists and Ronny. Ronny even taught the therapist what Eric had shown him how to do, and Charlie made remarkable progress. The University set up online classes for Charlie so he didn't fall behind the other students.

Ronny and Eric had drawn large animals in the first-semester class. Each night, they were to study their textbooks on the various things they might be running into during the day. During the day, they served two of the regular doctors as helpers, doing whatever the two decided to ask them to do. Not for the first time, Eric ran into a doctor who seemed to take an instant dislike to him. Ronny, on the other hand, was liked by the doctor. So Eric let Ronny take the lead, silently backing him up in caring for the horses and cattle they handled.

Ronny was fuming. That dodo of a doctor had Eric cleaning the stall for an old mare they were working on while he was helping by holding the mare by the halter as the doctor examined her and told Ronny what he was doing in his exam of the horse's legs and joints. He then showed Ronny how to pill a horse. That done, he had Ronny take the horse back to her stall.

"What did he say was wrong with her?" Eric asked as Ronny led the old mare into the stall and released her.

"Arthritis," Ronny said, trying to keep his voice pleasant. "He gave her something for the joints. He said the owners would probably put the horse down if she couldn't produce more foals."

Eric rubbed the mare's neck, whispering to

her as he had when Ronny had been sent to fetch her. No, it wasn't arthritis; he could feel some poison inside the bloodstream, causing the mare immense pain. Black walnut, it was black walnut or some part of it the horse was eating. "Ronny, tell the doctor that the mare eats black walnut bits.

"It could be in the bedding they are using where she lives," Eric said, then wheeled the wheel barrel off to dump the old bedding in the compost pile.

It isn't right, Ronny thought; Eric does all the diagnosing, and this creep takes all the credit, as he watched Dr. Bumbler, the name he called his instructor in his mind, walk off to inquire about the black walnut theory. The guy was too quick to accept the first thing that fit the symptoms. Chances were that the owners would go home and start using good bedding for the mare, and Old Bumbler would get all sorts of praise for Eric's find. But Ronny kept his mouth shut, hoping Eric would eventually stand up for himself. He knew that Eric had guts when he believed strongly in something. Trouble was getting him to that point. Look how he had hounded Ronny about Charlie.

By Friday, Ronny had had enough of Dr. Bumbler's treatment of Eric. He was seriously considering telling the guy off himself. He saw Eric touching one of the other doctor's bovine patients. He wasn't surprised to see Eric approach Doctor Benny, as the patient's owners called this doctor. Ronny couldn't hear what they were talking about, but Dr. Benny went over to the patient and began to look the cow over again. Soon, he had Eric holding the cow as he reached his gloved hand up the cow's rectum.

"To the right, yes, there," he heard Eric call out. Dr. Benny grunted and started moving his hand back and forth as he withdrew it from the cow. Whatever the item he pulled out of the cow was set aside as Dr. Benny quickly stepped towards Eric. There was a rushing gush as the cow emptied the backed-up stool inside her. Dr. Benny slapped Eric on the back with his clean hand and laughed at the amount of mess the cow made.

"Who are you teamed with?" Dr. Benny asked Eric.

Glancing over to where Ronny was standing, Eric nodded towards him, "Ronny there, we make a good team."

"No doubt. How would you like to spend some time helping me? I think my pair would suit Dr. Rich just fine," Dr. Benny said.

Eric motioned for Ronny to come over, and he explained what Dr. Benny wanted. "Sure, I'd be glad to work for you, Doc," Ronny said.

So, the next day, Ronny and Eric were under Dr. Benny's care. This was a new experience compared to Dr. Rich. Dr. Benny was a true teacher. He often had his students doing things they would never have had the opportunity to do if they were under another large animal doctor. Half the time, they had their arms up to the elbow in an animal. Much of the work had to do with calving and digestive problems. They learn the best method for drawing blood, giving medication, examining large animals, worming, and vaccinating. Calves were delivered with the help of the two students. They learned how to tell when a cow was about to calve and when it was in distress.

Eric and Ronny quickly learned to wear rubber boots when messing with cattle or horses. The odor of horse and cow followed them home and lingered even after bathing. The two young men learn to laugh about themselves when blasted by the foulest odors. Though it was hard work, the two were saddened to be sent on to the small animal clinic.

Working with small animals such as dogs, cats, birds, reptiles, rodents, and small exotic animals could be just as dangerous and as satisfying as working with the larger animals had been. The people who owned pets were often the problem.

Dr. Stoker had little patience with Floppy's owners. Twice, they had brought the little dog in complaining about intestinal gas being passed in the middle of the night by their little darling. Twice now, he had explained it was the food being fed to the little fellow, that no amount of medication would cure the problem, and that only changing what Floppy was being fed would work. "No food from the table," Dr. Stoker repeated.

"But, doctor, Floppy loves her little treats at dinner. You know we stopped giving her the fatty stuff," Mrs. Hebert said in her most innocent tone. "We only feed her the vegetables now. You wouldn't believe how much she loves her broccoli. It is just amazing."

With a deep sigh, Dr. Stoker tried again. "You

know how broccoli gives you a gassy stomach. What do you suppose it is doing to poor little Floppy here? It is upsetting her tummy and causing gas in the middle of the night. People's food is good for us but not for our little doggies. You are harming Floppy, feeding her from off the table. Feed her only the dried dog food. She is a much happier puppy, and your gas problem will disappear. Now promise me you will stick to the dry food I've prescribed," He told the owner sternly as he spoke.

"Okay, we will try." That didn't sound like a promise, more of a dismissal. From the corner of his eye, Dr. Stoker noticed his students trying hard not to laugh.

Once Mrs. Hebert was safely out of earshot, Dr. Stoker turned on the two young men. "This is not a funny situation. Sooner or later, they are going to bring Floppy in, and she will be too far gone with a heart attack or some other dietary preventable problem. As future doctors, it is up to you to do everything you can to prevent that happening. Call in the next client," he told Ronny.

The next patient was a rabbit. He was in a crate, and they could all hear the frantic scratching inside it. Once out of the crate, the problem was clear to Dr. Stoker, but he wanted to see what his students thought. For the next patient, he intended to turn over to them and observe. "Okay, you two tell me what you think is wrong with our bunny friend here," he instructed.

Eric and Ronny approached. Each of them looked the rabbit over. Ronny went first and felt the rabbit's body all over before looking at its eyes and into its ears. He stepped back and let Eric touch the rabbit. The fact that Eric didn't look into the rabbit's ears did not sit well with Dr. Stoker. So, he asked him his opinion first, figuring he had no clue. "Okay, Eric, let's hear what you say about the patient. Then, Ronny, I want your opinion. Eric, go," Dr. Stoker ordered.

"He has ear mites, plus he needs to be fed more greens," Eric said, stepping back to let Ronny speak his bit.

"I concur on the ear mites; I didn't pick up on the greens, though," Ronny said, looking down at having missed that information.

"And what would be your treatment?" said Dr. Stoker,

"Ivermectin," Ronny and Eric said at the same time.

Dr. Stoker took over then, explaining that everything the rabbit touched must be cleaned thoroughly, as well as the length and frequency of the treatment. Most importantly, the treatment needed to be repeated until all future hatches of the ear mite were dead.

Ronny and Eric alternated seeing sick animals for the rest of the day. One would be the attending while the other would run the lab test, checking for intestinal worms and heartworms. This was why they paired the students so that each would have hands-on experience and get used to running the lab tests themselves. There were a lot of repeat clients who came in for having stitches removed or having casts updated on growing pups, to more serious problems where the patient would have to stay for treatment or surgery.

While Eric ate it all up, feeling he was helping the animals, Ronny was nervous, always wondering if he was doing the proper treatment. He didn't have the ease of seeing what was wrong with the animal without running labs and now and then ordering X-rays. Dr. Stoker checked their results before giving each patient a rundown on the required medication or treatment. It was a busy day, although they saw no remarkable cases. Eric wanted to experience everything and was looking forward to doing surgeries. Ronny thought he had learned much about treating the owners that first day. He felt this was what he took away from that day of seeing real clients.

Dr. Stoker sat the two students down in his office. He took an extra-long time, it seemed to them, reviewing his notes for that day. When he looked up at the pair, they couldn't tell from his expression if he would blast them or tell them where they were lacking. Wiping his glasses, Dr. Stoker looked first at Ronny. His eyebrows knitted together as if trying to figure Ronny out. "Ronny, you seem to have a questioning approach as if you are searching for another answer to what you find with a patient. That is good. We should never think we know everything, not ever. To dismiss a possibility may be to miss the cause of an animal's problem. I think you will make a fine doctor if you keep this up. Only," he let that hang there for a moment, "don't second guess yourself into doing something costly and unnecessary. Think of the client's pockets. He is likelier to have his pet put to sleep if you order many tests that run the cost up so much he feels he can't pay the bill. Another thing I noticed is that you have a feel for the client, and you can talk to them politely so they understand what you intend to do and what they must do. That is very commendable."

Dr. Stoker turned his gaze towards Eric. "As for you, I think you are a lazy student. You manage to come to the right diagnosis but don't confirm your guesses before jumping in and getting the client all worked up. You could be wrong, you know. That is sloppy work; at some point, you will be wrong and lose a patient who could have been saved by simply confirming what you think is happening. I wouldn't want to be the person you have to explain how you lost their dearly loved pet to. That will be all for today. I suggest you both hit the books for a few hours before bed."

They were dismissed. Like that, they were sent off to think about what Stoker had told each of them. Ronny was floating on air while fuming over what the doctor told Eric. "Why didn't you say something and stick up for yourself?" he asked Eric.

"Because he is right. I don't do the tests, and just because I don't feel the need to do them doesn't mean I shouldn't. I need to have something to show the clients so they understand." Eric looked into space, feeling every bit of the disappointment Dr. Stoker had instilled in him.

It is seldom all sweetness when it comes to treating animals. When in pain, they are often fearful and cautious of being touched. They have no way of knowing you are trying to help, but they understand they will hurt if you pick them up. Back pain is often shown by a pet's reluctance to be held. They hide under things to avoid being bumped, picked up, or even petted if the pain is intense enough. Ronny encountered such a patient during his first solo session with a client. Dr. Stoker rotated from room to room, observing as each student tended to a patient. He was always ready to step in and take over if needed, and of course, he would give the final okay on any medications given out. This batch of students was due to rotate out at the end of two weeks to go into the surgery unit.

So it was when a Miniature Dachshund came in wrapped in a towel growling, the first thing Dr. Stoker thought of was a bad back as Dachshunds often had this problem. The frantic little woman who owned the Dachshund told Ronny how the dog had become fearful at first and then aggressive. Ronny was patient with the owner, telling her there were many reasons her little dog might feel this way and that he first had to examine little Taco. He unwrapped the dog as he talked, ensuring his voice was soothing, hoping to calm the patient and the owner. Ronny looked up and smiled at the owner, trying to get her to relax, and that was when Taco nailed him. The little dog frantically snapped repeatedly, puncturing Ronny's hand several times.

Eric came to help Ronny, thinking he could calm the poor dog, but one touch and he snatched his hand away. "Dr. Stoker, bring me a crate immediately. Hurry!" He called out since Stoker was with one of the other students. By the time Dr. Stoker arrived with the crate, Eric had the little dog tightly wrapped up in the towel again. He shoved the towel and dog into the crate. Leaning close to Dr. Stoker, he whispered, "Rabies."

Dr. Stoker looked sternly at him. "You can't tell that at a glance," he said, looking towards the owner. "Miss Harper, we need to run some tests on Taco. If you leave him with us, we will get to the bottom of his unusual behavior." Miss Harper nodded as she held back tears, then reluctantly left. Dr. Stoker took the dog and crate to the back to isolate the animal, just in case.

In the meantime, Eric demanded Ronny give him his hand. "Give me your hand. I have to heal you immediately," he said with urgency.

"No, it is just a few shallow bites; I've washed and disinfected it. You get weak, and Dr. Stoker is liable to use that excuse to kick you off the team," Ronny said in a low whisper.

"Give me your damn hand!" Eric shouted at him. He was too concerned about rabies to give a wit about losing his place in the rotation.

That fear in Eric's eyes finally convinced Ronny, and he placed his hand in Eric's hand. "Get ready to catch me," Eric told him. He went into Ronny's hand quickly, speeding as fast as he could to the bite marks. The deadly killer was there multiplying and starting to invade Ronny's blood. He killed it as soon as possible and fought it with savage energy, not even caring if it drained him completely. This was one of those things that needed to be attacked fast; you didn't have time to play with it, find what worked best, and just kill it. When finished, he looked up at Ronny with relief and passed out.

Ronny caught Eric and put him on the exam table. Next, he pulled Eric's cell phone out of his pocket and pushed the button on it he had seen Eric use when calling Bobby. "He's out," he said as soon as Bobby answered. "I think he needs that IV. Whatever, he healed me, it must have been bad, nasty, man. Hurry!"

Intending to jump all over Eric, Dr. Stoker arrived just as Bobby Jay pushed his way into the room with a backpack. Bobby began to set up the IV without looking up at Dr. Stoker, which was just about the last straw.

"Hold it right there. You can't come bursting in here," He said to Bobby, then noticed Eric on the table and turned to Ronny. "Did he pass out? Get a wet towel and then raise his feet."

Ronny stepped between Dr. Stoker and Eric, keeping him from interfering with Bobby Jay as he set up the IV for Eric. The man was used to doing this by now. He had the catheter inserted in no time. Bobby was worried about Eric, having never seen him this pale before. Once he was done, he sent Ronny to see what blankets were there. Then he faced the angry Doctor. Pulling out his ID, he flashed it before Dr. Stoker's face. "What has happened here is something you will never speak about again. Not even in your sleep are you to mumble about what happened here. This man is under the protection of the Secret Service. You may see me around from time to time. Ignore me. But do not ignore my subject. He is worth ten thousand of you. Do You Understand?" Bobby said.

"The boy shouldn't have made it this far in classes. He is lazy and does not do half the lab work he should. And how dare he to tell me that little dog had rabies in front of the owner. There is no way he can know what Taco has just by looking at him," Dr. Stoker was on a tear, worked up, and ready to let all his frustrations out on this stranger.

"Rabies?" Bobby looked over at Eric with an expression of awe. "He healed Ronny of rabies? No wonder he passed out. Good God, maybe I should call his mother," Bobby shook his head, "No, let him double-check Ronny first to see if he got it all. I can't believe it, rabies," Bobby's voice trailed off as Ronny entered with an armful of towels.

Dr. Stoker stood back as Ronny and the man in the black suit fussed over the goof-off Eric. He was surprised when the man in the black suit turned to him again and issued orders.

"This room is off-limits for now. We have to make certain nobody else gets wind of this. Your job is to make sure nothing, and I mean NOTHING, leaks out about this. If you fail, I will see that you are locked away in a hole so deep you won't see daylight ever again."

Bobby stared down at the doctor, aware that the man was pumped up with misplaced ego anger; he couldn't take a chance that the word that Eric had cured rabies leaked out. "If anyone asks, you will say that the dog made a huge mess here, and you have these two students cleaning it up. That will explain the towels and their absence. It would be best if you started tests on the dog who bit Ronny here immediately. Don't let anyone else attend to the dog. Once you confirm Eric's diagnosis, you'll know what to do. Oh, and find out if anyone at the owner's home was bitten."

Dr. Stoker tried again to talk some sense into this black-suited man. "That dog can't have rabies. All dogs are vaccinated against it. Besides, a house dog wouldn't have been exposed to rabies; a wild animal would have had to have bitten Taco for him even to be exposed." He stopped talking when he noticed Ronny had gone a bit pale.

"Rabies? He cured me of rabies? I thought he was freaking out over the dog biting me," Ronny stood staring at Eric's sleeping form, muttering to himself. "I owe him my life twice now."

Adjusting the towels around Eric once more, Bobby glanced at Ronny. "The motorcycle thing?"

"It was supposed to be me. Did he tell you that? I was supposed to be the one who lost an arm and had my legs ruined. He bugged the hell out of me until I decided not to buy the bike. Only Charlie took it for a spin. It was supposed to be me, not Charlie," Ronny said, condemnation in his voice.

"Charlie may have been hit even if it had been you. I understand he wanted you both to ride to the intersection. You were there to be with him, help him walk, help him maybe run again. He wouldn't have his legs working so well if not for you. Give yourself some credit, kid," Bobby said, even as he realized the doctor was listening. It's time for another talk with him.

Turning, Bobby backed the doctor into a

corner. "I can't tell you how special Eric is because if I did, you'd have to be locked away somewhere. All I can tell you is you have it wrong. He is not a lazy boy. Have you considered he doesn't need the tests to know? Think about that, and at the same time, think of what could happen to you if you breathe any of this to anyone," Bobby said in a low voice so close to the doctor that he could see age spots forming on the doctor's face.

Chapter Four

SMOOTHER GOING

Things changed slightly after Eric recovered and went home for the night. He had to pass up doing his run, but a difference in Ronny worried Eric. When they parted for the night, his friend seemed lost in thought.

The real change was in Dr. Stoker the next day. He stopped riding Eric about running the lab tests. Even though Eric was trying hard to remember to run them, he knew he often forgot in his eagerness to help a patient. Eric vowed to try harder to keep up appearances and do the lab work. His life was spent hiding who he was and what he could do. Camouflage, a life of pretending to be as expected, so he knew he could do this. It didn't matter that his mind had already jumped ahead to treatment and the urge to heal. He just needed to do things that seemed normal to the rest of the world, even though it would slow him down.

It was Eric's turn to solo a patient while Ronny

ran the lab test from the samples Eric took. Hiding just out of sight, Dr. Stoker watched everything Eric did. First, the boy rubbed the anxious dog on the head as he asked the owner what had caused him to bring the dog in. He seemed to be listening to the owner until he asked a completely unrelated question. "Has Jocko been in the laundry room lately?"

The owner looked puzzled as he explained how the dog wasn't eating. "My son locked him in there about a week ago. But he wasn't being cruel. He didn't realize Jocko had slipped in there behind him. Jocko was sleeping on a pile of dirty clothes when I found him. I don't think he had been scared while in there," the owner said, defending his young son.

"No, I didn't think he had been scared or upset, but dogs will sometimes chew on things that you and I would never think of them chewing on. What I'd like to do is take an X-ray of his stomach. This may tell us if he has some intestinal upset, which has caused him to go off his food. Is that alright with you?" Eric asked.

From his hidden spot, Dr. Stoker saw Ronny start setting up a film to take an X-ray in the machine even before Eric had the owner's permission. The two worked well together, no matter where they were in the teamwork. Not feeling any shame, Dr. Stoker listened to the two boys as they placed Jocko on the machine to take a picture of his insides.

"He has swallowed something, I think a towel. It is filling his stomach, so he can't eat food. We'll have to send him to surgery to have it removed. Let's lay him like this so the surgeon will have the best view of the item," Eric told Ronny as he stretched the dog out. All this time, the dog was remarkably calm. Once the picture was taken, Eric returned to the exam room with the dog, who was happy to see his owner yet still managed to give Eric a lick on his hand.

Stoker entered the radiology lab as if he were passing by and noticed Ronny developing the film there. "What do you have there?"

Ronny frowned at Dr. Stoker before answering. "Eric thought he felt something odd about the patient's stomach. We are just making certain, is all. You know, running the labs," Ronny couldn't stop his mouth from adding that little bit since Dr. Stoker had been riding Eric so hard over that subject.

Ronny held the processed film to the light so Dr. Stoker could see the towel inside Jocko's stomach. "Good job. I'm certain he has already had the owner sign off on the surgery. I'll personally do the surgery. Tell him I said he did good," Dr. Stoker said. It was the closest he had ever come to an apology to a student. But then, he hadn't done it face-to-face with Eric. Did that count?

For the first time since he had become a teaching doctor, Dr. Stoker felt he didn't have enough time with a student. Usually, he was just happy if they showed enough promise that he thought they would not kill the patient once in private practice. However, he kicked himself this time for not understanding one of his students. How could he have been so arrogant to have assumed the boy was just lazy instead of seeing the real genius the boy had? He had heard of people with unique talents in their chosen field who could leap ahead of others in seemingly magical jumps past what others were doing. He had always thought these people were just insightful and able to work things out in their heads instead of taking the long, tried, and true road others took. Now, he found himself confused and disbelieving his own eyes.

Stoker had insisted Ronny begin the rabies vaccinations even though the test had not been done on the dog they held in quarantine. The larger boy, Ronny, had insisted he didn't need the shots. That is until Eric had told him to take them just to be safe. It was as if Ronny thought that if Eric said so, he should take the shots.

And the dog that swallowed a towel. How had he known when all he did was pet the dog on the head? Dr. Stoker recalled all the times he had jumped on Eric for not doing the labs before pronouncing his diagnosis on the examined animal. He had been right every single time. And that only added fuel to Dr. Stoker's opinion of the boy's work. It was called luck, and if a student skated along on luck instead of knowledge when he went out into the real world, they would end up killing a patient. You needed to know instead of guessing. You had to know how to tell if your assumption was correct and run the test to prove it. Not guess. But then there was that Secret Service guy telling him the boy might not need to run the tests as if he knew something Dr. Stoker would never be privileged to know. He had to know, didn't he?

Eric was nervous as he and Ronny entered the surgical unit. Every student either looked forward to or dreaded this moment. Eric felt both as he and Ronny rushed down the hallway to avoid being late for the orientation. They managed to slip into the back of a group of students as a man with a clipboard walked into the room.

"My name is Dr. North. You, however, may call me any of the nicknames you think up during your time here," Dr. North paused for the expected nervous laugh, then continued. "Today, you are going to watch. By watching, you will memorize every move you see a surgeon make while operating. If you have a question, you should wait until the surgery ends, then speak up. You are not surgery material if you do not voice your questions. Why not? You ask. It is simple: you do not have the inquiring mind it takes to go in and explore for something you can't see on an X-ray. Not everything shows up. So when you suspect it is something the animal has swallowed, you have to look for it. I'm telling you this because the first surgery is such a case."

They followed as the doctor walked over to a holding cage where a thin Border Collie lay looking forlorn as if her best friend had just died. "This little lady is suspected of eating something blocking most of her food. Her symptoms have included vomiting and gradually wasting away. When we took a series of pictures trying to find a mass or object, nothing appeared. As you can see, the owners finally decided to bring the dog in, probably saving the dog's life. Let's begin the prepping," the doctor said, allowing two of his helpers to carry the dog to a table.

Eric couldn't help himself. He had to do it, even with Ronny trying to tug him back by holding on to his lab coat. Reaching his hand out, Eric momentarily touched one of the dog's paws. Abuse! The fear inside the dog screamed at him, and blackness threatened to take his mind over—starvation, long days and nights without food, and often without water. Nothing was blocking this dog's digestion system, nothing. The owner had done this to the dog.

As Eric stumbled backward from the dog, Ronny reached out and steadied him. There was an expression on Eric's face Ronny had never seen before. Anger poured off of Eric, so much that Ronny felt like ducking. "What is it? What is wrong with you?" Ronny asked. Anything that affected Eric this way had to be bad, really bad. The whole rabies thing still sent chills down Ronny's back.

Eric's eyes were cold and deadly when he looked up at Ronny. At that moment, he was the picture of his father, dark and brooding. "The guy was starving the dog to death. They can't do this surgery," he stated in a flat voice that said this isn't going to happen.

"Listen, you can't do that again. They are going to think you are weird. You'd be the freak instead of the doctor. Don't do it, Eric, please," Ronny whispered. He felt panic rushing through himself at the thought of Eric blowing everything. Bucking Stoker had been bad enough; the more people who knew what Eric could do, the worse things could become for him—an idea formed in

Ronny's mind. "Let me go get Stoker. He already knows you are different. Maybe he can help without this coming from you. Okay?" Reluctantly, Eric nodded, and Ronny slipped to the back of the students, watching the dog being prepped for surgery and listening to Dr. North drone on about how important each prep step was for a sterile field.

Ronny navigated the hallways of the University Hospital quickly. His only thought was that he had to get Dr. Stoker quickly before Eric did something weird.

Dr. Stoker washed his hands and pushed the door of the men's room open, stepping out into the hallway. He regretted his extra cup of coffee on the way to work.

"Dr. Stoker, please, you have to come right away."

The call sounded desperate, but Stoker was used to students thinking everything was an emergency. Looking down the hallway, he saw the boy teamed up with the weird kid rushing towards him. "Calm down. Now tell me what this urgent matter is about," he asked Ronny.

"It is Eric. They are to do an exploratory surgery on a dog that has been abused. The owner was starving the dog to death. He must have had a neighbor notice, forcing him to bring the poor dog in. Please, will you do something before Eric does?" Ronny gasped out while trying to get Dr. Stoker to start walking.

Reaching up, Dr. Stoker rubbed his eyes. God save him from stupid students, he thought. With a sigh, he followed Ronny. This would be tricky;

he would be stepping on someone's toes no matter what he did, and all for some mystical skinny kid. Some days, it didn't pay to get out of bed. Expecting an argument to be going on, Dr. Stoker stopped to observe the line of students waiting a turn to palpate the stomach of a dog lying on the prep table. The surgeon was watching each student attempt to find a lump or object inside the dog. Eric was last in line, with one person ahead of him.

Ronny went up behind Eric as if he had been standing in line the whole time. "What happened?"

"One of the others asked if we could try and find what was stopping the dog from eating. Lucky break for our canine friend," Eric said, then turned to Dr. Stoker. "This dog needs to be fed and cared for, sir, and taken from the creep who owns her.

Taking a deep breath, Dr. Stoker slowly let it out. He watched as Eric took his turn, palpating the dog. Eric's hands seemed to caress the dog, and then he slowly straightened up, motioning Ronny to step forward for his turn. He whispered to Ronny, "She is expecting."

Ronny felt first with one hand before using both to press the thin dog's belly between them gently. "Yes, I feel them too—two tiny marbles. Life starting up in pebble form," Ronny said, his face glowing with the incredible feel of young life between his hands.

"What?" Dr. North asked.

"She is expecting, sir. Two puppies. I didn't feel any obstruction. Did anyone else?" Ronny asked. All the students negatively shook their heads.

"So, all that you people learned could not

find anything wrong with the dog," he paused and looked at Eric and Ronny, "except you two, who found puppies. What does that tell us we need to do?" he asked, fully expecting them to all say to do an exploratory.

"Try feeding the dog to see if she can eat?" Ronny asked, hoping to take the spotlight off of Eric.

"Yes! Wait a moment, what did you say?" Dr. North asked.

"Feed the dog to see what happens. This way, we can see the symptoms firsthand," Eric piped up. Behind him, he felt Dr. Stoker step away and heard his footsteps heading back out of the surgery.

"Interesting idea. This might be a worthy project to let you witness why we need to go in and find the cause. Agreed," Dr. North said.

"Thank you," Eric whispered to Ronny. Ronny looked very pleased with himself.

It certainly was no surprise when the owner of the Border Collie did not return to see about the dog or pay the bill. Meanwhile, the Border Collie dog began to regain her weight, becoming a healthy dog once again. She was declared to be abandoned and up for adoption. The fact she was expecting did not appeal to the people looking to adopt a dog. Ronny and Eric felt responsible for the dog's plight. It was, however, the dog's sad eyes that had Ronny applying to adopt her. The problem was she wouldn't be allowed in the dorms. After debating with himself for several days, Ronny approached Eric about renting an apartment together.

Fully expecting Eric to agree to the shared

apartment idea, Ronny brought it up as they scrubbed up to enter the surgery. Today, they would be allowed to close up a couple of the animals being operated upon.

"I was thinking. You have your cat; if I were to take the Border Collie, we could rent an apartment together. It would be better than the dorms, and we could have some meals at home, saving us both money. That is if you don't mind living in the same apartment with me," Ronny said. He looked up when Eric didn't say anything. Eric seemed to be worrying about what to do. "It wouldn't hurt to look at apartments. Would it?" Ronny asked.

Finally, Eric spoke. "I guess not." He looked over at Ronny. "You need to know a few things before we look for an apartment, Ronny. I can't talk about it here. Okay?"

What could Ronny do? He didn't understand Eric's reluctance, and it hurt a little to think that as close as they had become, Eric didn't want to live with him. He nodded and shut off the water with his elbow. What was so bad that Eric thought he needed to know before even looking for a place to live? That thought kept running through Ronny's mind as he was first up to close on a spayed dog. Usually, he would be thrilled to be doing something he had only practiced on dead bodies, but his mind worried about what Eric wanted to tell him. In autopilot, Ronny grasped the inner lining with his pickups, threaded a stitch through it, and brought the needle through the other side. He was on the last stitch on the outer skin before he even realized it. Surprised, he looked up at the attending surgeon to see his reaction to the stitch line. "Step back and scrub out. You will learn about how you did when everyone else has finished. Sucks to go first, doesn't it?" Dr. Hilton smirked. Ronny nodded, letting the Doctor believe he was okay with waiting. It did suck to go first when you had to wait around to hear the results.

How did he tell Ronny about his hectic life? More critical was whether he should trust Ronny with the secrets of his life. These questions and more bombarded Eric as he stepped to the table to stitch up a cat spay. He knew he was doomed to live a lonely life unless he could find the one woman who would love him despite his nightmares, his sugar lows when healing, and his cat transforming into a panther when upset. It didn't seem fair to Ronny to expose him to all the crazy happenings in Eric's life. Ronny didn't deserve to have that burden on him for the rest of his life. His mind was off, thinking of all the damage that could be done to Ronny's mental health if Ronny were to step into his world. Eric, like Ronny, Eric did his stitching on autopilot. Only he caused a small amount of healing on the inside of the cat as he put the last stitch into the skin area. Dr. North's gruff voice said, "Step back and scrub out," which caused Eric to become aware of those around him. He nodded to Dr. North and stepped away from the table.

Eric glanced in the observation area to see Ronny looking at him as if concerned—nothing for it but to call Bobby Jay and seek his advice. "Bobby, I need to talk with you," he said into his phone. There was no way he would talk about this over the phone. They'd have to go to the park or someplace with wide-open areas to avoid being overheard. Reluctantly, he moved up next to Ronny. "I need to talk to Bobby Jay, then we can talk, okay?"

Ronny nodded and watched with troubled eyes as Eric slipped away from the class. He had forgotten. How the hell could he have forgotten the Secret Service was protecting Eric? No wonder he had put off saying anything about moving into an apartment together. There had to be restrictions on the poor guy. What was it like to live in a goldfish bowl with someone watching your every move? He'd be living in that goldfish bowl if they shared an apartment. He hadn't thought of that.

Bobby was waiting when Eric exited the surgery area. "What's up?" he asked, his brow furrowed.

Eric rubbed his forehead and kept walking as he spoke. "Not here. Private."

Now, Bobby Jay was apprehensive. Anything that required privacy had to do with the things Eric or his family could do or a threat to them. He began to hurry Eric outside and to the car, his eyes searching every spot and every move from a person just in case the threat was there. Once in the car and on the road, Bobby took a breath. "Okay, spill."

Eric looked away from Bobby out the car window and the campus grounds passing by as he spoke, "Ronny wants us to move into an apartment together for this last year so he can adopt Molly, the pregnant dog. I want him to have her, but is it fair to him to have to witness me having nightmares? And what about Bruce? He could put a real scare into the guy. This is my lot to bear; I don't know if it is right to give him nightmares, too. Then there is the whole 'Swear on your life' thing. He'd have that hanging over his head the rest of his life."

Pulling the car over to the curb, Bobby turned to face Eric. "So what are you going to do? Are you just going to spend the rest of your life without friends who know who you are? Wouldn't having just one friend you could talk to about a nightmare beside me be great? And Bruce, will he never be allowed to play with another animal friend or have someone you know pet him? I can understand how scary it must seem to let someone in and trust them to do what is right. To believe in you. But, you have to let a few people into your life. You don't deserve having to deal with life alone," Bobby held up his hand to stop Eric from protesting. "I think Ronny has already proved he will be okay knowing the real you."

Gulping to try and loosen the knot in his throat, Eric nodded. "Will you help me explain it all to Ronny?"

Bobby Jay slapped Eric on the back. "Of course, kid," he said, starting the car and heading back to drop Eric off to finish his class.

Stepping back into the small crowd that comprised their part of the Senior Class, Eric went to where Ronny was practically biting his nails, waiting for the results of his stitching up his patient.

"Bobby will join us to discuss an apartment," Eric said.

Ronny blinked, and thirty seconds passed

before he nodded in reply. He has changed his mind, Eric thought. He couldn't blame Ronny for changing his mind. Who would want to sleep in the same apartment as him?

"Ronny, if you have changed your mind, I'll understand. Look, you are my hero for taking Molly. Without you, her future looks bleak. Maybe you can move in with Bobby Jay and the night man. Bobby doesn't sleep much, and his place always has an empty bed. He has put me in it a few times. Don't feel like you have to put up with me."

"Shut up. Just shut up that nonsense," Ronny said, his voice gruff and angry. So, Eric shut up.

Eric felt he was attending his funeral when he met Ronny in his dorm room. Bobby Jay was carrying a briefcase, and Eric knew it held a lot of papers for Ronny to sign. That is, if Ronny even agreed to listen to all the restrictions in his life because of Eric. Neither of Eric's sisters had ever had any girlfriends to yak with or anything like a typical teenager's life. Eric certainly hadn't had any friends until Bobby Jay. Bobby was the closest Eric had been to a friend in his whole life besides Middy and Susan.

Ronny stood up when Eric and Bobby Jay entered his room. He meant it as a sign of respect for the Secret Service Agent, but it was also a sign that he was nervous. He sensed Eric's tension since he had broached the subject of their getting an apartment together. He thought the Secret Service protected Eric all this time because of his strange healing ability. Now, he wasn't so sure that was the reason. When Bobby Jay pulled a device out of his briefcase and started scanning the dorm room, Ronny wondered what he was getting himself into here.

Bobby's face was grave when he told Eric and Ronny to sit down. So much could go wrong during this conversation. Instead of helping Eric gain a friend he could depend upon, Bobby might lose that friend for Eric.

"Before we can even have this conversation, Ronny, you will need to take an oath and sign documents swearing you will never reveal in any form or means what you learn today. Should you break that oath, you will be labeled a traitor to your country and locked away for the rest of your life. Do you understand?"

Bobby paused and looked Ronny in the eyes with such a firm, commanding expression that Ronny felt he either had to make this commitment or refuse right this very moment. Chewing on his bottom lip, Ronny glanced over to where Eric sat. Eric had his hands clamped between his knees, his face sad as if he had already lost Ronny as a friend. Now that Ronny thought about it, he didn't know if Eric had any friends. No wonder they all had to go through this; just thinking about what it meant, the very idea he could be labeled a traitor to his country was some serious shit—poor guy.

"I swear to all the things you have said I must swear to," Ronny said before he could stop himself.

The breath Eric had been holding rushed out of him, and he nearly fell forward onto his face and the floor. He had been so sure this would be too much for Ronny. He didn't relax; they had to tell Ronny about Eric's weirdness and Bruce. Either one could drive Ronny away. Both might be the tipping point that drove Ronny to never speak to him again. He watched as Ronny signed the forms that bound him to the agreement. Ronny deserved to hear all the weird stuff from him. It was the least he could do.

"I'll tell him," he said to Bobby Jay. Bobby nodded as if this was a foregone conclusion. When the last form was signed, Eric stood up and faced Ronny. Dread filled him, and his flight instinct was so strong that it took all he had not to take off running from this place, which would see the death of his only friendship.

"You know I can heal," Eric began pacing back and forth. "You don't know that I have visions and nightmares that come true. Sometimes, I wake up in the middle of the night screaming or… weeping. Sometimes during the day, a vision hits me so hard that Bobby says it looks like I've frozen. I do not know how long I'm frozen when a vision happens. Sometimes, I can move, like pick up the phone and call my parents or Mids, my sister, to let them know what I've seen. The visions are seldom good. Often, they are of someone dying or being hurt, like the motorcycle thing.

"Bobby here and Higgins, my night guard, try to figure out where whatever I have seen will happen. If possible, they will stop it from happening. They don't always succeed. There is a time limit on my visions and nightmares. We usually fail if we don't find and prevent the instance from happening within two weeks. I used to read the paper and watch the news during those two weeks. I don't, can't, anymore. It is too much of a burden if we fail. That is what it will be like when around me. Your life will be filled with my screams in the middle of the night. And Me standing frozen for long moments. Or being frantic because we haven't pinpointed where something will happen." Eric paused in speaking a moment. This last bit had him cringing inside at what Ronny's reaction might be.

"Then there is Bruce."

"Your cat?" Ronny asked, puzzled.

Eric nodded. "Bruce isn't an ordinary cat. Well, he was, but we think him being so near death when I healed him caused him to be like he has become," Eric stopped speaking as he searched for the right words.

"What? Does he have seizures or something?" Ronny prompted.

Eric laughed, "It will be the or something. He changes."

"Changes how? Is he one of those cats that suddenly goes bonkers and attacks people?" Ronny chuckled.

Shaking his head, Eric's face sobered. "When upset, he turns into a huge panther."

What Eric hadn't expected was for Ronny to burst out laughing. "You guys! You are pulling my leg now. That isn't possible…," Ronny saw the serious expressions on Bobby and Eric's faces. "You're serious? But how? Why? I don't understand." Ronny looked back and forth between the two men. "Truly?"

Eric and Bobby both nodded.

Ronny sat back, gazing off into space.

Meanwhile, Eric was preparing himself to lose Ronny as a friend. He felt they had just reached the tipping point.

"Can I see him do it? Please. Just once," Ronny asked. He got up, eager to see this transformation.

At Ronny's request, a crease formed in the middle of Bobby's forehead to see Bruce transform into a panther. He looked over at Eric. "Is it safe? So far, Bruce has only seen us and that mugger who tried to shoot you."

"What? What mugger? What happened?" Ronny erupted with questions.

Bobby rubbed his eyes as if trying to wipe away this whole situation. He and Eric were breaking many rules set up to protect Eric and his family, just telling Ronny as much as they had. Before he could decide to allow this breach in telling Ronny about the mugger, Eric spoke up. "I was out jogging. I like to unwind at night by jogging while it is cooler out. Also, Bruce went with me, and we didn't see many people. So, that night, we were a bit ahead of Bobby. I've always been fairly fast running, and I decided to cut through an alleyway to make my turn to head back. Bruce had gone after a mouse or something that caught his interest and was a little behind me when I entered the alley. This guy steps in front of me and threatens me with a gun. He is out to rob me. Only Bruce sees him with that extraordinary eyesight he has. I heard him rumble in that deep way he has when he has transformed. I say something like, 'Oh, oh, you've done it now. You've made my cat mad'. About then, Bruce steps around me and takes the guy down. Bobby was there almost as fast. So, after mouthing the creeps throat, Bruce let the guy up and returned to standard cat form.

"The funny part was, well, maybe not funny to the guy; he kept screaming at Bobby and the pickup crew to shoot the monster cat. And Bruce was back in cat form acting like a sweet kitty twisting around the men's legs."

"Did the mugger have to sign all those forms too?" Ronny asked.

"No, I doubt that guy will ever see the light of day again. After all, he did threaten Eric with a gun. His freedom was over from that point on. We take protecting Eric's family very seriously," Bobby told Ronny.

Ronny looked sober for a moment. "When can I see Bruce? That is so cool he can change his form," he said, reaching out to punch Eric in the shoulder. He paused and looked over at Bobby. "There a rule against giving him a 'Buddy Punch'?"

Bobby smiled, "I think we can make an exception for you. From what I hear, Middy was punched all the time while she was in police training."

Whipping his head around to stare at Eric, Ronny blinked a couple of times. "You didn't tell me your sister is a cop."

"Police Officer. Don't ever call her a cop to her face. She is dangerous. You don't want her to dislike you. She will make your life miserable," Eric said, his face scrunched up as if in pain. "Come on, let's go see if Bruce is hungry." The way the color drained from Ronny's face was so funny that Eric couldn't help but laugh. That broke the tension in Ronny, and he punched Eric in the shoulder.

When they reached Eric's dorm room, Eric held up his hand in a waiting motion. "Let me go in first. Once he sees I'm friendly with you, he should be okay," he told Ronny. Eric opened the door and slipped in, leaving the door open just enough for Bruce to see Bobby and Ronny waiting to come in. Eric spread his legs and stood still as Bruce sniffed him all over. "Bruce, I want you to meet Ronny. He is a friend. No snacking on him. Understand?" Bruce rumbled under his breath and sat down, watching the door intently.

Ronny stepped inside the dorm room and stood still, staring at the large black cat watching him. "He is big," he said as Bobby pushed him the rest of the way inside.

Bobby stepped inside and closed the door. "Sorry, but we don't advertise Bruce being here."

Ronny grimaced as if he knew that but had forgotten. He never took his eyes off of Bruce, though. "When will he change shape?"

Next to him, Bobby sighed.

"Damn it, I hate having to do this," he said and pulled his gun out.

It was over in a moment that boggled Ronny's mind. One second, a black cat was in front of him, and the next, Bobby was pinned to the door by a large panther. The panther had Bobby by the throat as he rumbled softly to himself. Bobby put his gun away. Eric's cat was back to normal in the blink of an eye. Bobby rubbed his throat and glared at Ronny.

"Happy now?"

Ronny looked like he would faint momentarily, then he said to Bobby, "It happened so fast. Can I see it again?" He ruined his joke by laughing.

"Kids!" Bobby reached over to wipe some panther slobber on Ronny.

Ronny wisely kept his mouth shut for a bit. He walked over and sat down on Eric's bed. "What does he eat, steak?"

"Cat food. He is a normal cat for the most part. He reacts and changes into a panther when he feels a threat. Bruce, the Super Cat!" Eric said with a laugh. "We go running almost every night. Sometimes, it is just a quick jog, but we both love to run."

Rubbing his hand over his eyes, Ronny worried about what Bruce might do to Molly when they met. "Do you think leaving Bruce and Molly alone together is wise? I mean, would he hurt her?" He glanced at Eric to see what he thought.

Eric answered as best he could, shaking his head, "I don't know. We will have to see how they react to each other. Honestly, I'm not sure us moving into an apartment is best for you, Ronny. My life isn't all sweetness and cream. Bruce is just one thing in my life that goes beyond usual.

"And another thing, if we are going to move out of the dorms, I'd just as soon get a house with a bit of land Bruce and Molly could run and play on. I miss living on the farm with my family. A little land under my feet would feel good. I can afford it. We could live there and not worry about housing while we set up a practice. It would allow you to save up to buy your place. What do you think?"

Ronny had never considered things that far ahead. It made sense to save money up for a place of his own. But he'd put all the bills on Eric, which wasn't fair to the little guy. There was a lot to think over, plans to make or unmake according to what he decided overnight. "I think we should sleep on it. We both need to search our hearts and minds to see if we can make this work. I have Molly to consider. I don't want to put her in danger. She is going to be a mom."

Chapter Five

SLEEPLESS NIGHTS

It was a long night of tossing and turning for Ronny. He had a lot to think over. This whole nightmare bit, and mostly, the panther Eric had. On top of that was the oath he had formally signed to never speak about Eric and his family. He had leaned heavily on Eric last year, having him help him with Charlie and his studies. Charlie and he owed Eric more than money could ever buy. If not for Eric, Charlie would have never walked again. Would it be so bad living in the same house with the shrimp? And his cat? The fundamental stumbling block was Molly. Ronny had to be certain Bruce wouldn't decide to kill Molly. He could never live with himself if he rescued Molly only to put her in danger again. Molly had been through enough, and she would be a mother.

Determined to back out of living with Eric while still not knowing how he would keep Molly when she was released from the hospital, Ronny approached Eric before class.

Eric had been waiting for Ronny to leave his dorm room and nearly jumped when he finally saw him walking down the hall to the front of the dorms.

"Ronny, I have an idea. Why don't we introduce Molly and Bruce to each other and see how things go? We could meet up at Bobby Jay's place. Two secret service guys should be enough to handle anything our pets decide to do," Eric said before Ronny could speak up. Ronny nodded. The wind had left his determination sails before getting a word out.

For once, the day seemed to fly by quicker than Ronny wanted. He was scared, plain and simple. Not for himself. No, he was afraid something would happen to Molly. He had become very fond of the loving dog. She was so forgiving, trusting, and full of life. Bruce was dangerous when he changed from a cat to a panther. Look at how easily Bruce had taken down Bobby Jay. Eric trusted Bruce. It boiled down to whether Ronny had faith in Eric.

Pulling his car to the curb, Bobby Jay waited for Ronny to leave the University Hospital's Clinic with Molly. He had his reservations about this meeting between Molly and Bruce. His job was to protect Eric. The question was whether he would do that if he had to shoot Eric's cat. Bruce and Eric were already at Bobby's place, with his alternate watching over them. He would have sent the alternate to pick up Ronny but felt Ronny would be more comfortable dealing with someone he knew. Bobby released a relieved breath when Ronny exited the building and opened the car's back door to climb in with Molly beside him.

When the car with Ronny and Molly pulled up outside Bobby's place, Eric reached down and petted Bruce.

"You remember Ronny. He has Molly with him today. I know you have smelled Molly on me before. She is a good girl and has had a hard life. Please be nice to her," he told Bruce. The door was opening, and talk time was over.

Ronny clutched Molly's leash so tight his knuckles were turning white. He was prepared to pull Molly to safety and place himself between her and Bruce if needed. He looked at where Eric was stroking Bruce, wondering why he was doing this and risking Molly.

Molly's tail began to thump on the floor when she saw Eric. She started to scramble across the floor to Eric when Bruce moved, drawing her attention. Molly's whole physical reaction changed. Instead of charging across the floor to Eric, she laid down and turned her belly up to expose it. Her tail was wagging so fast it was creating a breeze. Slowly, Molly pulled herself across the floor to Bruce. She crawled a bit, then turned her belly up before crawling forward. When she reached Bruce, she wagged and wiggled so hard the floor vibrated. Now and then, she would flick her tongue out to lick Bruce on the chin. All while remaining as flat on the floor as she could be without sinking into it.

Forced to step forward as Molly made her way to where Bruce sat beside Eric, Ronny watched this interaction with Molly with wonder. What was she doing? Submissive, she showed the cat that he was the boss. That had to be what she was doing. Poor Molly. Maybe it was wise of Molly. Did she know about Bruce, even in his cat form? Animals could sense so much more than humans could tell with their puny senses. Now, would Bruce accept her?

Eric had been watching Molly's display, too. He had seen this reaction many times when he was growing up. His mother's dog was the dominant force in the animal kingdom on the farm where he was raised. Any animal that came in contact with his mother's Dog would demonstrate that they accepted he was the dominant animal. He had been prepared to block Bruce from hurting Molly if he had misjudged Bruce as trustworthy. He watched closely for any sign of aggression on Bruce's part.

Holding his head still, Bruce endured the licks from the dog, asking for acceptance. She was with pups. Bruce's protection suddenly extended to the mother dog and her unborn pups. She was his now. With a roar, Bruce transformed and laid down alongside Molly. He licked her head, allowing her to push her body up against him and snuggle there. The two of them lay there, and Molly finally became as still as she could, which wasn't possible for a Border Collie. Her eyebrows twitched as she looked around the room to Ronny and everyone else. And her tail kept wagging softly at the very tip.

Clearing his throat, Eric told Ronny, "I think Bruce just said, 'Nobody better mess with my dog.'" He grinned at Ronny.

Ronny was white as a sheet. He looked up to Eric before he could find his voice. "I thought he was going to kill her when he roared like that. You mean he was warning everyone he was protecting her?"

Nodding, Eric thought of what this meant. "We have to find a house now, right?" he asked Ronny.

The problem with house hunting was that Eric already knew what the house he was to buy looked like. He had visions of the house since he was a child, and in every vision, he was happy living there. He knew there would be several acres of land and an area for a vegetable garden behind the house, and the front of the house would have flowers everywhere. He knew the house; it was part of him. He just had to find it.

Impossible, Eric thought after two nights of looking at houses from the newspaper. He was starting to feel desperate, and that was beginning to affect his work. There were already surgeons who would not let him take part in surgery just because he was weird and did things they couldn't have done in a million years. Yes, he cheated by using his healing powers now and then. He could have spared all those poor cats, dogs, and other animals the pain of recovering from surgery by simply healing them before they had surgery. That he couldn't always heal them would eat at him, leaving him feeling wanting and a traitor to the animal kingdom. So, he threw himself into the impossible task of finding his dream house.

Bobby had had enough of Eric's gloom. "What's wrong, kid?" he finally asked him. When Eric told him about the house in his visions, Bobby held up a hand to stop him from continuing. "I have an idea. Why don't we make a drawing of this house you want and send the drawing to the real estate people? They will know if such a house with land is available, right?"

"Great idea, Bobby Jay!" Eric stood up excited over the thought of sending a drawing of the house out to the real estate companies in the area. He rushed to the small desk in his dorm room and pulled out a folder. "Here it is. I've known about this house since I was a child. Let's run off copies and send them off now."

Bobby chuckled, "Alright, partner. I'll see to it."

Eric and Ronny were standing in front of the house from Eric's dreams two days later. It was set on 20 acres of land, mostly woodland, but a cleared area around the house, making a large yard both front and back and to the sides of the house. "Perfect," Eric said. "Look how much room they would have to run and play in. I can make trails through the woods to run in, too. It's just what I wanted. What do you think, Ronny?"

Ronny's mouth was still hanging open at the size of the house and the land around it. Ronny found his voice at Eric's question. "You'll never be able to afford this, Eric. Let's look for something smaller, more in our budget range."

"Ronny, this is going to be my house. I've seen this house since I was a little kid. It looked a little different than it does now without the flowers that my visions had around it. Do you and Molly want to live here until you buy your place?" Eric asked.

"We do just let me help out at least with the groceries. I have a huge appetite," Ronny said with a laugh. In his mind, he was certain Eric wouldn't be able to get the house, but he wouldn't rain on his friend's dream.

That weekend, they drove to Ronny's parent's house and loaded up his bedroom. Eric, of course, had to buy a new bedroom set for his room. He also set up two spare rooms for his SS to occupy. They had no reason to travel back and forth from their apartment to cover Eric. This would save them all money in the long run, as Eric could use their help with his plans for the grounds and the house.

Finally, the two medical students packed their dorm rooms and placed Molly and Bruce in the car. It was time to go home.

Home. No place but the farm had ever felt like home to Eric. This acreage, this house was now his home. He had lived most of his life with this place at home in his heart, and now he was here at last.

Eric and Ronny stepped out of the car Bobby was driving. Molly and Bruce bounded out of the car together. One look at the large yard was all they needed. Molly fairly vibrated with excitement. She took off running in huge circles with Bruce running beside her. There was such joy in them that it made Ronny laugh. He pushed Eric and took off running. They ran around pushing and shoving each other while laughing and whooping it up. When they finally stopped, the two grinned at each other. "Pizza!" Ronny said, pulling out his cell phone.

Unfortunately, the one thing they had forgotten to do was buy groceries. For breakfast, the humans had leftover pizza. Bruce and Molly fared better with having their dog and cat food. Dishes and cleaning supplies were added to the list of supplies that were needed.

Monday morning, the two youths scrambled to dress, care for the pets, and make it to class on time. The two of them squeezed into the room, where they were briefed on the day's assignments just before Dr. North arrived. Dr. North's eyes flicked to Ronny and Eric as if he was well aware they had just arrived. "Today, we will begin to have each of you handling a surgery from beginning to end. We will only step in should things go wrong. By the end of the week, you will have all had the opportunity to prove yourself to be a surgeon. You are all up today, Mr. Toronto, Mr. Granger, and Mr. Harris. Should we have another surgery come in, Ms. Bell will handle it. The rest of you have studies to attend to and will assist when needed." Dr. North turned around and left the room without another word. The room buzzed with excitement. Hands-on. They were having hands-on for a change.

The first scream cut through the night like a knife, slicing Ronny's mind open and spilling him out of deep sleep. He leaped off the bed, his heart beating so hard he clutched his chest to contain it. At first, he thought he must have had a nightmare, but the sound of feet running from the bedroom beside him had Ronny open his door and follow. Another scream wrenched the air, sending chilling fingers of fear down Ronny's back. Bobby Jay, in his boxer briefs, jerked open Eric's bedroom door and held his hand up to stop the night man and Ronny from entering. Ronny stood in the doorway watching Bobby Jay as he pulled Eric into his arms and soothed him.

"It is okay, kid. I'm here now. Could you wake up and tell me what you've learned? I've got you. Wake up, Eric." He kept talking soothingly as he held Eric and rubbed his arm. Bruce had transformed and stood over the pair on the bed in protective mode. Ronny could hear the deep rumbling the panther was making.

Eric gasped and sat up. "He killed them all, the whole family. I tried to see out the windows for something to tell us where, but he just keeps killing and killing," Eric sobbed. "Even the baby in her crib." Eric clutched Bobby Jay's arm so tight that his fingers turned white. "It is soon, Bobby, real soon. We may already be too late."

"Okay, calm down. I need you to be rational. Start at the beginning," Bobby said, motioning to Higgins to place the recorder on the nightstand by the bed.

Leaning back against the bed's headboard, Eric began to speak. "It was nighttime. I must have been looking through the murderer's eyes, which is why I couldn't see out the window. He was enjoying killing them too much to look outside. He was approaching the house. It was dark, no lights on.

He licked his finger and touched the doorbell like he was marking it. Then he pushed the doorbell and waited. There was a hanging basket with those air plants that send out stalks with baby plants on them," Eric said, stopping. He closed his eyes as if to remember or block out the memories coming to him. "The numbers 5 and 1. I had forgotten that I saw those two numbers on the porch before the door opened…."

"Were they the first two numbers, the middle, or the last two numbers for the house?" Bobby asked, interrupting Eric.

"The first two, I think. Green. The house's siding looked green in the light that came on before the door opened," Eric said, his voice trembling as he related everything he could remember about the people, the furniture, and the age the baby appeared to be.

All the while Eric talked, the recorder was running. The night man plugged in a laptop and began to type in information as Eric described the family, their ages, sex, and anything about them that might lead them to who this family might be. The bit of the house number they had with the family information gave them three possibilities—three families who may be in harm's way.

Bobby Jay stood and left the room. When he returned, he was dressed with his weapon strapped on. This was part of the partnership he had with Eric. It was up to him to find and stop the crime scene Eric had seen. He was on the phone with the local detective he had befriended. "Yes, those addresses. We don't know if it will be tonight or when. Just send a car to them. Then let me know if they look like they have green siding in the dark. Yes, of course, this will be your take-down. You know I don't want any of that crap on me. Help me out here, Mr. Hero," Bobby said as he stopped the conversation. He looked over to where Eric was still propped against the headboard. "We have a decent chance of stopping this. Don't go getting depressed before we even know if we can. Try to get some real sleep."

Eric nodded, but his body still trembled, and his face was white as a ghost when he slipped back down into a prone position. Still in his panther form, Bruce lay beside Eric, putting one of his giant paws on Eric's chest.

Backing out of the room, Ronny felt his hands trembling. Nightmares. He had warned Ronny he had nightmares, but Ronny never thought he meant like this. This was horror being born. Ronny remembered Eric telling him he had a nightmare about him, so he was asking him not to ride a motorcycle. Did he dream of the accident? No wonder Eric had bugged him not to ride one. Ronny had lived through the horror of seeing his best friend crippled, losing an arm. It would have been him if Eric hadn't acted on his nightmare. Something happened in Ronny as these thoughts ran through his mind. He felt a fierce protectiveness come over him. He had thought he owed Eric for saving him more than once. Now that he had seen Eric's life firsthand, he knew he had to help protect him from the rest of the world. He'd help Eric in any manner he could. Nobody should have to go through that nightly hell.

Molly licked Ronny's face when he crawled back into his bed. Ronny hugged Molly to him. He could still hear those terrifying screams that had come from Eric. Part of him knew that he would be having nightmares tonight. Just hearing what Eric had described made him not want to go back to sleep. Holding Molly, he listened to the beat of her heart and slowly relaxed, drifting off into a dreamless sleep.

Bobby Jay came dragging in around two in the morning. He entered quietly, going first to check on Eric before finding his bed and falling onto it. It had been a rough night. He and the locals had stopped the home invasion, but not all the damage. The father of the family had been stabbed. When Bobby had left for home, he didn't know if the man was going to make it or not. Bobby sure hoped the man lived. He didn't want to have to tell Eric they had lost one person. The kid felt every failure and was hard on himself, thinking he should have seen the vision or nightmare earlier. Despite all the good he did, the kid still felt guilty over every loss. Dang it, kid, it is not your fault, Bobby thought as he dozed off.

Grumpy, Eric woke in a bad mood. He needed to run to clear his head of all the terrible things inside it. Bruce was clingy, staying at Eric's feet and winding around his legs. "You wanting a run too, Bruce," he asked. Bruce sat down, looking at Eric with wide-open eyes. "Not a run, then."

Molly licked Ronny's face, waking him up. He groaned and rolled over. All the horror of Eric's nightmare came flooding into his mind. Crap, it was real. Not a dream at all. "Come on, Molly. Let's make breakfast for Eric. I hope he likes burnt toast."

When Ronny entered the kitchen, the night man was already placing bacon in a skillet. He looked over his shoulder at Ronny. "You have time for a quick shower before breakfast is ready. Eric should be back from his run soon, so make it quick. He likes to shower before eating."

"What happened? With the nightmare, I mean?" Ronny blurted out. Eric's words about his nightmare had haunted his dreams all night.

"The father is in serious condition but should make it. The rest of the family are all safe. They will have nightmares over this but are alive," the SS man said.

Ronny turned the television on, looking for a morning news program. He needed to hear it for himself over the news, official-like. "Turn that off. We don't remind Eric of his nightmares. It is bad enough that he has to live through them to try to stop things from happening. Bobby let him know things went well before they started the run. Don't make him relive it."

Ronny nodded and turned the television off. He thought of all the times he and the other guys talked down to Eric. He had called Eric a shrimp. Ronny shook his head, remembering how shaken he had been hearing Eric tell Bobby about the nightmare. He couldn't imagine living that in his head. To see that sort of thing happen. Right then, he knew he'd never be as strong as Eric was on his worst days. "Do you make breakfast for them every morning?" he asked.

Chuckling, the SS man looked over at Ronny. "I do now that we all live together. I want to be able to sleep today when I go to bed. I think this will relax me enough for me to sleep."

After walking Molly, Ronny took a quick shower. He wanted to be dressed and ready to leave for the University as soon as Eric arrived. While staying with Eric, Ronny was learning a whole new rule book. Rule Number 1 was never to remind Eric of his nightmares. Ronny was confident there were other rules. After all, this was a house run by the Secret Service.

On the drive to the University, Bobby Jay had Ronny add his number to his list of contacts. "You are now under my protection, as is Molly. Should something bother you, a stranger you feel shouldn't be there, a box sitting where it should not be, anything at all odd, you speed dial me."

Ronny nodded, his face grim as if an added weight had been put upon his shoulders.

"Bobby, don't scare him like that. Hopefully, I'll see…," Eric shut up as they pulled into the parking lot. He nodded his head to Bobby.

There was Rule Number 2, Ronny thought, "Don't talk about such things in front of others." Poor Eric; he must have a ton of rules to follow.

Dr. North wasn't happy. Today, his two problem students will perform solo surgeries with an attending standing at their shoulder. He didn't like students who didn't mess up at least once before reaching this stage in their training. The skinny boy just rubbed him wrong. He didn't know what it was about the boy, but he set Dr. North's teeth on edge. North found himself second-guessing his diagnosis. He'd been so confident before, but now he wondered if he was making a mistake every time he started an exploratory surgery. That feeling of not being satisfied with his decisions was something he hadn't felt since he was a student himself. He wondered if he was wrong to hope the skinny boy messed up today.

Ronny and Eric were to be teamed for each other's surgeries. They would switch roles when it was time for Ronny to be the surgeon and Eric to be the assistant. They had just prepped Ronny's patient, a giant bear of a dog with numerous tumors, when Dr. Stoker entered and told them to stop. Dr. North was immediately there, questioning the interruption. "What is the meaning of this, Stoker?" he asked.

"I'm sorry, Dr. North, but I need these two. We have a bit of an emergency going on. I don't want to talk about it here. If you three will come with me, I will explain." Dr. Stoker said. Dr. Stoker led them to a small office after an attending and another pair of students took over Ronny's patient. "I have to make this short, so listen closely. This morning, we had three cats sent to us with an unexplained illness. By noon, five dogs had been admitted. When another cat came in, we quarantined it in the clinic. Something is out there infecting both cats and dogs. The symptoms differ slightly between the two species, but I'm convinced the same condition infects both." Dr. Stoker paused and looked over at Eric. "I need you. You are our best hope at solving this puzzle and stopping the spread of the infection."

Eric nodded and stood up, ready to help. "Wait. You need to inform Bobby Jay," Ronny told him. Again, Eric nodded; he didn't want to waste time. If something was spreading through dogs and cats, it meant whatever it was could cross-species.

When Bobby Jay's phone rang, he opened the door to the small office he had followed Eric and the others to. His eyes traveled over the two Doctors, stopping on Dr. North. "You may leave. I know you have other duties," he said.

Dr. North shook his head. "This involves the whole hospital. I need to know if I should isolate the patients in my surgery."

Bobby's eyes returned to Dr. Stoker, and he tipped his head, indicating Stoker should speak.

"You best do that. As a precaution, have them step in and out of bleach solutions. Wipe down all the cages with the solution. Nobody enters or leaves the surgery without gloves and feet covers. Go," Dr. Stoker sent Dr. North off as if the fires of hell were on his tail.

When Dr. North left, Bobby Jay was on Dr. Stoker, asking questions. "When was the first case reported? What have the local clinics found out so far? Have they found the source? Has there been any indication this can be transmitted to humans?" he paused to give the doctor a chance to answer.

"Just hold on a minute. This is a clinical problem affecting our hospital and the surrounding area, not some Secret Service thing," he said as he motioned Eric and Ronny to follow him.

"You don't know that for a fact. This could be

a dry run aimed at Eric and his family. Anything, anything at all that might threaten him is my business. I will protect Eric and Ronny no matter what you think...." Bobby was interrupted by Eric putting his hand on Bobby's arm.

"Their best chance is for me to look and see what is causing them to be ill. I can't... won't leave them to suffer," he told Bobby. "Please don't cart me off like a sack of potatoes, Bobby."

Bobby's face scrunched up like he was in pain as he looked at Eric's determined face. "You are going to do this whether I agree or not. So, some ground rules first. If I have to, I will stuff you in a hazard suit, understand?" Eric nodded. "Okay, gloves, mask, booties at all times. You will not reach up and scratch your nose or wipe sweat from your face. You will take a disinfecting shower immediately upon leaving the ill patients. I don't want to call your mother and father about this, understand?" Bobby threatened. Eric closed his eyes and nodded his head. The one thing he didn't want was to have his mother come to heal him. He'd seen her die when healing someone. No, he would not risk his mother. This could be something simple and easy for regular doctors to cure.

"Okay, just let me check it out. I'll try to restrain myself," Eric promised. He looked at Dr. Stoker before whispering to Bobby, "Just in case, get a couple of the Andy Bags."

Shaking his head, Bobby looked over at Ronny. "Ronny, take my keys and bring a couple of the IV bags from the trunk of my car along with a setup." He tossed his keys to Ronny and focused on Dr. Stoker. "I'm going to let Eric look at your patients." He turned to Eric. "Do you need to touch them barehanded?" Eric nodded. "Shit."

"Look," Eric said, trying to calm Bobby down. "These things happen all the time. It could be something simple. You are freaking me out, Bobby. Don't go into a panic. I want to take a look. I'll use one finger. One. Bobby, what will you do once I graduate and set up a clinic? Are you going to vet every person who brings a patient to me? Relax, man. Please."

Looking down at the floor as if ashamed of himself, Bobby nodded. "It is just I've seen Ebola. Stuff like this scares me."

"I'll be careful. Okay?"

Bobby pulled two protein bars out of his pocket and a bottle of brownish liquid, handing them to Eric. Eric grabbed the bars, stuffing them in his mouth and chewing as fast as possible. Then, he guzzled down the drink, handing the wrappers from the bars and the empty bottle back to Bobby.

Dr. Stoker watched all of this with great interest. It was as if the SS man was beefing Eric up before letting him look at a bunch of sick dogs and cats. How was Eric going to 'look' at the patients?

Out of breath as he had run the whole way to the car and back, Ronny handed Bobby Jay two IV bags. Bobby motioned for Dr. Stoker to lead them to where the isolated patients were kept. Just outside the door to the room Dr. Stoker was heading towards was a table with stacks of masks, gloves, and scrub boot boxes. All four of them suited up before entering the room. It was quiet inside the room, which was lined with cages, both large and small. Nine of the cage doors stood open, with the patients inside laying limp as if sedated. Two people were monitoring the sick animals, and both turned to see who was coming inside the room. "Tell them to leave," Bobby told Dr. Stoker.

"Please wait outside while we examine the patients," he told the two attending the animals.

Eric ripped the forefinger off his main hand's glove and walked down the line of cages. At each cage, he reached in and stroked his hand over the cat or dog inside the cage, letting his forefinger touch the animal's head. Reaching the last cage, he rubbed the dog's elongated head. Inside was a Greyhound, so still that at first, Eric feared the dog was dead. Instinctively, he strengthened the dog before stepping away. He was glad Bobby had given him the protein drink and bars when he felt the drain upon him.

Dr. Stoker and Bobby had been watching Eric as he went from cage to cage. They both looked expectantly at him when he walked to where they stood. "Draw blood from them all and send it to Poison Control. It isn't a virus or anything like it. This is a poison. I haven't seen it before. But they have all had a dose of it to various degrees," Eric said. He looked at Bobby with a plea in his eyes. "Let me rid them of it after the blood is sent off."

"We have things we can give them for poisoning. Why not let me start them on something and see how they respond?" Dr. Stoker said. He looked to Bobby Jay as if asking permission to treat his patients.

"Do that, but first draw up the blood we need.

With their huge poison database, Poison Control may give us the name of something to fight. I'll leave you doctors to do that while I arrange for a courier to come for the vials of blood. Be sure each vial is labeled and includes the owner's address." Bobby stepped outside the room to call for the courier to come to pick up the evidence of a mass poisoning of pets.

Chapter Six

KEEPING SECRETS

For two days, dogs and cats flooded the hospital clinic. Finally, the source of the poison was located. A warehouse where bags of cat and dog food from a particular company were stored and then distributed to local stores had a mishap with a chemical solution. The solution seeped through the plastic-wrapped bundles of pet foods, which were later sent to various stores. Once the brand name was known, people were informed of a recall by the manufacturer of that brand. However, they were not responsible for the contamination. They took it upon themselves to pay all hospital costs for the affected pets.

Eric faded into the background once the media became involved. If anyone asked him who had discovered the pets were suffering from the poison, he would point to Dr. Stoker. Bobby had already talked with the doctor, and Dr. Stoker played his part well, telling people that it was a hunch he had played.

When Ronny and Eric returned to Dr. North's care, they learned they had been put at the end of the line for doing their surgeries. In the space of a day, they went from riding the nervous thrill of actually being in charge of surgery to being low on the list to do surgery. "I'm sorry, Ronny," Eric said with heartfelt regret. He knew how long Ronny had prepared himself for doing the surgery he had been called away from. And it was all Eric's fault. His weirdness had done it. Just like Eric had worried it would.

By day five of the poison scandal, any part Eric and Ronny had played in it was buried so deep that nobody even thought to question them. Bobby Jay finally took a relieved breath and celebrated building a dog door for Bruce and Molly. Usually, he would have been totally against having a dog door in the house, but then, usually, the home didn't have a cat, which could turn into a panther. Besides, Eric had presented the case for the dog door very well, assuring Bobby that Bruce would be told to guard that door. Of course, there were the deadlocks that Bobby installed for when they weren't home.

Watching Molly and Bruce explore the dog door had everyone in the house chuckling. Molly didn't want anything to do with something that she thought would close on her and trap her. Bruce, on the other hand, approached the door with confidence. He rubbed his head and cheek pads on the door, claiming it was part of his territory. With a flick of his black tail, he pushed against the opening

panel and exited. Inside, Molly waited to see if
the door was eating Bruce. She touched her nose
to the door as if trying to smell where Bruce had
disappeared. At about that moment, Bruce pushed
back inside, startling Molly. Molly leaped back, then
watched Bruce go over and lay down as if nothing in
the world was wrong, and there wasn't some beast of
a door thing blocking the way outside.

Bruce tried again to get Molly to follow him
out of the dog door. She walked as far as the door
but scrambled back when he went through it, and the
door swung back into place. Bruce entered again to
lie down as if bored with the whole thing. Suddenly,
Bruce transformed. Doing her belly crawl thing,
Molly came up to him, thumping her tail on the floor
like crazy. He stood and stalked over to the door,
and Molly came behind him, crouched submissively.
He pushed the dog door open with his head and held
it there. Molly whined and tried to lick Bruce's face,
but he grumbled and stepped forward. Holding the
door open with his back, he rumbled as if to himself.
Molly crept forward to try to lick his face again, and
they were both outside the house. Bruce and Molly
returned through the dog door after running outside,
acting like little kids on a sugar rush. The lesson was
learned: the door was not some demon, but it was a
good thing.

The weekend was upon them, and Ronny
had a date with one of the cheerleaders. He always
had one girl or another thrilled to go out with him.
This time, however, he thought about Eric sitting at
home and decided to see if he could convince Eric
to double date with him. He'd even provide the girl

if needed. When he brought the subject up, he was shocked at Eric's refusal to even think about going out. "Why not? I could see if Brenda has a friend. It would be great for us two to go out together with our girls in our arms. Come on, do it for me," he said, trying to sway Eric into going.

Looking disappointed in Ronny, Eric shook his head. "Ronny, I'm not interested in going out with any girl. Haven't you ever considered who you wanted to spend the rest of your life with? Think about it. That person, the girl who will own your heart and you will own her heart for the rest of your life, shouldn't be some random girl you take out for a lark. I would have taken only her, my one, out. I'd have wanted to be the one who opened her up to laughter, joy, and every adventure in her life. But I already know that life is not something I can have. You've seen what my life is like. It is nightmares, screams in the middle of the night, horror upon horror. Suppose I was to go out with you and those girls. What are they going to think when I go into a vision trance? Or when I jump up and frantically yell for Bobby Jay? What if he comes running in with his gun out and sticks it in the girls' faces? Suppose someone is sick, and I accidentally touch them and pass out. Don't you see, Ronny? I can't do that to a girl."

A sick lump formed in Ronny's stomach. He had never thought of what Eric's social life would be like. It was zero, that's what it was, zero, except for him. And even though he hadn't sought to be friends with Eric, it was more out of needing him to help make Charlie whole again. As well as learning so much about healing, everything had been for Ronny's benefit, not Eric's. Even this house was because Ronny needed a place to keep Molly. He nodded to Eric that he understood. The reasons Eric isolated himself were valid, and he couldn't think of an argument to counter them.

Dr. North closely watched Eric as the young man began his solo surgery. He noticed all the touching the boy made before sedating the dog and prepping it for surgery. Eric had drawn a case of a dog with internal tumors approaching a size that crowded the dog's stomach. The dog was unable to take in enough nourishment to sustain itself. Also, the dog was aggressive, which Dr. North thought would be a problem for the young budding doctor. Only that didn't happen.

They brought Eric's patient in with a muzzle on his head. He is in pain, Eric thought, wanting to comfort the dog and ease his pain immediately. As he approached the table, the dog snarled at him. Eric touched the dog on the head, taking away all the pain. Instantly, a rapport developed between Eric and the dog. His patient understood Eric was there to help him.

Dr. North looked away when he saw Eric was going to take off the patient's muzzle. For a brief moment, he thought about not correcting Eric and allowing the boy to be bitten. But he couldn't sink that low. He looked back with his mouth open, prepared to stop the pending disaster from happening, and shut his mouth.

Eric rubbed the dog's head and told him what

he needed to do. Buster licked Eric's face and lay still to be sedated. Eric worked quickly, putting the dog to sleep and tubing him, then turning the dog over to Ronny to be prepped.

Disappointed in himself for wishing a student harm, Dr. North was puzzled over how that same student had calmed a patient Dr. North knew was aggressive. It was another weird check in the column for this student. The fact he didn't like Eric shouldn't count when he was instructing him. So why did he continue to feel angry at the boy? He understood why he felt enraged at Eric; it was so dumb to be angry about, and he didn't want to admit it. The boy made him feel lacking. There, he admitted it to himself. But it didn't make him feel any less angry.

While Dr. North was musing over his failings and his feelings about Eric, Eric had scrubbed up and was ready to start the surgery as soon as Ronny had the dog on the surgery table and ready. Eric knew he had needed to cheat some. He had to. One of the tumors had been resting right on top of the main artery. If Eric didn't shrink it using his powers, then he wouldn't be able to remove the tumor without killing the dog during the surgery. He had explained that to the dog and received a kiss for it. For the next thirty-five minutes, Eric removed the tumors and healed as much as he could without giving himself away. Buster would recover quickly from this surgery, and nobody would know that Eric had given part of himself to assure the dog that he had little healing on his own. By the time Eric put in the final stitch, his hands began to shake, and all his insides felt like they were throwing up.

As soon as his patient was in the recovery cage, Eric pushed Bobby Jay's number on his phone and sent a text that he needed bars and a drink. He knew Bobby would know what he meant. Eric still had to take part in Ronny's surgery. At least with a couple of protein bars and a drink in him, he wouldn't faint on Ronny.

Bobby Jay slipped back to where he knew Eric was waiting. He hadn't been far away the entire time the boy was in surgery. It was a weakness of Eric's to go on and heal any animal or person he came across. It was the same weakness the whole family seemed to have, that giving beyond sense bit. They hadn't warned Bobby about this or Eric's nightmares and visions. Maybe the others hadn't bothered to get to know their subject like Bobby. He could see how they might have thought this was a nonsense assignment, but Bobby had learned the truth about Eric. And the truth both scared him and made him feel a sense of awe. He'd grown to think of the boy as the younger brother he never had. When he handed Eric the two protein bars and the open bottle of energy drink, he looked him over with a critical eye. "You should rest and eat a meal," he told the boy.

Eric shook his head. "I have to help Ronny with his surgery. He was great being the other half of the team for me. I can't let him down," Eric said, gobbling the bars and guzzling the drink as fast as he could. He turned and rushed off to give Ronny the support he had been given.

Bobby shook his head at the thought of foolish kids. Only Eric was a man now, not some whinny kid. Heck, he had never been a whinny kid while Bobby knew him. Stubborn, yes. Foolhardy, most certainly. Never whiny. So Bobby went to stand just out of sight, ready to swoop in and take care of the kid when he passed out.

Ronny had wrestled the little ball of fluff into submission. The little guy had freaked out when he saw a syringe and needle coming towards him. "Now, calm down, little one. Eric, come take over; I'm sorry I tried to start without you," Ronny told Eric, and he let Eric take over, holding the little tan ball of terror. Immediately, the little one settled down and allowed Eric to roll a vein up so that Ronny could inject the sedative. Ronny often wished he had that gift of calming a beast that Eric had. But then, he didn't want to have the nightmares Eric had, so he would settle for trying to calm an animal the old-fashioned way. He was grateful Eric had been able to come to help him. He'd seen how Eric's hands were shaking after his surgery and feared the worst had happened. That Eric was sitting out in a car, hooked up to an IV himself. All was well now. Ronny knew he had this surgery in the bag. Eric was here.

The grin on Eric's face just would not let up. He felt as if he was flying from the euphoric feelings inside him as his row of students lined up to walk across the stage to be handed their diplomas. Ronny had already done his walk and given Eric a thumbs-up when returning to his seat. Eric took a quick look up into the stands where his family sat. His dad was beaming as if his chest was about to burst with pride.

Even his mother was smiling as she sat looking back at Eric. His sisters, Middy and Susan, were there. Middy is in her new police uniform, and Susan is dressed in an evening gown. He knew Susan had come straight from Washington, DC, and he loved her for coming here to suffer this crowd for him.

With so many people present for the graduation, it was hot, and Eric was sweating as he took the first step up the stairs to the stage. He felt a breeze swirl around him, cooling him down. That same breeze made his gown flap. He laughed and threw a thumbs up in Middy's direction, counting himself fortunate she hadn't lifted the material, exposing his legs. He crossed the stage to do the handshake and hear what was said to each graduate.

His years of study and worry had brought him to this point. He swallowed a lump in his throat, thinking of all the times he had thought he was beaten trying to get here. Now, he had the rest of his life in front of him. He'd start working with Dr. Monroe on Monday as an equal. He was not an equal, but he soon would be one.

He approached Dr. North, watching as the man was handed the solid-looking folder containing a message saying his certificate would be mailed to him. Eric knew the man had never liked him and thought it was ironic that Dr. North would be the one to shake his hand upon graduating. Eric sobered as he stopped in front of Dr. North. North grabbed Eric's hand with a firm grip as if determined to hold Eric there while he had his say. "I'm going to be watching you, Mr. Whiting. You best not do anything that might bring you up in front of a review board. Congratulations!" he said, handing the folder over to Eric.

Well, Eric thought, that went okay. And now I know he does hate me. Then Eric flipped his tassel over to the other side of his cap and held his folder up for his family to see. There were cheers and whistles from where his family sat and from many men in dark suits stationed around the area. He heard Bobby Jay shout, "Way to go, Eric!" And all was right in his world.

When the last speech was made and the hats all thrown into the air, Ronny's football team surrounded him, tossing him into the air. He was pounded upon the back, jabbed in the ribs, and whooped at by so many of his friends that he lost count of who he had talked to. Then, a hush fell over his friends as Charlie went to Ronny. Charlie was grinning ear to ear, walking straight and tall. He didn't seem aware he was missing an arm. The fact the other guys were acting as if he still had a disability in a hospital bed didn't seem to phase him at all. But Ronny saw the tension in Charlie's eyes. Ronny did the only thing he could do. He rushed at Charlie and barreled him over. He laughed as they fell to the floor and pounded Charlie's back. "You and I made it, Charlie. And they thought we were just dumb jocks! Yahoo, you old bear, we made it." He rubbed his knuckles on Charlie's head while Charlie laughed and brought his legs up to wrap around Ronny, pulling him off him. Then Charlie was knuckling Ronny's head. They sat up afterward laughing, and Ronny looked around for Eric. Eric should have been there; he had been responsible for Charlie's full function of his legs. He should be part of this celebration tussle. Ronny chided himself. He knew better than to think Eric would participate in anything that might draw attention to himself.

Surrounded by his family, Eric endured the many hugs, photos, and pats on the back. In reality, he was worried about his sister Susan. She was looking rather pale. He glanced over at Susan's SS man. Didn't the guy see her distress? The SS guy was looking everywhere but at Susan. He looked uncomfortable being near Eric's sister. He is one of those, Eric thought. The guy feared Susan would read his mind and find something damaging inside his head. It irritated Eric that so many of the agents freaked around his sister. Weren't they supposed to be the most trustworthy agents? Eric looked over at Middy's SS man. He looked haggard, as if he couldn't wait for his shift to be over. Another one bites the dust. Middy was hard on the SS covering her. She believed that she did not need babysitters. It was going to be an enjoyable night.

Eric had told his family he wanted a night just with them. They could eat and talk about what was going on in their lives. He did this mainly for Susan's sake. She seldom left her mountain hideaway to go out in public. That she was here showed how much she loved her family and was a testament to her love for them. Susan approached Eric, "Love you, but you have to stop worrying about me. It is giving me a headache. Go, run over and pound your friends on the back a bit. We'll meet you back at your house," she told him.

Eric hugged Susan to him. "Okay, I'm sorry. You have to eliminate that creep who is supposed to protect you. He doesn't seem to care what you feel," he whispered in her ear. Susan nodded, then waved Eric off to see Ronny. He knew she had picked up on some thought, some need of Ronny's to see him if only to wish Eric congrats.

Keeping an eye on the fellows surrounding Ronny, Eric walked up to him and raised his hand for a high five. "We made it," he said, turning to Charlie to do the same.

Ronny picked Eric up and spun him around a few times until Eric's stomach felt like it would rebel and make a fool of him among all these guys who had always looked down on him. But, he managed to stay steady on his feet and not throw up when Ronny let go of him. Charlie slapped Eric upon his back, staggering him just a bit before recovering his footing. "Easy, Charlie, I'm not strong like you. You about knocked me into tomorrow, and that would be a shame if I couldn't enjoy this night."

Charlie laughed and punched Eric in the shoulder lightly. "No worries, Shrimp. I'll take it easy on you. After all, you are a doctor now. I might need a stitch or two sometime," Charlie joked. Eric laughed, glancing over at Ronny to warn him not to say anything about how Eric could heal.

Looking uncomfortable, Ronny turned towards the rest of the guys. "Let's go party," he shouted, walking towards one of the exits.

Eric stopped him long enough to tell Ronny that he had his family to spend time with before they all returned to their various cities. Ronny nodded, grabbing Charlie and giving him a war whoop as he ushered the rest of his bunch to the parking lot. Higgins slipped out the door behind Ronny. He'd be tailing this addition to Eric's life for the rest of the night.

It was like a dream come true for Eric. The fact he held the evidence of having graduated in his hands was something out of a dream world. So many times, Eric had thought this day would never come, yet his family surrounded him in the house of his dreams with written proof that he had made it. Susan smiled at him with her, 'Yes, I know what you are thinking,' Look. He laughed and punched her gently on the arm. "You are so bad, Suzy. Don't you dare tell Mom and Dad I doubted I would make it." Her brow rose teasingly, wiggling her eyebrows, and she punched him back. They both laughed. It was a joke between them when they were children and Susan first came into her power. She would look at Eric in an 'I know what you did' look and smile in her most naughty manner.

Walking up to Eric, Middy put her brother in a headlock and knuckled him on the head. "Don't you go thinking just because you are a fully grown doctor that you can beat me," she said, having her wind whip him playfully.

He yelped and wiggled out of her headlock. "Don't come running to me when you scrap your knees then, young lady. I work on animals," Eric shot back at her.

Middy dropped down on her hands and

knees and bounced around Eric, her tongue hanging out and making a barking sound. Bruce suddenly pounced on her. Transforming, he held her down with one paw and roared in her face. "Eric, please get your cat off of me," Middy said, her eyes wide now that she saw the mighty panther Bruce could turn into.

Tossing the folder with proof of his achievement over his shoulder, Eric fell beside Middy, laughing. He tapped his hand on the floor while counting to ten. As he said ten, Bruce became a black cat again. Eric lifted one of his paws in the air. "And the winner is… BRUCE!" he declared as if an announcer.

"Children. It is time for us to go to the airport. Susan, we have arranged our flight plan to drop you off at your stop before taking Middy to hers. There is no sense in exposing you to more minds than necessary. Middy, behave," Felith said, and that was the end of their horsing around. Real life was upon them once more. Eric's mother and father would go back to the hospital, where his mother would heal someone on Death's door. Susan would return to her isolated mountain home. Middy, now a rookie cop, would arrest people.

On the return home after seeing his family off at the airport, Eric wondered what Ronny was up to with his buddies. "Your sisters are nice. The older one looks like she'd be a handful to watch over," Bobby Jay told Eric while he guided the car on the route home.

"Mids is just as powerful as she is full of

mischief. She used to give our Aunt Julian hell all
the time. Julian got on her bad side early on—a BIG
mistake. Don't ever cross Mids, Bobby," Eric told
him.

"What about the other girl, Susan? She
seemed okay."

"I feel so sorry for Susan. She can't be out in
public for very long. Every thought anyone thinks
around her pounds on her mind. She feels all
their emotions, all the anger, the hate, the despair,
everything. It is horrible. We do our best to protect
her, but she is needed often by…" Eric whispered,
"grandfather." He glanced over at Bobby Jay before
going on. "I'm only telling you this because you have
the clearance to know about us. Please, you can't tell
anyone else about Susan," Eric said, a haunted look
on his face. Bobby nodded, looking grim at this
added secret to keep.

Lights were flashing up ahead, and the traffic
had reached a standstill. "Looks like an accident of
some sort," Bobby muttered. Eric unhooked his seat
belt and reached for the door handle to get out of the
car. "Hold it," Bobby said, stopping him. "You can't
go up there as a doctor. You can render first aid, but
nothing more. But, before you do that, you must eat
protein bars and drink energy drinks. Otherwise, I'll
handcuff you to the car. Got it, kid? And be sneaky.
Don't heal a cut outright. Just press on it a moment
and act like that did the job. Anything worse, you do
only enough to save a life, nothing more."

"Okay," Eric said, nodding his head. He
opened the glove compartment and pulled out four
protein bars and two energy drinks. He had learned

to eat and down these boosts so they could start building him up. He was thankful he had Bobby as his SS security. He looked after Eric and even hooked him up to an IV when needed. Poor Susan didn't have anyone to help her.

While Eric was eating and drinking, Bobby maneuvered the car off the road and parked it out of the way. He checked his gun, then stuffed his pockets with bars and drinks for Eric. This was the real-life of taking care of someone like Eric. You had to be prepared to shoot a bad guy or boost your subject up. It was never dull. However, he could use a bit more sleep once in a while. He laughed at himself, wishing for sleep when there were people in need of protection. Right now, he had to keep the kid from killing himself or giving away his secret.

Eric's blood was rushing through his body super fast, or so it seemed, as he opened the trunk of the car and reached inside. For a moment, his hand hovered over the Medical Bag he had put together for when he had his practice. Then, his common sense kicked in, and he pulled out the high-quality medical kit they carried in the car instead. It was strange not to be able to act as a doctor, to pretend he couldn't do all the things he could do. Eric had learned to hide his talents or curses. But that didn't mean he liked having to do it.

It was a mess of cars blocking the roadway. It looked like one car was stacked on top of another in spots. Bobby flashed his ID and asked a trooper how he and Eric could help. "We are waiting for the medics to make it here. All this backed-up traffic makes it hard for them to get to us. We just redirected them to come to us in the other direction. Bit of a chance, but we need someone to tell us who is critical and who can wait."

Eric spoke up before Bobby could warn him off, "I can do that for you. I have some limited medical training. I can't do more than first aid, but I can tell you who desperately needs treatment." Bobby took a breath. Eric had handled that well. Then, it occurred to Bobby that Eric was used to having to downplay what he could do. He nodded his head at the kid to let him know he had done a good job explaining things.

"You go right ahead. If you can figure a way to mark each person with what you find out, it will speed things up," the trooper said, relief obvious in his eyes.

Bobby pulled a marker out of his pocket and showed it to the trooper. "We will mark their foreheads," he said.

Eric was already heading to the first car. Looking inside, he found a man by himself. He touched the man's forehead. "Drunk, nothing more." Quickly, he went to one of the cars with another one on top. A woman was in the bottom car. There was an infant strapped into its carrier in the back seat. The mother had a broken arm and a concussion. The baby was okay. "Broke right arm and concussion. The infant is okay." The top car was wobbling back and forth as Eric had examined the infant and mother.

"Careful, kid. That one may slip at any time," Bobby warned, but Eric was already squirming into the top car.

"Bar," Eric called out, offering a hand out the window. Bobby opened a protein bar and placed it in Eric's hand. Inside the car, Eric was applying pressure to an open hole in a man's chest as the car rocked again. This was the reason for the pile-up. The man had been shot and had gunned his car trying to get away, crashing into the car his car sat upon. The man was covered in blood, looking dead rather than alive. Eric did his best to stop the bleeding, repairing several main bleeders. He only hoped it was enough to save the man's life. There were others he needed to check, and he might need to heal them, so he had to save some of himself for them. "Bobby, write 'Critical gunshot' on the window. I've applied pressure bandages."

"Trooper," Bobby yelled at the man dealing with angry people who wanted to move on. He came running over to Bobby. "The man in the car up there has been shot. He is one of the first they need to deal with when the medics arrive," Bobby said, watching Eric back carefully out of the car's window.

"I'll call it in. If nothing else, it will get us some extra help here. Dang graduates are tying up a lot of our time," the trooper grumbled softly.

Bobby stuck close to Eric. Now that a shooter was involved, he was in SS mode. His eyes took in the slightest movement. A driver was waving a handkerchief out of his window frantically at them.

"Oh, no," Eric said as if his breath had been knocked out. "Bobby, that is Dr. North. Come give me a hand."

Swiftly, Eric ran to Dr. North's car window.

"How badly are you hurt, sir?" he asked the doctor while scanning the car. A woman and a little girl were strapped in the back seat. The girl looked to be asleep. The woman was weeping.

Dr. North grabbed Eric and half-yanked him into the car. "Airlift. Have them send an airlift for my daughter. She has a bad heart. We were taking her in for her transplant. Quickly, we can't delay," Dr. North shouted at Eric, his eyes wild with a crazed look on his face.

"Let me go so I can check her pulse," Eric reasoned with the overly stressed man. Glancing over his shoulder, he called to Bobby. "Get him off of me so I can tend the girl."

Bobby was instantly prying Dr. North's hands off of Eric. "Calm down. Let Eric do his thing. He can't help if you hinder him." He watched as Eric opened the car's back door and took the little girl from her mother.

Eric's face was grim. He looked up at Bobby and made a drinking motion with one hand. Raising his face, he parted his lips slightly. Closing his eyes, he concentrated on repairing the child's heart. As Bobby began pouring one of the energy drinks into Eric's mouth, Eric swallowed automatically. Once, he opened his eyes briefly and looked at Dr. North. "You need to start checking the other cars. Render aid, mark their foreheads with what is wrong with them. I'm going to faint after this." The last he said to Bobby Jay.

Bobby nodded, prepared to catch his subject. He snarled at Dr. North, "Get your butt moving. He is giving his all for your little girl. The least you can do is help out." He handed North the marker. For a moment, it looked as if the older man would protest or have a temper fit. He looked around as if realizing people were hurt in the other cars. Then, he glared daggers at Eric and went off to check on the occupants of those cars.

The child's heart was slowly healing. The trouble was that Eric wasn't as strong a healer as his mother. He was slowly becoming more potent as a healer. Still, he didn't have the inner strength of the rest of his family to act as batteries to help him heal. "Take me straight home," he mumbled, throwing his last bit of willpower into healing the final spot on the child's heart. As blackness took over his mind and he fell into Bobby's waiting arms, his last thought was to wonder if he had succeeded.

Catching Eric, Bobby Jay cradled him to him. He gave the woman a harsh look. "We were never here, understand? You and your husband must never speak of this, ever." Anger was in his words, and fear was in his heart as he ran with Eric's limp body in his arms to the car. Higgins was off protecting Ronny. He was on his own. He strapped Eric in, slamming the door to the car on his way around to the driver's side. He didn't look to see what else was going on. There was only one thought in his head: get Eric home and on an IV. Dirt flew from the car's tires as Bobby hopped across a grassy divider to a feeder road. "Dumb kid, you damn, dumb kid. Don't you ever think?" Bobby shouted at Eric's unconscious body. He drove like a madman.

Screeching the tires as they finally arrived at the house, Bobby leaped out of the car, ran up to unlock the door, and brought Eric inside. He did what he had to, rigging an IV for Eric and covering him nicely and snugly in his bed. He didn't object when Bruce transformed and came to lay with his panther body against Eric. Finally, Bobby sat down in a chair facing his subject. Now came the long wait for Eric to wake up.

Sometime in the morning, Higgins and Ronny came home and found their beds, unaware of Bobby and his vigil.

Chapter Seven

LIFE GOES ON

With a groan, Eric rolled out of bed. He felt like a truck had run over him and then back over him before driving off. A vague memory of a little girl with a heart failing flashed in his mind, making him draw a deep breath before trying to stand up. He needed food, and by the smell of bacon sneaking through his door, Higgins was cooking breakfast. Running a hand through his hair, Eric opened his bedroom door and slowly walked towards the kitchen with Bruce at his side. Flopping down in a chair, he almost groaned again. That heart was the hardest healing he had ever done besides Charlie's legs. He needed food and lots of it. A soft moan of appreciation escaped his lips when Higgins sat a heaping plate of food before him, "Thanks, I need this."

Trying not to look like he had the worst hangover of his life, Ronny entered the kitchen as Eric picked up his fork. One look at Eric and Ronny's headache became secondary. Eric looked like hell. "Man, and I thought I had a wild night. You look worse than I feel. What did you do, Shrimp, drink a whole bar out of beer?" Ronny croaked out in a whisper voice.

Eric looked up, startled. "Did anyone hear if that little girl lived? What about the guy who was shot?" he asked, concern written upon his face.

Higgins slammed Ronny's plate of food down before him and slapped the back of his head. "You had to get him started worrying, didn't you? I should slap that beer-soggy head off of you," he said, stomping back to the stove to make Bobby's food and his own.

Wisely, Ronny shut up and just ate his breakfast, wondering what he had missed. A little girl and a man shot? What happened while he and the guys were out whooping it up? Watching Eric eating like a starving man, Ronny realized Eric had spent his night healing someone instead of having a nightmare about them. Who? A little girl and a man shot, of course. Ronny flinched when Higgins banged a skillet down hard upon the stove.

"What's all that noise?" Bobby Jay asked, coming out of his room fully dressed. He, too, looked like he'd had a rough night. His eyes were bloodshot, and he didn't have that upright, I'm in charge look he usually projected.

"Sorry, sir," Higgins said, glancing at Ronny as if he still wanted to slap his head off. "Eat and go back to bed. I'm still good for a few hours. We need to stay home and recuperate. Ron Ron didn't come home until the wee hours after partying."

Bobby grunted and sat down at the table. "Thank you," Bobby told Higgins when he sat Bobby's plate in front of him and sat down with his breakfast.

Shit, Ronny thought, could I be any more of an ass? "Yes, thank you for making breakfast," he mumbled. Even though he didn't want to eat, he forced himself to fork eggs into his mouth. Higgins had cooked it, after all. He felt a little ashamed of keeping the SS man out all night. But it had been the last night of his being a student. Today, he had to take on the cloak of a full-grown man. His life as an adult began. Here he was, acting like a spoiled brat, not even thanking Higgins for cooking a meal.

He had stayed out most of the night with his friends. He'd felt like this was goodbye to his friends on the football team. He and Charlie were close, so he hoped they would continue to be lifelong friends. He'd wanted a night to remember, to be able to look back and think of the crazy night they had all spent drinking and whooping it up. Life was scary, and he'd had a taste of it with Charlie's accident and Eric's nightmares. Now, he was facing being a responsible adult who made life-and-death decisions in his practice. He'd be comforting people who lost an animal friend and, hopefully, be on the side of giving good news about a loved pet who would live for many years.

Ronny glanced over at Eric, feeling guilty that he'd had such a good night with his friends, and left Eric to face whatever had happened to him. Eric was sitting frozen in place, his fork halfway to his mouth.

"Bobby, something is wrong with Eric," he whispered urgently to the SS agent.

Bobby knew that look on Eric's face. The boy was having a vision of some sort. He'd be frozen like that until it passed. "Leave him be. He is seeing something. It is best to let him finish the vision."

Frozen, unaware that three people were staring at him, holding their breath, Eric rode with a family in their car. They were laughing as they butchered a road song. The baby started crying, and the mother leaned over the backseat to see if the baby had a wet diaper. She turned her head to tell the father to pull over so she could change the diaper. He grumbled, slowing down to look for a safe spot to pull over. Then he was slumped over to the side with blood dripping down his face. The car jerked to the side as he fell towards his wife with his hands still gripping the steering wheel. The vehicle crashed into mile marker 49 and continued down an embankment to smash into a tree.

Eric took a deep breath and came to his own body once more. His fork fell from his hand as he reached out to brace himself. Then Eric realized he wasn't in that car. He was home eating his breakfast. For a frantic second, Eric swung his head, looking for Bobby. When he saw Bobby, he calmed down enough to speak. "A family in a car. Driver shot— mile marker 49. The car went off the road down the side of the road and crashed into some trees. It will be hard to see the car from the road."

"Do you have a when?" Bobby asked.

"No... maybe, maybe now. They need to hurry. There are children in the car, one a baby," Eric was upset. He had been there with the family when it happened. It was like he was part of the family. He was scared, scared he hadn't seen enough to save them.

The two SS agents went into action. Ronny had seen them work as a team before, and watching the two of them reminded him of his football team. Each of his guys had a job to do. Bobby and Higgins were like that. Higgins pulled out a map and spread it on the table. He had barely eaten any of the breakfast he had cooked, pushing it aside to make room for the map. Bobby got on the computer and was pulling up topographical maps. They located two locations between them that could match Eric's vision. Meanwhile, Eric ate like a half-starved man.

Bobby and Higgins stood. They both looked over at Eric as if judging his condition. "I'll go, Sir," Higgins said. "You need to guard him. Call me if he sees anything more that might help." He gave a critical look at Bobby's plate. "And eat your damn breakfast." Rubbing his eyes as if weary, Higgins gathered the car keys, checked his gun, and opened the door.

Ronny jumped from the table and said, "Wait for me." Higgins scowled at Ronny as if he were about to blast the boy for thinking this was a beer run. "I thought you could use another pair of eyes. Okay?" Higgins gave a reluctant nod.

Once on the road with Higgins driving, Ronny explained his wildness last night. "Last night was a one-time thing," he stated, "It was, for me, the end of childhood, and today is the beginning of my adult life. I know that sounds lame. I am sorry you had to go with me. That meant Bobby had to stay up with Eric, right? That is why he is so tired today."

"He would have been up all night with him anyway, kid. Eric healed last night and nearly died on Bobby. He sat by his bed until he felt the kid would make it. Don't blame yourself," Higgins reassured him. "I bet the kid will go to work tomorrow, too. Bobby is going to have his hands full. The least I can do is stay up a few hours and let Bobby rest."

"Did," Ronny paused, unsure if he should ask about last night. "Did the little girl and guy who were shot survive?" he finally asked.

"Only a man was shot. He caused the pile-up on the highway by running up on the back of the car in front of him when he passed out. The little girl wasn't shot. It was her heart. Eric stopped the bleeding on the gunshot man, and then he healed the child's heart. That did him in," Higgins said, almost as if he was giving a report. "Keep your eyes down along the tree line here. Eric said the car went off the road and down an embankment."

Ronny kept hoping he would see the wreck of the car. But deep inside, he didn't want to find a vehicle with dead children inside it. Up ahead of them, they saw a plume of smoke rising. Dread took hold of Ronny, along with a sense of urgency. He started having flashbacks to when his best friend Charlie had been nearly killed when hit by a huge truck. Eric said there were little kids and a baby in that car ahead. What would they find? Little bodies? Nausea filled his stomach and forced him to sit back to calm it down. Ronny didn't want to throw up in front of an SS agent.

Parking on the side of the road, Higgins stepped out of the car and pulled out his cell phone. Knowing the truth, Higgins called the instance an accident to cover for Eric. That done, he took pictures of the opposite side of the road from the smoking car. Ronny was already scrambling down the embankment to the wreck. Higgins shook his head. The young didn't have any sense of self-preservation. The shooter could still be in the area watching them at this very moment. Higgins popped the trunk of the car, taking out the large first aid kit they carried in case Eric or anyone needed it. He grabbed the stack of blankets to keep their subject warm during those sugar lows. Shutting the trunk, Higgins scrambled down the embankment after Ronny. "Stand back. Let me check things out first," he ordered Ronny.

Ronny glared over at Higgins. "I've got this."

"No, you don't. You can't treat them. All you can do is give first aid. We have to be legal here. The fact we happened upon this accident means little if we injure the survivors before the medics can get here. So, back off," Higgins said, fully aware that there was an alert child in the backseat of the car. He was still pissed off at Ronny for drinking so much last night. If the boy was going to live with Eric, he needed to grow up and act like a responsible adult.

Ronny's head was still pounding, and he didn't feel up to arguing with Higgins. Maybe he was right. After all, Ronny was just an animal doctor and not trained to treat humans. It was as he nodded his head to indicate he would back off that Ronny noticed the little boy clutching his bloody sister to his chest in the backseat.

"Don't hurt my sisters," the child said.

"We are here to help," Ronny soothed. Higgins nudged Ronny with a blanket for the kids. "Here, let me put this blanket over you and your sister to keep you nice and warm until an ambulance can come to take you and your family to the hospital. Okay?" The little boy nodded, tears beginning to pool in his brown eyes. "Help is coming. You need to be brave for your Mom and your sisters. Keep your cool for them."

The child sobbed, "I think I wet my pants. They will laugh at me."

"No, believe me, nobody is going to laugh at you. Why, you are the bravest man here. Look at you. You are holding your sister, protecting her. I bet you even put that pacifier in the baby's mouth, didn't you?" Ronny said.

Sniffing up his tears, the boy nodded. They could hear sirens screaming in their urgent voices towards them.

At home, Eric and Bobby waited for what seemed to be hours for some word on what Ronny and Higgins found out. Bobby was worried about Eric, who seemed so down in the dumps. Finally, Bobby turned on the television for distraction. An update was provided about the interstate accident that occurred last night. There was Dr. North in all his stuffy glory, playing down his part in giving first aid to the people who were in the accident. The camera switched to the announcer. The man spoke with an uplifting ring. "What many of you may not know is that Dr. North and his wife were taking their daughter to the hospital last night to receive a new heart. While the girl's father took charge of the accident, hoping an airlift would arrive in time to transport his daughter to the hospital, a miracle happened. His sweet little girl's heart got better. She no longer needs to have a transplant...."

Bobby turned the television off. At least they had good news concerning the little girl. The phone rang, and Higgins told them the family was at the hospital. However, the father had died.

The nightmares stayed away Sunday night, and for once, Eric had a whole night of sleep. He and Ronny were up early because they had started working as doctors that day. Higgins made a huge breakfast, scowling only once at Ronny. Ronny wondered how he could get off of Higgins' crap list. He knew that much of it was because he worried about Eric as it was the whole wild-drinking party he and the team had. Glancing at Eric, Ronny raised his eyebrows and indicated Higgins with his head.

Eric mouthed 'later' back. The only person Eric could think about was Betty. He'd get to see her all day, every day this week. That possibility had his heart doing double time. Until he remembered he couldn't have a girlfriend. Or a wife. That dampened his mood, and he ate breakfast, feeling as if his world had ended once more. At least he had his work, and he could sort of help people. Yeah, even if it wasn't always successful.

After making sure Molly and Bruce were

happy and that Higgins could sleep without being awakened by either of the pets, Eric, Ronny, and Bobby Jay were about to leave. A car pulled up to the house, putting Bobby Jay and Higgins in super SS mode. Eric and Ronny were hustled to a bedroom while Bobby answered the door.

"They do this every time someone comes to the door?" Ronny asked Eric.

He nodded. "Mids and I don't have it so bad. My sister Susan is locked away in a room with monitors to see what is happening. There are snipers above her place to take anyone out who is a threat. Yeah, Mids and I don't have it bad at all." Higgins put a finger to his lips, shutting both of them up.

They could hear voices in the living room but couldn't understand what was being said. Higgins' phone vibrated, letting him know bringing Eric and Ronny out was safe. Ronny was tense; he hadn't entirely adjusted to this cloak-and-dagger world that Eric lived in and could feel his muscles ready to take a head-on hit. He was shocked to see Dr. North standing in the living room being talked to by Bobby Jay. Dr. North didn't look like the stern instructor who had given him and Eric so much trouble this last year of college. The man looked chastised and humble.

Bobby Jay patted Dr. North on the shoulder once he had finished informing him of the likelihood of spending the rest of his life in prison. "I'm happy for you. Miracles do happen," he said, letting Dr. North know how he should handle the gift Eric had given to his daughter. He indicated that Eric and Ronny were allowed to come over to them.

"Dr. North," Eric said, offering his hand.

Dr. North seized Eric's hand and noticed Higgins and Bobby both take a step closer to him. He shook Eric's hand and smiled, actually smiled. "I just came to wish you two boys well and tell you what a pleasure it has been knowing you. You both have bright futures ahead of you," he said, letting go of Eric's hand and offering his hand to Ronny.

Ronny shook Dr. North's hand as if the world had turned upside down. "Thank you, sir," he said in unison with Eric. Eric laughed, and Ronny relaxed.

They all hustled to the cars, except for Higgins, who yawned and sought his bed. Ronny couldn't help but wonder what was up with Dr. North. That whole scene was utterly unlike the man who had disapproved of Eric and Ronny so totally. He noticed that Eric didn't seem surprised by Dr. North or concerned over the man's out-of-character actions. His mind wrestled with what that meant, and then he remembered that Eric had healed someone Saturday night. "Was the little girl Dr. North's daughter?" he asked.

Eric nodded and turned his face to look out of the car window. He didn't want to be reminded of the people harmed on Saturday. Or those on Sunday. Yet, there they sat in his mind as he went over the events, wondering what more he should have done. Could he have prevented the father of that family from dying if he had the vision sooner?

The car pulled into the clinic's parking lot, and Eric straightened his shoulders. It was time to be a doctor, ease pain and heal, and do his weird-to-the-world thing secretly.

Glancing towards the back of the clinic, Eric could tell that Betty was already hard at work cleaning kennels and feeding the boarding dogs. His traitor of a heart quickened in his chest, and the cloud hanging over him seemed to lift a little. If that were all he had, that slight lightening of his mood, he'd have to live with it. A person could live with anything: nightmares coming to life, losing lives, loving someone from a distance, all of it was bearable, even if you had to work in secret every day for the rest of your life.

His resolve lasted until Betty walked up to pick up a dog for a bath. She had a bruise under her eye. Something Eric wasn't familiar with coursed through his body. It blanked his mind to everything else around him except that bruise.

"Eric, Eric," Dr. Monroe said again. It didn't penetrate Eric's mind that he was being called for an entire moment as he warred with himself over going and immediately demanding to know what happened to Betty's cheek or following her to the back and healing the bruise.

Ronny nudged Eric's arm, bringing him back from the brink of stupidity and doing something that would expose what he was to the world. "What?" he asked, his irritation clearly showing. Ronny nodded towards where Dr. Monroe stood, his arms crossed, scowling at Eric.

Eric turned his attention to Dr. Monroe, but his mind was on Betty and that bruise on her cheek. A wave of slow-burning anger raged inside him at the thought someone may have hurt her. He wondered if Bobby would look into it so he could keep his name out of things. Eric hated that he couldn't take direct action on his own. Every cell in his body was screaming at him to confront her and find out about that bruise. He had to be strong for her sake. No way was he bringing her into his nightmare world. But what if she was living a nightmare? Bobby would have to check it out for him. He had to.

"You will each take an exam room. From now on, you are doctors. It would help if you assumed the responsibility of your profession. If you have a question, be sure to contact me immediately. Do not second guess. Be certain. Now I will retire to my office. Oh, you must get a weight and history on each patient. Also, check and clean the ears if needed and clip the toenails. Most people who come in do not tend to these little things which can help a pet have a happier life." Dr. Monroe, having given them his instruction, retired to his office. He wanted to see if Eric would remember to first care for the patients in the clinic. He had plans for Eric, and this trial period would decide whether he put those plans into action.

Ronny looked stunned at Eric. His mouth was open as if he had questions he couldn't voice. Smiling, Eric motioned Ronny to follow him. "He is testing us. I think he wants us to make mistakes. Only, we won't make it that easy to take us down. First, we need to medicate and check the patients in the clinic. Back here on the computer, we look under 'In Clinic.' That file lists everyone who has stayed overnight and what medications or treatments they need. Let's see what we have. You make a list as I read things off," Eric told Ronny.

The two of them fell into a rhythm of medicating and treating the animals in the clinic. They each took a part of the list and worked as much as they had when at the college's clinic. Eric would often touch a dog or cat that Ronny was about to treat or medicate beforehand to calm the animal, so Ronny had no problems with the cat or dog. Twice, they worked on the same animal. On one, Eric held up a leg while Ronny changed the bandages and treated the wound on the large dog's leg. The other was a cat Ronny assisted Eric, who had to flush out an abscess. They were done in record time before the clinic doors opened for the walk-in clients.

Twice, Eric saw Betty walk up to pick up the dogs for bathing. Each time, his heartbeat quickened, and his anger at the bruise on her cheek grew. This feeling of rage was so unlike him. He wasn't like his sister Middy, who could hold a grudge for years. The thought of someone hurting Betty just provoked all his protective instincts. Yet, he couldn't do anything to protect her except talk to Bobby. All Eric had was nightmares to offer.

Overall, the next few days at work went well. Ronny and Eric handled all the clients while Dr. Monroe caught up on whatever paperwork he had to do. As Eric and Ronny walked to the car to go home, the vision hit Eric. He froze in place, his eyes wide, his features expressing horror. He saw his sister Middy kneeling in a pool of blood. Police officers were scattered on the ground around her, either dead or dying. Mids had tears and defiance on her face. She looked up, and it appeared she was screaming something. Then Eric came to himself. Eric fumbled for his cell phone, his hands shaking almost uncontrollably. He couldn't lose his sister; he wouldn't survive her loss.

When Middy answered the phone, Eric began to babble in a panic. "Wear your vest every time you go on patrol, Mids. I saw officers being shot and killed. You knew them. I saw you crying, Mids, alone on the sidewalk with bodies around you. Promise me, you have to promise me, or I'll come there and follow you around," Eric took a gasping breath. "Tell your security guy. Have Grandpa send more help. Do everything to keep safe, Mids. I can't lose you." Middy had always calmed him in crisis with a simple promise that she had him calming down. Eric made her promise to call him before she left for work and when she came home from work each day.

It wasn't until he hung up the phone that he realized Bobby Jay and Ronny were guarding him. Bobby was all business. "What was that about? Is there a threat directed at your sister?" he asked.

"I don't know. It looked as if her fellow officers were the ones who had been targeted. I made her promise to wear her vest," Eric told him.

"Let me see who is assigned to her," Bobby said, immediately pulling out his phone. He talked in a low voice for a moment before hanging up. "I know the guy who has her, and he is a bulldog. If anyone can keep her safe, it is him. Let's get you two home. I'm sure Higgins has prepared a meal and is fretting that it will get cold. We all know what a grump he can be when upset," Bobby said, trying to lighten Eric's mood. Ronny gave a little snort-laugh. He had been at the end of Higgins's disapproval and didn't want to face it again. Eric nodded. His mind was still in shock over the vision he had just had.

Expecting to have nightmares during the night, Eric was reluctant to go to bed. Weariness finally overcame him, making him bid Higgins goodnight and seek his bed. Surprisingly, he fell right off to sleep. The nightmares he had anticipated did not occur. Instead, he had dreams, real dreams. The problem was they didn't feel like his dreams. He was in a house that looked like a home anyone would love to own. The furniture was well cared for and made a person feel comfortable yet still had a look of elegance. Everything was neat and in its place. A large man sat in a very comfortable-looking chair, reading a newspaper. Now and then, he turned the page as if he were either scanning the pages or was a speedy reader. He held out his hand, and a woman was almost instantly there, placing a glass of what appeared to be wine in the hand.

Bruce transformed on top of him, interrupting the dream. When Eric had Bruce soothed back into regular cat form, the dream was just a foggy memory. As he drifted back to sleep, he wondered why Bruce had transformed.

The dream began with a child's happiness. A little girl had a stick in her hand, playing outside. She looked around to see if anyone was watching before sitting on the ground. With the stick, she began to draw something in the dirt of a flowerbed. It was hard to see the details at first, but a bunny shape appeared as the child became more focused on what she was drawing. From what Eric could see, the drawing was good for being done by such a small child. Suddenly, the child glanced over her shoulder at something. Quickly, she rubbed the picture out and placed the stick on the ground. Picking a flower, she turned and walked away.

It was like that all night; the dreams were different scenes of people. Sometimes, they were of a man watching television or reading a newspaper. Others were of a child drawing pictures of things and rubbing them out. Each time, Bruce transformed and woke Eric up. When morning arrived, he didn't feel as if he had rested at all. This night of just dreams instead of nightmares left him drained and wishing for some decent rest. Even the nightmares would be more welcome than these rambling dreams of people he didn't know.

As Eric dressed for the day, Middy called to check in. Eric was again thrown into the nightmare of a vision he had of her among her dead fellow officers. His worry about his sister sprang to the fore. She hadn't been dead in his vision, just so filled with grief and rage. Why couldn't he have had a nightmare that would help his sister catch a murderer? Eric knew that wanting to have a vision or nightmare about someone he cared about would only keep him from having either. He hesitated and concentrated on making it through breakfast and the rest of the day. Something was off. Why would a child need to hide drawing a picture? It felt so wrong.

Eric fretted over Betty, Middy, and some unknown child all day. He felt battered by the end of the day. This was the end of the working week, and over the weekend, he and Ronny would alternate days to come in, giving them each a day off. Before leaving the clinic, Eric went to the cages to hold the animals who were sick or recovering from surgery. He touched each head and checked to be sure they would each make it through Saturday without him. For some, he gave a tiny healing boost to their systems just to be confident they would continue to do well. As he left the clinic, he felt himself hoping for once that he had nightmares while he slept. People were depending on him—people he loved.

Throughout dinner, Bobby kept a wary eye on Eric. Something was eating at the kid, and that worried him. Some might argue it wasn't his job to ensure his subject's mental health. Those fools didn't know Eric and had never shadowed a superhero. Bobby had lost count of the times he or Higgins had gone out and saved someone's life because of Eric. Also, when Higgins had the headache from Hell, Eric cured it with just a touch. Bobby never thought he would feel awe for anyone he had been assigned to guard. Yet, here he was in that very position. Sure, the kid was reckless, but what kid wasn't?

Ronny was flying on a high. They'd had a perfect week at work. He had more faith in his ability to diagnose and treat patients. He'd even received a pat on the back from Dr. Monroe. How cool was that? He glanced over at Eric and grinned like a fool. "Man, we are the best damn doctors there are. We should go out tomorrow night. Maybe we can pick up a couple of girls."

A smile played on Eric's face as he nodded to Ronny. "Except I don't think either of us will have the time for more than dinner. Saturdays can be a killer. I'm glad you pulled it rather than me. Man, you are going to be dragging tomorrow night. We'll talk about going out when you get home tomorrow. That is if you have the energy to talk," Eric said, faking a knowing look at Ronny.

Later that night, Eric began to dream about the little girl again. She seemed such a sad child. It was as if all the joy a child should have in their life was sucked out of her own life. Eric wanted to help her, this dream child. He watched her do her drawings in the dirt and then wipe out any trace. She was an incredible artist and a child filled with fear. In one dream, the little girl was lying in bed. She looked feverish and was very still. A woman's hand kept refreshing a damp cloth on the child's head. For a moment in the dream, Eric was the mother, full of love and fear for her child. The dream changed, and the girl returned to her secret drawing spot. She stopped looking at the place where the flowerbed had been. Now, it was covered in cement. Nothing would ever grow there again. Not flowers. Not her pictures. Bowing her head, the little girl turned away, and Eric woke.

Chapter Eight

SEARCHING

When Eric woke up, it was morning. The day was in that dusty dawn stage. For a long moment, Eric lay there, devastated by the shattering of a little girl's secret life—a dream girl. There was one thing his family had taught him well, and that was never to give up. He needed help.

His mind was made up, and Eric looked for Bobby and Higgins. He found Higgins already up and mixing up what looked like biscuit dough. The man was a good cook, and Eric counted himself lucky to have him as one of his SS men. Like Middy, he had experienced some sour SS men during his childhood. Before Bobby Jay and Higgins took over, Eric didn't have anyone to talk to other than to lay down impossible rules for him to follow. Eric wasn't as much a rebel as Middy, but he didn't like the previous set of guys who had watched over him. Respect them, he did. Respect was different from enjoying a person. They had a job to do, and Eric knew that. True, it was their job to keep him safe. He had no trouble respecting them for what they did or had to put up with when shadowing him. It was just that he hadn't had anyone he could confide in for so long.

"Sit down. I'll have breakfast ready in a few minutes," Higgins said to Eric, nodding toward the table.

"After breakfast, we need to talk once Ronny goes to work. I need help, and you and Bobby are the only ones who might understand," Eric told Higgins.

Higgins paused, forgetting to stir the bowl of dough. He glanced over at Eric, a worried look on his face. It looked as if the kid was going to ask about sex. He started to say something, and then he continued mixing the dough. If the kid were in a romantic crisis, he'd best let the boss handle it. Giving sexual advice just wasn't his thing. Higgins' mouth twitched, and he rubbed his hand over his face, wondering how long he could delay this talk. If he didn't quit punishing his biscuit batter, the biscuits would be as tough as old shoe leather. In times like this, he wished he had become a plumber. Grumbling to himself, he started beating up the eggs for a while, then set sausage and bacon to cooking. He was so distracted he almost overcooked the gravy for the biscuits. By then, Ronny and Bobby had come to sit at the table.

Ronny was full of energy. This was his day to work the clinic alone. He was a little nervous but was mostly eager to spread his wings. This would be the first time Eric wasn't around to back him up. That was both a relief and a dread. For once, he'd feel as if he were in charge and not second-guess everything he did, wondering if he had missed something. But then again, what if he did miss something that Eric would have found with a simple touch? He had to know he was capable of handling things on his own. Shoveling eggs and sausage into his mouth, Ronny reached for the gravy and poured it over the hot biscuit on his plate. Looking up, he thought about how to thank Higgins and swallowed his mouthful. "Thank you, Higgins. This is the best gravy I've ever eaten."

Higgins grunted and nodded his head in return. His mind was on the talk he and Bobby needed with Eric. His breakfast tasted like sawdust in his mouth. He wasn't the kid's daddy, so why should he and Bobby be the ones to give this talk to the kid? Look at the kid pushing his food around the plate as if it grew on the trees outside. "Eat that food, Eric. I didn't cook it for my health, you know."

"Yes, sir," Eric said, sitting up and forking eggs into his mouth. He knew Higgins was mad about something, but right now, all he could think about was that little girl in his dreams and his sister Middy maybe facing a mass murderer. He was mentally marking the days off for the vision he had of his sister kneeling in all that blood. He wanted the vision to expire and all to be right in Middy's world. Waiting was like a shadow casting his world into semi-darkness. It had been so long since he saw the sun.

Bobby watched the other three at the table while eating his meal with gusto. Ronny seemed almost bouncing in his chair like a little kid waiting to go to the beach. The boy made Bobby smile as he remembered having felt like that. Higgins, however, was in a foul mood. Was he still mad at Ronny for getting drunk? Or did he have some other bug up his nose? The man was moody. This past week, he had been downright grumpy. Then, there was Eric. Something was up with the kid. He had that hang-dogged look of being crushed by something. The kid hadn't even run for the past couple of nights.

The moment Higgins left with Ronny, Eric turned to Bobby. "I need your help," he said.

"Sure, you have another nightmare? Tell me about it. I'll fire up the computer," Bobby said, getting up to go get the laptop they used to do searches.

"No, a dream. A lot of the same dreams," Eric looked down at the table before speaking again. "They aren't like my nightmares, which are like prophecies. These are like a part of a life, something that happened. It is so sad. There is this sweet little girl who has an amazing talent. If I ever see one of her paintings, I'll know she painted it. They are wonderful, Bobby, for such a little girl. She hides them. It is like she is afraid to let anyone see her draw. She draws in the dirt and then rubs it out. Here is the thing. Whomever she was afraid of must have found out. They had the patch of dirt cemented over, so she couldn't draw on it anymore. How cruel is that? And there are the dreams of a man sitting in a chair. It is like he thinks he is a king. He holds his hand out and expects a drink to be placed immediately."

Eric rested his face in his hands, covering his eyes. "I feel affection for the child as if she is mine. I want to protect her. To make it possible for her to draw and paint whatever her little heart desires. Isn't that weird?"

"That you care about a child? No, not at all. You forget I was there when you went into a pond and dove down to save a bag of kittens someone was drowning. I think you saw the fear and the longing in this little girl's face, and you want to help her, too. Let's analyze this," Bobby said again, getting up and going for the laptop. He sat back down and pulled up a text program. "Now, tell me what the area looked like."

"I can't. She is a little girl, about five years old. She isn't looking around. The only thing she is interested in is the picture she is drawing. It is all she cares about. She was never outside that yard. Once, she was in a bedroom, ill. I was with the mother at that time, not the child. All the mother saw was her child. I'm sorry, I'm no help this time. This one means so much to me, and I can't even help you." Eric stood up, pushing his chair back from the table. "I need to go for a run," he said, going to his room to put on his running outfit. Bobby jumped up, too. He needed to get ready to run with Eric.

"You don't understand. I think I'm going crazy. Will you recommend someone safe to have to examine my mental health? You and Higgins know why I can't go to just anyone," Eric explained to Bobby.

"Why do you believe you need such an

examination? Wouldn't it be more logical that this is just a dream such as average people might have?" Bobby asked. He knew he was treading on quicksand here. Someone like Eric was so unusual that nothing about him would be considered normal. Compared to Eric, he could not or would not use Normal.

Shaking his head, Eric tried to give Bobby's idea some thought. The trouble was he had nothing to which to compare the dreams. Sometimes, he had vague dreams that didn't stick with him. These dreams were too real, too emotional to him. They didn't predict anything. He could feel no time involved with them. She was a little girl. A little girl who is afraid of being discovered drawing. He felt love for her. How could that be normal? Or, as Bobby so carefully put it, average? He had to be crazy. Only someone insane would feel this sort of love for a strange little girl. "Because I feel so much love for that little girl. It is like she is my soul mate. Right at this moment, I would not hesitate to lay down my life for her. That can't be a sane way to feel about someone I haven't met. Can it?"

Struggling to think of anything that would convince Eric he was not insane, Bobby glanced out the window. This was damn serious. Where the hell was Higgins? Eric had outpaced him as usual on their run, but now that they were showered and dressed for the day again, Bobby still felt like he was falling behind. He hadn't considered that the kid thought he was going nuts. A thought occurred to him, and Bobby felt his insides turn over and nausea stir in his stomach. He hesitated to ask his next question, unsure he wanted to hear the answer. "Is it a sexual type of love?"

"What? NO! Bobby, if I thought that for one moment, we'd be at the doctor having me castrated this very moment. I've only seen the little girl's face once. That was when she was ill, and her mother was tending to her. Every other time, I've been projecting her, and she was so intent on getting one of her drawings done before she had to wipe it out that all I saw were her hands. Do you think that is why I'm dreaming of a little girl? Could it be something as sick and crazy as that inside me? Bobby, if it is, you have to kill me. Promise me you will kill me if that is the insanity that has hold of me. Promise!"

Eric was so worked up that he couldn't see Bobby's expression. He regretted having asked that stupid question.

"No, I don't think that, but I'd be remiss if I didn't ask you that question. I know we can rule it out. But, Eric, we need to figure this out. You can't go on the way you are right now. You know healing takes a lot out of you. Suppose something happens, and you need to go all-out healing. What happens then? Do you do a partial job? Do you faint before the person or animal is saved? You need to consider those things and not worry about a dream that may be just that.

"You know I'll do anything to help and protect you. I believe in you. Whatever it is, we must figure this out and get you past it. Now, let's go over it all again. Please start at the beginning and take me through each dream. Between us, we should be able to find some clue, some hint into the true nature of what you are dreaming. Okay?" Bobby looked at Eric while trying to look more hopeful than he felt.

Nodding, Eric started talking about the dreams. "The first dream was when she went over to a flowerbed with a stick. At first, I didn't know what she was doing. Maybe she was a little kid digging in the dirt with her stick. Then, the picture started taking shape. It was a rabbit with long, floppy ears. That rabbit seemed to come to life as she drew it. One ear dropped a bit at the tip as the rabbit's hind leg stretched up, scratching the ear. I've never seen such a detailed drawing in the dirt before. She looked over her shoulder and quickly rubbed the rabbit out, hiding her stick. She picked a flower and carried it off as if that was why she was out there all along.

"Then there was a dream about a man who seemed to think he was a king. He was reading the newspaper, and when he held his hand out, a woman stepped into the edge of vision and placed a drink in his hand. It was weird. A bunch of short flicks of the little girl sneaking in drawings in the dirt and covering them up. Then she was sick. I was with her mother at that time. She was worried and kept placing cooling cloths on the girl's forehead. That was the first time I saw the child except her arms and hands. She looked so helpless, a tiny little thing all pale and weak. Her hair was sticking to her face. She was a mess. I wanted to protect her, to take away her pain.

"Between these flickers, I'd see the man now and then. Always lording it up. He… he turned my stomach. That's about all I can tell you. I didn't see outside the yard, so no landmarks," Eric said, his voice trailing off as if feeling he had failed.

"Did you see anything in the girl's room? A picture, a doll, anything?" Bobby asked.

Eric sat with his eyes closed for a very long moment and thought of what was in that room beyond the bed. No dolls. He could see no toys—a nightstand beside the bed just beyond the little girl. Eric's eyes flew open. "A clock. It was old fashion, yet it looked new."

"Okay, we have something we can look up," Bobby said, smiling for the first time.

"There must be thousands of clocks that looked like that once," Eric complained.

"Yes, but you said it was new. So we are looking for someone who bought such a clock recently. Come on, kid, it is worth a shot. Isn't that better than moping around?" Bobby countered.

Eric looked up with a bit of hope in his eyes. "Yes." Some of the despair lifted from his shoulders. If there was something to the dream, some way to help this little girl, he knew Bobby would find it.

For the rest of the day, Eric looked at clocks online. None of them matched the clock in the dream bedroom. Even worse, none of the older clocks they found were still being sold. Those companies had either gone out of business or had discontinued the clocks at least ten years ago.

Bobby got up from the computer to start dinner since Higgins had remained with Ronny all day. He was still a bit pissed at Higgins, although he knew he was being unreasonable. Of course, Higgins would remain with Ronny. The big kid was now part of their assignment. Bobby cooked the only meal he was good at doing: BBQ ribs and potato salad, along with baked beans from a can. He was removing the foils off of garlic bread from the BBQ pit when Higgins and Ronny came home. Bobby watched as Higgins drifted over to the pit outside to help him carry the platter of ribs and the garlic bread inside the house. "Did you have the sex talk with the kid?" he asked. Now Bobby understood why Higgins had exited so quickly this morning. He had thought it was sex that was bothering Eric.

"No, it is worse than that. We are looking for a little girl and don't have any identifying markers to go by except a clock he saw. He is distraught over this one. Put your thinking cap on and get ready to spend a night on the computer," Bobby told him as he picked up the platter of ribs.

The two men entered to place the ribs and bread on the kitchen table. Bobby poured the baked beans from a pot into a bowl and removed the potato salad from the refrigerator. He looked to where Ronny and Eric were sitting, their heads tilted towards each other as Ronny held up a paper pad. "Yes, more like that. It didn't have any fancy things the clocks have now, but that is just about it. It was black. A small statue sat next to it. I just now remember that little statue. It was a bunny holding an umbrella," Eric was saying.

"Come and eat. We will need all our brain cells fed to figure this out," Bobby called to the two young men. He knew they were full-grown, but inside, he felt they were still like children. Eric always seemed so venerable. He was a strong-willed kid, and Bobby admired him for his ability to make something good come from his horrible nightmares.

The four ate silently for a few minutes, filling their bellies with good food. Bobby broke the silence, asking to see the picture of the clock Ronny had drawn. Looking it over, he was reasonably sure clocks like this one were no longer marketed. It was a typical old alarm clock wound with a key made of cheap metal. Only Eric had said it looked new. "I doubt anyone sells these any longer. You might find one at some junk sale, but I doubt it. You said it was new-looking?"

Eric nodded as he hurried to clear his mouth of food. He took a drink from the glass of iced tea in front of him before speaking. "It looked that way to me, but remember, I looked through the mother's eyes. I don't know if that was just the way she saw the clock or if it was, in fact, new. As Ronny was drawing, I remembered a tiny statue beside the clock. It was a bunny holding an umbrella. A white bunny."

"Alice in Wonderland," Higgins said. "When I was in college, my sister had something like that. It came as a toy in one of the kid's meals someplace had. That sounds like the white rabbit who was always saying he was late. It was the anniversary of the movie by Disney, and they promoted it with those toys. My sister collected the whole set."

"Great!" Bobby exclaimed. "We have two things to help us now. You get some rest tonight, Eric. You have to work tomorrow. I'll help Higgins with the web search before turning in myself. We've all had a rough day." Looking over at Eric, he could see the kid was about to protest, having to go to bed rather than staying up and helping in the search for his mysterious little girl. Bobby held up his hand to stop Eric from speaking. "Your job is to relax. Maybe you will see something more which will help us out. Besides, you will need all your strength to heal patients tomorrow. You know I'm right, Eric."

Reluctantly, Eric nodded and returned to eating his dinner, but his appetite was gone. For a few moments, he had thought they were making progress. Now, it was as if they had taken two steps backward. All he could do was hope to dream. Perhaps he would have nightmares that made him scream in the night.

Sunday started with a grumpy Higgins making breakfast and Ronny dragging around bleary-eyed. They had stayed up half the night trying to find Eric's clock. Even Eric was feeling cranky. His night had been filled with nightmares about his sister Middy. He kept seeing her kneeling among her fellow officers, tears streaming down her face as she screamed up at the world. A week had passed since he'd had the vision of this horror happening to his sister. They had a week to go before the timeline would have expired. That was how it had always been with his visions, as two weeks seemed to be the window for anything to happen. Two weeks of living with the pall of doom hanging over your head. What Hell must his sister Middy be going through right now? He had to get his head straight and have a dream or vision to help his sister. And help his soul mate, even if she was a little girl.

After forcing himself to eat breakfast, Eric and Bobby drove to the clinic. This was Sunday, so Betty was the only other person at the clinic. He'd use her help if needed to treat the in-clinic patients. He'd also handle any emergencies that may arise over the day and update the patient's owners on their pet's condition. It was about as easy a day of the week as any Veterinarian had.

Eric had worked weekends when he was a kennel boy for Dr. Monroe. Betty would have been in before or when Eric arrived. She should let dogs out, feed them, and clean their kennels. He didn't hear the dogs barking, wanting to go out or be fed. There was no sign she had been inside accessing the in-clinic files. The worry over the bruise he had seen on her cheek came rushing forward. Without a second thought, he rushed out to see if she was in the back, letting dogs out. No Betty. Perhaps she was just late. Eric tried to let that calm him down as he returned to the clinic.

The phone rang as Eric stepped back into the clinic to start treatments. "This is Dr. Whiting. How may I help you?" Eric said into the phone. He expected it to be the answering service calling about an emergency.

"Dr. Whiting? Oh, this is Betty's mother. Betty wanted me to let you know she can't come in today. It looks like she has that 24-hour bug I just recovered from. I'm so sorry," the voice on the phone said.

Relief rushed through Eric's body. She was okay. "Thank you for calling. Please tell Betty to take tomorrow off, too. We want her to be in top form.

I'll see to it someone covers for her. It was good speaking with you, Ma'am," Eric said. He felt lighter, as if a burden had been lifted from his shoulders. Only, what did he do now? Pulling out his phone, he grinned, "Bobby, I need your help."

Bobby Jay was out of the car so fast he ripped his suit coat on the door latch. His subject was in trouble pounded at his mind. Adrenaline rushed through his body, his gun was out, and his heart was pounding. It flashed through his mind that he should alert Higgins, but he dismissed that thought in favor of quickly making it to his subject. He'd been a fool to wait outside because he felt this was a safe area.

Eric opened the clinic door before Bobby reached it to break it down. Seeing the gun in Bobby's hand, Eric dropped to the ground. The training his mother had taught him and his sisters when he was little kicked in as he fell and rolled for the nearest cover. Then he realized no killer was behind him and laughed at himself. "Bobby, you scared the crap out of me," he gasped, laughing, climbing to his feet.

"What the hell! You aren't in danger?" Bobby barked at Eric. He was so pumped up he had trouble controlling his reaction to Eric's laughter.

"Oh, man! I'm sorry, really, really sorry, Bobby. I do need your help, though. Betty is sick, so I must work here and back in the kennels. Would you mind cleaning the cats' cages while I treat the patients? Anyone that needs medication outback, I'll give it to them. Once I'm done here, I'll let the dogs out and feed everyone. Tonight, I'll do it all myself, as I already know we are shorthanded," Eric said. "Just clean the litter boxes. I'll give them all freshwater and food."

Nodding, Bobby reluctantly went out back to take care of the cats. His body was still ready to pounce on anyone out to harm his subject. He didn't trust himself not to shout at the kid for scaring him. Good grief, this meant he'd be staying with Eric in the clinic from now on. He couldn't wrap his mind around not being on top of things should a threat happen. He knew the agent who was considered to be number one of all the living agents. Bobby realized he wasn't living up to what that agent believed. You never let your guard down, never. Everyone was suspect. No matter how aggravating your subject was, you always kept the subject insight. It was their job to protect the subject no matter what. Bobby felt he had laid down on the job, thinking Eric was safe in the clinic with him watching the outside. Wrong. So wrong.

Since knowing Bruce, Bobby had come to respect cats. Yet that same knowledge made him leery of approaching any cat. Having Bruce grab him by the throat instilled a slight fear of cats. He still liked cats. He didn't trust them to be nice. So, he was cautious when opening a cage door to clean out a cat's cage. The cats were mewing and pressing their bodies against the front of their cage doors, begging for attention. Most of them rubbed their faces on his hands or tried to get out of the cage. That is, all except for one. It was a tiny fluff ball of a kitten who looked so much like an owl with those big eyes and the still stare that Bobby wondered if it was a cat's toy. If so, where was the cat? Then that staring face swiveled to follow Bobby's hand. Bobby stopped, wondering if petting this strange-looking owl cat was safe. The cat's mouth opened, and this tiny whispered meow came out. Bobby chuckled as he reached over and stroked the kitten.

That was where Eric found Bobby when he cleaned the dogs' kennels and let them go out. Bobby was playing with the kitten. "Would it be okay to hold this one?" he asked. Eric nodded. Bobby still held the kitten once Eric was ready to leave for lunch. It had been a good day, after all.

When he lay down to sleep that night, Eric felt as relaxed as he could—the day had gone well, with Bobby forming an attachment to a kitten and Eric's mind being relieved over Betty. He was asleep within minutes of his head hitting the pillow.

The dreams were different, confusing Eric. The precious little girl Eric had come to look forward to seeing in such a short while was gone. In her place was a child a bit older, with legs too long and awkward arms. She was all elbows and knees. And sad, so sad. She never looked up. She didn't smile or seem to care about anything. It was as if she had accepted that her life would never have joy. One day, as the child dressed, something fell from her folded clothing onto the floor. She quickly looked around as if afraid someone had seen the object. Snatching it back off the floor, she secreted it in the bottom drawer of her dresser chest. Eric saw what she was hiding, but that was enough. It was the tiny rabbit statue all broken and glued back together.

Fortunately, Eric also caught a glimpse of the clock. It was the same clock; it only looked older and used.

A nightmare hit him in full force. It slammed into his mind, dark and filled with blood and tears. Murder. Someone was going to be murdered soon. Eric tried to take in everything he could see, but it was dark, and the killer was taking too much pleasure in watching the blood drain from his victim to look around the house he was in. The victim was a woman expecting a baby. A monster took two lives. Eric woke up screaming when he saw the woman's baby kick, and the killer plunged his knife into the woman's belly, killing the baby inside. Eric screamed in his dream, in the killer's mind, "No!" The killer's body shook as he pulled the knife out of the woman and placed his hands over the wound he'd just made. "No," the killer mumbled.

Eric jolted awake. What had just happened? Was such a thing possible? The thought that perhaps he could influence someone while in the grips of a nightmare terrified him. He didn't want that sort of power. It was too close to being like them, the monsters. Nobody should have such control over another being. Nobody. His mind seemed to be spinning. Where could he turn? He couldn't tell the SS about this development. Chances were that knowledge would leak out to someone else in the government. Then, he'd be used as a weapon. It is what they did. Eric remembered how terrified he had been when they took his mother. If not for their grandfather, she'd be locked up somewhere having experiments run on her. He couldn't lose his family, not again.

All the horror of when his birth family had been killed came rushing back to him. He had buried it deep inside him, never wanting to revisit that terrible time. He'd been so frightened of everything around him back then. His adoptive mom and dad had been there for him. They brought him into their world. It made him feel safe. Even Middy helped. He could remember her saying that she would protect him when she wasn't even a year older than him. Years. It had taken years to recover. He tried so hard not to run, screaming at every noise. What ended up helping him was his nightmares. He turned them into something positive. First to save his family, then to save others. Now, he could become one of the monsters in his nightmares, his visions. He wouldn't let that happen.

Eric rested his head back on the pillow and tried to get back to sleep. He had to have the strength to search his nightmares for something he could tell Bobby and Higgins about so they could find the pregnant woman and save her. No, speaking in their mind, only looking for evidence. It took a while until he finally drifted off to sleep. Nothing. He didn't have a dream before his alarm went off in the morning.

They were all seated at the table enjoying breakfast before Eric could speak to update Bobby and Higgins on the little girl. "Time travel," he said.

"What?" Bobby, Higgins, and Ronny all asked at once.

"Dream time travel. It is the only thing that explains things. Last night, the child was a couple of years older. The clock looked well used. She had hidden the Alice in Wonderland rabbit statue in one of her drawers. It had been broken into many bits and glued back together. All I can think of is traveling in time in my dreams. I mean, I do it going forward. Why can't it also be done going backward?" Eric asked, looking around the table for acknowledgment that he was correct.

Higgins rubbed his ear as if trying to massage the words into his brain. Bobby nodded like he had worked his mind through it all and agreed. On the other hand, Ronny sat with his mouth open and his eyes wide. A bug might have flowed inside that gaping mouth if he wasn't careful. "For real?" Ronny said when he got over the shock.

"What else can it be? I've seen the clock looking brand new. And I've seen it as if it has had years of wear on it. That little statue went from whole to a glued-together mess. What else can it be? It isn't a far leap from dreaming future events to dreaming past events," Eric reasoned.

They all nodded. Now, he had to tell them about the murdered woman. "I had another dream that was going to happen soon. A woman expecting a baby is going to be killed. It is a brutal killing, with the killer enjoying every moment of it. I didn't see anything to indicate where it will happen. All I know is it will be in a home in the bedroom. I hope we catch this guy. I hope we can save the woman. Nobody deserves to die like that. He used a knife. I can't tell you more than that at the moment," Eric didn't tell them he had spoken in the man's mind. He couldn't let anyone know what had happened. Getting up, he hurried to get himself together, waiting for Bobby and Ronny so they could go to work.

Chapter Nine

ADJUSTING

The week felt like it was creeping by. Eric threw himself into his day job, concentrating on healing as many of his patients as he had the energy to heal. Bobby was a constant inside the clinic now. It was like he feared to leave Eric even for a moment. That thought both irritated and reassured Eric. Nights were the worst time for him. Each night, he went to sleep filled with caution. The one thing he never wanted to become was one of the monsters of this world. The bullies, rapists, and the mental crushers all were monsters in Eric's mind. That incident in his nightmare with the murderer scared him. Eric believed he'd influenced the murderer when his mind had screamed out the word "No." The thought horrified him.

On the good side, the two-week window on his vision of Middy was about to expire. For once, he felt hopeful that a vision had been wrong. Middy's call before leaving for her night shift sounded so positive, causing Eric to laugh. It had felt good to laugh again, to have his sister teasing in that mischievous way she had. It was as if he could see her dancing out the door of her place going to work. He, in turn, felt content for the first time all week as he went to sleep that night.

Eric was sitting outside in what he thought was a garden. Quickly, he looked around, taking in as many details as possible in case this was a dream about a crime. It helped that lights were on at some little grocery store down the road. On the front of the store, a sign was blinking on and off saying "Dave's G." The rest of the sign was darkened, though. The garden in the back of the house where he sat was lovely. All manner of flowers had been planted and tended with care. Eric watched as a woman expecting a baby walked up the access road to the back of the house. She didn't seem to notice him when she entered the yard, going up to the house and entering it. Fear for her coursed through Eric's body. He knew she was the woman he had seen murdered in his nightmare. "Run," he tried to think to her. "Get out. Run," only she couldn't hear him.

He woke up to a phone ringing somewhere in the house. Minutes later, his bedroom door opened, and Bobby Jay entered. "Your sister's partner has been shot," Bobby said. "He is in surgery. She said not to worry you but to let you know she is okay."

Eric could feel the blood leaving his head at the words. It was starting. His nightmare was coming true. "Bobby, he is going to kill so many of her fellow officers. This is just the start of the monster after my sister." His face was stricken, and Eric continued, "The woman who is expecting, I saw a sign tonight for a corner grocery store. It had 'Dave's G' lit up. The rest of the sign was dark. You can see the sign from her backyard. The yard was turned into a flower garden. It is beautiful. Please find it and stop this guy."

"I promise you, I will find it. Try to get a little rest. Let me handle things now. I'll find this bastard," Bobby swore. He was more worried about Eric than finding a monster. But he'd do anything to ease the kid's mind. Never before had he seen Eric so shaken. It was like the kid's mind was wounded.

Walking swiftly back to his room, Bobby was already on the phone. He didn't care if he made every cop in the city mad at him; he would find the woman and save her if he could.

Eric sat on the side of his bed in his room, his face hidden in his hands as if that could keep the world out. He knew that nothing would keep the monsters out. His night job was to find the monsters before they could hurt others. This time, he couldn't fail. They had to find the expectant woman in time to save her and her baby. Bobby was right. He needed to get a little more sleep. Maybe he could see something more to help. He told himself not to think of what his sister was going through. But he did. Somehow, he had to stay sane and help Middy and everyone else with their monsters. Eric fell asleep with that last thought in his mind.

The morning seemed to come too soon and not early enough. Eric woke up worried that he hadn't found enough to save a woman and her baby. In his mind, he had shoved down his fear for Middy. He knew his sister was strong. What he didn't know was if she would be able to survive seeing so many of the people she knew and worked with dying around her. He thought he should call his parents and have them whisk her away somewhere safe. Someplace away from all the horror that would come into her life. Logic won out. Middy would hate him if he ever did anything like that to her.

Higgins kept a wary eye on Eric as he ate his breakfast. He didn't like the pallor of the boy's cheeks or the bags under his eyes. Bobby Jay was still out. Not having heard from Bobby since he had come to him in the middle of the night to tell him he was going out to save the pregnant woman. Higgins couldn't give Eric a report on that outcome. He could tell him that his sister's partner would be fine. He watched Ronny come stumbling in to take a seat at the table before he sat a plate in front of Ronny and sat down with his plate. "The news is good on Middleton's partner. He is doing great. They expect a full recovery," he told Eric, watching him and accessing his reaction.

Eric nodded, then looked around. "Bobby's not back?"

"Not yet. We should hear from him soon. It could be last night wasn't the night it happened. Bobby's on it now. The guy doesn't stand a chance between you two," Higgins assured Eric.

With his fork halfway to his mouth, Ronny looked up as if something had filtered into his brain. "What happened to your sister's partner?"

"He was shot," Eric stated in a flat 'I don't want to talk about it' voice.

Shooting Higgins a questioning look, Ronny decided his food was very interesting.

Bobby hadn't returned when it was time for Ronny and Eric to go to work. Higgins had lines on his forehead when he grabbed his car keys. This wasn't like Bobby. He'd have called or come back by now. He ran over the options in his head. He had to stick with their subjects above all. In case he couldn't contact Bobby or confirm Bobby was dead, he would have to call in another agent. Damn you, Bobby, he thought, don't you be dead. He'd have to ping Bobby's phone as soon as he had the kids situated. Or, he could have Ronny drive and ping him now. Higgins handed the keys over to Ronny, "You are driving, kid. I'll have my eye on you the whole way. I've been up all night, and it is best that I don't drive now."

Not realizing the strain Higgins and Eric felt from Bobby not checking in, Ronny snatches the keys from Higgins's hand like a child with a new toy. Higgins settled in the passenger's seat and immediately pinged Bobby's phone. His mouth hardened into a straight line as his jaw clenched. Bobby was at a hospital. Now that he knew where Bobby was, he could call the hospital for an update on Bobby if he didn't answer. He'd also find out if Bobby had been hurt or killed; for that, he needed to wait until out of earshot of the two kids. Higgins glanced in the rear-view mirror at Eric's pale face. There was no need to worry the kid until he knew

Bobby was hurt.

Higgins made Ronny and Eric stay in the car while he checked the clinic out. He was in SS mode all the way and wasn't about to let his subjects walk into an ambush inside the clinic. Stepping into the clinic after unlocking the front door, he swept each room with his gun drawn. As he rounded the door into one room, a girl's head jerked up from the printer with a paper in her hand. She blanched at the sight of Higgins and his gun. "We don't keep money here. And you look too old to be after d… d… drugs," she managed to stammer out.

Higgins rubbed his hand over his face. The kennel girl. He had glimpsed her the day he spent here with Ronny. "Sorry, didn't mean to scare you. I thought there was an intruder in the clinic. Just relax. I'll give the all-clear to the doctors. Uh, you have been out to the kennels, right?"

"Not yet. I needed the medication and bath list," Betty said, raising her hand with the list she had just printed out.

"Wait here, let me check it out first. You can never be too careful, little lady," Higgins winked at her, hoping she would relax before he went outside to check the kennels out. He was suddenly hit with a volley of barks from what sounded like a thousand dogs. Ugh, he thought to himself and quickly swept the yard, the runs, and finally, the kennel room. Satisfied, he returned to reassure the young girl that she could go on to work. Only Ronny and Eric were already there, telling her everything was okay. Not for the first time, Higgins felt the fool. He knew he wasn't, and he was only doing his job. If someone had been lurking inside or back in the kennel area to kidnap Eric, he would have found them. It was what he did. He protected the absolute fools. Only Eric wasn't a fool. He was a tool in bringing down killers.

"Higgins is the best cook around these parts," Eric told Betty. Higgins stopped and listened. He silently urged Eric to go on and invite her to dinner. When Eric walked away from Betty, Higgins sighed. The kid needed a girl in his corner. This Betty gal might be the ticket. He smiled at his thought while giving the kids the all-clear. Then, thoughts of Bobby were all he had in his mind.

Walking back outside with the excuse of securing the car, Higgins pulled out his phone and hit Bobby's number. Already, he was going over the list of people he would have to call if Bobby was dead. He almost dropped the phone when Bobby answered the phone. "Can't talk now. Breathe, that's it: in, out, in, out. Higgins, I think we are close. Hold on.... Push," a scream came over the phone, nearly deafening Higgins. "That's the way. You are doing great. Now relax and breathe. Higgins, I'm not sure how much longer this will take. I'll be there when Reba has the baby when I'm certain they are settled. I know you will keep the kids safe. I owe you one, Buddy." Bobby hung up on him.

What the hell? Who the hell was Reba? Higgins shook his head. It didn't matter. All that counted was Bobby was okay. He could take an easy breath of his own now.

Returning to the clinic, he found Eric and Ronny cleaning a ghastly looking wound on a little dog. The little thing opened and closed its mouth as if silently screaming until Eric touched the little guy. Higgins hadn't witnessed much of Eric's talents except the chilling screams in a nightmare and the frozen person version of a vision. So, he was enthralled with how a simple touch from the kid had the little dog at peace. Then he noticed the grimace of pain that flashed on Eric's face. The kid was taking the dog's pain into himself. Higgins was sure of it as the little dog softly licked Eric's hand. He could do one thing for Eric now: relieve the kid's worry over Bobby. "Talked to Bobby. He is at the hospital helping a woman named Reba have a baby. He isn't certain how long he'll be, though," Higgins said, watching Eric's face.

Eric's whole face lit up. "He did it! She is safe and has her baby. Her name is Reba," Eric said with a look of wonder. A huge weight seemed to be lifted off his shoulders as, for a few moments, he was allowed to be happy. Bobby Jay had saved the mother-to-be and was now helping her deliver her baby. What a wonderful day this was turning into. So often, Eric never knew the end of one of his visions, like the sniper who was never caught and appeared to have disappeared. But this one had ended with such a satisfying feeling.

Dr. Monroe had secured himself in his office after watching Eric and Ronny working for a few minutes. Eric wondered why his mentor had become so standoffish recently. He was worried that the doctor had become displeased with him. He knew he wasn't running as many tests as the doctor would have, but Eric didn't need tests. They were just for show. He didn't need them. Ronny made up for Eric's lack of testing and did very well in getting results quickly. Together, they were a great team. The question was, were they good enough to impress Dr. Monroe? For some reason, Eric had always thought he and Ronny would be working at Dr. Monroe's clinic until they could set up their own. Thinking things over now, he realized that had been a foolish, childish way of thinking. Things never turned out the way a person thought they would. He knew that more than anyone else. It was the things that made up his nightmares. That was the real world.

Right now, though, Eric was what was called happy. A woman and her unborn baby, correction, may be born by now that the baby was saved. Small victories had to be savored. Eric smiled as he gave Puddle, a very bouncy Pomeranian, a rabies shot. "There you go, Puddle. You get a good dog treat for being so well-behaved," Eric said, reaching into the treat jar to grab a doggy treat for Puddle. His mouth wanted to twitch into a smile as Puddle snatched the treat, then growled at his owner as if afraid the woman would like to eat his treat too.

"Doctor Whiting, you are so wonderful with my little Puddle. I wish I could take you home with me. Puddle can be a little devil at times. What is your secret?" Mrs. Addison asked.

"Puddle knows when he sees me, he is supposed to behave. I have given him a task to do, to be still. Maybe you should teach him the manners of a gentleman. You know our doggies like to be told what to do, to be given something to do so they can be proud of it. If you make him sit before handing him a treat or his bowl of food, he begins to be proud of himself. He'll still be your little darling, only sweeter." It was a talk Eric found himself giving over and over. People would go home and do the same things repeatedly so that the poor dog with them either takes over the house or becomes an over-excited ball of nerves.

As Puddle and his owner left, Eric disinfected the exam table. He felt someone behind him and felt a chill run up his back. When he turned to see who was there, Bobby was standing in the doorway to the lab. He had the biggest grin on his face as he looked at Eric. "It's a boy. She named him Robert Jay Turner. He is the cutest little red wrinkled baby I've ever seen, kid," Bobby said, his eye sparkling, unlike a man who had been up most of the night before should sparkle.

"You kept your promise, Bobby. I'm so proud of you. Did you catch the guy? Who was he? Do you think he will be a threat to the mother and baby?" Eric fired questions at Bobby.

"Hold on, kid. Let me tell you. Yes, the police got him. He had the knife out and was swinging at Reba. He had hit her, and she was helpless on the floor. The coward was going to stab her to death right where she lay. My police contact shot him, so, no, he isn't going to be a threat to her. She has a rough road ahead of her. The guy was her husband. It seems he didn't want to be saddled with a baby. He had himself a girl on the side and was planning on leaving with all the money from their checking and savings with the new girl. He was grinning like a demented fool before he was taken down.

"Reba went into labor and had latch hold of my hand. That woman has a powerful grip. I don't think Higgins could have pried her hand loose. I had to stay with her. After all, I promised you I'd save them. When we got to the hospital, the doctors couldn't get her to let go of me either. So, I ended up coaching her through the birth. You know, I never realized how long and painful a birthing can be. She'd scream, and I wanted to scream, too, as she squeezed the life out of my hand. About the time I'd get her relaxed, another pain would hit her, and off we'd go again. I was sweating bullets the whole time. Let me tell you, son, I'd rather face a volley of bullets than go through that again. But then, little Robert popped out, and it was worth all the pain to see that little messy baby," Bobby said, a wistful look on his face. "Get back to work, kid. I have to go make certain Higgins can drive himself home." He slapped Eric on the back so hard that Eric felt his teeth rattle.

Euphoric, Eric thought. Bobby looked euphoric, like a proud father. It was a good look on the usually serious SS man. Next thing they knew, Bobby could be passing out cigars. Eric laughed at the thought and sobered, wondering why he hadn't received the next patient's chart. Peeping out, he realized the waiting area was clear, and the clinic door had the lunch sign hanging in it. Dr. Monroe looked at him and motioned him to go to his office. Ronny was already seated in the office when Eric entered. The two friends exchanged a look, wondering what this could be about as they waited for Dr. Monroe to sit behind his desk.

Dr. Monroe pressed his fingers together and looked over them at Eric and Ronny. "You two haven't been here very long. I have to admit to watching you both very closely." He turned his attention to Ronny. "You tend to run a lot of tests. I've watched you double-check the results before you reveal them to the owners," he said, switching his attention to Eric. "And you seldom run any tests. The two of you have completely different methods of working. Yet, you work well together. I've seen you, Dr. Croft, ask Dr. Whiting to consult on cases. While you, Dr. Whiting, have never asked Dr. Croft to consult. I won't ask why this is because I don't want to know the answer. It is enough that the two of you work so well together." Dr. Monroe sat back and looked the two of them over. His expression was unreadable.

"I know you are both wondering what this is all about. I'm retiring. This clinic has been my life, and I do not want to leave it to go to just anyone. Eric impressed me when he was working for me. Now, you have impressed me, Ronny. I want you to become partners and take over the practice. You should discuss things with each other and let me know as soon as possible. I'm eager to go fishing. If you want the practice, we will have a lot of legal papers to file. I'll be a silent partner for the first year, and then the whole thing will be yours equally. I'm placing my trust in the two of you. Now go to lunch and let an old man dream of fishing."

The rest of the day went by with Eric feeling he was in a dream world where everything was beautiful. He wouldn't have been surprised if rainbows appeared in the sky while they were locking up the clinic. A murder stopped, a baby was born, and perhaps became partners with his friend Ronny. How could so much good happen within one day? There had to be a catch, some hidden disaster waiting to spring forth and ruin this wonderful day.

They were all happy to celebrate that the day had gone so well. Bobby called Higgins and told him to wait for dinner as they would go out. "And you get to pick the place. So, what are you hungry for tonight?" Bobby listened for a moment before laughing. "You got it, buddy." He looked in the rear-view mirror at Eric as he started the car. "You remember where we took Higgins on his birthday?" he asked Eric.

"The sports bar seafood place where everyone watched football and drank beer? Yeah. That is where he wants to go?" Eric said, feeling his head starting to explode from all the loud cheering and booing he had heard before.

"Yes. The food was great. I could have used less noise. But Higgins had a ball," Bobby confirmed.

"Can I bring earplugs?" Eric asked, hoping the answer was yes.

"And miss the whole experience? I don't think so. Besides, you need to hear me if I say duck. Remember the beer bottle?" Bobby laughed. "Eric had to dodge a beer bottle thrown at someone who had booed the hometown team."

Ronny spoke up for the first time, "Someone threw a beer bottle at Eric? Did you shoot them? Did they have to sign a million papers?"

"Get over the privacy papers you had to sign. Look where you are today. If it is so bad being around us, I can arrange an apartment for you," Bobby was irritated with Ronny. The guy just never let up about having to sign those standard forms. "Or, I can shoot you."

Ronny didn't know if Bobby was kidding about shooting him. He shut up just in case the SS agent was serious.

When they pulled into the sports bar's parking lot after picking up Higgins, it was already a quarter to eight in the evening. They had all changed clothes to avoid sticking out like sore thumbs while eating. Eric eyed all the huge trucks in the parking lot. There were even a couple of horse trailers parked in the back. He braced himself as Higgins and Ronny walked in ahead of him and Bobby, expecting to hear loud music or cheering fans. Higgins stopped just inside the door and looked around. The place was silent. Men sit looking up at the big screen televisions placed around the area. Higgins glanced up and took one look before shoving Ronny back out the door. Ronny was taken by surprise, nearly barreling Eric over as he was pushed hard out the door.

Higgins stood looking at Bobby Jay as if talking to him telepathically. Bobby's gun came out, and Higgins shook his head. "No, not that. Ronny, take Eric over there and stand while I talk with Bobby," Higgins barked at Ronny. Ronny's eyebrows shot up, but he did as he was told. He was already on Higgins' dirt list and didn't plan to make matters worse with the grumpy SS agent.

Once Higgins was confident Eric was out of hearing range, he spoke in a low voice to Bobby. "It's his sister. They are showing footage from this morning. Looked like a bloodbath. She was alive, though. What do you want to do, Boss?" he asked.

Bobby was immediately in super SS mode. "Keep the boys out here. Let me go in and see what it is all about. We can't keep this from him. Someone is bound to call him," Bobby said. Higgins nodded, walking off to join their subjects. He couldn't think of them as the kids, not when it came to his job.

"What's going on?" Eric asked the moment Higgins stopped in front of him and Ronny.

"Just hang here with me for a moment. Bobby is gathering Intel. Can you believe he is a godfather now? He'll have the kid wrapped in bubble wrap when it comes time for him to try to take his first step. Poor kid," Higgins joked. "And what is this rumor of you two becoming partners?"

Eric didn't seem to hear Higgins, so Ronny answered. "Dr. Monroe offered us the clinic as partners. We thought we'd decide tonight and maybe add that to this celebration."

"Yahoo! Way to go!" Higgins said, but his voice didn't sound or carry much in the way of cheer. Ronny glanced at him and realized whatever had made him back out of the bar was terrible.

The door to the sports bar opened, and Bobby came over to where they stood. "We are going home. I'll order some pizza. Get in the car." Bobby looked Eric in the eyes. "I have something to tell you," he said.

The air seemed to have been sucked out of

Eric's lungs. He knew deep inside it had happened. His nightmare about his sister Middy had come true. "How many were killed?" he asked.

"You knew?" Bobby said.

"Yes, I saw it happen. Middy's alright, isn't she? In my vision, she was alright, but the others... so many others. How many?" he asked again.

"Eleven. Two were not police officers. It happened this morning," Bobby said, watching the scowl forming on Eric's face. He continued, "The SS has been trying to keep your sister's name out of things. You guys have to be kept a secret, you know that. Calm down, Eric. I'm sure your sister will call you once she has been debriefed. They are going to question the shit out of her. You know that. Eric, she has the best of us with her. He'll keep her safe."

Eric snorted, "It's more like she will keep him safe. You don't know my sister; she is a force to be reckoned with. I almost feel sorry for the creep who has stirred her wrath."

Blinking in surprise, Ronny couldn't keep quiet. "Why?"

"She is likely to blow him clean to Mars," Eric turned away before they could see the concern he felt. He wished he had been wrong. This was not something he wanted his sister to have to experience. "Pizza, here we come," he threw over his shoulder, trying to put the others at ease.

It was fortunate they had access to excellent legal advice, Ronny thought as he and Eric sat down to review all the various papers that had to be looked over and signed involving the clinic and the property it sat upon. He knew that Eric was footing most of the bills on this great legal advice they were receiving, but that didn't make him feel any less thankful there was someone to explain all the legal gobbled-goop. He would have scratched a hole through his scalp if he had been alone.

Kendall Jones looked over his glasses at Eric and Ronny, watching their faces as he began to speak. "This is an amazing deal you came upon. The land alone is worth twice what the owner is asking. Even if you demolish the clinic and sell the land, you will have double the investment. I take it Mr. Monroe is slightly senile?"

"What? No. He is our friend and an amazing doctor. You are out of line suggesting such a thing," Eric said, standing up and pointing to the door. "Out. Get out of my house."

Ronny stood too, uncertain as to what had Eric so riled. "Easy, he doesn't know the man like we do. He is just doing his job."

"He made Dr. Monroe sound like a senile fool. I will not let that pass. People have to stand up for each other," Eric said, staring Ronny in the eyes as he spoke. "If someone were to come up and say something bad about you to me, I'd punch him in the nose."

A snort came out of Ronny before he could contain it. "You could try at least," he managed to get out. Then, he could not hold the laughter such an image brought to his mind any longer and burst out laughing.

Eric looked at Ronny, bent over, laughing like an idiot, and pulled a straight face. "Well, I would sic

Bruce on them and scare the crap out of them." For all of two seconds, he kept a straight face before he was laughing too. Sobering, he looked at the door the lawyer had gone through. "I guess I best ask Bobby to look into another lawyer for us."

"I think that would be a good idea. Maybe let him talk to them beforehand, with his gun out," Ronny said, smiling. He was worried about Eric. Something was off about him. He supposed having his sister in danger might have something to do with how Eric sometimes snapped when talking, but that wasn't the whole problem. Whatever it was, Ronny hoped it would clear up soon. Ronny had never realized how much he liked the old Eric, the quirky, thin, geeky guy who had helped him so much with Charlie and in class. That guy was gentle and wouldn't hurt a fly. Not at all like this more surly version was becoming.

There was a tentative knock on the door. Eric stood up, but Bobby appeared out of nowhere and approached the door. Eric noticed that Bobby had become a by-the-book man. He didn't know why, only that it was irritating him. They had a great working relationship. Eric thought of Bobby and Higgins more as friends than SS bodyguards. Now this is by-the-book crap. Don't get out of the car. Don't open the door. It felt like a needle poked in Eric's eye whenever he said don't. Glancing up at the door, Eric almost swore. He didn't because he wasn't raised in a home where swearing was the usual family tone.

"What do you want?" Bobby asked the lawyer standing outside the door, looking as if he had swallowed his tongue when Bobby greeted him with his gun in hand.

"I wanted to apologize. Mr. Whiting is correct. I was way out of line speaking about Dr. Monroe in that manner," Kendall Jones said. "If they give me another chance, I'd like to represent Dr. Whiting and Dr. Croft in this matter." He looked past Bobby to where Eric and Ronny stood.

"Dr. Whiting, you want me to allow this cur back inside?" Bobby asked without looking back at Eric.

Did he? Eric knew he had been unreasonable, just like he knew why his temper had flared. There was a little girl in his dreams he couldn't help. "Let him in. Let's get this over with. Ronny and I are raising our offer," he said, looking over at Ronny. Ronny nodded; he thought it was only fair.

After much thought, with minimal input from a now polite lawyer, the two partners had what they thought was a fair offer. They shook hands with Kendall Jones, agreeing to meet with Dr. Monroe in the morning, and finalized everything. Soon, Eric and Ronny would become the owners of the clinic. Eric felt sadness at the thought of Dr. Monroe retiring. He admired the elderly doctor and counted him as a friend. To lose one of his few friends was indeed a sad day. He may continue to be a friend, coming to dinner now and then and advising them on new problems that might come up.

After eating dinner, Eric went for a run. Bruce kept pace with Eric while Bobby Jay tried to stay up with the pair. He noticed that Eric didn't wait on him like he usually did. Something was driving the boy to be thoughtless and reckless. Bobby had become used to Eric considering him when they ran. He knew Eric was faster than he was and younger, but the boy had always shown consideration for the SS agent. This time, Eric ran as if the demons of hell were on his heels. Perhaps they were, in the kid's mind. After all, his sister was in constant danger; he had all those nightmares to contend with, and he was in love with a little girl in his dreams. All that must be like hell to someone like Eric. The kid had a fixed-it obsession. As much as Bobby wanted to help Eric, he didn't know what to do.

Chapter Ten

AVOIDANCE

That night, Eric tossed and turned, trying his best to get to sleep. However, he didn't want to dream again and take a chance of controlling someone in the dream. At the same time, he wanted to dream, to check on the young girl he had been dreaming about, and to have a dream about his sister's monster. Dream, don't dream. The effort to do either seemed beyond him. So he fought with himself whether to get to sleep or not.

Bruce finally gave up on sleeping on the bed by Eric, and the cat growled before jumping off the bed and finding a spot in a padded chair to settle down. Usually, Bruce would sleep for a while before starting his patrol of the house. The cat watched the house each night, checking each room for intruders, mice, or men. Often, he went out the doggy door to check on Higgins, who was doing his patrolling. Higgins would pet the cat now that nobody was watching. It was their little secret that Higgins liked Bruce.

The exception to Bruce's patrolling was on nights when Eric was caught up in a bad nightmare or dreamed about the little girl. The little girl provoked such sadness in Eric that the cat felt he had to be there to protect his person.

Exhaustion finally had its way with Eric, and he fell into a restless sleep. Things swirled through his sleeping head, bringing regular nightmares of monsters under the bed and in the closet. Those he could deal with. Where the others, the real monsters, made him scream in his sleep. Then there she was. At least he thought it was her, his dream girl, his soul mate. All he could see was the back of her head as the person he was in crept up on the girl. No, not a girl, but a nearly woman. He could see the clock looking ancient beyond her as she sat on her bed. Her head was bent as she looked down at her lap.

The man who Eric saw through looked down into the girl's lap. She was reading a book that made Eric's breath catch. It was the book he had given Betty. Huge hands reached down and snatched the book up. Betty looked up with sorrow, and those hands ripped the book apart. One of the hands hit Betty across the cheek. "Stop!" Eric silently shouted. The hand reaching out to grab Betty's hair stopped clenching into a fist. The man turned away from Betty, taking the book's remains.

Eric woke drenched in sweat. Bruce was lying on top of him in panther form. Eric rubbed the broad head of his cat/panther. "It is okay, boy. I'm okay now," he soothed. Bruce flicked his tail and stomped out of the room as if he didn't care about Eric. Eric lay on his back, staring up at the ceiling. Betty had been hurt because he had given her a book. No wonder she was so quiet at work. Someone, he suspected it was her father, was harming her at home.

Would she have been hurt worse if he hadn't said something to the monster who hurt her? He hadn't said it to him; he'd made him stop. Horror and relief warred inside Eric. He had seen that bruise on Betty's cheek himself. Would she have had more bruises if he hadn't done the one thing he didn't want to do? Did something good come from this monstrous thing he had done? Is that how monsters justify hurting others? He didn't believe that. No, people hurt others because they thought everything was about them. They felt slighted in some manner, real or imaginary. Usually, that slight was more imagined than a fact. He didn't want to be that sort of monster or any monster. There had been enough monsters when he was a child.

Curling up on his side, Eric debated going out for a run. It wasn't fair to Higgins to have him follow him when he ran at night. If he laid here, he might fall asleep again. He didn't want to take a chance on speaking out in his dreams to anyone, to be a monster. Eric thought about calling Middy to talk to her, but she was working out on patrol or sitting behind a desk since her partner had been shot. All the people he could have turned to were either asleep or busy.

At some point, while Eric was arguing with himself, he fell asleep. A man wearing a stocking mask held a gun on an elderly man behind the counter at a pawn shop. Eric knew it was a pawn shop because, behind the older adult, a sign was blinking, saying so. Jim's Stuff to Trade, the sign said. The man with the stocking mask looked to be shouting at the older man as he waved the gun around. The older man clutched his chest, gasped for breath, and fell across the counter. "Get help." The words had spilled out of Eric's mind before he could think about it. Only, he was telling himself to get help, not the robber.

His nightmare continued. The robber picked up the store's phone. His hand shook as he dialed 911. He did not speak and left the phone beside the older adult.

Eric woke with his heart beating so hard it felt as if it would burst out of his chest. Did he help that man? Was it him, or did the robber have a bit of human left in him? He was more confused than ever now. What if he could help the people in his nightmares? Was that what this new thing was about? Or was he fooling himself and trying to make it into something good? Then, there was the fact most bad men and women repeated the crimes they did. So, was he letting the person get away so they could harm someone else later? He was intelligent; at least, he thought he was reasonably competent. Then why couldn't he sort out what was going on inside him? Was he a good person? Or was he turning into one of the monsters he had nightmares about?

It was difficult for Eric to look at Betty now that he knew the child in his dreams had been her. He had learned so much about who she was as a person from those dreams. Knowing how much she loved to draw and create with her hands made him ache inside with the pain she had carried all the years growing up at being denied that one pleasure. He wanted to wrap her in his arms and comfort the child inside her. Then there were his feelings for her, those things she could never know. Everything inside him longed to give her all the drawing and painting tools she needed to make her happy. Only how could he when he knew to give her those things would cause her pain at home?

Catching up one of the dogs running in the clinic's exercise yard, Betty could feel Dr. Whiting's eyes on her again. He had been so kind to her at first. Now, he seemed to be trying to ignore her, but he wasn't. And that was what worried her. Did he find her so repulsive now that he would fire her? This job was the only thing in her life she had to love. Every moment here was a joy to her. She got to befriend all these fantastic dogs and cats and even interacted with the doctors sometimes when they were working on a patient. It was one of her dreams coming true. It was the only dream that she had left. She was so afraid of doing something wrong that she worked extra hard to do what was right. Lately, she felt she was walking on thin ice. If one wrong step is taken, this dream world will be gone. She'd be plunged into the cold waters of nothingness. Betty felt tears threatening, which was just stupid. She hadn't cried since she was a very young child. This job was worth fighting to keep. She felt she had to stand up to someone for the first time. This job was too precious for her to lose.

When Betty applied to Dr. Monroe for a job doing the kennels, she thought her heart would rupture from beating so fast and hard. That couldn't compare to how she felt approaching Dr. Whiting in the office. She stopped and watched him for a moment before tapping on the door. He looked so tired as if he hadn't been sleeping. Silently, she thought about her nights and the nightmares that plagued her. She'd trade her nights for his anytime. She tapped lightly upon the door. "May I come in?" she asked.

"Of course, Betty, anytime. Is something wrong? Do you need help with anything?" Eric had stood upon seeing Betty. He motioned to the chair in front of the office desk. Once she was seated, he leaned against the desk in front of her. "Now, tell me what is on your mind."

Looking down at the floor, Betty tried to find the courage to speak her mind. Nobody listened to anything she had to say when she talked, which wasn't often. She was taking a big chance saying anything now. Only she had to know if he intended to fire her. "I would like to know if you are intending to fire me. If so, how long do I have before I leave?" she blurted out.

"What? Why would you think something like that?" Eric asked, genuinely shocked that she would think something was so terrible.

"You've seemed angry lately with me. The only thing I can think of is that you will fire me. If you give me a chance, I'll work harder. I don't have to take a lunch break. I could come in earlier and have all the dog's cages and the kennels cleaned and the yard picked up before you even arrive if that will help. You won't have to see me. I could go out the side gate to get dogs brought in. Anything," she said, trembling as she fought the tears she never cried.

Eric knelt in front of Betty, taking her hands. "Betty, I am not mad at you. I might be mad at myself, and I'm sorry if you felt that feeling was directed at you. I haven't been sleeping well. So, if I seem grumpy, that is all about me, not you. I don't have any excuse for being the grump I've been lately. My sister is having a bad time, and I'm worried about her. But that is no excuse. I don't want you to leave. You are so good at the clinic. It is why I want you up here more than in the back now. Do you know nobody else has your touch with the dogs and cats?" he laughed. "Even that devil cat has started behaving himself. He once hissed at me, and I threatened to bring my cat Bruce in to visit him. But you don't have to threaten him. He sits back and lets you clean his cage. Don't ever think I'm going to make you leave. You have a job as long as I'm partnered in this clinic. Understand?" he asked.

That last bit broke Betty in pieces. Nobody had told her anything good about herself. A lifetime of tears broke through the barrier she hid them behind, and she sobbed.

Eric folded his arms around her thin shoulders when the tears started. He wanted to take away the pain she was having, to keep her safe. The bad thing was she felt so good in his arms. It was everything he knew holding her would be. He was so screwed. Here he was, skating on thin ice, and it was breaking the wall he had tried so hard to keep around his heart. "It's okay. I'm glad you told me what was upsetting you. I'll try to leave my grump at home. You'll see. I'll be Mr. Sunshine. Only you can't tell anyone. Dr. Croft will tease me to death. I can hear him now, 'Mr. Sunshine, I need some light over here. Shine on me.' I'm sure he can think of inventive ways of making fun of me. So, our little secret, okay?"

Betty wiped her eyes, ashamed of having broken down that way. It had been such a relief. She had thought her world was ending, and instead, it was growing brighter. Mr. Sunshine. She smiled and nodded at Eric.

Both relieved and scared about Betty staying, Eric knew he could only take it one day at a time. He felt so much peace when he held her during those brief moments he comforted her. Reality had set in with an emergency banging on the door where the lunch sign hung. There was no time to indulge himself in the comforting feel of holding Betty.

A frantic woman was at the door. The front of her blouse had blood and hair on it. She looked like she had wrestled a demon and just got away. When Eric opened the door, the woman headed back to her car, which was pulled up in a haphazard way next to the door. Throwing open the back passenger side door, she frantically waved for him to come over. A dog that would have rivaled the size of his mother's dog lay on the back seat. The dog's huge, broad head hung off the car seat, dripping blood onto the carpet of the car. "He was lying in the road. I almost ran over him. I thought he was dead and just stopped to move him off the road. Then he growled at me. I didn't know what to do. So I pulled him by his back legs into the car and came here. I can't lift him. You need to help him; please get him out of my car so I can go to work," she rambled on that way as Eric touched the dog's head to access him.

Eric's mouth became a thin line as he clamped it shut in anger. This woman at least brought the dog in, even if she only wanted to dump him off and go to work. No matter how much he wanted to tell her off about just dumping the dog and leaving, he knew she had tried to do the right thing. The trouble was he didn't think he was strong enough to carry the giant beast into the clinic. Pulling out his phone, he buzzed Bobby Jay. "I need your muscles to carry a dog in," he said as soon as Bobby answered. He knew Bobby was probably just inside the door watching him anyway. The man had been hovering over him a lot lately.

Bobby opened the door to the car where Eric was attending his patient. One look at the dog had him pausing, "Holy crap, he is a monster."

Eric grimaced at Bobby, giving him a little head wave to indicate Betty and the woman. Usually, Eric would have called Ronny to do the heavy lifting, but Ronny was occupied with cleaning a sedated dog's teeth in the back. They were planning on working through lunch and going out later tonight. It was something they had planned on every night since their celebrations had been cut off, with Middy on the news in the blood bath. There always seemed to be something that would come up to stop the four of them from going out.

"Take him to surgery. I will have to do a lot of

work on him." Eric said.

Betty approached the woman, thinking she'd get the contact information for the doctors. The woman slammed the car's back door. Before Betty could stop her, the woman jumped into the car and took off. Betty tried to memorize the car's license plate number. Hoping she retained it correctly, she rushed after Eric and Bobby, stopping at the front desk long enough to scribble down the number on the plate.

"I need an IV set up, and someone needs to call for pizza. This room will be off-bounds until I'm done here. Bobby, you know what to do. Betty, bring some towels and hot water bottles to place around this big fellow," Eric said. "I wish I had a battery." He mumbled under his breath.

Brow furrowed, Bobby headed to the car to fetch several IV bags. As he walked, he speed-dialed a pizza place to have them deliver six pizzas fully loaded with everything extra. It wasn't the meal he would like to see Eric eat, but he was here alone with no Higgins to make up a good meal for them. He had learned quickly that getting food and IVs hooked up and in Eric was vital. Bobby didn't like that Eric was already telling him to get the IVs. That meant the dog had a lot of damage. A lot. Should he call Higgins and wake him up to come, just in case? No, Higgins needed some rest. Bobby didn't like leaning on Higgins when he could handle things himself. Slamming the trunk of his car shut, Bobby placed the IV bags and the catheter in a plastic bag. There was no sense in advertising what he was doing.

The extra-large doorway into the surgery was

closed when Bobby got back to it. He turned the handle and slipped inside with his bag. Eric was gowned up as if preparing for surgery. He handed Bobby a pair of gloves when he entered. "Once you have me hooked up, put these on. I've set aside the instruments that would normally be used. You must bloody them to make it look like they have been used. The fingers of the gloves need blood on them. But keep an eye on me. If you see me starting to faint, make me stop. Once I start, it isn't easy to know when to stop. We have to make it look as if I did surgery on this guy," Eric explained.

"Got it. Where would you have been cutting him?" Bobby asked.

"His head and his belly, possibly even the chest. He must have been hit by a huge truck. I figure the woman won't be back. I'm glad she brought him in. She saved his life," Eric said as he pulled the high stool Dr. Monroe had taken to sitting on while doing surgery over and sat down. He didn't talk after that. He was inside the dog, hunting down the worst areas and doing quick patches to keep the dog alive long enough for him to heal him completely. The dog was a mess. Organs had been bruised and torn. The brain alone was in dire need of work.

Eric concentrated on the skull and brain after his first quick fix trip through the dog's body. He had never treated a brain before, so he wasn't sure if he was saving the tissue he was forced to reattach. He knew they said brain tissue did not regenerate, but it did relearn. So, there must be some hope for it. He fixed any bleeders he found and sent healing into all the tissue so there was no brain swelling. The skull seemed eager to accept Eric's healing, but Eric had barely started on the skull when someone pulled him away from his patient.

"Eric, stop, stop it. Can you hear me, kid? Stop now and rest." Bobby was shaking him, Eric realized.

He slumped into Bobby's arms, blackness threatening to take him over. He gave a weak nod, pulling back into himself. "Pizza," he mumbled and heard Bobby chuckle.

"Okay, but sit on the stool and don't pass out. Deal?" Bobby said. Eric nodded. "Here," Bobby said, placing an open bar in Eric's hand and opening a drink bottle. He watched a second to be certain Eric was eating and drinking before slipping out of surgery to get the boxes of pizza that had been delivered.

Ronny and Bobby carried the huge dog Eric had worked on to the recovery room. He barely fit into their largest cage. "There you go, Tiny. Have a good sleep. I know I will tonight," Bobby told the dog, petting the sleeping dog's head.

"Tiny? You have to be kidding. This thing is like a horse," Ronny complained.

"Shush, you'll make him feel bad," Bobby said, giving Ronny his 'I'm serious' look.

Betty had come up behind them and saw the look Bobby gave Ronny. "Do I put that on his record?"

"Sure, why not? It is as good a name as we have for him right now. I will see to it Dr. Whiting takes a nap in the office. Nobody is to disturb him. Dr. Croft will be your go-to if anyone has questions. Understand?" Bobby said, looking at Betty. She nodded, and he regretted seeming so stern. He knew it was hard for the shy girl to be up in the front when most of her time was spent in the back. Eric had made it clear he wanted her to be used more in the front, though, and nobody would question why he was making that call. "You've done a wonderful job. Keep it up," he said before hurrying to help Eric to the office.

Letting Bobby support him, Eric made his way to the office. He was so far gone that he could barely think. He knew and voiced one thing, although he was scarcely whispering. "We need to set up a room with a cot for me. Maybe a small add-on. Someplace I can treat the bad ones and pass out on a cot."

Bobby nodded. The thought had already crossed his mind. He'd look into having that expansion done tomorrow. There wouldn't be any more hiding in surgery. He could see how impractical that was already. This was his subject's clinic, and they had the right to ensure it was suitable for Eric. They needed a room where his special IVs could be stored out of sight. And the energy bars and drinks. He'd need a cot and table to set up a meal. Plans were swirling in Bobby's mind as he propped Eric's feet up and placed a pillow behind his head. Permits and construction plans. They'd need to check out companies ahead of time. Do that now. Get everything lined up. The list was growing in his head.

After fetching a blanket from the car to cover

Eric as the lad slept, Bobby returned to check on Tiny. It's funny how he felt so responsible for the dog. He had to belong to someone. They would come to claim him and pay his bill, and he'd never see Tiny again. Poor guy, he was so huge and so helpless. Bobby thought that made him feel such an attachment to the big dog. His subject thought him the big, strong guy, yet sometimes Bobby felt helpless. And tiny. He just had to suck it up and be the big guy those times. Poor Tiny, when could he ever be just a happy pup? Bobby sat on the floor in front of Tiny's cage, rubbing the dog in one of the few places where fake bandages weren't covering the dog. This was how they would justify Eric charging people for his healing. Faking the surgeries a normal Veterinarian would do.

Betty was bringing a dog up to the front desk when she heard the moan coming from the Doctor's office. When the owner took the dog, she returned to the office. Slowly, she turned the handle on the office door, opening a crack. Peeking in, she saw Dr. Whiting with his arms stretched as if trying to stop something. Suddenly, he stood up and took a staggering step towards her. "Bobby. Get Bobby," he demanded.

Now scared, Betty ran to the recovery room, where she saw the man who was always in a suit she heard called Bobby. "He is asking for you, hurry. Please hurry."

There was only one 'he' about whom Bobby was concerned enough he would rush off, leaving the helpless Tiny. Eric.

Reaching the office, Eric fumbled with the

phone as if frantic about calling someone. "Easy, tell me who you need. I'll call them," Bobby said. Briefly, he thought about calling Ronny into the office. Ronny handled all the patients alone while Eric rested after his massive healing. No, he'd wait to see what was up. It could be a police business. "Sit back and relax. Talk to me," he urged.

"My sister. I need to help. Mom won't be able to handle this alone. Call my sister Susan. She has to come too. We all need to be there. Now. Right now. Get a plane. I have to go," Eric was in a panic. He was so worked up that he barely made sense as he talked.

Bobby placed a hand on Eric's shoulder. "Okay, I've got it from here on. You eat a couple of bars and have a drink. I've got this. Please give me your phone so I can get Susan's number. I'll make the travel arrangements. I'll have Higgins pack us each an overnight bag. Do I need to call your mother too?"

Shaking his head, Eric whispered, "No. Mids was on the phone with her when the vision came to me. I… I have to go. It is bad, Bobby, horrible. Ronny, get Ronny so I can tell him." Eric fell back in his chair, clearly still in the grip of his healing weakness.

"Okay, I've got this, Eric. Relax," Bobby soothed. It had to be something terrible for the kid to be this upset. Quickly, he scanned Eric's phone and found his sister Susan's number. He called her as he walked to the entrance to the lab room to stand where Ronny could see him. Ronny looked up at Bobby, and Bobby indicated that he needed to come to him. "Susan? Ah, Tex. This is Bobby Jay, Eric's SS man. Middy needs Susan's help. Eric is about to have a fit worrying over this. It has to be bad. Tell Susan that Eric says all of them are needed. I've no information about the crisis, but it isn't good. Thank you. I'll see you there." Ronny was standing in front of Bobby.

"What's up?" Ronny asked.

"Something to do with Eric's sister. He and I are going there as soon as I can get us a ride. You will be solo here, holding down the fort until we return. I think Eric will have to brief you on things. Go to him. I have a flight to book and to notify Higgins to pack bags for us. You have this?" Bobby said.

"Yes, sir," Ronny replied. He didn't blink an eye at the sudden change in the situation. Bobby patted Ronny on the shoulder as he turned away to call Higgins.

They are so organized, thought Ronny. Not only did a car arrive to take Eric and Bobby Jay to the airport, but a man was also left to guard Ronny. Realizing he would be watched over even if Eric wasn't there was weird. Whatever this emergency with Eric's sister was, it had to be bad for the number of agents to become involved. Higgins was left to be with Ronny at home and care for the animals. Another agent was sent with Eric and Bobby to cover the nights. Thinking of Bruce being without Eric, Ronny worries. How were they to control the transforming cat?

Eric was on his phone at the airport. The fact

he was talking to his cat wasn't apparent at first. To anyone listening, he was trying to reassure a child or girlfriend that he'd be home as soon as possible. Only the roar that responded was strange.

They were rushed to a hospital once the plane landed. Eric was the only one with any idea of what was going on from his vision/nightmare. He and his family surrounded Middy, giving her all the support a family so close could provide. There would be none of the bickering most groups had over who was in charge. Only one person led this family. The SS surrounded their mother, escorting her to the room where Middy's Secret Service Agent lay dying. The moment he touched the patient, Eric thought he would pass out. Never had he felt so much damage in a person or animal. Crushed. The man was crushed, literally. His mother abolished him for trying to help her heal. Eric was scared. Fear for his mother was like a dark blanket smothering him. There was no time for him to wallow in fear. His job was to be a battery for his mother. He ate when told to eat. He rested when everything inside him screamed that he had to give more of his energy to his mother. She was the healer. She was the one they had to save. They were just batteries to boost her up so she could heal. His sisters placed their hands on his mother. Their father's hands were the first and the last to support their mother each time they, as a team, returned to healing this mountain of crushed flesh. Eric had also felt the brain tumor inside Middy's SS man. That also had to be healed. They ate, rested, placed hands on his mother, and the cycle repeated.

There was still so much bruising when Eric's mother finally agreed they were done. If she and Eric had been left on their own, they would have continued healing, but then, his mother might have died. That was the cost of healing, giving so much of yourself that nothing was left inside you to support your life. Thankfully, his mother had his father to look after her, to make her stop when he could. Eric did one last trick, trying to ward off the possibility of blood clots from all the bruising. His mother had reconstructed bones, nerves, muscles, and so much more. All nature had to do was heal the surface bruising. Reluctantly, the family split up, returning to their own homes. Still, Middy and her SS man were in their minds and hearts.

Higgins walked his second round of patrolling the outside of the house. He wasn't used to not having Bobby Jay in charge of things. Twice, he tried calling Bobby to see how Eric's sister was doing, and he heard Bobby's lockdown recording on his phone. It meant he was in a situation where no incoming or outgoing calls could be made. That worried Higgins. Finishing his patrol, Higgins went into the house only to have Ronny come charging at him, ordering him to get the car. "Calm down. What is the problem?" he soothed.

"Molly. Molly is having the puppies. We need to get her to the clinic," Ronny practically yelled at Higgins.

"Kid, you do know dogs have puppies all the time at home," Higgins said, wondering if the kid had finally lost his marbles.

"Right, I knew that," Ronny took a deep breath and returned to his bedroom. He knelt just inside his closet and started speaking softly to Molly. "It is going to be okay, girl. We are going to get you through this. I'm here," his voice seemed to catch in his throat. A roar from Eric's room startled Ronny so much that he fell back. Molly zoomed out of the closet, running so fast past Ronny he didn't have a chance to grab her. Bruce. A deep-seated fear hit Ronny upside his head. Bruce was going to eat Molly! Jumping to his feet, he rushed after Molly.

Higgins saw Molly run into Eric's room and followed her. Bruce was upset. The cat had been depressed since Bobby Jay left with Eric to solve his sister's problem. If Molly had felt Bruce needed her so much, she had left the nest she had made to have her puppies. The cat must be in bad shape. He had just stopped to see what Bruce and Molly were doing when Ronny tried to yank Higgins' gun out of his shoulder holster. Higgins acted on instinct and flipped Ronny over his shoulder while holding the hand gripping his weapon. Ronny was yelling at him as they tussled on the floor. "I have to shoot him before he eats Molly. Let me have your gun. Give it to me. Give it to me!"

"Stop," Higgins ordered. "Stop now, or I'll bust your jackass head open." Higgins yanked his gun free from Ronny and tapped him on the head with it. "Now get up and apologize to Bruce."

Ronny's face was so red it looked like he had spent the day on the beach without sunblock. "He isn't eating Molly?" he asked as if he just realized how he had been behaving.

"No. Will you behave if I let you up?" Higgins asked, looking at Ronny as if he was disgusted with him.

Ronny nodded and slowly stood up. Fearing the worst, he looked over to Eric's bed. Bruce stood on Eric's bed in panther form, his huge tongue licking Molly's head as Molly lay panting like mad with labor pain. "Oh," he said, feeling like such a fool. He started to walk over to the bed to be with Molly, but Bruce raised his head and looked at him, changing his mind. He paced back and forth, lost in worry over his Molly dog. She shouldn't have to go through this alone.

An hour passed, then two, with Bruce standing over Molly and the two of them panting as if sharing each labor pain. Ronny paced like a nervous wreck. He lost track of time, walking out to the kitchen for a drink of water and back to Eric's room. Ronny heard Bruce roar. He dropped the glass of water and ran. Skidding to a stop a safe distance from the bed, Ronny heard a tiny voice. Molly was cleaning her first puppy off while Bruce licked her on the head. Ronny felt something like pride filling in his heart's blank spots. Forgetting to be afraid of Bruce, he knelt beside the bed, watching a tiny replica of Molly squirming closer to her. Ronny reached out and rubbed the little puppy on the back. There was a small white blaze down the pup's forehead. "Blaze. Your name is Blaze," he told the little one. It dawned on him that Bruce allowed him to be there and touch the puppy. All was right in his world, and the cat finally accepted him.

Chapter Eleven

BETTY

Bobby Jay had been shaken to his core upon seeing Ritter so damaged. He had to be all SS man, appearing unmoved and uncaring. Inside him was the worry his subject was going to kill himself, helping to heal his friend. Nothing had prepared Bobby Jay for what they witnessed at that hospital. The sheer power of one thin woman had him wondering how many other amazing people there might be in this world that nobody ever knew existed. And he, Bobby Jay, was privileged to protect one of them.

Eric slept off and on as they traveled home. Bobby knew Eric was worried about his cat Bruce. He hadn't been able to talk over the phone to the cat as he'd first thought he could. Someone higher than Bobby Jay had decided no communication with the outside world would be allowed. Bobby knew this was more to block anyone than the family discussing what had happened at that hospital. Still, it cramped Eric's plans to keep Bruce calm while he was away from him. Keeping Bruce calm was a must.

Bobby Jay dozed briefly on the flight home. His sleep was filled with images of Ritter crushed and bloody. This was followed by snatches of what he feared they would find upon returning home. His sleeping mind conjured up scenes where Higgins and Ronny were on the floor, their throats ripped out. Bruce was standing over them, roaring.

At last, the car from the airport pulled up to Eric's home. He bounded out of the vehicle, barely pausing long enough to snatch his travel bag out of the car's trunk. The house looked quiet and dark. Why weren't the lights on? Bobby Jay dropped his bag and pulled his weapon out, motioning Eric to return to the car. Eric shook his head. His friends and cat were in that house. If something was wrong, he needed to be there to help and heal them.

Slowly, Bobby cracked the door of the house open. Silence. Where the heck was Higgins? Bobby searched the entrance room for a clue about what was happening. It was too dark to see much, but the little Bobby could make out looked normal. Crouching, he made his way towards the kitchen. Higgins was usually in the kitchen this time of day. Pots were on the stove, meat was laid out to be cooked, and vegetables were ready to be prepared, but there was no Higgins. Over and over, Bobby repeated to himself, "Please don't make me have to kill Eric's cat." He was about to explore the rest of the house when the lights suddenly came on, making him jump and swing around, almost shooting Eric behind him. "Didn't I tell you to get in the car?" he whispered gruffly to Eric.

Before Eric could answer, the door to the utility closet opened, and Higgins stepped out. Higgins threw his hands up upon seeing Bobby's gun. "Dang it!" he said as if trying not to speak too loudly. "You about scared ten years off my life. Put that fool thing away and keep quiet. It would help if you didn't wake Bruce up. Poor guy hasn't slept much." Higgins said, chuckling softly, and motioned for Bobby and Eric to follow him. He led them back to Eric's bedroom and eased the door open. There was Bruce in panther form, lying on his back on Eric's bed, his legs sprawled to the side as he lay on his back, snoring. Molly was lying on top of Bruce as if she had been holding him. Her belly was no longer enlarged with expected puppies. Molly's eyebrows twitched as she looked from Eric to Bobby. Her tail flicked softly at them before curling up on Bruce with her two wee pups.

Higgins motioned for Bobby and Eric to follow him and gently shut the door back. "Dang, the circuit breaker flipped off. I had to find the thing and get the lights back before cutting my fingers off chopping veggies. Ronny should be home soon from a last-minute emergency. How did things go with your sister?"

The tension drained out of Bobby as he flopped down in a chair. Finally, they were at home. He allowed himself a moment to relax as he listened to Eric and Higgins's talk. Soon, the kitchen was filled with the aroma of delicious food cooking.

Bobby sighed in contentment. His subject was safe. Suddenly, Bobby realized Molly had puppies while they were gone. "When did Molly have the pups?" he asked, changing the subject from the serious discussion about Eric's sister and Ritter.

Higgins' mouth twitched. "The first night. I thought I was going to have to shoot Ronny once he found out she was in labor. For a dog doctor, he pretty much lost his marbles. Molly tried to be sneaky and have the pups in Ronny's closet. Only Bruce became upset that Eric was gone and transformed. Either that or he knew she was about to give birth. You know how Molly becomes when Bruce goes all Mighty Panther on us. She heard him roar and left poor Ronny sitting in front of the closet as she took off to find Bruce. You should have seen Ronny trying to wrestle my gun from me to shoot Bruce cause he thought the big guy was going to eat Molly. How Molly managed to get up on your bed, I'll never know. But there she was with Bruce standing over her. Both of them panting like mad," Higgins paused and looked at Eric. "We may have to get you a new mattress. She had the pups up there. Anyway, they panted, and Ronny paced for half the night. Then, the first pup arrived. They all made such a fuss over that first little one. It was another hour before the other little one popped out. By then, Ronny was passed out on the floor because Bruce wouldn't let him in the bed. Bruce was sitting up there next to Molly, looking like he was the proud daddy of her puppies. All he has done since is puppy-sit. Poor guy hasn't even eaten. Ronny was dragging when he went to work this morning."

Higgins shook his head, "Those two will be very happy you are home."

Eric slept for eighteen hours straight once his head hit the pillow. He slept so soundly that the panther, dog, and puppies in his bed didn't register in his sleeping mind. This was normal after using his healing powers or acting as a battery for such a prolonged time as had happened to heal Middy's SS man. On the plus side, such usage also increased his powers. He just had to recover first and not have given so much of himself he died. Dying could be the downside of using his healing power. However, if he were revived, there would be a massive increase in his powers from then on. Nobody else knew these facts. It might scare people to know he and his siblings became more potent after stressing themselves using their powers. Call it a scientific fact, like practicing with a musical instrument. You learn how to play and practice until you play well—or, as a surgeon, you become the best in your field—practice made perfect… at a cost.

Bobby Jay wasn't given a day off to rest, though. He took Ronny to the clinic and watched him while Eric slept and rested. Bobby noticed the staff seemed to look to Ronny more as their boss than they did before when Eric had been there. He hoped this was a good thing, that Ronny could take some of the weight off of Eric's shoulders. Another change was that Eric's healing room was finally finished and furnished. Now, there would be a place where Eric could recover from healing without people wondering what was wrong with him.

On the second day, Eric was back at work, and one of those needing him and his talent came into the clinic. It was a cat that had been impaled upon a garden stake when dropped out of a second-story window by the owner's little girl. The child was in tears, clutching her 'kitty' to her chest. Why did the mother let the little girl hold the cat? Eric didn't know. This had to be traumatic for the little girl to know she was responsible for her cat being hurt so badly.

Ronny kept shaking his head as if he was sure the cat was already dead as Eric touched the silver, long-haired cat on the head. Eric glanced up at the woman and the little girl before speaking. "If you wish, you may sit in the office while I work on your kitty. I promise to do everything I can to make this little one well," he said, going over to squat in front of the little girl. "Why don't you go with your mother? If you have nap time, you might as well go home. Either Dr. Croft or I will call you as soon as surgery is over." He patted the child on the head, seeking out her terror to relieve it.

The mother frowned down at him. "Don't make promises you can't keep. We don't believe in coddling her. Life is hard. She needs to learn this lesson," she said.

"I have made a promise, and I will keep it. Now, please go so I can get started," Eric said. Not waiting to see if she left, he picked up the silver cat and returned to his private room. Now, it was up to him to keep a promise to a little girl.

Ronny was left to handle the day-to-day business of giving vaccines, worming, and the everyday problems many owners brought with their pets. His mind constantly worried about what was happening in the back room. He had seen Bobby Jay going into that room with Eric. That must mean Eric would be hooked up to those weird IVs again. He was there draining himself to healing by touch or whatever method he used. Was it magic, voodoo, or just something Ronny couldn't understand? Whatever it was, it both awed and scared Ronny. Thankfully, it was a busy day, and Ronny was stretched to his limit just seeing patients. Near lunchtime, he called in for pizza, remembering to order several extras for the vast intake of food Ronny had learned Eric needed when healing.

Once in his healing room, Eric shaved the areas around the garden stake on each side of the silver cat. He disinfected the area and the nub of the stake on one side of the cat left from cutting it off. She lay very still in a semi-coma state. Every bit of the cat's being was pushed to keep her alive. She had nothing to spare for staying awake and alert. Pulling the stake out of the cat was bound to cause more damage. However, Eric was reluctant to open the cat up and cause all the trauma of surgery. The garden stake was made of wood and might leave bits of the green stain or wooden slivers from the stake inside the cat. Eric would not only have to heal and repair all the tissue that had been destroyed, but he needed to destroy all the particulates remaining in the tissue.

Taking a deep breath, Eric cut off the end of the garden stake as close as possible to the cat's body. He treated the area with disinfectants and began working the stake out of the cat's body. His face paled as he absorbed all the pain the cat would have felt if he hadn't taken it into himself. Dizziness swept over Eric when the stake pulled free, but Eric couldn't stop now. He had to stop the bleeding and seal off areas that threatened to rupture.

Bobby called to Eric to stop and rest before realizing that Eric was too far into the healing to hear him. He had learned so much from Eric's father on how to take care of Eric. He began to talk the kid down, telling him what he needed to hear so he could stop on his own. "You aren't going to do this little one any good if you pass out. Stop for now, take a break, and rest. Our food should be here soon. Sit back and eat an energy bar. You have to stop now, Eric, but just for a bit. Come on. Let me put some hot water bottles around this little guy." Bobby didn't think Eric was hearing him until Eric slumped back. Bobby placed a blanket around Eric's shoulders.

Ronny had his hands full when the pizza arrived. He knew it needed to get to where Eric was holding up, doing his impossible healing as fast as possible. Seeing Betty taking a dog up to go home from a bath, he told her to take four boxes back to Dr. Whiting's exam room. It wasn't until he washed his hands and prepared to go to the office for his pizza that he remembered nobody was supposed to see Eric healing. That had been the whole reason for building the private room. Rubbing his eyes at his brain-dead move, he rushed back to see if he could get to the room before Bobby Jay opened the door. The door was unlocked! Ronny opened the door a crack and looked in. What he saw had him rushing in, slamming the door behind him.

Bobby Jay caught Eric as he fell out of his chair. The boy had insisted on healing a bit more before the food arrived. His heart had stopped. While Bobby was positioning Eric's body on the floor to start chest compression, someone knocked on the door. He needed help, and he didn't care who that help was, so he rushed to the door, reaching out to pull Betty and the pizza inside. "Drop those on the floor. Get over here and breathe for Dr. Whiting while I do the compression. I have a rolled towel under his neck to help keep his airway open. Give him three good breaths, then sit back." He didn't give Betty a chance to refuse as he dragged her over and pushed her down to her knees. Grabbing the blanket he had put around Eric's shoulders earlier, he covered most of Eric's body and began CPR.

Shaken, Betty did as she was told. She breathed for Eric twice more and felt his neck when ordered by Bobby Jay to check for a pulse. She was scared. Dr. Whiting was dead. That thought shook her to her core. He was so gentle and kind to her. He had left her little gifts and never even told her he had done so. Why did someone so gentle and honorable have to die while others who were monsters lived? Dr. Croft came rushing in just as Dr. Whiting took a deep breath. Betty rocked back on her heels, her face white and her heart pounding. They had saved him.

"What the hell happened?" Ronny growled at Bobby Jay.

Bobby glanced at Betty and gave her a little smile. "You did well. I'm glad you were here," he told her. She dropped her head as if embarrassed to have received praise. Looking up at Ronny, Bobby's expression became serious. "We need to order a defibrillator in case this happens again. It's my fault. I should have made him eat before he started working on the cat. I was stupid, stupid, stupid. Make sure the door is locked. I need to talk with Betty," Bobby said, looking over to where Betty was adjusting the blanket and moving it up to Eric's neck.

Nodding, Ronny did as he had been told. He nearly tripped over the pizza, managing to avoid making a mess with their lunch. He could hear Bobby telling Betty to make hot water bottles to place around Eric after he was moved to the cot waiting for him. Ronny joined Betty in preparing the bottles of hot water. They used two-liter plastic Coke bottles, getting the water as hot as possible before placing them around Eric's sleeping form.

Bobby moved them aside to set up another IV, placing it in Eric's other arm. He turned both drips up reasonably high and plopped himself into Eric's empty chair. Eric had scared the crap out of him. He'd nearly lost the boy. This was after he had seen how stressful this healing was on them when Eric's mother had healed Ritter. How could he have thought one drip would be enough? Because it had been enough the other times Eric had fainted. Only he didn't faint this time. He died. Good grief, he had involved the girl, too. Could he be any more of a screw-up? And he thought this assignment was just punishment. To watch a dingbat teen who had no sense. Now, he realized this assignment was a great honor. Maybe he was the wrong man for the job. That thought bounced around as he tried to figure out what to tell Betty. She'd have to sign the nondisclosure agreement. Wouldn't Ronny be pleased about that?

Sighing, Bobby held his car keys out to Ronny. "Go get my briefcase out of the trunk of the car. I'll have that talk with Betty while you are doing that."

Ronny could feel the blood draining from his face as he realized Betty would have to sign some of the forms he had been made to sign. As much as he grumbled about signing those papers, he didn't wish anyone else the same experience. He gave Betty a look of pity before taking the keys and leaving.

Standing, Bobby Jay had Betty sit in the chair he had vacated. "I'm one of the Secret Service agents assigned to keeping Dr. Whiting safe. He is a very special person and must be protected at all costs. As you have just witnessed, he is extremely delicate. We protect him from his folly and any person wishing to harm him. You mustn't speak of what you saw here today or what you have been told. We take protecting Eric very seriously. You will have to sign some papers swearing to never speak or reveal in any manner what you see today or on any other day concerning Dr. Whiting. Do you understand?"

Betty's eyes grew huge as Bobby talked to her. She tried to speak when he finished, but her voice wouldn't work. She nodded her head instead. Betty glanced over to where Eric slept and found her voice. "Will he be alright?"

"Yes, this time. He will be upset he didn't finish healing this cat, though." Bobby said, trying to make Betty smile. Ronny walked in with Bobby's briefcase. "Thank you, Dr. Croft. You do the skin sutures, which Eric would have done to make it look like the cat had surgery. Then go back to work like normal."

Ronny nodded and sliced the skin on the cat to make a suture line, which he stitched up. He turned the cat over and did the same thing to the other side. "That should do it. We put her in recovery now until Eric has a chance to check her out to be certain he got everything. Betty, it would help if you ate after signing those papers. I'll eat in the office to head off anyone coming in. You will assist me in the exam rooms for the rest of the day." Ronny was brisk and forceful in his quarterback mode. Behind him, Bobby smirked to himself. This was a side of Ronny he hadn't seen before.

The dream began as it had so many times before, with Eric seeing the girl, now a woman, Betty, in her home. She was sitting on her bed, staring off into space. There was a difference to her that Eric could not figure out. Her look was different, as if she had matured overnight. Part of the difference was that Eric was not looking through another person's eyes. He wasn't the mother or the father. He was just a mist of little form watching over his soul mate. A form of no substance incapable of defending her. It occurred to him that he had only been able to help her when he commanded the father to stop. Did he have to be a monster to stop a monster?

His dream shifted, and Eric realized it was more of a vision of the future than a dream. It was like when he had dreamed of this house as a child. His mother, her hair nearly completely silver, was in

the kitchen of their home farm. She had just picked
up the last dish from the kitchen table and was
turning to place it in the sink when it seemed like the
air near her ruptured in a burst of energy, pushing
his mother against the sink. Out of nowhere, a
man stumbled forth and laid a body on the table.
Eric could hear him speak, which was unusual.
"Grandmother, heal him, please. I need to go back."
The man was gone in a blink, leaving a sonic sound
behind. The noise in his dream shook Eric awake.

Grandmother? His child or Middy's child?
Like his house, it would be years in the future. A
boy? One of them would have a boy. A son? He
might have a son. A huge grin spread over his
face. For a moment, he let himself enjoy this secret
knowledge. A child would mean a wife. The boy
must be Middy's son. That made more sense as he
often saw things going on with Middy. He'd felt so
proud there for a moment, thinking he had a son.

Pulling the covers back over him, Eric closed
his eyes, seeking to rest a little before morning
showed up. He slipped into another dream; at least,
he thought it was a dream. He walked into the
clinic to see the waiting area completely changed.
Gone was the dull green color of the walls. Instead,
they had been painted a soft coral color. There
were pictures on the walls Eric hadn't seen before.
Beautiful images of what looked like the patients they
treated. Each dog, cat, bird, and other assorted pet
was depicted in cute poses as if listening or looking
at someone with adoring eyes. Eric wondered who
had painted these beautiful captures of their patients.
He saw the cat he had just worked on, which had

been speared with the garden stake. A dog Ronny had treated. Everywhere were patients he knew and some he didn't.

There was no signature on the paintings. There was no indication of what incredible artist had produced such beauty for the clinic. Then, he knew. Going into his office, he saw a picture on his wall. He did not doubt who had painted it. It hung behind his desk in wondrous testimony of the person responsible for all of them. It was a rabbit with one ear flopping over as it scratched the ear with its hind foot. Betty.

The smell of bacon cooking woke Eric. He stretched and prepared himself for a short run before breakfast. There was a lot to think about. Somehow, he had to make the dream of all those wonderful paintings come true. It was the one thing he could do for Betty. Maybe he could never have her for his wife, but he could make one of her dreams come true. It was possible. He just had to figure out how.

Why did he have to pull duty with a runner? Bobby mulled over his past sins, wondering if this was a punishment from some divine being for something he didn't realize he had done. His eyes scanned the trees along Eric's path for his short morning runs. Something was up with the kid. Heck, something was always up with the kid. With some nightmares and some personal crises, the kid was a magnet for trouble.

All thoughts he was having fled immediately when Eric pulled up and turned around abruptly, heading back towards the house. Bobby did a quick scan before sprinting after Eric. Well, that was different. Eric hadn't even worn Bobby to a nub before returning to the house.

Back at the house, Eric quickly showered and dressed for work. He was at the table in six minutes, ready to lay out a plan for the guys. Higgins banged a plate before him, evidently in a grumpy mood again. Ronny sat next to Eric, giving Higgins a wary look. Bobby Jay planted himself directly across from Eric and stared at him as if expecting him to explode. Eric waited until everyone was seated and had started digging into their breakfast before he spoke up. "I had a dream vision last night. I want us to discuss it and set it into motion. This involves the clinic, so you have a say in what we do, Ronny," Eric said, looking at Ronny stuffing bacon into his mouth next to him. "Because this involves Betty, you two need to advise me on the wisdom of implementing this plan." Eric waited for Higgins and Bobby to nod their heads before going on.

"You remember how Betty always wanted to draw pictures but was denied as a child? Well, I want to give her that childhood dream of hers. This is what I saw in my vision. We had repainted the walls in the reception area with a light coral color. It brightened the room a great deal. But, here is the thing. Pictures of the animals we have been treating were hung on the walls. They were wonderful paintings capturing the personalities of each dog, cat, bird, and even a lizard we treated. Betty had painted them. My question is, how can we do this without upsetting her home life? And do you approve?"

Bobby rubbed his face as if scrubbing some fog from his mind. "Crap! This is a problem. I can understand you wanting to do this for her, but, kid, this could be dangerous. From what you learned in your dreams, this father of hers is a regular tyrant. At the very least, you'd be making her home life troublesome. At most, the father could take it out on her or come after you. A bully like that is used to getting his way. He feels everything he wants is all anyone should ever want. They need to bow down to him and make him feel powerful because they are weak in his eyes. It is like lighting a fuse to mix things up there," Bobby said, glancing over at Higgins to see if he was on the same page as him. "Let us talk it over and get back to you. Don't do anything until we have had a chance to assess possible threats."

So much for dreams, Eric thought. The bit of brightness that had flooded his heart was covered with a heavy hand.

Everything was going so well that it was scary. Eric's nightmares were quickly figured out, and several people and families had been saved from tragic happenings. Eric and Ronny decided to include their helpers at the clinic in the decisions to remodel the clinic. It was no surprise to Eric when everyone decided the walls should be painted a light coral. The receptionist helped rearrange the furniture in the waiting area, revealing a talent for designing an open and pleasant arrangement. If anyone had an idea, Ronny and Eric would seriously consider it. Days turned into weeks as the clinic slowly transformed into the image Eric had seen in his vision. He felt happy and relaxed for the first time in a long while.

Eric waved goodbye to the little girl clutching her kitten to her chest. The child told the kitten that she had to be given shots sometimes. Eric smiled as he wiped down the exam table to prepare for the next patient. It was then the vision hit him. His sister Middy lay on an exam table looking pale and still. Her SS agent was holding her hand, refusing to let go as the doctor was explaining something to him. He shook his head in shock and anger.

A gasp escaped Eric as the vision left him. Middy was in serious trouble. He had to go to her. Going to the exam room where Ronny was putting ointment into a dog's eyes, Eric motioned for Ronny to come to him. Ronny gave the dog's owner the ointment tube and instructed him to do the treatment once each morning and night for a week, then bring Piggy back in so Ronny could see how the eye was healing. He waited until the patient and owner left before going over to Eric. "What's up?" he asked.

"I have to go help save my sister. It didn't look good. You can call in one of the substitutes on the list to help out for a few days. I'll call and update you when I can. We'll have Higgins come for the rest of the day. He has to bring our go-bags anyway. I'm sorry, Ronny, for leaving on such short notice." Eric explained.

"Don't be, man. I understand. You go and save your sister, alright? I can handle things here." Ronny told him. He had realized that there would be times when Eric dropped everything to help his family.

As Eric turned away to notify Bobby Jay they

were leaving, he saw Bobby already on the phone. "Yes, both of our bags. Pack extra Andy Bags and the usual bars and drinks. I need to order a flight, and we will leave as soon as you arrive. Don't worry about the cat. No, don't bring him. Yeah, yeah, I owe you one." Bobby hung up and immediately punched in another number. Since their trip to heal Middy's SS agent, Bobby had been preparing for the possibility of having to take Eric to help his sister again or attend her funeral.

Looking up, Bobby saw Eric watching him. "Do you need to change any patient appointments?" he asked.

Nodding a yes to Bobby, Eric made quick calls to his patient's owners. He also wanted to get the sketch pad and pencil set he had in the car to leave in the back for Betty to find. He was hoping she would make a few drawings in it so he could use that to get her to do the paintings for the lobby. For now, he'd leave the sketch pad back in the kennel. Right now, nothing, not even getting Betty to start drawing, was more important than getting to Middy. His stomach hurt with the sense of urgency that had a hold on him. He was thankful that Bobby had overheard him talking to Ronny and that he didn't waste time asking him what was happening. That was the upside of having a constant watchdog keeping you in sight all the time. They tended to get things done.

The moment Bobby Jay pulled into the hospital parking lot where Middy lay dying, Eric scrambled out the door of the car and took off running. He'd seen how bad things were in a vision on the plane. It ate at him that they had so far to travel before he could help his sister. He went as swiftly as he could to where he saw a group of police officers standing in the hallway. From there, it was simply a matter of looking for where the SS had blocked people from determining where Middy was staying. Rushing past the serious-faced SS, Eric opened the room door and entered. "Am I in time? I started as soon as the vision hit me. It is bad, isn't it?" He gasped, trying to catch his breath as both the horror of losing his sister and the dash to get here hit him. His mother's words chilled him to the bone.

"I'm not going to lie, Eric. This is the worst stuff I've ever seen. We have to fight with all we have. Any ideas?" she asked him.

"We can either take turns, or both of us hit it with all we have," Eric mused.

"We can't afford to faint. We are the only thing standing between death and Middy," Felith said. "We do it in short bursts, clearing as much of it as possible. And we must keep going back over the areas cleared because this thing doesn't stay clear. It is fast and evil. I make a little progress, then have to go back and clean it up again."

That explanation from his mother scared Eric more than anything. He was barely aware of his father hooking up an IV to him. He heard Middy's SS agent say, "I'll do him." And they all began to eat the protein bars and drink the bottles of energy drinks.

Eric gasped when he first felt the thing inside his sister. He pressed his hand tightly against her arm and fought beside his mother, trying to save his sister's life.

Chapter Twelve

DESPERATE TIMES

Pure fear had a hold on Eric as he and his mother took turns healing his sister, Middy. This thing that she had been poisoned with was, as his mother had said, 'evil.' It was trying to devour Middy from the inside. Even though they were making slow progress, Eric knew that sooner or later, their strength would end. They'd died, and then Middy would die. With only Eric's father and Middy's SS agent acting like batteries to boost his mother and him, Eric knew they were fighting a losing battle. He thought about Bruce, Ronny, and Higgins and how they would be upset when he died. He wouldn't give up, even if it meant dying. Middy had always been strong for him; he would be strong for her. "We need real food inside us to boost us up," Eric said, his voice so weak they could barely hear him. "Bobby Jay," he called out, and almost instantly, Bobby was at his side. "Bring us a huge meal, you know the sort." Bobby nodded and was on his phone before he reached the divider curtain. Eric wasn't done giving orders, "Mother, next break, you try to sleep a few minutes, then we switch, and I'll do the same. This thing is almost stronger than both of us, and we need to hit it constantly, so we will rest for a while when we can. That way, it won't have a chance to undo what good has been done. Constantly attacking it will hopefully wear it away. It is going to be a long night."

With the meal arrived Susan and a young boy. "I want you all to stop thinking this is impossible. I've brought two new batteries and plenty of food. My sister is a fighter, so buck up and start thinking more positive thoughts." Susan told them.

Hope, she had brought them another battery, and hope.

They had needed that bit of hope as the terrible enemy ravished Middy's body almost as fast as they could heal her. Eric knew they were making progress, but it didn't seem enough. It was a race to the finish line. The question was, 'Would they crash and burn before winning the race?'

Time sped up, taking its toll on the two healers and their batteries. Eric's mother was the one healing while Eric ate yet another protein bar and drank an energy drink. He knew they were all reaching the end of what little they had left to give in saving Middy. Eric's brain seemed to be inside a vat of molasses, sluggish and difficult to hold himself awake and aware. The following healing push might be the last one he'd ever give. He could feel the life draining away from his body. He didn't care. He had to save his sister. He had to.

The following two hours passed, with every touch sending agony through the healers and their batteries. Eric was on one of the frequent breaks they had to take now while his mother worked on Middy. Suddenly, his mother called to them. "Come quickly. I have it isolated in one small spot. We need to all work at once to finish it off. Eric joins me; everyone else supports us."

Eric's father called Susan's SS agent, Tex, to bring in the doctor and two crash carts. They all knew this was it. They either would succeed or fail. Once this push was over, they might not be alive to carry on.

Eric and his mother, Felith, attacked the last bit of horror, drawing relentlessly on the two batteries they each had. Felith could feel the darkness starting to creep up on her, and she pushed harder. She couldn't, wouldn't let her daughter die. Eric was just as determined, fighting his darkness as his strength began to wither away. It was a suicide attempt given by both healers at the same time. Darkness took them over, and they fell into the waiting arms of two SS men. York, the young boy who came with Susan, was already down. Susan was swaying and went down with a thump. Ritter, Middy's SS agent, and Fred, Eric's father, just slipped to the floor holding their healers. It had been an all-out effort by them all. Their last thoughts were 'Middy live'.

Doctor Pierces', who had only been allowed to observe up to that point, eyes went wide, but she didn't hesitate to wade in and start checking pulses.

The two who had been touching her patient were in cardiac arrest; the rest were out cold, although the boy barely had a pulse. She needed help, but one look at the SS men standing over her told her nobody else would be allowed in.

Bobby Jay appeared as if out of the blue. He ripped Eric's shirt off and lubed the paddles of one of the defibrillator machines. Not waiting for approval, he shocked Eric as if he had done this many times before. He started the machine to charge again, even as he felt for a pulse on Eric's neck. Ignoring everything around him, Bobby Jay concentrated only on Eric. This was his to-do, and part of this partnership was keeping Eric alive. "Come on, Eric, Bruce will kill me if I return without you. Then, they will come to shoot Bruce or send him to the gas chamber. You don't want that, do you?" That seemed to work, and Eric took a deep breath before rolling to his side and falling into a deep sleep. "Blankets and six cots," Bobby Jay called out to the men in black waiting outside the curtains. They were men used to there being such emergencies. Not only were blankets brought, but warm blankets.

Silently, the SS watched over their subjects, their faces grim. What they thought could not have been more apparent was that this was the long vigil, the waiting period until they knew that once more, their subjects had pulled off another miracle and lived.

Bobby Jay watched Eric closely. The boy had died. How did he protect him? Twice, he had come close to losing this seer/healer. Twice. He'd have

to make arrangements for a portable defibrillator—
something he could carry with them no matter where
they went. And speak to the other protectors to
ensure they also brought one. This job had taken on
a whole new form. It wasn't a place yourself between
a bullet and your subject thing anymore. We have
to adjust and adjust again as things develop, Bobby
thought. He'd thought a gun, maybe a tracking
device, would be all he'd need on this assignment.
Now, he was including medical equipment. What
would he need tomorrow or the next day? It wasn't
only the kid's future he was protecting. He had
become involved and allowed himself to be used.
He'd learned that nightmares could be stopped. That
is if you have a seer as your subject.

"Buckle up," their pilot called back to Bobby
Jay and Eric as they approached the landing. Higgins
and Ronny should have a hot meal waiting at home.
At least, Bobby hoped so. His subject was still rather
pale and weak from saving his sister. And the nut
heals that little bird when he is weak after healing
Middy. Bobby wouldn't have believed a wild bird
would up and claim a person like that little fellow
had Eric's sister. But, he would have never believed
anything that had happened since he'd taken this
assignment. He knew one thing for sure. He was
glad they were on his side of the law.

The drive home was unremarkable. When
they pulled up to the house, Bobby was again
reminded of how weird his life had become. No
sooner had the car stopped than a roar sounded
inside the house, and Bruce came bounding out of
the doggy door they had installed. Only Bruce was

in panther form, which meant he was emotionally upset. The enormous black cat bound from the house to the car, joyfully knocking Eric down at seeing him. Molly came on Bruce's heels but kept back, waiting for permission to approach Eric and Bobby.

Finally, Bruce became a typical house cat's regular-size or extra-large size. Molly approached to show her joy in the reunion with Bobby and Eric. Her approach was one of shyness and gentle licks. Eric took his time with both animals, letting Bruce calm down and telling Molly she had not been forgotten. Ronny and Higgins stood on the porch, watching the scene play out.

The men settled around the dinner table, waiting for Higgins to dish up the hearty stew he had made with cornbread and broccoli. Eric thought he smelled Blackberry pie. He ate the first helping of stew in silence, needing the nourishment to bring him back to a healthy level. When the second heaping bowl of stew was put in front of Eric, Ronny could contain himself no longer. "What happened? You look like death not even warmed over, man."

Eric glanced up at Ronny and chuckled, "Thanks. I can count on you to tell me how handsome I've become while visiting my sister." Eric seemed to gather his thoughts before he went on. He frowned and looked to Bobby Jay for the go-ahead since he didn't know if he could talk about something so classified.

Bobby nodded, "It's okay to tell him. I'll shoot him if he tells anyone else." Bobby gave Ronny a look that said he meant it before returning to his meal.

"It was something stolen from a highly classified and secure Lab. It's a horror. It was eating at Middy from the insides and destroying her. Mom wouldn't have been able to kill it on her own. We... we almost didn't kill it. Every time we cleared and healed an area, it would start eating away at it again. If Susan hadn't brought York with her, we all would have died trying to kill it and still lost Middy. Susan has an adopted son, or maybe he is like a ward. But he can do the battery bit. And Middy's SS agent, Ritter, became a battery. Nobody but us kids has ever been able to do the battery bit. It just goes to show us that all a person has to do is believe they can do something to do it," Eric said, leaning back in his chair and closing his eyes.

Bobby took over, explaining how things went. "It was touch and go the whole time. We had all of them hooked up on IVs. And stuffing bars and drinks down them every time one paused," he stopped speaking, staring down at the table, his food forgotten as the memory of all the subjects dropping at the end hit him. "Eric's mother finally got the thing corner. Eric, his mother, and all four batteries were at the limit of their strength. I thought of knocking Eric out to get him to stop and save him. And I think the rest of us had reached that same conclusion where we would lose one subject but save the rest. His mother called them all back to it, and they went after the thing with everything they had left inside them. The batteries lost consciousness, and Eric and his mother both died. I could have killed him for putting me through that if he hadn't been already dead." The last bit came out of Bobby in a whisper. He glanced over to see if he had upset Eric, but Eric was sound asleep.

Eric threw himself back into work, trying to forget the horror that had almost taken his sister and the rest of his family from him. He knew his own heart had stopped, but that didn't upset him as much as thinking he could have lost even one member of his family. He cuddled each patient he treated that first day, taking solace in each patient's love for humans. That helped him to erase the fear which lingered inside him. He was quieter on the ride back home that first day. Something inside him felt as if there was more horror to come. It was as if he could feel something stalking him and the others.

Throughout dinner, Eric remained quiet, his mind trying to understand why he felt this foreboding. He didn't see the looks passing between Higgins and Bobby. Nor the shadow of worry in Ronny's eyes. After dinner, Eric put on his running shoes and took Bruce to run through the woods on the trail they had made for that purpose. Running usually cleared his mind and gave him a little peace. That evening, there didn't seem to be any peace for Eric. No matter how long he ran, his mind still raced with worries, and that odd feeling of danger was draped across his shoulders.

Watching Eric head for the shower, Bobby Jay shook his head and plopped down in one of the kitchen chairs. Higgins placed a hot cup of tea before Bobby as he sat down. "Okay, spill. What happened with his sister?"

Rubbing his forehead, Bobby gathered his

thoughts before speaking. "It was that thing which was developed. You remember, they hushed it up quickly and tried to pretend they had never made it. It was bound to kill his sister. If the whole family hadn't come to save her, they wouldn't have been able to manage it. Not even his mother's remarkable ability was enough to kill it. The worst part was having to stand by feeling completely helpless. Tex, Miss Susan's man, made us all count mentally not to stress her more than was needed. I never realized what it must be like for him to care for her. This snooty doctor kept trying to see where the healing was going. We just about ran out of supplies. Higgins, it was like being on a battlefront with supplies running low and your men stretched beyond endurance. The whole family was so pale and drawn towards the end that we knew things would not end well."

He paused, and a haunted look came into his eyes. "He died. Our boy died. And his mother. The rest of the family went down like wet noodles." Bobby stared off into space for a moment. "But, we got them both back. And his sister was saved. I never felt so damn useless as I when watching them all do their thing," Bobby said, slapping his hand down on the table. "We need to order portable defibrillators. I want them delivered by tomorrow. We can't be unprepared should his heart stop again." Higgins nodded and pulled the laptop over to him.

Standing just outside the kitchen, Ronny listened to what Bobby was saying. He tried to wrap his mind around everything Bobby was telling Higgins. It just all seemed like something distant that happened to strangers in someplace far away. His mind didn't want to process it. Life, for him, had taken a left turn the day Eric came into his life. This certainly was not the life he thought he would be living. He had never believed he would be partners in a clinic so soon after becoming a Veterinarian. The world seemed to be spinning faster and faster, with so much being crammed into each day: weird, frightening things and miracles. He never thought he'd live in the same house as a cat who could change into a panther. Or be friends with a real mystical healer. Nobody would ever believe him if he broke his vow and talked about what happened.

In his room, Eric had fallen into a restless sleep. Darkness swirled around the edges of his dreams, whispering silent threats. The visions began. He saw Bobby Jay walking around the car, his gun drawn. There was this loud sound, and Bobby flew back, landing on the pavement in front of Eric. Blood bloomed on the shirt Bobby wore, covering his chest. Eric rushed forward, placing his hands on Bobby and sending his mind into Bobby's body as fast as possible to seek out the damaged area and start trying to repair it. But, every time he succeeded in healing, another spot would bloom. Throughout the night, he healed Bobby repeatedly in an endless looping nightmare. Until he woke up yelling, "Watch out!"

Heart pounding, Eric looked frantically around his bedroom. Bobby wasn't lying bleeding. It had all been so real. He had been sure Bobby would be lying on the floor bleeding out. The knowledge that Bobby was okay washed over him, leaving him feeling weak and relieved. Then, the worry set in. How could he stop the nightmare from coming true? How could he save Bobby?

He didn't dress for running; he ate breakfast in his bathrobe. Eric waited until everyone was seated with a steaming plate sitting in front of them before speaking. "I want you both to wear vests from now on. Even here. You get up, dress, and put on your vests. Could you do this for me? Okay?"

Bobby studied Eric briefly before answering, "Certainly, you are the boss." He tried to lighten the mood but immediately realized Eric was serious. "A nightmare?" he asked.

Eric nodded. Picking up his fork, Eric ate slowly as if still trapped inside his mind. The problem was that his nightmares nearly always came true. He couldn't bring himself to talk about the nightmare. It was still too real for him.

When Eric walked into the clinic, he did a double-take as he saw the coral-colored walls. He had forgotten all about the redecorating that they had started. That remembrance made him wonder if leaving the sketchpad for Betty had worked. As much as he would have liked to have gone in the back and checked on the place where he had left the tools for drawing, he didn't go. He had to keep himself out of the picture. Hide. He was always hiding. Secreted away from the rest of the world, he did his unofficial job of dreaming nightmares.

One good thing had come from going to heal Middy and dying. It was evident to Eric on the very first animal he healed when they went into the clinic.

His healing power had increased a great deal. He wasn't up to his mother's level yet, but he was healing his patients faster with less effort. Eric didn't think Bobby would agree that the death had been worth it for that bit of gained ability.

Eric petted the Chihuahua, which he had healed of a damaged heart on the head, and offered the little dog a treat. Then he gave the child hiding behind his mother a lollipop. Smiling, Eric told the woman who owned the little dog that the dog would be fine. He gave the little dog a harmless shot they had created for such occasions. People needed to believe he cured their pet with medicine, not by laying-on-hand magic. "Now remember no more candy or anything else but his regular dog food. You are to use this measure to give him his food. Getting overweight is bad for this little guy. And only two treats per day," Eric told the owner. "You take good care of him; he will be around for many years." Eric gave the owner the measuring cup he provided for dogs and cats. Each cup was designed to fit the animal's size to help prevent overfeeding. Sometimes, the most challenging part of healing and keeping an animal healthy was convincing the owner to feed and exercise their pet correctly.

A vision hit Eric in full force as the owner exited the exam room. To him, he was no longer in the exam room but in a parking lot somewhere. He left the car he was in to follow behind Bobby Jay. Bobby waved one hand behind his back, motioning for Eric to return to the vehicle. There was this loud sound that exploded in front of Bobby. Bobby flew backward, his chest blooming red with blood. Eric rushed forward, placing his hands on Bobby's chest. There were so many bloody places covering Bobby's chest. "Watch out!" Eric called out as the vision began to loop around again.

The exam room returned in focus, with Eric kneeling on the floor with his hands extended over nothing. He blinked; for a moment, he had trouble believing this was the real world. The vision had been so intense, so vivid. Rising, Eric returned to clean the exam table and ready the room for his next patient. He was situated in the rear of the clinic because his visions hit him at odd times of the day. He could have some privacy if healing had drained him too much. Bobby Jay ran interference for him, making it clear to all the clinic personnel that he would never be disturbed. This placed Ronny in a difficult position as he had to take on everything to do with treating patients when Eric was out, sleeping off a healing drain. As a result of the distance Eric had erected, the employees had come to consider Ronny as the big boss and Eric as a hired hand.

"You okay?" Bobby asked, stepping into the exam room. He noted the still distant look in Eric's eyes and mentally kicked himself for not being there when the kid needed him. Man, he reminded himself, not a kid. He still considered Eric the youth he had been assigned to protect. Back then, he thought Eric would be some spoiled rich kid to whom he'd have to lay the law down. He'd been wrong, totally wrong. The memory of Eric rushing into the park's pond to save a pillowcase of kittens being drowned flashed in his mind. "A vision?" he said, trying to get a response out of Eric. He didn't like the closed-off expression on Eric's face. Eric nodded and leaned on the exam table as if to support himself.

"Are you wearing your vest?" Eric asked, demanded.

"Yes. I believe in you. I'm certainly not going to question anything you tell me to do for safety. Do you feel up to telling me more about what you have seen?" Bobby inquired, not wanting Eric to close them out of anything that they might be able to help with.

For a moment, Eric felt lost. How could he explain away losing Bobby? He had failed in his vision. Sure, he didn't see the ending, but it had defeated him. Taking a deep breath, he finally responds to Bobby. "Later tonight. It has me upset at the moment. Let the next patient come back."

It worried Bobby that Eric kept reminding him to wear his vest. Whatever his vision was about, it must involve either Higgins or himself being shot. Or them both. Somehow, they had to relieve Eric's mind of that worry. And be extra alert because if they went down, who would stand between Eric and a bullet? They needed details, something to work with and to arm themselves. Knowing in advance could only be a plus in protecting Eric and Ronny. Maybe they should start bringing Bruce to the clinic with them. Bruce had great instincts. He certainly wouldn't allow anyone around Eric with a gun. How could he convince Eric that bringing Bruce would be a good thing? Except if Bruce transformed in front of other people, there would be hell to pay. Eric might have to surrender him for testing. And

Eric would never do that. Scratch the plan to bring Bruce. Back to square one. Protect Eric, and don't get killed.

Dinner was ready when Bobby brought Eric and Ronny home. All the guys had time for was a quick romp with Bruce and Molly with her pups. Higgins had adopted one of the pups, and it was fun watching the oh-so-serious SS agent play with the puppy. That night, however, the romp was short, and the men gathered at the table to eat and discuss Eric's latest vision.

Eric did not want to talk about the vision, but he knew his SS buddies might glean something from the vision he could not see. "It starts with you exiting the car ahead of me. You walk around the car, draw your gun, and put one hand behind your back to wave me back to the car. That is when it happens. It is like a cannon goes off or a bomb explodes. I don't know," he paused, shaking his head. "You fly backward, and there are all these places on your chest bleeding. I kneel to heal you… only I can't seem to stop all the bleeding. Every time I get one spot stopped, another starts bleeding. I keep healing and healing, and you are getting weaker and weaker. Then, it starts all over again. I try yelling, 'Watch out', but it doesn't help. I fail, over and over I fail…," Eric's voice fades to nothing as he puts his face in his hands, trying to scrub away the horror of that failure.

Silence reigns for a long, eternal moment before Higgins finally breaks it. "So, just you and Bobby are in the car? Do you see where you are? Do you hear anything? And what time of day or night is it?" He peppers Eric with basic questions, trying to draw Eric back into the here and now.

Blinking, Eric sits up a little straighter. His face is still a map of defeat, but his eyes have a little more life. He closes his eyes, attempting to recall the vision as it had unfolded repeatedly in his visions. "We stop in a parking lot. Bobby tells me to stay in the car. He rounds the car to my side and pulls his gun out. He is strolling across a paved parking lot. I only see him and get a vague impression of a few cars in the parking lot. None are close, though. I couldn't see anything that caught Bobby's attention as his body was blocking it from me. He walks forward on my side of the car. I get a bad feeling, almost like I'm reliving a vision, and exit the car, determined to warn Bobby. Bobby twists one hand behind him, motioning me to get back. A loud sound goes off, and Bobby is blown back. Something stings my face. I rush to Bobby, my hands sending strength and healing into him. I seek out the worst spots and start to heal him. Then the blood and the vision will begin all over again."

"So it repeats. Next time, try to look beyond the parking lot. Look for a building, a street name, anything that will give us a lead," Bobby said.

Eric nodded. Bobby was right; he should have been looking around to see where it was. Bobby was hurt. Instead, he panicked because it was Bobby, and he failed. Bobby had been dying right before his eyes. And nothing he did would stop the bleeding. He shouldn't bleed like that. Something had to be wrong with Bobby. Reaching out, Eric grabbed

Bobby's hand and dove into his body. There must be a reason he couldn't stop the bleeding.

Startled, Bobby almost snatched his hand back from Eric. The closed eyes and deep concentration look on Eric's face stopped him. He had seen that look when Eric was healing. Only Bobby didn't have anything wrong with him. Did he?

Releasing Bobby's hand, Eric opened his eyes. "Vitamin K," Eric said. "I want you to start taking it today. Or let me give you an injection of it when we get to the clinic in the morning." He looked over at Higgins. "Give me your hand," Eric demanded. Higgins' eyebrows twitched up and down, and his face was sour, but he gave Eric his hand.

Again, the deep concentration came to Eric's face. He didn't take a long time with Higgins. Yet, when he let go of Higgins' hand, he seemed to wilt slightly. "You are okay. Ronny, let me examine you, too."

Nervously, Ronny gave Eric his hand. The time Eric had detected rabies in a dog that had bitten him flashed in Ronny's mind. He didn't hesitate to let his friend do his thing for him. Ronny felt he was forever owed Eric, having been saved more than once by his friend's weird powers. He was relieved when Eric said he was okay.

"But," Eric added, "we must get you a vest too. I don't know what is going on. We are not taking any chances on any of you being hurt. Got it!"

Grim thoughts raced through the minds of Eric's companions. They knew that for Eric to be this upset, whatever he had seen had shaken him up.

As they cleared the dishes, Eric froze in vision

mode. Three men stared at him, waiting for him to come out of the vision and tell them what he had seen. Dread sat on Bobby and Higgins' shoulders. They glanced once at each other, the silent exchange between them saying, 'Gear up; we have to be ready.' Higgins readied the laptop, and as he did, he realized he didn't feel the many aches and pains that had become normal in his life. The kid had healed him. I've got your back, kid. No matter what happens, I've got you, Higgins thought.

"A house on Seldom Street. I think it is a drunk man coming home. He has his key out when someone comes up behind him and puts a gun in his back. It is a robbery gone bad. Bobby, it would help if you had your cop friend patrol that street. It felt like just after dark," Eric told them.

Relief washed over Bobby. This was something normal, something he could deal with and solve. He looked at Higgins, who was already calling up information on the street Eric had mentioned.

Chapter Thirteen

RAW

The next few days saw nerves fray. Eric tensed every time they pulled into a parking lot, expecting the worst. The vision, which had been on an endless loop when it started, stubbornly refused to come again. Eric was determined to learn as much as possible from the vision and pass it on to Bobby and Higgins. The more they knew, the better prepared they were for when the vision came to life.

Bobby wanted to rid himself of his vest. The thing was hot, and he could feel one seam rubbing him raw under his shoulder holster. All it took was a glance over at Eric sitting so straight with that haunted expression in his eyes to keep him wearing the dang vest. He'd wear it through Hell if it would relieve Eric's mind. That was the problem with protecting someone like Eric. You ended up being punished in uncomfortable ways to have the privilege of protecting them. He was so lucky to have been assigned to Eric. Bobby laughed at himself as he reached up to wipe the sweat off his brow. Yeah, lucky. He jerked to attention when Eric yanked his phone out and answered it.

Bobby listened to Eric's conversation with his sister, Middy, not feeling the least bit of shame. Listening was a part of his job. He heard Eric agreed to video consult on surgery for a dog his sister found. The doctor on the other end of the call wasn't thrilled at having someone telling him what to do. Then Eric soothed the hurt ego of the man he was talking to. It was something the kid did automatically. He always played himself down and boosted up the other guy. Bobby used to think the kid was a little wimp. Now, well, he knew just how wrong his first impression of Eric had been. Anyone who had the sort of nightmares Eric had and managed to turn them into something positive could never be called a wimp. He had more courage than Bobby had. Imagine facing those demons every night.

The consult on the surgery took some time out of the day. Eric's time on the phone gave Bobby a break from all the drama he had felt from Eric's vision. Only that, too, was a problem for Bobby. He had time to consider his death. Was he prepared to die? He had a will, but had he updated it lately? Another thing was bills. Was there anything he hadn't paid off? When was the last time he had talked to any of his family? Thinking of his death brought out a whole truckload of things he needed to check on. This job. Who could he trust to look after the kid?

Ronny tried not to think of them being in some future danger. He liked to live in the moment. He'd grab onto any happiness he could find. Already in his life, he had to come to terms with two possible grim futures, which was enough for him. His friend Charlie had taken the first hit meant for him. Every day, he lived with the guilt of Charlie being hit by that truck instead of him. The scare with the rabies was next and had shaken him to his core. He could have died a slow and agonizing death from that dog bite if not for Eric. He didn't value Bobby's life any less than anybody else. He was having a hard time believing someone as good at his job as Bobby would walk into danger like that. After all, he had been forewarned. Undoubtedly, the SS man would be too alert to let something kill him now.

Higgins scrubbed the kitchen until he wore out the sponge he was using. His mind considered different ways to solve the kid's foreseen danger. The trouble was he didn't have any clues, and there was nothing he could research on the Internet or figure out on his own. He was used to having some clue to wrap his mind around, no matter how slim it might be. When he started looking things up for Bobby Jay, things he didn't believe were real, he was like a newbie to the online search. Now, he set up things to pull up any database with one keystroke. You have one word of a store logo; he could find the store or stores in the area. Give him the color and shape of a building he could locate by satellite. He could pull up anyone's phone records, birth dates, places they visited, and anything about a person. But he couldn't find an unknown parking lot from the future.

Every time Bobby and Eric left the house, he insisted on knowing exactly where they were going and when they would be there. If the plans change, Bobby better call him and let him know. A week and a half was the time limit left on this threat to Bobby Jay's life. It was a damn eternity. Each time the phone rang, Higgins expected it to be a call that Bobby was down or dead. Without Bruce, Higgins would be tailing Bobby's car day and night to hell with getting some sleep. How could any of them sleep with something like Bobby's death hanging over their heads?

Higgins stopped scrubbing and tried to relax, realizing he had gotten himself worked up again. How did he know? Well, the black panther breathing on his neck was a good clue. Higgins laughed, closed his eyes, and counted backward from one hundred. After a few moments, he opened one eye and petted the black cat, licking his hand. He scooped his puppy off the floor and took the pets outside for the last walk. It was time to pretend to sleep.

Robberies and domestic violence were the only things Eric dreamed about the next few nights. Every time he saw a parking lot, dread filled him. He was having trouble eating and sleeping. He found some relief at work in the distraction of healing his patients. Gone was the excitement over remodeling the clinic. All that occupied his thoughts was the sight of Bobby bleeding to death. He gave Bobby Vitamin K and checked him daily to ensure his blood would clot. The only other thing he could do, since he wasn't dreaming or seeing a vision of the scene where Bobby was dying, was to make sure his own body was fully charged. He had to be ready to heal Bobby.

There were four days to go before the two-week limit on his vision of Bobby Jay dying was over. Eric was almost a walking zombie. He had lost weight, and dark circles were under his eyes. His partner Ronny was beginning to show wear. Four days. If they could make it those four days and maybe two days more, then Bobby would be safe. Four days. An eternity.

Needing a moment alone, Eric walked out of the clinic on the pretense of checking on a dog he had treated. Taking the oversized Rat Terrier out of his boarding cage, Eric placed him on the countertop in the kennel room. It was when he saw the sketchpad he had placed there, hoping to entice Betty to do the drawings. Once Jumper was back in his cage, Eric pulled the sketchpad over and opened it.

He forgot to breathe.

The first picture was his rabbit. It's funny how he considered it his dream vision of a painting on his office wall. The truth was this was Betty's rabbit. It was a rabbit Betty had dreamed about since she was a little girl. Eric had lived those dream moments with her while sleeping in his bed. And here, at last, was the thoroughly done drawing. It was wonderful. She was so talented. He had to figure out how to get her to do the paintings he had seen in his dreams. Eric looked through the sketchpad for ten minutes at one fantastic picture after another. When he pushed the pad back where it had been lying, he realized that for those few minutes, he hadn't worried about Bobby dying. He took a deep breath. Life restarted.

Bobby. He needed Bobby to come to the rescue again. It was the only way to broach the subject with Betty. Bobby had to be the one to discover the drawings and heap praise on Betty. Then, with Ronny's help, Eric could appear surprised, and somehow, they would convince her to paint the pictures for the clinic.

That evening, Eric sat down to dinner feeling lighter inside. One burden was about to be lifted off his shoulders. Higgins glanced over at Bobby and raised his eyebrows in question. With a shake of his head, Bobby shrugged his shoulders. For once, Ronny picked up on the silent communication between Bobby and Higgins. He frowned and looked over at Eric to see if he had seen the little look pass between the two SS agents. It was frustrating that Ronny always felt two steps behind the two agents. True, it was their job to be on top of things, but wasn't that part of his job? Wasn't he supposed to pick up on the silent signals from each pet that came to him with some trauma or illness? Then why couldn't he see what was happening in his home?

Picking up his fork, Eric began to eat his roast and potatoes with vigor. He was eager for everyone else to fill their bellies up so he could tell them his plan for Betty and her drawings. He was enjoying his dinner for the first time since his vision of Bobby. That thought dampened the glow inside him, and he slowed down his eating as he remembered all the blood seeping out of Bobby's chest. The gloom began to close in on him again, smothering the bit of joy he had felt before. He was completely unaware of the looks passed between the three men at the table with him as his mind went over and over the problem of keeping Bobby alive.

"You have something you want to tell us, so spit it out," Higgins said as he got up from the table to bring them a slice of hot fudge cake with a scoop of ice cream.

Eric looked up, startled out of his gloomy mood. "Oh, yes. Betty did some secret drawings of the patients we see every day. They are wonderful, beautiful. I have a plan on how we can discover them," Eric paused and looked up from his plate, some of the earlier lightness coming back into his life. "I think either Bobby or you, Higgins, should discover them. That leaves me out of the equation. Then, well, maybe Ronny can come up with the idea of having her paint pictures of the drawings for the clinic. It keeps everything more believable, and I'm not involved in any of it. We can offer her two hundred per painting. I'll pay for them so the clinic won't be out of pocket. But, here is the thing: it will be by donation, so the clinic makes the checks. What do you think? Will it work?"

Higgins rubbed his chin, his mouth scrunched to the side as if he was thinking hard about it. Bobby was already nodding his head yes. While Ronny just negatively shook his head. They were all staring at Eric as if he were a cauliflower that suddenly had sprouted up in a row of beets. "It keeps me out of sight. I won't even be in the picture, so to speak.

Come on, guys, what's wrong with it?" Eric said, a hint of desperation in his voice.

"If we all play our parts, it could work," Higgins said. He flicked a look at Bobby to see if he agreed.

Bobby turned towards Ronny. "This places a lot on you. Are you willing to participate in Eric's plan?" he asked, having seen Ronny's initial reaction.

Feeling pressured, Ronny didn't know what to say. He knew this was some vision that Eric had had. He just hadn't figured that he was included in pulling it off. There he went, upset over having to take part in a ploy to get a shy girl to paint pictures for the clinic. Hadn't he just been feeling left out of things a moment ago? You can't have it both ways, he told himself. "Okay, but I need you guys to guide me through this. I'm not much of an actor." Ronny laughed as if he were making a joke, and some of the tension left him as Higgins muttered something that sounded like, 'That's for sure.'

Higgins looked at Eric and smiled. The kid was eating his cake and ice cream with a smile.

They talked about how to approach Betty and what they would say until Bobby called a halt and ordered Eric to bed. Eric felt good about their plans. He had faith in his vision of Betty's drawings becoming master paints coming true. Bruce joined him on the bed, and the two communed for a while, with Eric rubbing and petting the cat as he purred his contentment. It had been a good evening. Sleep came without the feeling of dread that had accompanied it lately. And that was all it took to release the nightmares locked inside of Eric.

The first dream was of Betty. He saw her set up in the back of the clinic with an easel painting one of the pictures he would buy from her. There was such a graceful movement in her painting. Before their eyes, the little Chihuahua Twigs came to life. He had the cast on his leg from when he had broken it jumping off the sofa at his home. His good paw was planted on a bag of chips, and in his mouth was a potato chip. The painting captured the personality of the mischievous dog. "Wonderful," Eric whispered in his dream. Betty jumped and looked behind her to be sure nobody was watching her. He could have kicked himself. He'd have kept his mouth shut if he had known it was a vision. A couple of times, he spoke during a vision and saw the person he was in react. It had scared the heck out of him. He didn't want to be a person who controls another. Never. Ever.

It could have been the dread he felt at having misspoken in the Betty vision that caused the vision with Bobby to appear. Immediately, Eric knew it was the vision of Bobby dying. The moment they pulled into the parking lot, the horror-filled Eric nearly paralyzed him. But he had a job to do. He had to find clues to relay to Bobby and Higgins. He made himself look out the window on his side of the car. There had to be a reason Bobby had motioned him to stay back. If he could find the reason, maybe he could prevent Bobby's death. There was an older model car with the trunk open and a tire leaning against it. He told himself to look for the plate number, but Bobby blocked the view, motioning him back. Scrambling out of the car, Eric tried to reach Bobby before it happened. He was fast, but the blast was more rapid. Bobby was thrown back, and the horror began all over again. Blood everywhere. This time, it didn't flow as freely as before. Eric almost got ahead of it. Almost.

It started over again. They pulled into the parking lot, and Eric wasted no time. He looked for the license plate to see the number, ignoring the tire. Only half the plate was visible. EC92, Eric burned that part of the number into his brain. Over and over, he said it. "EC92, EC92, EC92". Bobby blocked the view and was thrown back. Frantically, Eric healed each spot that bled.

He woke with a start and reached for the tablet by his bed. Quickly, he wrote down what little he knew of the car. Then he went to find Higgins. Higgins could start the search by tracking down the owner of the vehicle. He could also put in the information that it was a small bomb that had struck Bobby. They had four days to end this. To save Bobby Jay.

Higgins was outside patrolling the area when Eric found him. He briefly outlined what he had seen in his nightmare. The SS man nodded, his face solemn. He headed inside to begin the search for a car his subject had seen in a dream. Having given Higgins the notes he had made of what he had seen, Eric returned to bed, hoping to get more information from his dreams.

There were no more dreams of Bobby, though. Eric dreamed of an angry father berating his little girl for daring to draw a picture. A Betty dream. This type of dream had become so familiar to him that he didn't try to pick it apart or find why it appeared. He just let the dream happen. As much as he wanted to comfort the child in the dream, he didn't try to speak. Speaking in his dreams, he considered a temptation. It was something that verged on trying to control another person's will.

Morning came with the relief of waking up. There was a slight hope inside him that Higgins had found that car in his dream of Bobby. He had to make himself go for his run instead of seeking out Higgins. Afterward, he showered and dressed for the day.

Ronny was already sitting at the table when Eric finally allowed himself to enter the kitchen. Bobby was close to Eric's heels. The runs were always more challenging for Bobby, although he was fit; wearing the vest during the run didn't allow him to breathe or cool down sufficiently. Eric sat down with Bobby plopping down beside him. They looked up expectantly at Higgins as he sat their food before them.

"Let me get some food inside me, and then I'll tell you what I found out," Higgins told them. He noticed Ronny looked up from his plate with a question in his eyes. For the first time, Higgins realized how it must be for Ronny to live with them and always be the last to know what was going on between Eric and the agents. The boy was the last to learn about something happening or what they were investigating. It had to grate on the lad. Higgins mulled that over in his mind as he ate what his evening meal was for him. Finally, he sat back to give his report. "The partial plate number you gave me, Eric, brought up several vehicles. I eliminated all the newer models and have it down to ten older model cars. I printed out pictures of the types of cars that comprised those ten. I want you to look at the pictures and tell me if you see the type of car you saw in your dream. What happens after that, we'll have to figure out." He gave Eric a folder with pictures of the suspected cars inside it.

Opening the folder, Eric felt a chill. Inside were pictures that might lead them to find the man or woman in his nightmares. The person who hurts… kills Bobby Jay.

The third picture was of the car Eric had seen in his vision. He picked up the photo and stared at it for a long moment. "This one," he said, handing the picture to Higgins. "That is the car I saw. Tell me you can find out who the owner is and end this threat."

It had to be that one, Higgins thought. The others he could account for and ease Eric's mind. But, this one had been turned over to a junkyard. They'd have to physically search to see if the car was still there and if it had been processed into scrap metal. "That is the one at a junkyard. It has a chance of being turned into scrap metal. We have to go there and find out. I can do that before it closes this afternoon. First, I need to take a nap."

"Why can't I go? I could check it out during my lunch hour," Ronny said. He saw the negative look on Higgins' stern face and pressed his case. "Look, I'm part of this too. I need to feel I can contribute at least a little to your work. All I will do is see. I could say I'm looking for spare parts for my old car, trying to get it to run. That will work. Right?"

"One of us will go with you," Bobby stated firmly. He could see the kid wanting to feel like part of the team, but they couldn't risk it- risk him. He was a subject now because of his relationship with Eric. He was not an agent nor a secret weapon like Eric.

Nodding, Ronny was pleased with himself. He had managed to wiggle his way into the inner circle. He took a deep breath, both relieved and elated. Things were looking up.

At lunch, the three of them went to the junkyard to investigate car number three. After parts for the old beat-up fixer that his dad had bought, Ronny acted like a teenager. Eric was the buddy brought along for moral support. Once again, Bobby witnessed Ronny's acting ability.

"I need a starter, a water pump, and the passenger side door. If you have an old wreck around here of the same type as this clunker my dad gave me, it sure would help. I'd be willing to take it apart myself, with Jimmy's help," he told the man in charge of the place. As he spoke, he indicated Eric with his head, indicating he was Jimmy. "Heck, if the whole thing doesn't cost too much, maybe I could pull it home and use the needed parts. What do you think, Uncle Bob?"

Bobby had to hand it to the kid; he could put on a show and make you believe in it. "You'd best take it to my place. Your dad will kill you if you start bringing junk home," he said, playing along with a look of you must be out of your mind.

"Really? You'd let me work on the car at your place. Uncle Bob, you are the man!" Turning to the person they were trying to sway, Ronny looked at him hopefully. "Tell me you have something that will work."

"I had a car that would have been perfect for you to get your parts off of, but it went into the crusher yesterday. Sorry, son. Try me again in a couple of weeks. Those older cars are always being sent here when the owners buy something new," the man said, dismissing them and going over to another junkyard addict looking for a deal on something.

Car three was a no-go. What did they do now?

Disappointment hung heavy in the car as they drove back to the clinic. The stop to pick up fast food didn't brighten Eric and Ronny's expressions. Bobby knew these things didn't often pay off, but he was disappointed. There was a heaviness upon him as if he was being sucked down into a black hole. So much depended upon them having a breakthrough in this case. Not the least of which was his own life. More than that was the feeling he would let Eric down if he did die. The kid would blame himself.

They sat around the main office like bumps in their seats instead of forceful men. The food tasted bland, and the drinks didn't satisfy the thirst inside them for knowledge. Pulling out his cell phone, Bobby updated Higgins by message since he didn't want to wake the man who had stayed up all night getting the lead they had just checked out. Car number three had been crushed. Just like their hope. Like hell!

Bobby slammed his hand down on the part of the desk he was using as a table for his food. Eric and Ronny gave a startled twitch and looked at him as if he had lost his mind. "No more moping around. We have just begun to fight whatever this is. So, Sad Sacks, perk up. Heal some pups and kitties. Go on, get to it," Bobby said.

Eric stood and put the trash from his lunch away. He straightened up a little, but the wear of worry still lingered on his face. When he was a little boy, his mother had never let anything stop her. She'd be near death and still go on. He remembered the times she had left her sick bed, barely able to move, and went to take over doing the dishes from his Aunt Julian. He'd often wondered what gave her the will to continue. Now he thought he knew. She wasn't about to let the rest of them down. Mentally, he shook off the disappointment, the feeling that they were not making progress, and the fear of Bobby dying. He would continue and save Bobby. First, he had pups and kitties to heal. Eric's shoulders went back, and his back straightened the rest of the way as he prepared to face whatever was thrown his way.

Ronny couldn't shake the sense that they had lost their one shot at finding someone dangerous. He gave Bobby a scowling look as he prepared for the after-lunch rush.

For the third time, Bobby checked on Eric. Higgins was out tailing Ronny on a date with some gal he had taken an interest in. That left Bobby to watch over Eric as he slept. The kid's sheets were twisted as if he had battled sleep coming, but finally, Eric was asleep. Taking care not to make any noise, Bobby returned to the living room. Eggshells, he thought, it is like walking on eggshells around here. Keeping the kid safe was wearing him down. Just rest, kid, he thought to Eric. The boy needed a few nights of regular sleep instead of worry and nightmares. Bobby almost envied Higgins tailing after Ronny and his girl. That was something normal. Normal. People thought what was normal couldn't compare to watching over Eric. There was nothing normal about having nightmares every night or seeing things that hadn't happened yet. The kid needed to rest and sleep. Who was he trying to fool, himself? Eric needed to have a nightmare and give them some clues to solve this thing hanging over them.

Bobby walked softly back to Eric's room and looked in on the kid. He couldn't tell if Eric was dreaming or in a deep sleep. Bobby felt so helpless. This thing, the nightmare, was something he couldn't fix for Eric. If he could, he would go into that nightmare world for Eric and save him from all the fear and worry.

Frustrated, Bobby stepped out on the porch with Molly to let the dog and her rapidly growing pups run around before he drove himself mad with worry. Automatically, he searched the grounds around the house with his eyes, looking for anything out of place. The dogs ran and played a bit before doing their business. Molly herded her pups back to the house, tongue flipping up and down in her grinning mouth as she panted. Bobby gave her the hand signal to remain quiet. She had learned to be a shadow when everyone was worried about Eric. The whole household revolved around Eric and his mood.

Bruce growled. Everything flew out of Bobby's head, but his job was with that cat growl. A rolling, eerie sound sent a chill down Bobby's back. He crouched, sweeping the yard and the porch with critical eyes. What had the cat sensed? Molly pushed past Bobby, herding her pups through the dog door inside the house. That set off alarm bells for Bobby Jay. A mother protecting her babies. He motioned Bruce to follow him and set off rounding the house to check all sides. If something was out there, he needed to know which direction it was coming from. He would take a few steps and check Bruce's reaction to see if the cat was upset. Nothing. Not a snarl or a growl the whole trip around the house.

Tense. His body was so tense he could almost feel his muscles tightening up, ready to spring into action. He kept his breathing even and slow, not letting the adrenaline cause him to make a sound. Slowly, he opened the door with his security card. Securing the door and barring the dog door, Bobby allowed a soft breath of relief to escape his mouth. His steps were smooth and measured as he approached Eric's room. With his left hand, he pushed the door open, prepared to shoot anyone who wasn't Eric: nothing, nobody but his subject, asleep, tangled in the sheets.

I'm losing it, Bobby thought as he carefully shut Eric's bedroom door. This whole thing has me spooked like some newbie on the job. Still, something had caused Bruce to growl. Maybe it was a coon or opossum. He had trouble believing Bruce would go off over a coon. Eat it, yeah, he might change and eat the poor thing. But he wouldn't warn against it.

Pulling out his phone, he tapped the number for Higgins. "How is it going with the lovebirds?" he asked when Higgins answered.

"That boy is so smooth the little gal is moonstruck. It almost turns my stomach to watch. Is the kid okay?" Higgins said.

"As okay as ever. Sheets and bedding are a mess. And Bruce growled at something outside. That is why I called. Be careful when you return. It may have been nothing, and he hasn't alerted since, but there is no sense taking chances." Bobby warned.

"You need us to come in? I won't regret pulling the plug on this romance early. Just let me grab Ron Ron, and we'll be there."

Bobby considered having Higgins do just that for a second, then shook himself at how stupid he was. "No, let Ron Ron stay out as late as he wants. Someone needs to get a little action around here. It sure isn't going to be our boy or us," Bobby told Higgins with a chuckle. And it was true. Neither of them had a life. They lived to keep their subjects safe. Bobby had a dim memory of going out on dates like Ron Ron… Ronny was on. This assignment ended all thoughts of having an everyday life. He watched Bruce stalking across the floor to where

Molly lay curled up with her pups. The cat turned his head and stared at Bobby as if trying to tell him something.

"Bobby!" It came from Eric's room. That panic-sounding call had Bobby running full out down the hallway to open Eric's door. Eric was kneeling by his bed, his hands stretched as if covering something on the floor. Damn, the kid was caught up in a nightmare. Should he wake him up or let the dream play out? Walking over, he squatted down next to Eric. "I'm right here, Eric. It is okay. I'm okay. Look up in your dream. Look up and tell me what you see."

He was dying. Bobby was dying, and he wanted him to look up and see what was around them. "I can't, Bobby; I have to heal you."

"Just look up as you heal me. You can do that for me, can't you, kid?" Bobby asked, wanting to reach out and wake Eric but afraid to touch him.

Eric raised his head and stared off across the bedroom. The kid looked almost as if he was about to cry. That touched Bobby more than anything, and he wanted to stop this thing from happening and causing Eric so much pain.

Chapter Fouteen

STRETCHED THIN

Two days to go before they could breathe without worry was what Eric thought when he woke up. Three to be safe. He took a shower and dressed for work, not even realizing he hadn't gone for his morning run. When he went to the kitchen, Higgins was still sorting out what he would cook for breakfast. He glanced up at Eric and raised an eyebrow in question. "What?" Eric asked, puzzled.

"I've never seen you willingly skip your morning run. Have you discussed this with Bruce?" Higgins said, motioning toward where the black cat sat before the door, staring at Eric.

"Oh. No. Bruce understands, though. I have info for you. At least, I think it is info...," his voice trailed off. Eric tried to sort out what he had seen last night. Only he wasn't confident he had been having a vision dream. While Bobby had been bleeding to death on the pavement in front of him,

he had also been squatting beside him, talking to
him. How was that possible?

"Sit down and tell me about it while I get
breakfast going," Higgins said, pointing a finger at
Eric's usual chair. With little effort, Higgins threw
the ingredients for the biscuits together. It wasn't
long before he had the dough ready and formed into
rounded shapes on a baking pan.

"I'm not sure this was a real vision dream,"
Eric began. "It started with the same car and the
tire leaning against it. I didn't get to see anything
new before... Bobby... But then something odd
happened. He squatted beside me as I tried to heal
Bobby."

"The guy by the car did?" Higgins asked,
puzzled.

"No, Bobby. Bobby was on the ground and
beside me at the same time. He kept telling me to
look up. He said to do it for him. So I did. I didn't
think I could, but I didn't want to disappoint Bobby.
So I forced my head up and looked. The explosion
had pushed the car away. It was, for certain, a bomb
of some sort. Funny thing, though, where the tire
had been was some round disk thing as large as the
tire had been. The tire was gone. I pulled a bit of
it out of Bobby's vest, and," Eric stopped speaking,
sitting forward, his head in his hands as if beaten.

"What else?" Higgins prompted.

Eric couldn't speak for a moment, shaking
his head as he relived trying to heal Bobby again.
"Nothing. Everything went black. I don't remember
anything until I woke up this morning."

Bobby Jay had been standing in the doorway

about to enter the kitchen dressed for the early morning jog they usually did. He stopped and stood quietly, listening to Eric tell Higgins about the dream. He hadn't believed that Eric had heard him last night. It wasn't until he heard the kid saying he saw him in his dream that he realized he had penetrated the boy's awareness enough to include him. "I was there," he said, going over to sit at the table. "You called out my name while in the grip of the vision dream. I could tell it was the one where you were healing me. So, I sat beside you in the bedroom and asked you to look up. I didn't believe it would work. It seems I was wrong. You talked about the disk setting where the tire had been. It means that the explosion's force was concentrated in our direction. This has a stink of intent."

Higgins and Bobby shared a look. What that look meant, Eric didn't know. He set that puzzle aside to think about it later. He had to keep Bobby safe for another few days if he could. Tension knots in his shoulders and neck hadn't been there before.

As Higgins began to place plates of steaming food in front of Eric and Bobby, a groggy Ronny came stumbling out of the bedroom to plop down at the table. "About time, Ron Ron. I was beginning to think you'd sleep till noon. You look like you are about half here as is," Higgins said, placing Ronny's plate in front of him.

"I'm up and fully functional, old man," Ronny shot back at Higgins, then blushed and ducked his head down to spoon eggs into his mouth and hide his red face. Some tension left the others at this batter between Higgins and Ronny.

Soon, they finished with breakfast and were on their way to the clinic. A car set next to the clinic's front door with a heavy-set woman behind the wheel. She opened her door when they pulled up and ran to their vehicle. "Hurry, Pumpkin was hit by a car. He needs help. Please, doctors, you must help him."

Pumpkin, if Eric remembered right, was a hugely overweight Saint Bernard. Eric had tried to make the woman understand that she was not doing Pumpkin any favors by overfeeding him. He and Ronny approached the rear seat of the woman's car. It would take both of them to carry the dog inside. How Mrs. Carmichael managed to get Pumpkin into the car was one of those things that went beyond explaining.

It took all of them to carry Pumpkin into the clinic. Eric directed them to his private healing room immediately. Pumpkin's skin had been jerked half off his body by the car which had hit him. The dog was a quivering mass of raw flesh and pain. Embedded in the raw areas of the dog was a lot of debris. Bits of roadside gravel and grass contaminated the whole region. Ronny looked up at Eric and just shook his head. He was at a loss on how to treat such a massively damaged area.

"Take Mrs. Carmichael to the waiting area and convince her to go home. I'll start cleaning the area. We need to keep the tissue moist until the skin can be pulled back up over it. Could you take me off the books for patients?

While Ronny carried a whole load of daily

clients, Eric worked over Pumpkin's mangled body. All of the skin ripped free from Pumpkin's body was still attached. It looked like the fat on the dog's body couldn't hold on to the skin when the force of the car dragged Pumpkin along the road. Occasionally, Eric would send healing force into the large dog, keeping the tissue from becoming infected with bacteria. All morning, Eric cleaned the dog, and Ronny, Bobby, and Betty came in from time to time to help him along. The constant strain of fighting off the invasion of infection was taking its toll on Eric. By eleven that morning, he was needing an IV for himself. Bobby cared for Eric, hooking him to one of the life-saving Andy Bags. Betty was not allowed to enter the healing room after that.

As Bobby Jay inserted the catheter into Eric's arm, a vision hit Eric. He saw Middy lying pale and limp among what appeared to be a destroyed building. She looked at first dead but then took a breath. The vision flashed forward with Middy being held in Ritter's arms and him trying to force some of the protein drink down her. Eric's sister was near death. Gasping, Eric came out of the vision. He tried to pull his arm away from Bobby, but Bobby was too strong for him to break free. His first instinct was to go save Middy. Feeling frantic, he looked around the room he was in confused. The vision had been so clear he thought he was there with Middy and Ritter. "I have to go. My sister needs some Andy Bags. Ritter doesn't have any. I have to go. Unhook me, Bobby," he said, still trying to pull away from Bobby's hold.

"Calm down. One of us will take her the

Andy Bags. Let me call Higgins. There is a box of them at the house that just came in. Higgins can prepare a package and take them to your sister. You have Pumpkin here to heal. You don't have to do everything. We are here to help. You know that. Let us help you. Okay?" Bobby reasoned with Eric.

Eric's senses finally registered where he was and what he had been doing. Bobby was right. He couldn't leave Pumpkin when he knew that the dog's only chance of living was for him to heal him. "Okay, we'll do it. Get one of you on a plane to be there on time. He has to go straight to the hospital. By the time he lands, Ritter will be nearly at the hospital with Mids." Eric thought for a moment. They would need someone else to help Ronny cover the clinic while Eric healed Pumpkin. This would be an ordeal-type healing where he could only do so much and have to rest before doing more. It meant holding up here in his healing room day and night. "Go, set things in motion while I'm still able to function," He told Bobby, waving his hand to shoo him on his way.

Reluctantly, Bobby nodded. First, he adjusted the liquid flow into Eric's arm before walking out the door to talk to Ronny and call Higgins. Bobby called Higgins, knowing he was waking the man up. "Eric's sister is going to die unless one of us takes some Andy Bags to save her. Get half of the new box of bags and some setups. Call the airlines or arrange for a private plane for the trip. I have to talk to Ronny and let him know we will be shorthanded. Drop by here with the package and the flight info. Sorry," Bobby said, watching Ronny giving a puppy her first shots. Ronny was going to have to suck it up and stay at home until they had Higgins back.

Handing the little girl the puppy starter kit they gave out to all new dog owners, Ronny smiled at her. He pulled the dog brush out of the kit and showed the little girl how to brush her puppy. Then he gave the little girl a necklace with the words 'I Love My Dog' on it. He could see Bobby hovering in the lab room. Eric could need help, so Ronny wasted no more time seeing the little girl and her mother out of the exam room with the now happy puppy.

"What's wrong?" Ronny asked right off.

Shaking his head to ward off any more questions, Bobby pulled Ronny back into the lab room. "It is his sister. He can't leave Pumpkin to save her. She needs to be on the IVs we hook Eric up to, or she will die. That means Higgins has to take them there and hook her up. We don't have time to wait. Higgins is on his way here, and the flight has been arranged. This means you can't go out on dates until Higgins returns. Understand? You have to stay at home."

Why Higgins? They just excluded him from the whole thing again. "I'll do it. You need Higgins here just in case Eric's vision comes true. I can care for Eric's sister and leave you guys free to double-team Eric." Bobby was shaking his head, about to lay into Ronny, but Ronny wasn't finished. "Listen, I owe Eric. I need to do this to help relieve his mind that his sister is okay. Please don't deny me this chance to help. Please," Ronny said, ready to beg if needed.

His brow furrowed down so low his eyes were hooded; Bobby stood in thought. The kid had a point. If something did happen to Bobby, Higgins needed to be here to take over. The problem was that it left Ronny unguarded. Ritter would be there, Bobby told himself. It made sense to keep Higgins here. All they had to do was get him on the flight there safely. Reluctantly, Bobby nodded. "What about the practice here? Eric won't be in shape to see clients," Bobby said.

"I'll see if Dr. Monroe will come. If not, there is a Temp Agency," Ronny said.

Driving through the security gate from the runway, where he had seen Ronny safely on his way to save Eric's sister, Higgins glanced off across the airport's parking lot. The trouble with parking lots was that they all looked the same if you didn't take in the bigger picture of the surroundings. Eric's vision only showed him a small slice of where Bobby was hurt. It could be any place. Any place in the whole world. Every parking lot was suspect in Higgins' mind. Bobby Jay was the best partner Higgins had teamed up with as a Secret Service agent. He wasn't going to let some scumbag take him out.

Higgins saw parking lots everywhere: grocery stores, shopping centers, schools, theaters, fast-food places, banks, and bus stations. They needed Eric to see anything indicating what parking lot they wanted.

Then there was the car. Bobby had already tipped off his contact in the police force regarding the type of car and the danger of approaching it. But what if a person not connected with the law found the car? Would the bomb be set off? The clock was ticking; they had to find the vehicle.

Back at the clinic, Bobby was thinking along the same lines as Higgins as he watched the guy who had been hired to pinch-hit for Ronny. Having stationed himself between the exam room and Eric's healing room, Bobby was ready for about anything. He'd ensure this new guy didn't steal anything or damage the reputation Eric and Ronny were building. Protecting Eric was Bobby's primary objective. He didn't trust anyone he hadn't vetted himself.

A vibration started in Bobby's pocket. He checked the screening on his cell phone and immediately turned toward Eric's healing room. Looking over his shoulder, he checked on the hired doctor and was pleased that he had just started examining a new dog. Turning, Bobby went to Eric's room and slipped inside.

"I need a meal, then a nap. I don't care what you order, so long as it is hot and filling. Oh, and protein." Eric said as he sank upon the cot in his healing room.

The phone rang at one of the places Bobby used at times like these. When Eric needed food, Bobby looked over at the patient. The dog looked in better shape than Eric did. The once quivering mass of flesh now showed signs of having the skin reattached. Bobby glanced back at Eric, noticing that he was fast asleep already. The kid jerked in his sleep; his hand reached out, and he mumbled something—the vision. Bobby was confident Eric was reliving or instead dreaming the vision again. "Thank you for calling. Please press one if you want to review our specials today." Said the voice on the phone. "Press two to order." Bobby pressed two. He quickly gave the order, ensuring enough for the entire clinic. The workers here had become used to the frequent gifts of unexpected food given to them by the doctors. All Bobby wanted to do was get to Eric and try to guide him through the nightmare he was having.

Hanging up, Bobby squatted down next to Eric's cot. "Listen to me, Eric. You need to look up and see what parking lot you are in. This is important. Look up and remember what you see. I know you can do this, kid. Could you do it? Could you do it for me? Look up at the buildings and anything surrounding the parking lot. Look!" He continued speaking urgently but softly, hoping to penetrate the vision dream and reach Eric. He had managed it once before. He could do it again.

A soft knock upon the door broke into Bobby's concentration. Reluctantly, Bobby stood up and went to the door, slipping out it to prevent Betty from seeing Eric hooked up to the IV. Betty carried several pizza boxes with three bags stacked on top. "Thank you, Betty. I'll take two pizzas, and let me look in the bags. One of them is for Dr. Whiting," Bobby said, sorting through the bags to find the one with chicken in it. He smiled at Betty when he had the bag and relieved her of the top two pizza boxes. "Now, you and everyone else enjoy the rest. We appreciate all the help you all are giving to the doctors."

He watched Betty return to the front office before entering Eric's room. Bobby knew Eric was sweet on Betty, and it concerned him that the boy didn't have a love life. It would take a very special woman to live the life Eric had. Shaking his head, Bobby went over to wake up Eric.

Eric wondered how he ended up in the clinic when he opened his eyes. He had been trying to see beyond the car with the blast plate. Bobby had insisted he look around. The ghost Bobby in his dream had told him to look up from the bleeding body he knelt over. He had seen the car, that dreaded car which represented Bobby's death. The car was smoking, and parts of it had ignited. Look beyond the car, he told himself. Heat waves made the sight beyond the car blurry, yet he saw something. A broken R hung limply from the front of a building. Focus. Concentrating, trying to ignore the bleeding Bobby in front of him, Eric tried to get the name of the place where that broken R hung. That was when Bobby woke him up.

Sitting up, Eric grabbed Bobby's arm and pulled him closer. "A place with a broken R hanging from it. That was all I saw," he said in desperation. "The car was on fire and blocked a clear sighting. Bobby, what does it mean?"

"I don't know, kid. I'll find out, though. Then we will get this bastard." Bobby said, relieved that Eric finally had a clue for them to follow up on. "Let's eat so you can finish healing this poor dog."

They ate in silence. Eric focuses on regaining his strength to try to finish healing his patient. In contrast, Bobby sat eating and did not taste the food. He was on a guilt trip over having used Eric. Part of him felt Eric was a gift, a person who could help prevent a crime or at least see justice done for the victims of crime. The other side of him worried that he was using the kid. Was he causing Eric to have all these nightmares of horrible things being done to innocent people? And he had just finished trying to manipulate the kid during one of his nightmares. But wasn't it worth it if it saved someone in the future? How do you justify using someone as gentle and kind as Eric? The whole thing sometimes made Bobby feel disgusted with himself. Then they caught a guy before he could kill someone, and that seemed to make all the rest of it worth doing. Only, did it?

Weariness sat on Eric, feeling like a mountain he had held up forever. His body wanted to lie down and sleep until next year. His mind would have none of that, and it was determined to heal Pumpkin. Perhaps he was doing too much so soon after all the energy spent healing his sister Middy. This time, the fatigue seemed to wrap around him in a smothering hold, hurting his head. For him to have a headache was unusual. He pushed the pain away and concentrated on eating as much food as he could fit into his stomach. He had a dog to heal, a life to make right again.

Instead of napping as he had initially planned, Eric went back to healing Pumpkin again. He had Bobby renew the fluids flowing into his body and placed a hand on Pumpkin's head. Pumpkin was the most prolonged healing Eric had ever done on his own. There was so much skin to reattach, and the blood was constantly encouraged to flow through to keep the tissue viable. If he couldn't keep the blood flowing through the tissue, it would die, and Eric would have to remove that portion of the skin. It had to stay alive, and there was just too much of the skin to regrow it all on his own. Then there was Middy. His sister had almost died. What if she needed him again? Everything turned dark as Eric passed out from sheer exhaustion.

Bobby laid his subject and, yes, his friend down on the cot and covered him up. Carefully, he inserted a second catheter in Eric's other arm and hooked up another Andy Bag. He placed an electric blanket over Eric, tucking it around him. Setting the blanket to warm but not burn, Eric, the SS agent, turned to check on the dog being healed. Satisfied, Bobby left the room, closing and locking the door. He had to watch the stand-in doctor and inform Higgins of their latest clue.

The clinic was quiet when Bobby stepped out of Eric's room. No yapping dogs or cats meowing could be heard. What now? Bobby wondered. Silently, he crept along the hallway until he could see the exam rooms. Nobody was working. Itchy, wound tight with everything with Eric, Bobby almost pulled out his gun. Then he heard low voices coming from Ronny's office. "So, do doctors buy lunch every day?" That would be the stand-in doctor talking. Bobby relaxed a little and walked towards the office. He noted the lunch sign hung on the front entrance and shook his head at himself. Just the crew eating lunch and not some dire problem.

"No, but they do buy lunch fairly often. I think it has something to do with Dr. Whiting feeling sick." Bobby heard the receptionist say.

"I wondered why he wasn't doing his share of the patients this morning. What is it that he has?" The stand-in asked.

Bobby stepped into the office before anyone could answer the question. "Dr. Whiting has low sugar blood. On days when he feels he can't leave his patient, we order food for everyone. He is a very generous man," Bobby said.

"It must eat up the profits to feed everyone like this as often as they indicated. Is there a business manager to regulate such spending?" Dr. Burrows asked. "Surely you want to recover the cost of acquiring and remodeling the clinic. Spreads like this seem a little overboard to me."

"Is that why you became a veterinarian? To make money?" Bobby shot back at this guy, questioning Eric's reasons for healing.

"Well, yes. And I like animals. Working with them like this seemed a good fit for me. I get paid for doing something I enjoy," Dr. Burrows said, unaware he had irritated Bobby Jay.

"Let me tell you about the first time I met Dr. Whiting," Bobby said. "He wasn't a doctor then, just was in training to become one. He was jogging, and I foolishly decided to jog with him. He is fast and soon outpaced me. We were approaching a pond in the park when suddenly, he sprinted right into the water and dove under. I had no idea what was going on. But, he came up with a pillowcase and several drowned kittens. He worked to save them all, but only one lived. Anyone who will go into a pond to save kittens from drowning doesn't care about the money. They care about the patient." Bobby had a scowl on his face when he finished his tale.

"What's he doing now?" Dr. Burrows asked, realizing he had stepped out of line. This was a cushy job, and he wanted to return here next time they needed an extra hand.

"Healing Pumpkin. And yes, he did have a low sugar level. Thus, the food. Now, eat up before your lunch hour is gone," Bobby said, indicating he was done with the conversation.

Dr. Burrows stood up. "I'll go help him."

"No. You are here to take the exam room. When and if he wants help, I'll let you know. Sit down," there was no mistaking the command in Bobby's voice.

"Look, I was just wondering why you went to the expense of feeding everyone. I'm fine with following the rules here. Okay?" Dr. Burrows said, trying to make amends.

Eric had removed the catheters from his arms when he woke, and his head hurt too much, so he could not sleep. He looked for Bobby and came up behind him, hearing the exchange between the two men. He felt like his head would crack open from the pain inside it and had come seeking out Bobby to see if he would leave long enough to get something for it. But he had an answer for Dr. Burrows. "We are a team here. No one person is more important than the next person. My family has always felt that everyone is equal and should be treated that way. For Bobby and I to have a hot meal sent in, everyone should share it. The only thing we go by is how trustworthy and honorable a person is." He held onto the door frame, keeping himself standing. "I need you, Bobby," he said, trying not to collapse in front of everyone.

Eric healed and rested all evening and into the next day's afternoon. He finally had the skin attached and blood flowing through it. He managed to leave his room long enough to use the bathroom. Passing Bobby, who was checking on the new guy, he told him he needed help. The killer headache had him almost incapacitated now.

Entering his healing room, Eric explained to Bobby how he needed to suture the edges of Pumpkin's skin together. The problem was he needed someone to turn the dog and hold him while he sat and did the suturing. "This is purely to cover how Pumpkin was healed. People will see the sutures and assume what they will. It explains things in their minds." Eric gave a weary sigh. "I can't last much longer, Bobby. I've done all I can with Pumpkin without dying. He probably doesn't need an antibiotic, but we'll send him home with some in case I missed something."

Nodding, Bobby began setting up a suture tray for Eric. By now, he knew just what Eric needed and wanted. Out of the corner of his eye, he studied Eric. Something was wrong. It's more wrong than healing fatigue. He started to ask but then clamped his mouth shut. Explaining might take up too much of Eric's remaining energy.

Carefully, Eric pushed the suture needle through one edge of Pumpkin's skin. He had all the torn, loose skin reattached and the blood flowing through the connective tissues. All he had to do was make these long suture lines connecting the two edges of the skin. He went slowly, making his sutures evenly spaced and as professional as possible. It took all his focus, every bit of his willpower, to push that suture needle through one side of the skin and then up through the other side of the skin. Hiding his skills from others required cosmetic actions such as bandages, sutures, and sometimes braces. There were days when he spent more time putting cosmetic coverings on an animal than he did healing it. It was all part of the act, the cover-up.

Today, however, his head hurt almost too much even to make his hands do the suturing. Sweat dripped off his forehead before he was half done with the suturing. He wasn't aware of the time passing. All he could think about was pushing through the next stitch. Twice, he sat back and put out his hand towards Bobby Jay. The SS agent would place an energy drink or protein bar into Eric's hand. Eric would gulp whatever was in his hand and start working on Pumpkin again.

Bobby's mood is grim as he helps Eric with Pumpkin. His gut was telling him that his subject was in danger. Whatever was going on with the kid was serious. He had watched Eric heal often enough to know that he was pushing himself beyond the resources in his body. Several times, Bobby glanced over at the defibrillator machine, wondering if he needed to start it charging up.

"Now turn him," Eric said, his voice almost a whisper.

Gently, Bobby rolled Pumpkin up on his side.

Already, Eric had stitched up one side of Pumpkin's body and across the dog's back. This final row of stitches would go down Pumpkin's other side almost to his hip. Pumpkin was no longer a quivering mass of raw flesh. He looked almost back to his old self minus his fur except for the stitches. Bobby looked around the healing room at the bloody gauze and lap sponges. It certainly looked as if Eric had been performing surgery in here. Most of it was from cleaning the debris out of Pumpkin's flesh before Eric had begun to reattach the skin. The workers would not have reason to question what went on in there. Now, if they convinced Dr. Burrows, they had it made.

It took another twenty-five minutes before Eric finished the last suture in the long line from Pumpkin's shoulder down to his hip. Fatigue kept causing Eric to stop. If he could quit letting himself reach out and boost the dog's blood system, he wouldn't be in quite so bad a shape. But instinct took over, and he'd find his mind roaming through the connective tissue, ensuring blood flowed and bacteria were not breeding. When he tied the last suture, Eric leaned back in his chair and closed his eyes.

"Lay down and rest now, then we'll move Pumpkin to recovery. I know he will sleep for a good while yet. What do you want us to tell the owner?" Bobby asked.

"Tell them he will recover but needs to rest and only be slowly walked on his leash until the skin has completely reattached. Also, give them one of the weight loss diet plans. And the antibiotics I prescribed. Have Dr. Burrows make up the label and count out the pills," Eric said and looked over at the cot where he usually rested. The headache would ease if he laid down and kept his eyes closed.

"Get some sleep. I'll take care of everything else. You sleep for now," Bobby said, offering to help Eric get to the cot.

"I can't sleep. I'll rest, though maybe that will help just to lay here in the dark and rest," Eric said, wobbling to a stand. His legs didn't want to hold him up, but Eric was as stubborn as his mother and stumbled, walking to the cot. He would have fallen onto the cot if Bobby hadn't gently lowered him.

The SS agent placed a blanket over Eric and turned all but a small lamp off. Burrows wanted to help. He could help him move Pumpkin to recovery. But first... Bobby draped a beach towel over the IV stand and down across where it was hooked to Eric's arm. There is no sense in taking chances. Once done, he gave a searching look at Eric. Eric laid flat on his back with one arm up, covering his eyes. Something was wrong. Bobby felt it in his gut. Giving himself a mental shake, Bobby silently went out the door, securing it behind him.

Bobby checked on Dr. Burrows. He didn't trust this man. For one thing, he asked too many money questions. Someone interested in how much Eric and Ronny made could be looking to take them for some of that money. Eric had to be protected from the slime bags of the world. Everyone was out to exploit someone like Eric. The scientist would love to get their hands on him and make him dream on command. How President Whiting had managed to keep Eric out of the government's hands was a mystery.

Dr. Burrows was washing his hands when Bobby approached him. "Okay, Doc, you wanted to help. Come with me. We need to move Pumpkin to a recovery cage. Then, you will write the prescription and fill it out, which Dr. Whiting ordered. If you are the one who is here when Pumpkin goes home, the owners are to do slow walks until Pumpkin returns to have his stitches removed. Also, we are handing out a reduced diet plan and a measuring cup for his meals. I may be taking Dr. Whiting home shortly so he can rest. Are you good to work till closing?"

Giving Bobby a frowning, puzzled look, Dr. Burrows said, "But he has only seen one patient in two days. I've been swamped all day." Something in the way Bobby looked had Burrows shutting up. His lips were tightly pressed together as if he were suppressing his anger at being used the way he had worked today.

Bobby touched his lips, indicating they needed to be quiet. He unlocked Eric's healing room and went in. Fortunately, they had a dog-sized gurney to transport Pumpkin to recovery. The hard part would be lifting the dog from the treatment table to the gurney and into the recovery cage. Bobby carefully transferred the IV hooked up to Pumpkin to the holder on the gurney. He motioned for Burrows to take one end of Pumpkin while he took the other end. Together, they lifted the colossal dog over to the gurney. Bobby placed a large beach towel over Pumpkin and ensured his IV line wasn't kinked. He saw Burrows look over at Eric and shake his head.

We can scratch this one from future jobs here, Bobby thought to himself.

Chapter Fifteen

A BOMBING HEADACHE

As much as Bobby wanted to monitor the temporary help, he knew Eric needed to be taken home so they could watch over him. Something was up with Eric, and it didn't feel right.

It took an hour and forty-five minutes before Eric was strong enough to walk out of the clinic looking halfway normal. The headache was almost more than Eric could withstand. He was unaware of the things around him as he walked to the car with Bobby. Getting into the car, he leaned back and closed his eyes. The sound of Bobby entering the vehicle from the driver's side penetrated the lancing pain in Eric's head. He felt Bobby lean over and pull Eric's seatbelt across him, then heard the click of the seatbelt fastening.

Bobby chewed on his lower lip, considering whether to ask Eric if he was alright or keep his mouth shut. The kid was his responsibility. It was up to him to keep him safe, even from himself. Bobby started the car and headed in the direction home. As they approached the main highway, it was apparent that it was backed up, and nobody could get on it. Mentally, Bobby plotted out an alternate route home. It would take longer to go the back roads than on the highway, but it didn't look like the main highway would clear soon. Out of the corner of his eye, he saw Eric flinch when he turned the car sharply around a corner to escape traffic.

"Okay, spill. What is wrong? Don't try to bluff your way out of this. Just tell me," Bobby said once he was driving smoothly again.

Eric didn't answer right away. When he did, his voice was strained as if speaking hurt him. "Headache. I have a bad headache."

Bobby took a deep breath. "Okay. Unless you can heal it, I'll stop and get you something to take. Can you heal yourself?"

"No," was the whispered reply.

Bad headache? How bad was it that Eric couldn't tolerate it? Thoughts of brain tumors flashed in Bobby's mind as he watched for a store or shopping mall along the roadways. Nothing. They were in some residential areas. Bobby was surprised at the neighborhood's size as it hadn't looked that large on the maps he had studied to lay out travel routes. There had to be a store near such a populated area. He saw a sign alongside the road stating several businesses were ahead.

A small group of stores and shops was on the right side of the road. Bobby turned the car into the parking lot and heard Eric make a slight sound of pain. "I'll be right back," Bobby said now, more worried than ever about the kid. He thought he heard Eric say, "Wait," as he exited the car.

"Wait," Eric called, his voice sounding weak. As painful as the light was to his eyes, Eric opened his car door and stepped out. He saw a car with a tire leaning against it and a man at the opened trunk of the vehicle. "Watch out!" he shouted at Bobby as he stumbled out of the car. Fear leaped full force upon him as his nightmare unfolded in real life. Bobby was going to be killed unless he could stop him.

Bobby heard Eric's warning and immediately reacted. His first instinct was to protect Eric. Spinning around, he launched himself at Eric, knocking him to the concrete and covering Eric's body with his own. Bobby flipped over; he lay on top of Eric while he pointed his gun in the direction of the car with the tire next to it. That was when it happened. The tire next to the vehicle exploded outward towards Bobby and Eric. Bobby's hands stung with the force of the rubber from the tire and the contents. Whatever flew at them was red, redder than blood. It splattered over Bobby and Eric and hit the side of the car over their heads.

Momentarily, Bobby was blinded by the yuck upon his face. Quickly, he swiped his arm over his face and looked for anyone who could have triggered the explosion. He saw a woman running away holding her child and an older man waving her to hurry to him. Whoever had set this bomb off was gone or hidden. Bobby became aware of Eric struggling beneath him.

"Get off! Let me heal you, let me heal you,"

Eric said, panic evident in his voice, his heart racing with the terror of his nightmare upon him. He had to heal Bobby. This time, he couldn't fail. He tried to buck Bobby off him enough to unpin his arms so he could touch his flesh and start healing him. "Damn you, Bobby! Get. Off. Me."

Realizing how upset Eric must be at thinking his nightmare had come true, Bobby rolled off the kid.

"It's okay. I'm alright," he soothed while scanning the area around them. Where had the bomber gone? Sirens were screaming in the distance as people slowly gathered from nearby stores. He had to get control of Eric and get him safe from everyone's eyes. "Get in the car and lay down. I'm okay. You warned me in time, kid. Do as I say now. We are in damage control mode. You know what to do. You have a headache and were trying to sleep in the back seat when all this happened. Go on."

"Let me touch you first," Eric demanded. He reached out and touched Bobby on his neck. After a moment, he nodded. "Tell them I have a migraine, and we stopped for some pain killer. I took care of your hands," Eric said, crawling into the backseat and allowing Bobby to close the door on him. He had to do damage control on himself. Swiftly, Eric took off his lab coat from work and used it to wipe his face and hands down. He wiped every spot he thought might have been exposed with the lab coat. He finished just as the first police car pulled into the parking lot. Sitting up, he schooled his face into a look of confusion and fear. It wasn't hard to do as he was confused, and the fear from earlier was still upon him. He stuffed the lab coat down the back of the seat out of sight. Hopefully, they had covered up any involvement Eric had in this horror. As Eric punched the last bit of lab coat inside the back of the seat, he saw all the red stuff he had wiped off his forehead and arms. So much red.

Once the officials arrived, clean-up began in earnest. Bobby stepped forward to speak to the first officer on the scene. "It blew up right in front of me, Officer. A man was standing towards the rear of the car. Leaning against the back fender was a tire. That is what contained the bomb."

Bobby looked down at his hands, which made the officer look at them, too. "Oh, man! We need to transport you to the hospital. Come have a seat in my squad car," the officer said. Is anyone else injured?"

"Hold on, I'm okay. This is just that gunk that was in the bomb. I suspect it is ketchup. It makes me think of French fries," Bobby said. "I think I need that aspirin for my head now." Bobby laughed. "I just stopped to get aspirin, not a bath in ketchup."

The detectives arrived, and Bobby perked up when he saw that his police contact was among them. He waited for Harry to make his way over to him. "Well, Old Sod, imagine you being here. Let me guess, you were out for a stroll, and this bomber happened along?" Harry said.

Bobby started to rub a hand over his face and reconsidered as his hands were still covered in Ketchup. "My subject has a headache. Anyway, we stopped to get him some aspirin. This bomber was a surprise to me. Harry, I need to get my subject away from here. This is the sort of crap I'm supposed to shield him from. A babysitter's job is never done," he joked. Harry had often called him a glorified babysitter.

"Seriously?" Harry had a look of disbelief on his face. "You mean you are actually on the job and not just bullshitting me?"

Looking disappointed in Harry, Bobby shook his head. "I've never bullshitted you, Harry. I've always given you a reasonable excuse, yes. That, too, is part of my job. Honestly, we stopped to get some aspirin," Bobby waved his hand towards the car that had been involved in the bombing instance. "This is all yours, buddy. Just keep us out of it. Okay?"

"What did your… subject see?" Harry asked.

This was the moment Bobby dreaded. He'd have to out and out lie to a man he respected. "He was out of it with his migraine and resting in the back seat. He didn't see a thing." There, he had said it, and it made him feel rotten. He sucked it up, though, because he would do more than lie to protect Eric.

"I need to confirm that for myself, Bobby," Harry said. He continued when Bobby Jay frowned at him. "If I don't talk to him, someone else will ask him questions. I don't think you want that to happen. Do you?"

Shaking his head, Bobby glanced at the car where Eric sat, leaning back against the seat as if in pain. "Okay, but if you upset him, don't be surprised if I clock you one. I take my job seriously. Babysitter or not, I'm the meat shield between him and anything bad." He waited until Harry nodded before taking him over to the car. Bobby kept running all the possible outcomes from Harry meeting Eric. So many of them were not good. In the best case, Harry went away believing Eric was an innocent bystander who didn't witness a thing. The worst case was that Harry saw through everything and began to pressure Eric to have nightmares on demand. Bobby did not want to end up having Harry sign a stack of nondisclosure documents. That would put a heck of a strain on their relationship. Bobby motioned for Eric to lower the window so they could talk as he tried with his eyes to indicate Harry.

Giving in to the throbbing pain, Eric looked pale and drawn. Bobby's look in his eyes made him wary of this man. "Did you get the aspirin, Bobby?" he asked.

"No, sir. Something came up," Bobby said, glancing over at Harry. "This is Harry Brothers. He has a few questions for you. I know you are feeling poorly, but you must do this." Turning to Harry, the SS agent cautioned him to be brief and not to ask personal questions.

Harry pulled out a recorder and turned it on. Bobby reached out and turned it off. "This has to be an off-the-record interview, Harry. Otherwise, you won't be able to question my subject. Okay?" Bobby said.

His mouth clamped rather tightly, and Harry nodded. "Okay, Mr...?"

Eric looked over at Bobby to confirm it was okay to give his name. Bobby gave a slight nod. "Whiting," he said.

"I see. Okay, then. I only have one question.

What, if anything, did you see before or during the bombing?" Harry asked, an edge of wariness creeping into his voice. He had heard gossip about how President Whiting made people disappear if they threatened his family.

"I was out of it for the most part. I have this killer headache. Bobby was going to run into a store and get me some aspirin. I'm not sure what happened besides a loud noise," Eric said, reaching up to rub his forehead where it throbbed.

His mouth twitched like he wanted to ask more; Harry didn't believe Eric for a moment. The detective backed down. "Thank you. That is all I needed." Bull, Harry thought, this guy was outside the car. That wasn't red hair gel in his hair. He wanted to call him on it. To haul him in and make him sweat until he learned the truth. But he owed the SS agent several times over for helping to prevent some nasty shit from going down. The truth was he had come to trust this secretive man. He nodded to Bobby to let him know he was done.

"Harry," Bobby called out as the detective started walking away. Harry turned back to Bobby. "Call me when you find out what went on here." Harry nodded again, keeping his mouth clamped firmly shut.

Eric lay in the back seat and closed his eyes momentarily. "Let's just go home. I think if I lay in my bedroom with the lights off, I'll go to feeling better," he mumbled. Covering his eyes, he tried to relax. This had to be what people called a migraine headache. He couldn't remember ever having a headache before. That wasn't true, Eric thought. I did have a headache once on the night Billy, their goat, was hurt. His first vision was that night when Billy needed help. Since then, his powers have grown. He didn't have headaches, and he didn't catch colds. The only so-called illness he had was the nightmare visions. Perhaps that was why the headache hurt so much. It could be he was being wimpy because he had never felt this sort of pain before.

By the time they pulled up to the house, Eric's pain was like having an endless scream inside his brain. When Eric stumbled, stepping out of the car, Bobby supported him the rest of the way into the house. "Let me call a doctor," he said as he helped Eric to the kitchen table.

"No. No doctor, no hospital," Eric said, his voice more a whisper than anything. He held on to Bobby's arm as he spoke. "You have to promise me no doctor or hospital."

"But…"

"Promise me," Eric pleaded.

Looking down at the miserable expression on Eric's face, Bobby couldn't help himself. "Okay," slipped out of his mouth before his mind could control it. He glanced over at Higgins, whose face was a stone wall.

Higgins shook his head and turned away to dish up the steaming chicken stew he had made for dinner. Bobby Jay may have promised not to take the kid to the hospital, but he hadn't. I'll wait for a while, and if the kid hasn't improved, I'll haul his ass to the hospital myself, he swore to himself. He placed Bobby's bowl in front of him, then scooped the best parts of the stew into a bowl for Eric. Taking the bowl around to where Eric sat, he reached out his free hand, putting it on the kid's forehead, pushing Eric into an upright position. "Don't slump at the table. Have some respect for the cook," Higgins abolished Eric. Hot forehead but cool cheek. That puzzled Higgins.

Bobby and Eric waited until Higgins was seated at the table with his bowl of stew before eating. Bobby broke off a hot portion of bread from the oven for Eric and himself. He passed the bread to Higgins, who gave him a questioning look. Bobby shrugged.

The kitchen was quiet for the next few minutes except for the sound of spoons scooping up chicken stew. Finally, Higgins broke the silence. "Ron Ron is due back later tonight," he stated gruffly. "Do you want to pick him up, or do you want me to go after him?" he asked Bobby.

"You go. I need to wash all this creepy ketchup off me. I think a hot shower will do Eric some good," Bobby looked over to where Eric was slowly spooning stew into his mouth. It looked like the kid was concentrating hard on getting that spoon into his mouth. You have to give him credit, Bobby thought; the kid has just gone through a bombing and looks like death warmed over, yet there he sits, forcing food into his mouth to please Higgins. "Let me shower now, then go. I've got things here."

Did he? Bobby wondered if that was the real question. He had made a promise to his subject which he might not keep. He couldn't keep it if this headache were more than just a headache. His first duty was to protect Eric, even from himself. As much as he longed to linger in the shower and triple suds his body up to get rid of the sense of guilt he felt at having lied to Eric. Bobby rushed through the scrubbing. He was rough cleaning himself, scrubbing his face and upper body so hard he almost raised a rash. Too soon, he was done and in sweats.

Higgins took off as soon as Bobby entered the kitchen again. He wanted to pick up Ronny and have him back here so his mind wasn't split between worrying about Ronny and Eric. He also needed to be here if he had to knock Bobby out to haul Eric to the hospital.

Unable to voice his need for help, Eric motioned Bobby Jay over to help him get to the bathroom. The headache was causing problems with his vision. Every gleam of light was like a knife stabbing into his brain. If he hadn't felt ketchup still on his skin, he would have skipped the shower and gone straight to bed.

"You need help?" Bobby asked, his voice hesitating. It was apparent he didn't want to help Eric into the shower.

"No, I'm fine," Eric managed to tell Bobby. Shutting the door to the bathroom, he sat on the side of the tub to undress. Eric didn't bother to put his clothes in the laundry hamper. For once, he was not the son his mother raised. Instead, he was the child in need of feeling the warmth and the comfort of a bed. Or hiding in a dark closet, only he had outgrown running for the closet whenever he was scared. So he stood under the hot water spray and let it soothe him.

The vision hit him as he stepped out of the shower to grab a towel. He fell, slamming into the floor, his body stiff with the rigor of a vision upon him, not even aware he fell.

Bobby heard the noise of Eric's fall and nearly broke the bathroom door off its hinges, rushing inside. Eric was like the statue he appeared to become when he had a vision. That was the only thing that stopped Bobby from moving him. This was one of those things he often worried about. What could he do should a vision hit Eric at a bad time? He was finding out the hard way. Instinct kicked in after that first moment of indecision. Running to the hall closet, he grabbed several blankets and a pillow. The blankets he spread over Eric to keep him warm. The pillow was placed under Eric's head so he wouldn't face plant into the bathroom's hard tile floor when he came out of the vision. Now, he waited. Sinking, Bobby settled on the toilet seat, prepared to keep vigil.

"Hurry, we are late," the young boy yelled, taking off at a run. A wind stirred his hair, blowing it into his eyes as he ran. "Mom is going to be mad. Give me your hand." The vision seemed to zoom forward as the two boys entered a house.

"Grab your bags. We have to go," Middy told the boys. She held tightly to a little girl's hand as if afraid to let go.

The scene changed to the cabin of a plane.

York, Susan's adopted son, was holding a small child close to him, playing paddy cakes with the child. "Paddy cakes, paddy cakes, bakers man. Roll the dough, roll the dough as fast as you can." Men were loading the plane with boxes and a few bits of furniture. Goldie, their dog, lay next to York, her eyes twitching from person to person.

Again, the scene switched. This time, it centered on a burned-out husk of a home. Smoke curled up into the sky from Eric's house.

Things flashed through his mind, horrible things. People lined up and shot in the streets. Beatings, torture, and people hunting through the garbage for scraps of food or clothing. Massive graves. One horror after another hit him until he wept for the whole country. His world was dying. He and his family were in hiding.

With a gasp, Eric emerged from the vision to find himself on the bathroom floor, covered in blankets. His eyes seemed blurry until Eric realized he had indeed been crying. Slowly, he straightened his body and sat up.

Bobby Jay handed Eric some clothes to put on. The SS man's face was stern-looking as if he were holding himself in tight check. He exited the bathroom and closed the door so Eric could dress.

What the hell had the boy seen? Since this assignment, Bobby has witnessed Eric having a vision many times. Never had he seen the kid cry. Come close, but never cry. Never. It had taken all his willpower to keep from pounding Eric with questions. Something, some instinct, told him now was not the time to question his young charge.

When Eric opened the bathroom door and came out, Bobby knew he had made the right choice. Eric's eyes looked haunted, but he walked alone as if his strength had returned. "Shouldn't Higgins be back with Ronny?" he asked Bobby.

"Soon. Those two probably had some catching up to do. I swear they are like two spoiled little boys at times," Bobby said, trying to lighten the mood.

"Yeah, I know. I think Ronny feels left out of things. Maybe we should include him more. He needs a go-bag like the rest of us to have ready," Eric's voice trailed off at the sound of a car pulling up outside, letting them know Higgins was back with Ronny. He didn't say they all needed more than just a go-bag. They needed a place to go. When the time for the vision drew near, they would have to salvage as much as they could from the house before it burned. Bruce, Molly, and the pups had to be moved by then. And it all had to be done in secret.

While Eric was trying to come to terms with the vision he had just seen, Ronny and Higgins arrived home. Ronny was grinning ear to ear. "Your sister is getting married," he blurted out as soon as he saw Eric.

"What?" Eric's mind had gone completely blank at Ronny's words. Finally, the word 'married' sank into the deep blank hole of Eric's mind. "To Ritter?"

"Yes! He calls her 'Cupcake'. Man, I thought I was going to be shot when I tried to get the Andy Bags to her. I never want to see that many guns pointed at me again. My life flashed through my mind. I had to scream that you'd sent me to stay alive practically," Ronny took a breath after rapidly spilling out how he had been considered a threat to Middy. All the time he was talking, he watched Eric for his reaction. He hadn't expected him to receive the news of Middy's coming marriage so calmly.

Nodding, Eric returned to the first far vision he had seen—the young man delivering an injured man to his mother. "Then the popper is Middy's son," he muttered more to himself than to Ronny or the two SS agents.

"Popper?" Bobby asked. This might be the opening to discover what Eric had seen in his vision. He watched Eric closely, waiting for an answer.

"Yes, I had a far vision of a young man popping into my mother's kitchen with a man to be healed. He called her 'grandmother'. At the time, I didn't know if this would be my son or one of my sister's sons in the future," Eric explained.

Ronny started roaring with laughter, so much that he almost rolled around on the floor. "What's a popper?" Ronny asked.

"Oh, I just think of the power as being that. It is someone who can pop from one place to another. It's like if you wanted to go to the store but didn't want to drive. You think the store and pop, you are there. Mother can pop people away from her. It isn't quiet, though. It makes a sonic boom sound when the person leaves the area," Eric saw the confused expression on Ronny's face and went on. "It is caused by air that is replaced. The surrounding air rushes in to fill the vacant space from the air that went with the person leaving, and BOOM!"

"Cool," an excited Ronny said. "Can you do

that?"

"No, nobody except mother can that I know about. But, this guy could, in my vision. He popped into the kitchen, then popped out, making a booming sound. And yeah, it was cool," Eric said with a slight smile. "Anyway, sometime in the future, Middy, or one of us, has a son who can pop from place to place. And Middy is getting married. So I concluded the boy is hers."

It took two days before the locals had sorted out the bombing instance. An illegal had taken offense at what the butcher shop in the small shopping center sold. It didn't matter to the man that it was what was sold at all the butchers in America. He thought that the country should conform to him, to his country's beliefs. This man had decided to protest using ketchup to represent blood on the following customer who pulled into the center. Nobody had been badly injured or killed, but the act was a form of terrorism. Had anyone known Eric had been hit by the bomb, things would have been worse for the bomber. Bobby's friend Harry had omitted any reference to either Bobby Jay or Eric Whiting.

The vision Eric received of the distant future cured Eric of his headache. Eric realized that as his healing powers increased, so did his vision range. The troublesome thought for Eric was the whole speaking when in a vision bit. The idea of influencing another person in that manner upset him no end. He wanted to think he was a good person, not some mind bully. He had to clear his mind of all the negative thoughts they had a wedding to attend.

Chapter Sixteen

BEAUTY

Freed from the horror of the vision of Bobby's death, Eric's thoughts turned to Betty and how to get her to use her talent to turn the clinic into a place of beauty. They had been sidetracked from the plan to bring out Betty's ability to draw by the need to save Bobby and Middy. Now, except for a few dreams about a thief, they had time to set their plan.

Higgins had pulled the short straw. On the following Sunday, when Ronny had the treatment and checked on the animals, Higgins was to discover the drawings during clinic duty. He didn't want to be part of this whole 'wow, these are great' thing. For him, telling such a lie was hard. He was a tell-the-blunt-truth type of person. People irritated him no end with their shallow lies and pretenses. So it was when he did pretend to take a casual stroll back into the kennel room his expression was one of extreme displeasure.

Betty was freshening the water and litter boxes for the cats boarding. She had finished letting the dogs out and had cleaned their kennels. That grumpy man with a sour face came in just as she placed Fussy Nut's litter box in his cage. Fussy saw a chance to escape and took it. He charged out of his cage, managing to scratch Betty, and then he took off towards the kennel room door. "Catch him," Betty called out.

Startled by the girl's shout, Higgins slammed the door shut and crouched, ready to take on anything. He hadn't been prepared for a fur ball with fangs and claws. Fussy tried to run under the annoying human blocking the doorway. Higgins countered, dropping to his knees and making a wall with his arms. He grabbed at Fussy, missing and receiving a long scratch on his hand. Fussy scaled the bathing tub, reaching the countertop.

Before Higgins or Betty could grab the cat, Fussy scrambled and ran the countertop. Anything in the way scattered off the counter onto the floor. Fussy made his escape under the cat cages. He looked out from his safe spot, glaring and growling at Higgins as if to say, 'You are dead meat.'

"Same to you, you little devil," Higgins hissed at the cat.

Betty nearly laughed at how the sour-faced man spoke to Fussy, but she was afraid to laugh. "Maybe I should get him," she said timidly, not daring to look at the cross man.

"No, Ma'am. It is my job to protect you. Stand back, please," was Higgins' automatic response.

He could shoot the cat. Yeah, that would go down really well with his subject. So scratch shooting the little demon. If this was a wounded animal on the side of the road, how would he handle it? He'd pull a blanket out of the car's trunk and wrap the creature in it. "You want to hand me one of those big towels on the floor, Miss Betty?"

More wary of the man than the angry cat, Betty crept over and picked up one of the beach towels she used to dry the dogs she bathed. Moving slowly so as to not alarm Fussy Nut, she approached the hand Higgins held behind him for the towel. Carefully, she placed the towel in his hand, making sure he had a hold on it before she released her grip. As she stepped back, Betty realized she had forgotten to breathe.

Evaluating the situation, Higgins saw three escape routes for the cat. One was back out the way the cat went under the cages, and another was to run to the other end of the cages and out that way. Lastly, the cat could exit the hiding spot and scale to the top of the cages. They had to block off two options so the cat could only come out from under the cage in one direction. "Take a handful of those towels and stuff them under the cage beside the cat. I'll push that large container of food up against the other side. Then I think I'll be able to reach under the cage he is hiding under, using this towel as a shield. What do you think?" Higgins asked Betty.

Not expecting to have to give a response, Betty froze for a moment, then nodded. She grabbed up three of the towels and began walking along the line of cages, whispering to each cat or small dog in them. She was attempting to seem normal and not a threat to Fussy Nut. When she reached the cage next to Fussy, she crammed the towels under the edge, making as much of a blockage as possible. She glanced to be sure the grumpy man was doing his part and not looking at her, then took a relieved breath.

Once the cat was barricaded in, Higgins motioned for Betty to stand back. He wrapped the towel around his hand, ensuring he could move unhindered. He admired the calm way the girl had walked the length of the cages talking to the animals and decided to try that. He spoke in his most relaxed, persuasive voice as he slowly approached Fussy Nut. "Okay, how about you and I call a truce? You let me pick you up and return you to your temporary home. And I won't shoot you. Okay? Who knows, maybe you are a nice little kitty under all that growling exterior. Like I'm a nice man. Let's both be nice for a change."

He was at the cage front. The cat would have to go through him to get loose again, and that wouldn't happen. Shoving the towel under the cage with his hand, he grabbed the cat and pulled it out. It all went remarkably well. Higgins carried the hissing, clawing cat to the cage Betty held open and deposited him. He watched the girl close and lock the cage door before backing away.

As he backed up, Higgins stepped on one of the bottles lying on the floor and fell on his butt. He laughed at himself until his eyes fell upon a page of the open sketchpad on the floor. He picked up the sketchpad and stared at the picture drawn, frozen at the sight.

Hearing the grumpy man fall and then let out a laugh, Betty whirled away from trying to soothe Fussy. With horror, she saw the man had the sketchpad she had thought Dr. Whiting had left her. She had been so stupid, so very stupid drawing. The man would be angry, and she would lose her job. Why didn't he say something? Why wasn't he tearing all the pages up and throwing them at her? Was he going just to kill her?

Amazed, that was what Higgins felt. He forgot the role he was supposed to be playing in this deception. He turned the page to find another drawing that took his breath away. The girl had talent, just like Eric said. He didn't have to pretend his part now because it was true. Looking up at Betty, he saw the resigned look in her eyes. Poor little gal denied it all these years. Not anymore, not if he had anything to say about it. And he sure did have a say. "Ma'am, you are the greatest artist I've ever seen. I've been to some fancy art museums, but never have I seen such talent. May I show these to the doctor? Please?" he begged.

"He'll fire me. I don't want to lose my job." She almost sobbed when admitting her fear.

"No, he won't. I promise you neither he nor Dr. Whiting will ever fire you. Ma'am, I keep my promises. That is a fact," Higgins stated with such certainty Betty thought he might mean what he said. Against her own will, she nodded.

At Betty's nod, Higgins sprang to his feet like a teenager. "I'll be right back. Stay here, Miss Betty."

Walking with purpose in his stride, Higgins entered the clinic. He could hardly wait to see these drawings as paintings. It wasn't that he hadn't believed in Eric's vision of Betty's painting on the clinic walls. He just had thought the kid was love-struck and his perception warped by man longings. Now Higgins could see why Eric was so taken with the paintings in his vision and believed in this girl.

Tucking the sketchpad under his arm, Higgins stopped and watched Ronny examine one of the clinic's sick dogs for treatment. The boy looked like a proper doctor as he looked the dog over. He needed to try getting over his irritability at the boy. So he got drunk when he graduated. Didn't most boys do the same thing? And going after a pretty gal that was just part of the old sex glands kicking in. The kid would grow up and learn a pretty face wasn't everything. Eric seemed already to have a handle on the whole grown-up bit. He was too old for his age. Enough, Higgins thought, they had a job to do, a part to play.

"She is scared," Higgins said. "She is afraid you will fire her over her drawing in this sketchpad. You better damn well reassure her."

Ronny looked up and saw the sketchpad tucked under Higgins's arm. "You got it?" he laughed at his own words. "Of course you did. You can do anything. Is it as good as Eric thinks?"

"More than. Anyone who doesn't think so is blind. We have to commission this girl to do the paintings for the clinic," Higgins stated as he handed the sketchpad to Ronny.

Ronny wanted to snatch the pad out of

Higgins's hands. Eric had built this girl's talent up to be some wonder of the world. Ronny had trouble believing such a drip of a girl was a great artist. He took the pad and turned to the first page, and his jaw dropped.

"That was my reaction, too," Higgins said.

"I need to go talk to her and do my part. Give this pup half a cup of food for now. I want to be certain he can hold that down before we feed him more," Ronny said, already on his way out to the back of the clinic.

She thought about just gathering her things and leaving the clinic. Why wait around to be yelled at? Why not just go and find some other job? Because a grumpy man made her a promise, she believed him. Maybe.

Putting a smile on his face, Ronny entered the kennel room. Betty jumped when he stepped into the room. "Higgins showed me these wonderful drawings of yours. We've wondered what pictures to put on the reception and exam room walls. What better than pictures of our patients? You have solved all our problems," Ronny paused, noticing Betty's eyes widen. "I'm sorry. I did come on rather strongly, didn't I? I am just so excited. We want... need you to paint your drawings into pictures of different sizes. The clinic will pay for you to paint them. Name your price."

"Yo... you want me to paint pictures? I can't," Betty said once she found her voice.

"Why not? We'd commission you to do the work. We'd even give you time free from your duties here to do the paintings. The clinic could draw up a contract if you want one. Just think of your work on display for everyone to enjoy. Do you realize how happy people will be to see their dear pets when coming here?

"I'll talk to Dr. Whiting. I know he will love the idea. Why don't you think about it overnight? Dr. Whiting and I will come up with an offer per painting. You think things over but don't feel pressured into accepting. Of course, we want the paintings, but we all want you to be happy working here. I'm just so excited about these wonderful drawings. I'd like to see them come to life. So please forgive me for coming on so strong. I'll let you get back to work." Ronny backed out of the kennel room, hoping he hadn't made the shy girl decide to leave the clinic.

Higgins was waiting for Ronny to get back. A lot was riding on the kid playing his part. "Well?" he asked the moment Ronny entered the clinic.

"She said she can't. But I left her thinking about the idea. I hope I didn't come on with too much force. She is a shy person. They can be harder to deal with than someone with more confidence," Ronny told Higgins. "It is like a soft dog. Like Molly. We have to talk calmly to her. You know how she shrinks into herself if you aren't gentle. Whereas you could whack Bruce over the head, and he'd give you a dirty look, then eat you. Understand?"

"Ron Ron, I have spent my life protecting people too dumb to live. I'm not one of them," Higgins abolished.

Right. Stick your foot in your mouth, why

don't you? Ronny told himself. Then, anger of his own seeped into Ronny, "Neither am I. My name is Ronny, not Ron Ron. I know you think I'm dumb, but the truth is I'm just young and trying to enjoy what life I have. You guys have shown me the underbelly of life. I've seen how fast a life can be taken from someone. So, I go out on a date now and then. I whoop it up when some landmark is reached in my life. But, like it or not, you must accept that I'm also part of Eric's life. I'm his friend, the only friend he has besides you two." Ronny shut up, figuring he had overstepped again and was about to be on the receiving end of Higgins' grump. The way the SS agent was staring at him made his blood run cold.

"Agreed. From now on, you are going to play your part in things. Of course, that may mean more hiding than carrying the football into the goal zone. Suck it up, and put on your man pants," Higgins finally said.

"Perfect," Ronny said, smiling.

From Eric's expression, nobody would realize he was excited and very nervous. Today, he would play his part in having Betty paint pictures of the clinic's patients. He straightened the papers and pens on his desk for the tenth time while waiting for Betty to come. Bobby had gone back to tell her Eric wanted to see her and her sketchpad. The waiting was beginning to get to him. This was just too important to mess up with a bundle of nerves. He closed his eyes and began to count. There was a soft knock on his office door at number three hundred.

"Come in," Eric called, softening his shoulders. His sister Susan had told him he was often too stiff and straight when tense, making him look stern while nervous. And Susan always knew what Eric was thinking. Susan would have known he was terrified if she had been here now. "Did you bring the sketchpad?" he asked, trying not to appear overly eager.

Betty clutched the sketchpad to her chest as if to protect it. There was no way she could tell from Dr. Whiting's face and manner how mad he was that she had drawn pictures. Determination filled her, but it was fading fast in the face of fear. She felt so exposed, so lost as to what she should do, how she should behave. Experience had taught her to hide her need to draw. She had pretended for so long not to care that outwardly, she never admired a picture or showed emotion when some wonderful painting made her want to cry or smile like the sun was shining. She hesitated just inside the doorway.

"Do you mind if I look at the pictures? Everyone says they are so fabulous. Ronny, Higgins, and Bobby are all so excited. They are like little kids at Christmas. Please, may I see them?" Smiling, Eric extended his hand toward Betty. This was the moment when she either trusted him or not. His heart pounded as he tried to keep his smile soft and inquiring.

Caught. She had been found out and revealed. There was nothing she could do but hand the sketchpad to him. As Betty handed the sketchpad to Eric, she felt her life was slipping away. There would be nothing left for her now. The job she loved would be gone. This kind man would fire her and scowl at her for daring to draw the animals who spoke to her creative side. Even as she placed the pad in Dr. Whiting's hand, she could see images in her mind of the animals, and her hands wanted to draw them.

Dr. Whiting seemed focused on the sketchpad. He had said the others acted like little children, but he was just as bad. She watched his face, waiting for the anger to come out. For her world to end.

Slowly, Eric turned the pages, looking at each drawing. He had thought they were incredible before, but they were even more impressive than he remembered. He was so lost in the pictures he forgot to speak to Betty and reassure her that everything was okay. He could only manage one word when he finally looked up at her. "Wow!"

He turned back to the first picture he wanted for his office. The bunny picture. "I think this one is my favorite. I love how you have caught him scratching his ear. It is so life-like. I want it for my office," Eric paused, realizing he hadn't convinced Betty yet to paint the pictures. "I'd be willing to pay you separately for just this picture. The rest the clinic will buy if you agree to paint them all for us."

Eric looked Betty in the eyes, his heart in his throat. He'd get down on his knees if that were what it took to convince her to paint these into pictures for the clinic, for him. He'd have a part of her with him then forever. "You have such a wonderful talent. We probably will be underpaying you if you agree to do this work for us. As I said, I want this first one for myself. I'm willing to pay you one thousand for this one picture. Please say you will paint it for me."

For the most prolonged moment, Betty's mind was blank. Nothing made sense. It was like being in the middle of a desert all your life, and suddenly, you were in a boat in the middle of the ocean. She had been waiting for something completely different than the words Dr. Whiting spoke. She didn't want to wake up from what must be a dream. Yet, she had to know. "I'm not fired?"

Eric tried to put Betty at ease, hoping his expression didn't change due to his confusion. "Certainly not. If anything, you are being promoted. This is a big promotion, and I'm asking you to take on extra responsibility. Please walk through the clinic with me. We'll look at each room so you can plan out what pictures would be best for them. The hallways should be lined with smaller paintings of every patient you wish to paint. What do you think? Two large pictures per room. And the one for my office will go on that wall. I can almost see them now hanging on the walls."

Finally, Betty's mind processed the fact she was in an ocean. Looking over at the wall, Dr. Whiting had indicated she, too, could see her bunny on that wall. A large picture with only a few flowers surrounding her bunny. The colors were in her mind, and her hands longed to paint that picture. Only, she couldn't. "I can't," she finally admitted.

Can't, not wouldn't. There was a reason Betty felt she couldn't take him up on the offer to be the clinic's artist. "My offer was too low. I understand it wasn't reasonable of me to think we were worthy of your talents. Please agree to help us decide where we can purchase pictures for the clinic. I shall grieve not having this wonderful bunny for my office. Will you help with the decorating? I'm willing to donate an area just for you to study what you plan to put in place of your pictures. I'll even provide paints for you to match the color of the test pictures with the clinic's walls. I'm out of my depth here. Decorating isn't something I'm good at doing. Will you accept the added responsibility of the decorator? It means a slight pay raise and a room to retreat when you have the time."

She blinked, her mind having to shift gears once more. A room of her own? For a wild moment, possibilities flashed in her mind. The pay raise bit didn't even register with her. The thought of a room, a place all her own, took her breath away. Then she remembered to breathe. "Why? Why do you want me to do this?" Betty asked. It had to be a trick, something to put in front of her to be jerked away should she reach out her hand.

"I have faith in you, Betty. I believe in you and your talent. But this is your decision and yours alone. As much as I want that bunny picture, I'd rather see you happy in your work than burden you with doing something you don't want to do," Eric confessed.

"You really would let me paint my bunny?" Betty asked, still not believing him.

"Yes, I'd pay you well for that one picture. It has captured me with every line of the bunny's form. The life you have given that bunny is beauty caught in action and preserved for all time. But I can understand your reluctance to share something so beautiful," Eric said. "I would be honored to have whatever help you give."

"Okay. On the condition that nobody else knows I've painted the pictures," Betty said, giving in to the temptation of seeing her drawings come to life.

If you think about it, the SS was good at keeping secrets. They were constantly in positions where they could overhear the secrets of rich and powerful people. The SS shadowed figures of the government and their families. Therefore, an SS agent needed to be above reproach. Higgins was thinking of the irony of his life since being assigned to protect Eric. Of all the secrets he expected to keep, this one had never presented itself to his mind. So now he was protecting an artist from being discovered.

He didn't protest the concept; it was the fact that this artist deserved recognition for her work. She shouldn't have to live in fear of being discovered. 'The Grumps' settled on him as he entered the darkened clinic to collect the first painting. His job was to take the painting out in the dark of night and have it framed. The idea was that Betty was to appear to buy the paintings once they were all finished.

Bobby and Eric visited the framing shop to pick up the first painting. Eric's painting for his office of the bunny was ready. Higgins had done his part in taking the painting to be framed. Bobby would pick the painting up, supposedly as a gift for Eric. This was the start of the discovery of the artist who would paint pictures for the clinic. Eric and Ronny had always taken photos of the patients they treated. So, they were to be the pictures given to this mystery artist used to paint the images for the clinic. This was the cover to hide Betty's secret. It was the condition she had placed upon the contract with the clinic and Eric. It was not needed in the contract other than to reassure Betty. The team was already committed to doing whatever was required to keep Betty safe. Things had shifted from Ronny being their secondary subject to Betty slightly above Ronny. They wouldn't have admitted this out loud, but inside each SS agent, that shift had occurred.

Eric had his secrets, one he was keeping from everyone. His vision of the future haunted him day and night. He kept hoping to find some clue as to the cause of his whole family going into hiding. Soon, he would have to reveal the truth and let the SS do their thing. They would have to make plans. The future hinged on the SS preparing a haven for all of Eric's family.

As secrets go, Ronny's was perhaps the most common of those held within any circle of people. He was in love. He did not consider what that meant to his love life when he accepted the conditions placed upon him to share Eric's life. The fact that a grumpy SS agent would follow him on his dates had not entered his mind. The knowledge that he was being watched put a huge crimp in romancing a woman. Knowing he had eyes on him when he was seriously in love caused him to have trouble expressing his feelings to the girl who had won his heart.

Higgins arrived at the clinic just as it was closing. He had come to be part of the unveiling of Betty's first picture. It was to be a private unveiling held in Eric's office. The scent of gumbo and other tempting dishes filled the car as he pulled up to unload the dinner he had prepared for them to enjoy on this special occasion. Higgins smiled as he lifted out the pot of hot gumbo. This was made from a recipe his grandmother had given him. She was from Louisiana and had made the best gumbo in the world when she was alive.

Betty was in the back, puttering about doing little things that could have waited until the next day while she waited to be called up for the event. She was nervous, even feeling a bit sick to her stomach. This painting of pictures went against all the rules which she lived under. She would be in trouble if her father learned about her secret painting. All the dogs in the kennel were quiet, having sensed her unease. She had just handed out the last treat when she heard her name called. This was it. She was about to sell her first painting ever. Taking a deep breath, Betty slowly entered the clinic's back door.

Eric felt like a little kid on Christmas morning. He had left the bunny painting wrapped by the framing shop. Betty needed to be there when they peeled the paper off the painting. When Eric called Betty for the unveiling, Bobby Jay locked the front door behind the last clinic employees. Eric wanted this moment to be unique for her. She deserved all the fuss they could make over her accomplishment. He had withdrawn cash to pay her for the painting to avoid leaving a paper trail.

He wanted to take Betty out to dinner to celebrate, but that, too, would have drawn attention to her. Instead, Higgins had cooked a special meal for them and brought it to the clinic. They knew keeping Betty too long at the clinic would bring suspicion about why she stayed late. Every moment of the time was planned out to be brief and memorable for Betty.

Ronny helped Higgins unload their meal from his car. He had wanted to invite his girlfriend to this dinner. But this was Betty's secret to keep, and he had grown fond of the shy girl. His stomach growled as the wonderful aromas invaded his nose. Next to him, with his arms full, Higgins raised an eyebrow. Ronny almost ducked, then chuckled at his reaction. As Ronny chuckled, Higgins was struck by how funny Ronny was with his never-ending appetite, and he gave a little snicker of a laugh. That set Ronny off, and soon, the two of them were laughing so hard that Gumbo almost sloshed out of the pot.

Bobby Jay stood frozen in place for a moment. The sight of Higgins and Ronny carrying on like two young boys was so unusual that it took him a moment to process the information his brain was receiving. The two men saw Bobby and sobered, then Ronny's stomach growled loudly, and they laughed again. Bobby smiled as he helped the two giggling men set up the meal. That boy could put the food away, he thought.

Eric cleared his throat behind his three

companions. The two SS agents' backs went ridged. Ronny blushed. Betty, standing beside Eric, managed a slight smile. Seeing these stern men relaxed was a real treat for her. Her whole life was spent in sober obedience. "You three want to let us in on what is so funny," Eric asked.

Ronny's stomach growled again, and Bobby hooked his thumb in his direction. "The kid is hungry. You think we brought enough food to fill his endless pit?" Bobby said.

Eric put his hand to his chin and appeared deep in thought. "He'll just have to wait. Gentlemen, may I introduce the best artist in the world. Here she is, our own Lady Betty," Eric said, giving Betty a slight bow and waving his hand in her direction. She blushed deeply, her eyes wide and her lip trembling. Eric said, "Today we unveil her first masterpiece, 'Bunny.'" Carefully, Eric tore the brown paper from around the bunny painting. Once the picture was revealed, the room went silent.

The quiet unnerved Betty. Doubt crept into her mind as she wondered if they didn't like her bunny. "I should pay you more," Eric said. "Bobby, help me hang Bunny, please. So we can view it in its rightful home."

Bobby was quick to help Eric hang the picture. Then they all stood gazing in wonder at Bunny.

Ronny's stomach growled loudly, breaking everyone from their muse. "We best eat before this boy starves to death," Higgins joked.

It was over too soon. Eric had wanted to

linger in his office with his friends and Betty all night. But the reality was there with them, lurking in the corners of their minds. They enjoyed the meal prepared by Higgins and were in the company of each other. Most of all, they admired the bunny picture. Eric slipped an extra five hundred into the envelope of money he handed Betty, feeling very satisfied with the transaction. Eric watched her face closely when he paid her. You could tell a lot about a person by how they accepted or gave out money. She managed to surprise him.

Betty stared at the envelope Dr. Whiting had placed in her hand for a long moment. Until now, she had not believed he had meant what he said about paying her for the pictures. Now, with an envelope of more money than she had ever seen before in her hand, she didn't know what to do with it. If her family found the money, it would go badly for her. But Dr. Whiting might be upset if she didn't take the cash. He seemed so happy at the moment. The dinner, the money, and even her bunny picture seemed like some fairy tale come true. There was no place in her life for fairy tales. "I can't take this," she finally said. "The picture is a gift for all you have done for me. This money would cause problems. Please keep it."

Eric placed his hand over Betty's, folding her fingers firmly around the envelope. "You have earned this. We have a contract, remember? You have kept your part of our agreement so far. Let me do the same. I don't want the money to cause you problems, but perhaps we can figure a way for you to have what you deserve in payment for your remarkable paintings," he said, glancing over at Bobby as he talked. "Ideas?"

It was Higgins who answered. "We set up an account in which to deposit the money. Betty will be able to draw out the funds whenever she wants to," Higgins smiled at Betty. "I can make this an almost invisible account. One day, you will be ready to take control of your life. When you are, the money will be there for you. On that day, young lady, I'll let out a whoop of joy for you."

Blushing, with a hint of a tear, Betty handed the money envelope to Higgins. "Thank you." Her arms reached out of their own and hugged the surprised SS agent. Turning, she hugged Eric; it was a quick, embarrassed hug. She backed away quickly. "I best be going. Thank you, thank you all for this special moment." Betty hurried out the door and out of the clinic. Behind her, she thought she heard Higgins say something that sounded like, "If you don't marry her, I will." But she had to be wrong. She wasn't marrying material.

That night, Eric was practically floating. He was so happy for Betty. At least her lifelong dream was coming true. And, thanks to Higgins, they had devised a method of paying her. Life at the moment was good. Yawning, Eric showered and fell into his bed. Bruce climbed onto his chest and swatted playfully at Eric's nose. Eric laughed and reached over, picking up a cat toy attached to a wand with a string. For a few minutes, he played with Bruce, letting the cat chase the squeaky mouse toy around and around on the bed.

Placing the toy aside, Eric petted Bruce, smiling to himself. What a nice way to end his day enjoying a game with his cat. His eyes drifted closed, and sleep claimed him. A dream hit him almost immediately. Betty was hugging him, but she didn't let go this time. He held her in his arms, smelling her scent as he inhaled. His dream self daringly nuzzled her neck. Betty turned her face to his, and they started to kiss.

The nightmare vision hit him like a blast of cold water. Betty sat stone-faced upon the edge of her bed as the person he was inside waved one of Betty's blouses in front of her. He pointed at a tiny spot on her sleeve that Eric almost didn't see. "Paint! This is paint! Don't even try to deny it. You know what happens when you disrespect me. This time, you are going to feel it for more than a day," the man he was inside of ranted at her. His big hands gripped her blouse, ripping it into shreds. Then he pulled back his arm, making a fist. "Stop!" The mental shout was out before he could keep it contained. Eric flinched. He had sworn he wouldn't do this talking in a nightmare again. Only, this was Betty, the woman he loved.

The man hesitated long enough for Eric to gather himself. What if he told this monster of Betty's never to touch her again? Would it work? He doubted just telling him to stop would work. This was a man who enjoyed harming a little child. Why would he quit harming her now? "You have harmed her for the last time," Eric said. "I am inside you now and will make your life hell if you disobey me. You will leave her alone and let her live her life. Always remember, I AM WATCHING YOU!" The big man's hand shook, letting Eric know he was getting through to him. "I see you," he added in the most sinister whisper he could manage.

Eric woke in a cold sweat. He was evil. The proof was in what he had done: manipulating someone with fear. He was a monster, as guilty as one of the murderers Bobby caught and put away. Evil.

Bruce jumped on Eric's chest and transformed. The panther held Eric down, staring into his face. Then he rumbled at Eric just before licking his face. Unbidden, Eric wrapped his arms around Bruce's thick neck and hid his face in the cat's black fur. Bruce didn't know that Eric was a monster.

Chapter Seventeen

CONFESSION AND TRUTH

Breakfast the following day found Ronny irritable and Eric pale and drawn. At first, Bobby thought Eric and Ronny had had a falling out between them. He knew Ronny was the only real friend the kid had in his life besides Higgins and himself. Any trouble between the two young men was of great concern to Bobby. Being the team leader, it was up to Bobby to sort this problem out. He just needed to know what had started the rift between the two friends. He gave Higgins a questioning look, but Higgins was still filled with the afterglow of their unveiling of Betty's first picture. The normally grim-faced SS agent whistled as he set their plates on the kitchen table.

"Blueberry and peach pancakes this

morning, Boys. And I made my special omelet. You've never had an omelet like this one. Eat up, or you will turn the cook grumpy," Higgins said, digging into his breakfast. "We did a good thing for once. That little gal has so much talent. I tell you, when I saw the finished painting, I choked up."

"Yeah, I bet," Ronny mumbled.

For the first time, Higgins became aware that Ronny was in a bad mood. He glanced at Bobby, looking for some clue as to what had the usually carefree kid so down. Bobby just shook his head. They all ate silently before Higgins noticed Eric looking super pale. He studied Eric for signs of illness. Then he looked back at Ronny. Something was up. Couldn't he enjoy one morning of feeling good without worrying about Eric and his friend? His fancy breakfast was wasted on this bunch of sad faces. He should send a plate of his pancakes to Miss Betty. She was bound to enjoy them. "I'll make a plate of pancakes for you to take to Miss Betty today. She deserves a little pampering." Higgins frowned at the others. "And don't you all go in looking like a sack of rotten potatoes either. Perk up, or I'll serve you burnt beans for dinner," He grumbled at the others. That would teach them to spoil his morning.

Giving Higgins a troubled look, Eric sat up a little straighter. Try as he might, but he still couldn't shake his worry. Only yesterday, he had felt like the world was set to right instead of it being a place where people killed people and monsters like him lived. He gave Higgins a slight smile and nodded, trying to project feelings that weren't inside him.

Ronny cleared his throat before speaking, "I won't be here. I have a date."

"Okay, change of plans. Bobby and Eric will have leftover gumbo. I'll eat some a little early," Higgins said.

"No!" Ronny said rather sharply. "I mean, you guys all eat here. I want to go on my date alone," he held up his hand to stop Higgins from protesting. "I want to be alone with Brenda. I can't relax and kiss my gal knowing you are stalking me."

"You won't even know I'm there, kid. I can watch over you without you or your gal seeing me. I'm like the wind," Higgins joked.

"I'll know you are there! Don't you understand? I can't be myself. I'll know you are out there somewhere, watching. Just stay home and let me have a normal date. Okay?" Ronny reasoned. "I need to have a normal relationship with my gal. She means a lot to me. She may even be my future wife. Either back off, or I'll have to find other housing."

Higgins was ready to agree and then shadow the kid without him knowing about it.

He nodded, "Okay."

"You are just saying that, aren't you? Tell me to my face you will not try to be sneaky and follow me," Ronny challenged.

Higgins had the decency to blush. Still, he couldn't allow Ronny to go out unguarded. He looked to Bobby for guidance, raising his eyebrows.

Maybe it is time for Ronny to find his own house, Bobby thought. It would take some of the stress off of Higgins. "How about you let Higgins come along tonight," Bobby raised a hand to stop Ronny from speaking and continued, "Tomorrow, we will start looking for your own house or apartment. First, let me lay down the rules. It has to be in a secure neighborhood. Fenced-in alarm system and security guard included. Second, your relationship with Eric appears professional from now on. These things are for your protection, understand?"

Ronny slowly nodded. What would happen to his friendship with Eric if he went off alone was something else he hadn't considered. Ronny glanced at Eric to find him deep in thought. "Buddy, I don't wish to break us apart, but I need to have a life outside of what is going on here," he said, a pleading note in his voice.

"You are right. I think it is time for you to make your own home. I knew this was only temporary anyway. Don't worry, I'll be okay,"

Eric reassured Ronny. Ronny needed to distance himself from him. After all, he was a monster.

"Then it is settled. This evening, Higgins will eat early and watch over Ronny and Brenda. Eric and I will have the rest of the leftover gumbo. I won't mind that one bit," Bobby smiled at everyone, trying to lighten the mood. What had started to be a feel-good morning had turned into one of gloom. Rising from the table, Bobby said, "Let's get this show on the road. Remember, you need a happy face, for Miss Betty's sake. Don't make her think you regret her having made the bunny picture."

Betty, Eric thought, he needed to be strong for Betty. Standing, he mentally straightened his shoulders and put on as near a happy face as he could manage. Ronny was leaving, and he may have brain surgery to take away his vision power. It wouldn't be all that bad. He could live an everyday life. There would be no need for the SS to watch him any longer. He'd be a doctor if he retained the knowledge. There was no way to tell what else would go when he lost the visions. It didn't matter. At least the monster in him would be gone.

Life goes on no matter what your internal struggles may be. A man was waiting outside the clinic when Bobby pulled the car into the parking lot. Usually, that meant an emergence of some sort. Bobby had been brooding over how to get Eric to talk to him on the drive over, and now there was no time left to speak.

Eric scrambled out of the car with Ronny hot on his heels. They both knew a waiting patient meant an animal in need. The owner was holding a towel-wrapped bundle in his arms. "Thank God you are here," Perry Jones said, his voice indicating he was in a panic. "Snuffles is having the puppies. She has been panting like crazy. Something is wrong. I know she is suffering, Doctors."

"Let's get her inside so we can examine her. Bulldogs often need to have C-sections because their puppies' heads are so large. But let's not go there just yet," Ronny soothed the owner while Eric unlocked the clinic and held the door open for them to enter.

Once they had Snuffles on a warm beach towel, Eric let Ronny take over and went to the back to treat the in-clinic animals. He wasn't surprised when Bobby came back to give him a hand. This was to be expected. The SS agent had taken to hovering around Eric lately. Silently, they gave out the medications and checked and cleaned any wounds or sutures that needed to be treated.

Bobby waited until they were flushing out an abscess before speaking. It had taken him that long to work up the nerve to talk to his subject. "Tell me what is wrong, Eric. I can't fix it if I don't know what is going on with you." He watched as Eric worked on the cat, his mouth set in a grim line.

Taking his time cleaning the abscess, Eric finally finished and medicated the cat before rubbing it on the head and putting it back in its cage. He sighed. Bobby shouldn't have to deal with this monster inside him, but he deserved to know what was happening with Eric. "After we finish treatments, and in my room. This isn't for anyone else to hear," he said as he washed his hands and cleaned the exam table for the next patient.

Cleaning up after the last treatment, Eric tried not to show his dread of what he had to tell Bobby Jay. He had come to look up to this SS agent, his friend. To ruin that with his confession tore his insides up. There was nothing left to do that would delay the inevitable truth being told. His shoulders tense, Eric led the way to his office. He walked over to his cot and sat down to see the bunny picture.

What was so wrong that Eric felt nobody else should know about it? Bobby was beginning to dread hearing this thing that his subject was hiding. The kid looked as if he were heading to the electric chair. Was he dying? Was that it? The kid was sick and didn't want others to know about it. "Are you sick? You know I'll take care of you no matter what it is. I'm here for you, kid. You aren't alone in whatever is going on with you."

"You can't fix this, Bobby. It isn't something you can do to make it go away. It is inside me. I'm a monster," Eric stopped, unable to say more until he gathered his thoughts.

"No, you are not a monster. You are, if anything, an angel put upon the earth to help others. I've watched you die, Eric. Give up your own life to heal someone. A monster wouldn't do that, and they would not sacrifice themselves for someone else. So get that bullshit right out of your head," Bobby said, having to hold back so as not to yell at the kid. What a stupid thing for him to think. He didn't have a mean bone in his body. Now Bobby was angry, wanting to lash out at something. This was not good. He had to keep it together no matter what. That was his job. He had to be in control when everyone else was in a panic.

Eric shook his head and held up his hand to stop Bobby from going on. "You don't understand. People hear me when I'm inside them in a vision dream. I... I threatened Betty's father in one last night. He was going to hit her, Bobby. I didn't know what to do. Anger took hold of me, and the monster came out. It threatened him. I told him I would always be watching him. To let

Betty live her life. I bullied him. And, for that moment, I didn't care that I was scaring him. That's what monsters do. They hurt people. They don't care about anyone but their selves. I don't want to be a monster like them. Let's see if the vision dreams can be surgically removed."

Unable to speak, Bobby stared at Eric as if he had lost his mind. Ironically, that was what Eric thought was happening to him. He felt some monster was hiding inside him to take over and make him harm others in his dreams. The kid had no idea how much good he was doing. Of all the things that Bobby had thought might be bothering Eric, this had not entered his mind. How could he fix this? An idea began to come to Bobby.

"Okay, if that is what you want, I'll look into it. I don't want to, but I'm on your side no matter what. I'll miss knowing the good that your visions do. Since you and I teamed up, we've saved a hundred and ninety-four lives. I don't think anyone has ever saved as many people as you have just by dreaming about them. True, a few we've lost, but even when the father in that home invasion died, we managed to save the rest of the family. The mother and children I keep tabs on because they wouldn't be alive if not for your sacrifice, your nightmares. And your sister. Ronny said she was about to check out when he arrived. You did that," Bobby paused to let his words sink in. "I'll start researching possible surgical solutions tonight. I won't let you down, Eric. We are a team." Bobby shut up and sat back.

Eric gazed up at the bunny picture. It was so beautiful. How could anyone hit a little girl for having such talent? Someone who was a monster could and would. He was so confused now.

The rest of the day, Bobby worried about whether he had said the right thing to help Eric get over his doubts about himself. He didn't know what else to say or do. Eric hadn't said don't bother looking into surgical procedures. This meant that Bobby was obligated to consider whether something like that was possible. Could the gift of nightmare visions be cut out of Eric's brain? He didn't want to face such an outcome. For Eric to stop having his nightmare visions was almost a crime. Never had Bobby felt he was doing something so worthy before. He was helping Eric save lives. The thought of another family not having Eric's dreams warn them in time to be saved just was very bad. They needed to escape all the drama, at least for a night.

On the drive home that night, Bobby broached the subject of Eric and himself going out for the evening since Higgins and Ronny would be gone. "I think there is no reason we shouldn't enjoy a night away from home. Ronny and Higgins will be out. Why can't we go out?" He watched for Eric's reaction in the rear-view mirror.

Eric looked up as if surprised. For a second, his face brightened, and then reality took over. "Ronny and Higgins both need cars. I don't see a way for us to go out unless we tag along with Higgins," he reasoned.

It's not an all-out refusal. Bobby would take it as a yes. "No, but we rent a car on the way home. Ronny can drive this one since it and the driver have tons of insurance. Besides, it has a tracker for Higgins to follow. You and I will take the rent job," He smiled at Eric. "Might be fun doing anything we want. Start thinking of what you want to do," he said as he pulled into a car rental place.

What did he want to do? It was some-thing he had never considered before. They could eat out if it didn't hurt Higgins' feelings. He liked that Mexican place where they ate when he was at Middy's. There was bound to be such a place here, somewhere. Then he wanted to buy another nature book for Betty. Betty must need some more paints by now. But then what? Something just for fun. What was fun? Take in a movie? They could watch any movie at home. What did he like to do? He wanted to run, ride horses, and visit animals. He liked museums.

None of those sounded like fun for Bobby, though. "What has your brow all scrunched up?" Bobby asked, interrupting Eric's thoughts.

"I can't think of anything that would be fun for you too. I mean, the things I like I don't think will be on your list of fun things," Eric admitted.

"What sort of things?" Bobby pestered.

"Running," Eric said and heard Bobby groan. "I want to eat at a good Mexican place. I like museums, riding horses, and visiting animals." He looked up at Bobby. "I told you that you wouldn't enjoy them."

"Wait a minute; there are possibilities there for me. Not the running, though. We can do that at home; I'm all for Mexican food. Museums are not open late enough for us to enjoy one of them. Nor is the zoo. I'm thinking we can arrange a place to go horseback riding. I think we can talk someone into renting us a couple of horses. Why don't we look into those two things?" he said, pulling his phone out as he exited the car to go into the rental place, motioning Eric and Ronny to join him.

As he ushered the boys into the car rental office, he talked to Higgins about the Mexican food and the horses. For once, he felt he had devised a positive plan they both could enjoy. The more Bobby thought about it, the more the idea grew.

As Ronny got behind the wheel of the SS car, it occurred to him that Eric had never gone out and done something that he enjoyed. He was glad Bobby was taking Eric out. And now he was leaving Eric behind so he wouldn't be there to make Eric at least laugh. The thought put a sadness inside him. Then, thoughts of Brenda entered his mind, and he knew that this whole moving-out thing was something he had to do. He checked in his rear-view mirror to see if Higgins was following him. Of course, he was. His temper surged until he remembered this may be the last time Higgins followed him. For the first time, he relaxed as he drove to pick Brenda up from her place.

Frowning, Higgins dropped back a bit from his tailing of Ronny. Not too far back, as he had to be prepared to zoom up and pro-tect Ronny should he be threatened. What the kid didn't know was that, for a while, someone would be following him. It wouldn't be Higgins, as he was recognizable. But, someone would be assigned to shadow the kid until they felt he was no longer in extreme danger.

Bobby and Eric left soon after they had followed Ronny home and cleaned up. They wanted to get the riding in before dark as that was the time limit at the horse ranch. They had changed into casual clothing and dressed for riding. When they pulled up at the ranch where they would be riding, Eric practically bounced in his seat with suppressed excitement. Bobby felt a bit excited himself. It had been a long, dry spell for him. He missed riding.

Two horses were saddled and waiting for them. Bobby looked at them with a critical eye. No, these would never do. He held up his hand in a stopping motion to Eric. The boy reacted immediately, going into defensive mode. "It's the horses, and we are not riding those. We want horses, not something little kids are taught on."

Looking at the horses once more, Eric agreed. These poor things had no life to them. He needed to touch them. "I'll need to touch them. They look in pain."

Reluctantly, Bobby nodded. "Just no deep healing. I want to ride tonight."

It was Eric's turn to nod. "You pick out our rides. I'll help these two."

Approaching the horse wrangler, Bobby didn't give him a chance to start his welcome speech. "These two will not do. It was explained on the phone that we are experienced riders. Let me look at your string of mounts. I'll pick two out unless these are your best," Bobby said.

The wrangler sighed and motioned Bobby to follow him. "You need to understand, ninety percent of the people who call in say they are experienced when they have never seen a horse before. We can't risk lawsuits," he said, glancing back at Eric petting the two trainer horses. "Your partner seems to like them."

"He is concerned about them and wants to make them feel better," Bobby said, giving the horses in the corral a once-over. "The black and the pinto. Let's hurry before we lose the light."

The wrangler smiled. "Most people look at the pinto and think she is a kid's horse. You and I know better."

Bobby and the wrangler quickly saddled the horses. Eric patted the two trainer horses goodbye and mounted the pinto. They didn't take off like two wild, inexperienced riders but allowed the horses to warm up. Bobby grinned at Eric, confident that this would not be the last time they would ride together as they trotted the horses off on a winding path.

An hour and a half later, the two men dismounted. Unused riding muscles let them know it had been too long since either had been on a horse. They didn't care. They might smell slightly horsey, but this night was one of joy. And they still had a marvelous meal waiting for them.

Eric felt so relaxed when they finally reached home that he had no trouble going immediately to sleep. For once, he felt at peace. Different dreams flitted through his sleeping form. They were dreams he never dared to let himself dream. He saw himself kissing Betty, taking her horseback riding, and slipping a ring on her left hand. Eric woke with a start. What? What had startled him awake? It wasn't until he realized that he hadn't had any nightmares that he knew it was because he felt he was missing something. Had the nightmares become such a constant in his life that he didn't feel normal without them? I won't let that thought ruin my first good day in years, Eric told himself and laid back down. Soon, he fell asleep.

Around three o'clock in the morning, the vision hit him hard. He was in the father again. The man was in a rage for some reason. He had his wife by the throat, bashing her face with his fist. "Stop it!" Eric shouted at him.

For all of a second, the man stopped hitting his wife. "Nobody tells me what to do, nobody," the man snarled. The man swung his head to the right and looked at Betty. She was in a heap on the floor, still. Only the slight movement of her chest showed life.

Horror caused Eric to wake up screaming. He rolled out of bed and stumbled towards the bedroom door.

Bobby was up and running at the scream from Eric's room. Higgins isn't home yet, he thought, drawing his gun. Bobby had been waiting for Higgins and Ronny to return. It was up to him to protect Eric and remain alert until Higgins could take over. Nothing was going to harm Eric, ever. The door busted open as he reached Eric's bedroom, and Eric stumbled out.

"We have to go now!" Eric shouted at Bobby upon seeing him. He grabbed Bobby's arm and tried pulling him towards the house's front.

Not questioning why his subject was in such a panic, Bobby used reason to try to calm him down: "You are in your pajamas, kid. At least slip some pants on and shoes."

"What?" Eric asked before Bobby's words reached his brain. "Okay, get the car started. He's killing Betty and her mother. I need to heal them."

Taking his phone out, Bobby asked Eric, "Do you know her address? I'll have the police and an ambulance sent. They can get there faster than we can."

Momentary relief flooded Eric's system. He ran to his computer and pulled the clinic's employees' files. "3415 Rosewood Lane," he told Bobby.

Speaking on the phone to his detective friend, Bobby repeated the address. "3415 Rosewood Lane. That's correct. Send an ambulance. You said you owe me one. I'm calling it in. Nail this creep, Harry. Oh, please send someone to notify my subject right away." There was a hardness to Bobby's voice. He wanted there to be no mistake about what he meant.

"I'm ready," Eric said beside Bobby.

The kid was dressed. Bobby rubbed his forehead as if his head was starting to hurt. "It is best if we leave this to Detective Brothers. There is an ambulance on the way. They will be taking anyone hurt to the hospital."

"Bobby, she was lying in a heap, barely breathing. I can't stay here. I need to touch her. I have to know she is okay," Eric took a breath, "Betty's mom was being beaten and strangled. She is going to need me, too." Seeing how doubtful Bobby looked made Eric desperate. "Please," he whispered.

"Damn," Bobby mumbled under his breath. He looked away as if seeking some solution, some way to keep Eric home. That 'Please' had ripped deep inside him. Closing his eyes in defeat, Bobby nodded. "Let's wait until a patrol guy tells you Betty is hurt. Then, we find out what hospital they are being taken to. No argument. You will appear to be a boss concerned about his employee, right?"

"Yes, sir." Eric would have agreed to wear a wig and high heels and dance through hell, anything to get to Betty. He had to make sure she was okay. "How long?" he asked.

The crunch of tires outside the house answered Eric's question. Shortly, there was

a polite knock on the front door. Bobby went
to the door, looking through the security lens.
Harry Brothers himself had come to give Eric
news of Betty being hurt. "Harry," Bobby said as
he let the detective in.

Harry looked around the room he was
in, thinking to himself how much he liked this
house. It was nice, yet simple. He spied the pale
young man holding onto the frame of a doorway. "Mr. Whiting, earlier we received a call of
trouble at the home of one of your employees…."

"Is she okay? How is her mother?
Where did you take them?" Eric was unable to
keep up the pretense any longer. He needed to
know Betty was okay.

"Eric, give Harry a chance to tell you.
Interrupting will delay knowing," Bobby said,
sounding more like a father than an SS agent.

Harry watched this interaction with
some amusement. So this is what a glorified
babysitter did. He gave Bobby a little knowing
smirk before continuing. "The mother is critical and in intensive care. She may need surgery
before the night is over. Rebecca has external
bruising to the face and some internal from the
brief report I received over the phone. The doctors believe she will fully recover in time.

"The man who did this is dead. Unfortunately, he pulled a gun and threatened to shoot
his wife when officers arrived on the scene. He

made the mistake of trying to shoot one of the officers."

Eric sagged against the door frame he had been clutching in relief. When he looked back up at the two men who were watching him, his mind was set. "Bobby, we have to go. I need to see the mother first; she is the worst off. Let Higgins know the plan. I'll go eat while you call him," Eric turned to Harry. "Thank you, sir. It means a great deal to me that you came here."

Harry raised an eyebrow at Bobby Jay when Eric rushed to the kitchen. "Well, he seems polite, at least," he commented.

"You don't know the half of it. He is the most stubborn, careless, and bravest person I've ever known. His ordeal tonight isn't over yet. There is a box in that closet that I may need later. I'll grab other supplies if you take them to the rental car. Higgins has my car shadowing Ronny. The rental doesn't have squat in it." Bobby was putting some trust in Harry's hands. He hoped he hadn't misread the man.

An hour and forty-five minutes had passed since Eric envisioned Betty's family. To Eric, it was an eternity. He would have run inside the hospital the moment they arrived if Bobby hadn't warned him not to draw attention to himself. He knew that, but his need to get to Betty was overriding his common sense.

The detective, Harry Brothers, followed them to the hospital. Higgins said he and Ronny would be there before long. They had arrived at the house from Ronny's date just as Bobby and Eric were leaving. Higgins had insisted they both take showers and change out of their clothing, which smelled heavily of cigarette smoke.

Walking with quick, measured steps, Harry took Eric and Bobby to the intensive care unit to see Betty's mother. Bobby carried the backpack he had learned to bring when there was a chance Eric would be healing. Harry kept glancing at that backpack. He saw some of the things Bobby had placed in that backpack. There were many questions in his mind. Why did they need IV hookups and those brownish IV bags? Then there were the drinks and some bars of food. What the hell was going on?

It was clear to Bobby Jay that Harry would corner him at some point and bring up the things they were about to do tonight or, instead, this early morning. But, right now, he had to get his boy to a patient before the kid broke down. They entered the mother's room, and Bobby went pale. This was so much worse than Bobby had imagined. No wonder Eric was in such a hurry.

The woman in the hospital bed had been beaten and strangled. Her face barely looked human. She was on a ventilator to keep her breathing. Bobby immediately pulled the curtains to keep anyone from seeing inside the room. He placed a chair close to the bed and made Eric sit in it. Next, Bobby handed Eric a protein bar and a drink from the backpack. It wasn't until then that he turned to Harry. "You need to step out and see nobody disturbs us. We are too exposed here. I know you have questions, but those have to wait," he told the detective. "And I have some papers for you to sign when we are done here."

Papers? Nondisclosure. Shit! No wonder Bobby never spoke of his subject. Harry slipped out of the room and guarded a secret he had yet to learn.

Washing the last bite of the protein bar with the energy drink, Eric reached out and touched Betty's mother. First off, he caught the bleed into her brain and took care of it. Then he healed her airway, ensuring he didn't do so much that his secret would be revealed. If he hadn't had two meals before coming to the hospital, he would be running out of life force by now and need a rest. But, the meals, the boosts, and his recent increase in healing from dying helping his sister saw him merely sagging, not wasted entirely. Thankfully, he had some reserves left for Betty. Once Eric was satisfied that his illegal patient was out of danger, even though she still looked critical, he stopped. "Call the doctor, Bobby. I think she needs to come off the ventilator."

Before doing what Eric asked, Bobby
cleaned up any evidence they may have left. The
bar's wrapper and the empty bottle were secreted
in Bobby's backpack. The chair moved back in
its place.

Harry flinched when the door behind
him opened. He glanced back into the room
and saw the curtains were open again. The room
looked the same way it had been when they
arrived. He watched Bobby go to the nurses'
station and heard him ask for a doctor to visit
the mother's room. "What's up?" Harry asked
Bobby when he returned to the room.

"Betty's mother needs the vent removed,"
Bobby said. "And Eric needs to see Betty." Higgins came rushing towards the two men before
Harry could ask any of the questions burning
inside him.

"I brought the go pack and resupplied it.
Next time, I use the rental." Higgins stated flatly,
giving Harry a stern look. "The kid okay?"

"Other than near out of his mind over
Betty being hurt, yeah. He is done with the
mother, so we must go to Betty's room. Where
is Ronny?" Bobby asked, looking back down the
hallway.

"Shit." Higgins snarled, then marched
back down the hall to find his wayward charge.
A doctor brushed past Bobby, sweeping into the

room where Betty's mother lay like an avenging angel. Bobby sighed and followed him. "Move out of the way. You shouldn't be here," the doctor barked at Eric.

"Yes, sir," Eric mumbles, backing far enough for the doctor to examine his patient. "I think she is waking up."

The doctor threw an annoyed glance at Eric. "Who made you the doctor here?" he grumbled at Eric. Betty's mother began to cough and make choking noises. Immediately, the doctor was focused on her. "Be calm. You have a tube down your throat to help you breathe. If you relax, I can take it out now that you are awake and functioning."

Bobby gave Harry a little shake of his head as if to indicate a 'duh.' Eric was on the move by then, motioning to Bobby to follow. "He has this. I need to see to Betty."

Falling in step with Bobby, Harry was thinking hard about what he was witnessing. Facts as he saw them. 1) Bobby's subject thought he was some faith healer. 2) It was a secret. 3) Bobby believed it. His respect for the SS agent slipped upon coming to these conclusions. "So, his is a sort of faith heal?" he asked Bobby once there were no ears near which might hear him.

A heavy sigh escaped Bobby. "Wait until you've read over the documents you need to sign. I'll blow your socks off, then. Right now, I must ensure my subject doesn't die."

Bobby quickened his steps to catch Eric before he entered Betty's room. "Eric, stop. Eat and drink before you go in there. I'm afraid you will forget once you see her."

Nodding, Eric waited until he had gulped down two energy bars and finished off two of the protein drinks before opening the door to Betty's room.

Chapter Eighteen

SAFE

When Eric finally laid eyes on Betty, he stopped dead still, not approaching or retreating. His heart just seemed to stutter. Bobby is about to walk around Eric and block his view of Betty when life returns to Eric's still form. Before Bobby could protest, Eric was at Betty's side. He reached out his hand and gently cupped her face with it. Quickly, he sought out the worst of her injuries. He was working on the last spot while deciding how much of the rest he could heal without questions being raised when Betty woke up.

Opening her eyes, the first thing Betty saw was Eric's face. She never cried, but tears ran unbidden down her cheeks when she saw Eric. "My mother is dead," she stated in a flat statement.

"No, she is okay. We made certain of that. Your mother and you still have your whole lives ahead of you. Don't you worry about anything, I'm here. I've got you." Eric thought he was being reassuring, but the opposite seemed to happen. Betty began to sob and shake. Instinct took over, and Eric sat on the side of her hospital bed, pulling her to his chest. She cried into his shirt as he rubbed her back and whispered over and over, "It is okay. I'm here for you."

Bobby Jay slipped out of the room, pushing Harry ahead of him. Eric and Betty deserved some privacy. He glanced around for Higgins, spotting him with Ronny, who looked woebegone. He motioned him over. "You have him until I get Harry to sign some papers. Leave them be. I watched until I was certain he was done doing his thing. Our boy used some sense for once. I'm not sure we will get him away from her tonight, though."

"It is about damn time he gave in to his feelings. I only wish this hadn't happened for him to do it," Higgins said, darting a look at Harry. He turned and motioned Ronny to come on over. "You'll be happy to know someone else will do some signing."

Ronny ignored Higgins for the most part and immediately asked Bobby about Betty. "Is she okay?"

Bobby shook his head. "Physically because of Eric, but emotionally, she is a wreck. We are giving them some alone time. Stay with Higgins. Harry and I have some business to take care of." Ronny gave Harry a look of sympathy, nodding that he understood.

Curious, Harry followed Bobby to the parking lot. He had to admit to being intrigued by all the mystery and wanting to see what Bobby was hiding. He watched as Bobby searched the parking lot for his car—not the rental, but the vehicle he usually drove. "You going to tell me why all the cloak-and-dagger nonsense?" he finally asked.

"Get in the car," Bobby said as he opened the trunk and removed a black briefcase. He was quick, but not so fast that Harry didn't see the portable defibrillator or the case of protein bars inside the trunk. After refilling the backpack, he left it in the trunk. They had Higgins pack if it was needed again. Right now, he had to make someone he considered a friend fill out endless forms swearing to die before revealing the truth about Eric.

Settling down in the car, Bobby looked over at Harry. "You will have to sign these nondisclosure documents and swear to never speak about or reveal in any manner what I will tell you tonight. If you break this oath, you will be imprisoned for the rest of your life. Do you understand?"

"You're joking, right?" was Harry's first reaction. Things like this didn't happen in real life. It had to be a joke.

"No, Harry. I'm dead serious," Bobby said, looking Harry in the eyes.

"Shit!" Harry swore, taking the papers from Bobby; he didn't read them; he just began to scribble his name on every line Bobby indicated. After signing the last page, he raised his right hand and swore never to reveal what was told him tonight.

After securing the documents Harry had signed in the briefcase, Bobby sat back and sighed. "You asked if Eric was a faith healer. The answer is no. He is a true healer. But it costs him and drains his life force. He has died a few times from healing. The kid has it rough, and I'll do anything to protect him. All the times I've called you with a tip have been because of him. He has visions, true visions. Mostly, they come in the form of a nightmare. He'll wake up screaming in the middle of the night from them. The first time, I was like you, thinking it was all bullshit. But then, I couldn't take the chance he was right, and he was. He saved a couple and their baby that time," Bobby sat back and looked off into the early dawn. "Sometimes, I fail to locate the person or persons in danger. He blames himself for those times. It isn't always possible to find someone when all you know is the shadowy outline of a building. That bomb he saw it way before it happened, but all he had was a parking lot. He thought I would die in that bombing. It had him scared, silly. The thing is, we only happened upon it because of his headache. He'd had the nightmare about it so often that I was ready when he yelled at me. That is what saved us both. My hands hurt badly, but he healed them before you arrived."

Harry's brows were pulled down in a dis-believing frown. "And you expect me to believe in this bullshit? Bobby, I'm not stupid."

Looking disappointed in a man he thought of as a friend, Bobby nodded. "The oath you swore and the documents you have signed are binding for life. You will never speak of, write about, nor reveal in any manner anything you may know now or in the future concerning my subject. The penalty is harsh, and confine-ment is for life upon breaking this agreement. Do you understand?" he said in a dry tone.

"Yes, I understand," Harry said, realizing he may have lost a friend. "Will you still call me with tips?"

"Yes," Bobby said in that same flat tone. "I best get back to work."

For two hours, Eric held Betty, giving her

comfort and love. Higgins took Ronny home so they could prepare for the day ahead and get a little rest. Bobby stood vigil over Eric while Harry went and questioned Betty's mother. He learned of the numerous beatings the woman had received and how she had protected her little girl by instructing her on how to behave. They lived in a hell made by the husband. Her husband had started beating Betty earlier that night. He went crazy when his wife tried to stop him from taking it out on them. She had thought Betty was dead. Nobody wept for the man who had been killed. All they felt was a relief.

Finally, Betty was ready to see her mother for herself. She needed proof of seeing her to allow her mind to accept that her mother wasn't dead. Following Bobby's instructions, Eric had a nurse come to help Betty into a wheelchair. Bobby had Eric push the wheelchair while he stayed alert to the danger to his subject and Betty.

They had just exited the elevator on the intensive care floor when Eric stopped walking. He stood with his hands clamped on the wheelchair, frozen in place. Thankfully, the hallway was empty. Bobby muttered a near-silent curse once he noticed Eric was in a vision. Betty reached up to touch Eric when he didn't move her forward. Bobby stilled her hand, shaking his head no. To Betty's credit, though she looked confused, she stopped and sat quietly.

A family was getting in their car as they strapped their toddler in the backseat and secured a boy who appeared to be around four in his booster seat. Two masked men ran out of Clyde's Mini Mart. The men forced the parents away from the car and took off in it with the children in the backseat. It was a soon vision. Eric came to his senses, looking around in a panic for Bobby Jay. "It is happening now, Bobby: Clyde's Mini Mart, a family. Masked men pushed the parents away from the cream car they were strapping their children in and took it. Now, Bobby. Now." Eric said, his voice holding panic.

"Calm down, Harry is still here. I'll get him on it right away. You stay with Betty." Bobby said, immediately striding the last few feet to where Betty's mother was resting. He opened the door to the room but stayed where he could still see Eric and the hallway. "Detective, we need you. Now," he called to Harry.

Looking up, Harry blinked. His mind has been mulling over the papers he had signed and the tall tale Bobby had told him. He didn't, couldn't believe it for one moment. But something was going on. Betty's mother had been in terrible shape. Harry had seen enough victims of violence to know her jaw had been fractured.

Yet, here she sat propped up in the hospital bed with only noticeable bruising. Biting his lip, he followed Bobby into the hallway.

Bobby walked to where Eric was still standing with Betty. "I'll take her in to see her mom. You tell the detective what is going on. He is signed in." With that, he took Betty from Eric and left.

"There is a family stopped at Clyde's Mini Mart. Two masked men, one short, one tall, push a man and woman away from their car and steal it." Eric took a deep breath before going on. "Two small children are in the backseat. Please save them. It is a 'now' thing, so it is about to happen. Or has."

I have to treat this as a phone call, Harry thought. He hated being made a fool, which his mind told him would happen. His heart was shouting at him, and if children were in danger, he couldn't take a chance. It's better to be the fool than wrong. Pulling out his phone, he had the dispatcher send the closest car to check things out. Almost immediately, he received a callback. "Brothers," he barked into his phone.

"This is Officer Murphy. We have two slimeballs in custody. The two children are safe in their mother's arms. I thought you'd like to know, sir," Murphy reported.

"Good job. You are a hero, Murphy." Harry hung up. He had some fences to mend.

Turning around, he was about to tell Eric that he had done well, but the guy was gone. Glancing down the hallway to the mother's room, Harry saw the door closing. Fences. The gates in those fences were rapidly closing, and Harry didn't want to be shut out.

Betty was holding her mother as the woman sobbed against her. This scene had played out many times in their lives. Betty's face was sober, with no tears, nothing but the comfort she offered her mother. The mother was an emotional wreck. Bobby and Eric stood tight-lipped beside each other.

Finally, Eric couldn't take standing back any longer. Betty shouldn't have to carry this burden alone. Walking over, he touched Betty's shoulder to let her know he was there. Her mother repeatedly said, "We can't return to that house."

"You don't have to go back. Betty can set up a new place for you to live in. I'll help her if she wants. You rest and recover, and everything will be taken care of by the time you are released," he promised.

"How will we pay the rent and bills?" her mother wailed.

"Betty has a job. With her salary and the extra work she is doing, I don't see a problem," Eric said. He was aware Bobby was listening, ready to step in and stop him if he said something that would lead to questions about himself.

Her mother stared at him and Betty for a moment before nodding. She dried her tears, and Eric stepped back by Bobby to let the two women talk. They whispered, their heads together, planning the future.

Bobby pulled Eric out the door and gave him a thumbs-up. "For a moment, I thought you were going to take them home," he said, then grinned at Eric.

Shaking his head, Eric looked sad. "No, I think they have had enough horror."

"You realize that Betty has already signed the forms?" Bobby asked.

"My fault, it is all my fault," Eric mumbled, turning away.

Bobby grabbed Eric by the shoulders and spun him around to face him as Harry walked up. "You listen to me, Eric. None of this is your fault. You saved them from dying. If not for your vision, Betty and her mom would be dead. Don't ever repeat such nonsense or think it. We don't have a woodshed, but I'll beat your butt just the same. Got it!" he gave Eric a little shake before letting him go. "Go see if Betty is ready to return to her room." Having dismissed Eric, Bobby turned to see what Harry wanted.

"I apologize, I'm sorry I doubted you," he said in a rush to ward off being dismissed like Bobby's subject had been. "I won't again.

You are my friend, Bobby. I don't want to lose that friendship. You have my pledge of silence on paper, but I'm extending my hand in friendship," Harry said, offering his hand to Bobby. He didn't think Bobby would take his hand for a moment, then Bobby grabbed Harry's hand in a tight grip and shook it.

Betty was due to be released from the hospital in the morning, so Eric spent much of his day hunting for houses she might like. When he had several he approved of, he gathered photos of them and the area surrounding them. Ronny was left to handle the clinic with Higgins. With pictures in one hand and a small bonsai tree in the other, Eric and Bobby returned to the hospital.

He was so nervous when he entered Betty's room. Uncertain about whether he had overstepped boundaries, Eric held his breath as he approached Betty. "Hi," he finally managed to speak. He extended the bonsai towards Betty, watching her face light up when she saw it. It was his first time seeing her reaction to one of his gifts.

"It is beautiful," she said. "It is a forever gift. Thank you."

"A forever gift. I like that idea," Eric said before he could stop his mouth. He hadn't intended to say the words out loud. "I have something else for you. Please tell me if I've stepped out of line." With that, he handed Betty the stack of photos. "Since your mom doesn't want to return to your old place, I looked at what was available there. These are what I found. If you don't like them, you can stay in a hotel until you find a place you like."

Taking the photos, Betty looked down at the first one, then back up at Eric. "We can't afford this. I thought you had pictures of apartments," she protested. Then she hung her head and froze.

She's afraid, Eric thought. "I'm sorry, that was stupid of me. I should have asked what you wanted before doing anything. Or better yet, left you to do it all. It will be the hotel then. Whatever you want is what we will do. The clinic will pay the hotel stay as a bonus for your beautiful pictures."

With her eyebrow furrowed, Betty was lost in thought for a moment. Then it suddenly hit her: She didn't have to hide her painting. "I can paint at home," she whispered, as if afraid to voice it out loud.

"Yes, you can paint anywhere you want to paint. People are going to buy everything you paint. Don't sell anything for less than five hundred. They are all worth more than that." Eric confirmed.

"We could buy a house," she said in wonder. "May I see the pictures again?"

"Of course, they are yours." Eric's heart hurt for all this woman had missed out on while living with a monster. Watching her face as she looked over the pictures of the property he had brought, Eric saw hope bloom. She had finally realized she was free to live.

"This one. Could my mother and I see it tomorrow?" she asked.

Eric smiled, and this was the one he would have picked. "Yes, I liked that one too. We'll take you to see the house. And, if you let us, how about a nice meal before or after? It could be to celebrate getting out of the hospital. Would you like to go show your mother the picture?"

After pushing Betty in a wheelchair to her mother's room, Eric and Bobby stepped into the hallway to give the two women privacy. Bobby was watching Eric closely. He had never seen Eric looking so happy. Eric seemed content and at peace. If being with Betty for a few hours made this much difference in Eric, they had to get these two kids together. How was the question? He was glad Betty had already signed the nondisclosure agreement. Maybe he would talk with her and work a little magic simultaneously. "I need to talk with Betty when we return to the room. I'll have Higgins come get you if you don't want to be there," he told Eric.

Eric's face paled before he shook his

head. "No, I have to face her sooner or later. There is no sense in putting it off. I knew this would happen after I thoughtlessly ran off at the mouth in front of her." Gloom and loneliness sat on his shoulders once more.

He stayed quiet as they returned Betty to her room. She was more cheerful and excited about the house than before talking to her mother. This was a side of her that Eric and Bobby hadn't seen before. Bobby hoped he wasn't stealing her joy by doing his job.

Bobby waited until Betty was in bed before clearing his throat to begin his speech. Eric stepped away but sat where Bobby could see him as Bobby started to speak. "What you overheard in the hallway is one of the things that required you to sign several nondisclosure documents and take that oath. Unfortunately, this happened. I apologize for burdening you with this secret," he paused to let his words sink into her mind.

"Dr. Whiting sees visions, doesn't he?" Betty said, glancing at where Eric sat slumped in defeat.

"Yes, when awake and has a vision, he freezes in place. At night, while Eric sleeps, the visions are more frequent, and they come in the form of nightmares when he sleeps. It is why he never tries to get close to anyone. Nobody would understand. Plus, if someone sees him do his thing, they must be processed like you. And I think you know what else he can do," Bobby said.

"He can heal. Is that why you had to give him CPR?" Betty asked, having put all of the pieces together.

"Yes, but it costs him to heal. That is why we built a private room for him to work in. How can you explain how a near-death pet is suddenly fully alive? We have to pretend he did it with surgery and medicine. Now, I need you to renew your oath. Do you swear never to reveal in any manner the things you have witnessed here in the hospital or may see in the future for the rest of your life under penalty of life imprisonment? Do you so swear this oath?" Bobby asked.

Betty looked over at Eric, who sat pale and tense against the wall. "I do solemnly swear never to reveal these truths which have been revealed to me today," Betty swore, then addressed Eric. "Does this mean I can now help you when you heal?"

Surprised, Eric looked up. A little color came back to his face. "I don't see why not. That is if you want to help." A small sun ray seemed to shine through the gloom he was feeling.

"Yes, please," Betty said. And Eric smiled once more.

It took a while for Betty and her mother to heal and adjust. They finally moved into Betty's house from the hotel. Betty returned to work and had a key card to enter Eric's healing room. She insisted on helping him with each healing he did. In the privacy of his room, he received calls from his family. That was how she learned he was also a battery for his mother when she healed.

In the meantime, Ronny found a house and moved out, taking Molly and one of her two puppies. Bruce was upset, mourning Molly. He would call for her all day and night, then lay moping, looking pitiful. The cat only calmed down and slept when Eric was home.

Higgins set up a direct connection to the clinic so Eric and Bruce could see each other. Eric would take breaks and talk to the large cat, which seemed to pacify Bruce. He would lay on Eric's bed, watching Eric as he spoke to him.

That was how Betty learned about Bruce. She was wiping disinfectant along a suture line Eric had made as a cover for healing a dog when Eric sat down at the computer to talk to Bruce. At first, she thought he was talking to her. "You should go out and play for a little while. Or take a nap."

Betty looked over to see if Eric was having a vision. He had his back to her, and she could see a black cat on the screen past him. "I'll take you for a long run when we get home. It would help if you didn't grumble at Bobby. It isn't his fault your Molly moved with Ronny."

Bruce roared and transformed. Eric gave him a knowing look. "It hurts, but she and Ronny are happier. He even plans on getting married. Bruce, be happy for Ronny. You still have me and the others."

Bruce's huge panther head filled the monitor screen for another moment, and then he became a black cat again. "Magic," Betty whispered.

Closing his eyes, Eric tried to center himself before facing Betty. "Of a sort. Bruce shifts when he is upset. He is gentle but misses Dr. Croft's dog, Molly. He thought Molly was his. When Molly had her puppies, he transformed and stood over her the whole time."

"I'd like to meet him. He is beautiful," Betty said.

"Really?" Eric asked, wondering if he could dare to have her over for dinner.

"Yes, I love all animals. You can trust them," Betty's voice drifted off.

She looked sad, and Eric looked for something to cheer her up. "Tomorrow night? Higgins has been after me to invite you for dinner some night. You could see my place and Bruce."

"Could I? I'd like that. I've never had

dinner at anyone's house," Betty said, her eyes sparkling.

Bobby went out and said good night to Tiny. The colossal dog pressed against him, nearly pushing him over. "Do you think you could get along with a cat, Tiny?" Tiny twisted his head and looked up at Bobby. "Is that a yes? I've been considering asking your doctor if I may take you home. Sound good?" Tiny's huge body wagged. "Okay then. It is a go." A good feeling filled Bobby as he hurried back inside to take Eric home.

Higgins looked Bobby and Eric over suspiciously. They seemed too happy. Setting dinner on the table, Higgins took his seat while mulling over what was up with the two men across from him.

They all ate silently, enjoying the homemade chili Higgins had cooked. Bobby broke the silence. "I'm going to adopt Tiny. He has been alone long enough that if someone wanted him, they would have been looking for him. If either of you has an objection, spit it out now." He looked first at Higgins and then at Eric.

"Bobby, this is your home too. I can't believe you would think you aren't welcome to do as you like here," Eric said. He looked over at Higgins.

"What? As you said, Eric," Higgins shrugged, uncomfortable with them both staring at him.

"Then he comes home tomorrow," Bobby said, smiling.

"Now for my news," Eric began. I've asked Betty to have dinner here tomorrow. She wants to meet Bruce. I know it is short notice, Higgins. Sorry."

Higgins sat up straighter in his seat and tried to suppress a grin. "Don't worry your little head one bit. I know just what I want to cook. I've been planning on an all-seafood night. We'll have fried catfish, shrimp, crab salad, coleslaw, and baked potatoes. I'll make some wild black-berry pie with homemade ice cream for dessert. There is one catch," Higgins paused and looked at Eric. "You have to make me a promise."

Eric gulped. He didn't like the gleam in Higgins's eyes. "What?" he asked.

"When you tell her good night, you have to kiss the girl, or the deal is off," Higgins said with a raised eyebrow.

"But…."

"No buts. That's the deal. I've waited long enough for you to listen to your heart. She has been read into the program and knows all about your nightmares. She isn't running away. Neither should you. Man up and take a chance on living," Higgins told him. Red-faced, Eric reluctantly nodded.

That night, Eric dreamed real dreams.

They were filled with Betty and him kissing. Sometimes, she would run away from him in terror. Betty sank against him other times, and he'd feel her heart beating wildly. His mind battled with his heart. The mind told him she wouldn't fare well in his world, and the other gave him hope of having a life with the woman he loved. He woke up wondering if happiness was possible. Higgins had said she hadn't run away when she signed all the papers and was told the truth about him. That much was true. Yet, knowing what he was and living with his nightmares were completely different things. A tiny seed of hope had been planted within him, and his heart had latched on to it, hanging on with all its strength.

At breakfast, Higgins was practically floating on air. He whistled as he was cooking breakfast. Then, he winked at Eric when Eric stumbled to the table, looking all rumpled as if he had tossed all night. Bobby was almost as bad. He looked like a kid on Christmas morning, eager to open his present. Eric, however, was nervous. This day could be a new beginning in his life or end all his distant dreams.

On the drive to work, Eric had two visions. The first was an early morning robbery at a corner stop and shop store. Nobody was shot or harmed in any manner except for mental stress. Bobby had seen Eric freeze in place and had pulled his phone out, placing it in the hands-free port on the dash. Bobby waited for Eric to come out of vision mode.

A gasp escaped Eric as the first vision stopped. He felt he had enough information that the police could immediately catch the robber. Turning, he opened his mouth to tell Bobby Jay about the vision when vision number two hit him. He was inside a ten-year-old little boy. The boy was running. His arms were full of school books and a bagged lunch. Reaching the corner at a crosswalk, he dashed across the street. Tires screeched as a car ran through the stop sign, and the driver saw the boy too late to stop. The car hit the child, throwing him well off the road. The little boy landed hard as the car picked up speed again and sped off.

"First, a mini-mart called 'All We Missed' was robbed. The thief wasn't violent. Immediately after that, I saw a boy hit by a car. I think it was the robber fleeing the scene. The boy was on his way to school. He was thrown off the road, Bobby. I don't think people will see him. It has to be a school near the mini-mart. Please get Detective Brothers on it. The boy may still be alive," Eric said in a rush of words.

"You get that, Harry?" Bobby asked.

"Yeah, I'm on the way there now. I'll let you know what we find," Harry's voice said over

Bobby's cell phone.

Eric worried about the little boy he had seen in his vision all morning while treating patients. While he worried, Betty finished her morning chores and retreated to her office to paint. There, she was free to express how she saw all the animals they treated in the clinic. Her days were spent in joy instead of fear. And she owed it all to Dr. Whiting. Something sparked inside her the first time she looked at the tall, skinny man. She didn't know how important he would become in her life. Tonight, he would show her his home and his fantastic cat. A cat named Bruce. Her heart felt as if it was singing.

Entering the clinic's computer files, Bobby changed the records to show him as the owner of the massive beast of a dog named Tiny. When Tiny was officially his, Bobby walked to the kennels in the back and took Tiny to the bathing area. "You and I are a team now, Tiny. You will have regular baths and mind your manners. Up you go," Bobby told Tiny. He took off his suit coat and rolled up his sleeves. Tiny turned his head, licking Bobby's face, and then sniffed Bobby's gun. "Yeah, that is part of me, so get used to it," he told Tiny, drawing his weapon so Tiny could look it over. While washing Tiny, he looked out the window over the tub, keeping an eye on Eric.

Towards noon, Harry called, letting them know they had found the robber. He had killed himself wrapped in guilt over hitting a child. An hour later, they found the little boy barely breathing, but in time to save him. A weight lifted off of Eric's shoulders. Now, he could worry about presenting Betty to Bruce.

Although Bobby planned to take Tiny home first and pick up Betty, things changed. What he hadn't counted upon was that it was harder for Betty to go home after work to her new house. Eric and Betty had decided that she would go with them. Thus, Eric and Betty end up in the back seat, with Tiny riding shotgun in the front seat.

"We are not certain how Tiny and Bruce will react to each other," Bobby explained as they pulled out of the parking lot into traffic. "So, do me a favor and stay in the car while they meet." He watched for Betty's reaction in the rear-view mirror. Her eyes widened a little, but she nodded.

Eric reached over the seat back and touched Tiny. "I think he understands, Bobby."

"He may, but what about Bruce?"

"Bruce will be accepting. I've put my scent on Tiny." Eric calmly stated. "Just let them work it out."

"I'll try, but for once, I understand how Ronny felt about Molly meeting Bruce." Bobby's doubt was apparent.

They were home too soon, as Bobby still felt a bit of fear. He had felt Bruce's mouth on his throat when Bruce was upset. Once more, he cautioned Betty to stay in the car, and as he exited, he let Tiny out of the vehicle. Blaze flew full force out of the dog door, heading towards Bobby. The young Border Collie slammed on the brakes when he saw Tiny and skidded to a halt.

Bruce walked out of the dog door at a lazy pace. He had smelled the intruders who arrived with his people. He grumbled to himself and sat down, eyes on the first intruder. He watched Blaze make a sliding stop, then turn around and head back to him. The pup knew who was in charge here. The intruder stalked toward him as if he owned this territory. Bruce waited while twitching his tail until the beast was almost upon him before transforming.

Back by the car, Bobby tried to stay calm as Tiny neared Bruce. So far, Bruce hadn't transformed into a panther. Bobby didn't know if that was a good sign or not. When Bruce did change suddenly, Bobby found himself taking a step forward. "Wait," he heard Eric say behind him, and he stopped, never taking his eyes off the scene before him.

Tiny stopped. He stared at the beast in front of him. Something exciting clicked inside

Tiny. He crouched his front end down and gave
a stiff-legged pounce. It was a way of saying
come on, let's play. He pounced again and did
an awkward turning spin to pounce once more.
He stepped closer to Bruce, lifting his paw and
waving in front of the panther. Bruce leaped forward, and the race was on; not that Tiny could
run fast, but he gave it a try. After a short run,
the two fell to the ground, wrestling like two
small boys. It was a brief encounter, stopping
with the pair lying side by side, looking pleased.

"Well," Bobby said as he opened the car
door for Betty, "I think that aged me by a few
years."

"That was beautiful," Betty exclaimed.
"They bonded with a game of tag. I've never
seen Tiny look so content."

Looking over at Tiny, Bobby agreed that
he looked content.

When Bruce saw Betty, he turned back
into a cat and approached with a lazy walk. It
was Eric's turn to be nervous. He relaxed as
Bruce wove around Betty's legs, rubbing against
them. Betty squatted down to scratch Bruce's
ears. Bruce began to purr, and Eric could breathe
again.

Dinner was full of good food and Higgins' tales about life around Bruce. "Bruce
roared about then, and Molly took off as fast as a
bullet and straightened to him. Ron Ron started

trying to wrestle my gun from me to shoot Bruce because he thought Bruce was going to eat Molly. Bruce was having an expected father type of breakdown standing over Molly, panting harder than she was with each labor pain." Higgins said as he gathered the plates off the table. "I thought I was going to have to sedate both him and Ronny."

Soon, it was time to take Betty home. Higgins gave Eric a pointed look to remind him he had to kiss Betty. Blushing, Eric walks with Betty out to the car. "He is not going to give it up," Bobby whispered.

Eric looked at Betty. The trouble was, he did want to kiss her. Carefully, he leaned in. "Thank you for coming," he said, then gave her a light peck on the lips before she slipped into the car.

Chapter Nineteen

FUTURES

On a Friday, Ronny announced he was marrying Brenda over the weekend. He asked Bobby if he should include Eric in the wedding plans. "He will want to come, but let's make it more of a boss attending type thing," Bobby told him. "Send the invitation through the mail. The more you seem separate from him, the better for your safety."

"But, he is more than just a boss. He is my friend, Bobby. And you are telling me to treat him like crap. I don't know if I can do that. It is bad enough not to be able to come to visit. To kick him like that isn't fair to him," Ronny protested.

"Don't you think I know that? Listen to me. When some people thought his grandmother held the secret to curing the flu, which killed so much of the world, they took her. Her husband was beaten and locked in a cell while a doctor dragged her away. She couldn't give them a cure because She was the cure. So they put her in a room with no light and locked the door. I'm not going to let that happen to Eric. Are you?" Bobby asked.

With a gulp, Ronny shook his head. "No."

"We take protecting him very seriously. You know what he can do besides healing. Some people and countries would kill him to prevent him from using that skill. I'm going to do my best to keep him hidden. Okay?" Bobby drove his point home, knowing he was scaring Ronny. Ronny nodded, unable to speak from the lump in his throat. Satisfied, Bobby left Ronny's office.

In the back, Eric was working on how to ask Betty for a date. "Would you like to go to the zoo on our day off?" he mumbled, not looking at her. When she didn't answer, he dared to look up at her and blushed.

Betty wasn't sure she heard Eric correctly. "Like a day trip?" she finally asked.

"Y… yes. We could take one of the cars, and Higgins and Bobby could follow us. I'd make sure they didn't walk too near us. Would that be okay with you?" he said, worried that he'd overstepped and ruined the friendship that had started between them.

"Okay, if I can take a sketchpad," Betty said.

Relief made Eric feel weak for a second, but he stiffened his legs and smiled at Betty. "I work this weekend. Would next weekend be okay?"

Betty smiled back at Eric, nodding. A date! She thought he was asking her on a date, feeling confused and elated.

That night, Eric explained what he wanted to his two SS friends. Both looked anything but pleased. Higgins broke the tension by slapping Eric on the back. "Way to go. You won't know we are there. I'm like the wind, and Bobby is the invisible man." Bobby laughed, and all was right with the world.

That night, Eric went to sleep with a smile on his face. He dreamed that Betty married him. They were at home when Betty's water broke. "Mother, it is time. Where do you want us?" Eric called out. Bruce roared as Eric's mother entered the room. Things flashed forward to his mother, Felith, placing a baby in his arms.

The nightmare started almost immediately after he held his baby. He was caught up in the dream again. It wasn't the first time, nor would it be the last time. There was more of a feeling of urgency as the young man in his dream popped out of thin air into his mother's kitchen. He left as soon as he had the injured man he carried settled, leaving the words "I have to go back." hanging in the air. Then flashes of Middy and Susan with their families came in hurried exits from their homes. Seeing his own home, a smoldering husk of ash preceded the beginnings of horror: deaths and beheadings in public. There was so much death that Eric woke up weeping. He knew it was time to tell Bobby Jay about the dreams.

Eric went for his morning run, something he had neglected doing lately. He was trying to outrun the nightmare, only he knew he couldn't. Bobby tried to keep up, but he might as well have been racing a hurricane's wind. Bruce stayed close to Eric, glancing back to see where Tiny and Blaze were. Tiny was slow and unable to keep up with Bobby, while Blaze ran circles around Bobby and Tiny.

New worry began to form in Bobby's sweat-covered head. Something was wrong with Eric, and it didn't look like anything good.

Higgins finished cooking breakfast as Bobby and Eric showered and dressed for work. Bobby had given him the look when they had returned from their morning run. The something is wrong look. The animals felt it. Blaze was glued to Higgins' legs as if needing comfort.

Higgins sighed; they had one night of happiness; it would have to be enough to hold them for whatever was coming.

The three men sat in silence around the table. Eric didn't even pretend to try to eat as he mulled around in his mind how to begin what he had to tell the others. Finally, he just started talking. "Do you remember when I mentioned the dream about a popper being born into the family?" he asked, waiting for them to nod. "That was the start of a recurring dream. It is of the future, a distant future—maybe six or seven years from now. Middy has two boys and one girl in the dream. Betty and I will have a baby, and I don't know the sex as all I see is the birth."

Higgins got a goofy grin, and a moment of happiness hit him and Bobby before Eric went on. "Then Middy and Susan are being rushed out of their homes. The feeling is urgent. Next, I see this house burned to the ground, and the real nightmare begins. Horror after horror in flashes as if there are too many of them to focus on. People were shot and left in the streets, heads cut off on television as warnings. People are eating garbage. On and on until I wake up."

There was no happiness on Higgins's face now. He was in SS mode, ready for action. Bobby was deep in thought, and then he spoke. "I think we need to prepare somewhere to move the whole family when the time comes. Maybe underground. A conference call with the others is the first thing to do. We'll start stocking future supplies as well," Bobby said and continued to throw out ideas until they had to leave for the clinic.

On the drive to the clinic, Eric said he'd marry Betty as soon as she was willing, and they needed to consider Ronny. Bobby began to have a headache as the enormity of everything sank in. First, they needed a safe place to house a large group of people and supplies to ride out the storm.

On Sunday, Ronny and Brenda were married. Ronny solved the invitation problem by issuing a blanket invitation to the clinic. Eric asked Betty to go with him to the wedding. The two were just general guests, with few people talking to them. It was a simple wedding without all the big displays in the little church where it was held. Betty thought it was terrific. Brenda wore a white wedding gown, and Ronny wore a dark tux. They made a beautiful couple. The whole time, Eric worries about how to protect the wedding couple in the future.

On Monday, Eric worked the clinic alone, with Ronny taking a few days for a honeymoon. Betty proved to be a great asset. The two of them could keep up with Monday's heavy client flow.

Bobby spent his time watching over Eric, seeing that he ate and drank what was needed to keep him going. And making constant calls. The search for a place to hide Eric's family was underway. They were looking for a long-term solution, much as they would prepare for the after-effects of nuclear war. There were already many hidden bunkers that existed. These were ruled out as anyone who could uncover a family already hidden from the world could easily penetrate the secrets of the government.

On Wednesday, Ronny was back at work. He glowed with happiness around him that Eric couldn't help but envy. He counted the days to the weekend when he and Betty would go to the zoo. The rest of the week went by with no difficult healing for Eric and only two nightmare crimes to solve. Fortunately, with Detective Brothers read into the program, things went smoothly.

Saturday arrived slightly overcast, and Eric nervously waited to pick up Betty. He had Bobby give him a refresher course in driving since he hadn't driven after leaving home for college. Someone in the SS was always driving him whenever he needed to go anywhere. This time, the SS was to stay out of sight to give Eric and Betty the illusion of being alone. So, he was twice as nervous about being responsible for driving safely.

Turning the corner on Betty's road, he saw her standing by the road, waiting for him. Carefully, Eric parked and exited the car to hold the car door open for her. She looked so beautiful to him that his heart almost stopped. He was aware of a silly grin on his face but couldn't keep it in. "It is looking a little like rain. Hope that won't ruin our day," he said.

Betty slipped into the car with a graceful move that took his breath away. "I like the rain. It washes the earth and gives life to everything," Betty told him. They talked about all the wonder of how life depended on water at the zoo.

After parking, Eric looks around to try to locate Bobby and Higgins. Neither man was in sight. That started Eric worrying about them as he had come to feel like they were a part of him, always there to make everything right for him. Soon, he pushed them to the back of his mind as Betty became excited about the seals in their aqua enclosure. She quickly opened her sketchpad and captured the seals in their playful moods.

They ooh and laughed from one habitat to another, only stopping to eat hot dogs and rest their legs now and then. They were approaching the very back enclosure containing Water Buffalo when it started to rain. Betty raised her face to the rain and let it soak her, laughing as the fat raindrops hit her skin. After a moment of enjoying watching Betty, Eric spread his arms and joined her. Soon, they were both wet. Then, the rain shower moved on, leaving them refreshed. Turning Betty toward him, Eric kissed her. It wasn't a scared peck this time, as he had already made love to her in his dreams.

Something shook the fencing beside them, breaking the spell upon them. One of the Water Buffalo had run into the fence, but not on purpose. Eric could see the milky film over Buffalo's eyes. Immediately, Eric reached a hand in the enclosure, touching the confused beast. Bobby appeared out of nowhere, ready to stop Eric, but Eric waved him off. So, the SS agent blocked Eric from anyone who might happen by. "Stand on the other side of Eric so nobody can see what he is doing," he told Betty.

Betty nodded, stepping so she was facing slightly towards Bobby yet covering what she could of Eric. "He is healing the Buffalo, right."

"Yes. Let's hope it isn't a deep heal," Bobby said. "This is one of the things we protect him from. He sees a need for healing but doesn't consider how it exposes him."

Eric sagged against the fence, and Bobby caught him. "Can you make it to that bench?" Bobby indicated a stone bench in the shade.

"Yes, let me go," Eric said, straightening up. He took Betty's hand, leaning into her as if whispering. They strolled to the bench and sat down. Eric pulled the protein bar out of his pocket. Bobby had slipped it in there. Opening the bar, he ate it in silence. They sat there like tourists enjoying a spot of shade. "I'm sorry," Eric said. "It looks as if our zoo visit is over. I'll have Bobby drive us someplace for a meal."

"I've had a wonderful time. And you are very heroic—that poor Buffalo. I'm so happy you were there for it. This day I will always remember."

Eric looked at Betty to see if she was humoring him. Her face was almost glowing, and her eyes held a sparkle he hadn't seen before. A weight lifted from his shoulders, "You didn't think I was weird? I'm no hero. Bobby and Higgins are the heroes."

"No, it was the most daring thing I've ever seen. You are a hero. People don't see your invisible cape." She said.

A month later, Eric and Betty were married in a quiet little ceremony with just the family, the SS agents, Ronny, and his wife. There would be no record of the event, nothing announcing to the world that they were alive. Their life in hiding had begun.

The End

COMING SOON

The next book in the series.

Even Thoughts Hurt